D1094164

THE HEDGEWITCH OF FOXHALL

ALSO BY ANNA BRIGHT

The Beholder

The Boundless

The Song That Moves the Sun

The Hedgewitch of Foxhall

ANNA BRIGHT

HARPER TEEN
An Imprint of HarperCollinsPublishers

HarperTeen is an imprint of HarperCollins Publishers.

The Hedgewitch of Foxhall
 For information address HarperCollins Children's Books, a division of HarperCollins Publishers, 195 Broadway, New York, NY 10007.
www.epicreads.com
Library of Congress Control Number: 2023937096
ISBN 978-0-06-308357-8
Typography by Corina Lupp
23 24 25 26 27 LBC 5 4 3 2 1
First Edition

To Grandmother and Mamaw.

Thank you for
a childhood full
of magic.

PRONUNCIATION GUIDE AND TERMS

Ffion: FEE-un

Taliesin: tal-ee-AY-sin

Dafydd: DA-vid (the "a" is like "apple")

Mathrafal: MA-thra-val

Osian: OH-shan

Powys: PO-wis

Brycheiniog: Bri-KHAY-nee-og

Gwynedd: GWIH-neth

Afanc: AH-vanc

Ceiliog neidr: KAY-lee-og NAY-der

Draig goch: dryg gokh

Gwiber: GWY-ber

Arianrhod: ah-ree-AN-rhode

Mam-gu (grandmother): MAM-gee

Llafnau (blades): HLAV-nye

Ap (son of): ap

Vch (daughter of): ferk

Diolch (thank you): DEE-olkh

Arawn: ah-ROUN (rhymes with "clown")

Annwn: AH-noon

Ten Years Ago

FFION

I was seven years old when I met wild magic.

I shouldn't have been out at all, what with it being midnight and there being Mercian soldiers at work only a few miles to the east. But I was a stubborn little gremlin even then.

It was my mam-gu's fault, really. Earlier that day, she'd shown me some amber she'd found in Foxhall Forest, and I'd thought the stones looked like a fistful of honey. "Why didn't you bring me some?" I'd asked. Amber made for powerful protection charms.

But my grandmother told me it would serve me better if I got it for myself. She hadn't told me it would take half the night to find, though. Nor had she told me what to say to Mam when she scolded me for disappearing for hours after dark. But that was a problem for later. Besides, I wasn't alone, not with Cadno trotting after me, red tail swishing as he snuffled at the roots of trees.

Mam would've said I didn't need a protection charm, as long as I didn't go looking for trouble. But with Dad gone half the time, and Mercian soldiers digging ditches and piling up dirt only a few miles off—well.

I was a witch from a long line of witches. I already knew better, even as a child.

As I came to a glade of naked birches, my irritated sigh smoked on the air. Mam-gu had found the amber in a stand of pines; it was late, and I was certainly already in trouble, and these still weren't the trees I wanted.

But when the dragons emerged into a strip of moonlight, I forgot about charms, or trees, or trouble. I forgot about everything.

They were dreigiau goch—red dragons. Red like cinnabar or copper or blushing dawn, red like foxes or flame or fresh blood or madder dye. There were six of them.

The larger adults had flanks grown over with lichen and mushrooms and ivy, but all of them were scaled and horned, with power in their wings and chests and jointed legs. They looked like fire and moved like water, like boulders tumbling downhill; they were the brightest things in that winter forest.

Later, I would learn that the color of a dragon's scales reflected the heat and age of their flame. I would learn that dreigiau goch could fly from one Welsh kingdom to another, farther than gwiberod or afancs or ceiliogau neidr, without even stopping to rest. I would learn how easily they could destroy farms or fields.

As a child, I only knew that they were made of magic.

I stepped into the glade slow as slow, making myself smaller than I already was, knotting my hair around my fist so it wouldn't catch a sudden breath of wind and spook them.

The largest of the six—it must have stood twenty-five hands high, it *must,* I was little and all the world was large but I knew the beast was truly massive—hung back. So did the other full-grown dreigiau.

But the smallest dragon stepped forward. The forest was quiet enough that I heard its amber claws clinking against pebbles on the ground, like rain falling on glass.

I waited, breathless, for it to come to me. And it did.

The smallest dragon's back came as high as my chest. I longed to run my hand over its side, to see if its copper scales were cold or if it would feel warm like the horses stabled at the Dead Man's Bells. But I didn't move a finger.

It pawed at me gently, lifting one blunt-clawed forefoot to nudge at my bare shin as if to ask *what are you?* It sniffed at my kirtle, too, snorting and sneezing when it reached my underarms; I'd been as ill-washed a child as I was a woman. When a laugh rippled out of me, the little dragon startled back, like it was surprised to find me as loud as any bird in the woods.

"I'm sorry," I whispered, desperate to save the broken moment, watching it watch me out of curious gold eyes.

But when the largest of the six roared a soft summons, even I wouldn't have dared to disobey. The smallest dragon bumped me once with its head, then turned back toward the others and galloped with them into the woods.

I'd stared after them, watching their scales shimmer until they faded out of view, feeling the woods fall silent once more.

In that moment, something in me fell silent, too. Something that would always be listening and looking.

I would search for dragons in later years. I would search the roads for gwyllgwn, the rivers and lakes for ceffylau dŵr. I never found them.

And I was never the same again.

1

FFION

Foxhall Forest, Powys, Wales
Spring Equinox, AD 796

The Mercian soldier couldn't see me when he fired the shot. But I saw him. I saw his arrow fly through the cold, wet dawn.

The stag was grazing down the ridge, crowned head low. And the soldiers were much, much farther into our territory than they should have been. I dropped into a crouch behind a holly bush, putting a hand on Cadno's scruff.

Maybe the soldier was fooling around, or maybe he was just a bad shot. But his arrow flew wide of the beast's torso and buried itself in its right hind leg.

Whether the hart lived or died, it would suffer.

The forest felt as it always did, close and full of secrets. But it felt a little less secret, a little less magical, as the animal let out a bellow of pain and ran crashing through the tree line.

I wondered what the Foxhall would have to say about this. Not the hart; they wouldn't care about him. But maybe they'd care about Mercians straying farther into our kingdom than I'd ever seen them.

Probably not.

The Foxhall—the coven for which our town was named, for which the forest was named—was untouchable. They wouldn't trouble themselves over a few Mercian soldiers, or read anything into their presence here. And the stag was just a stag, after all.

If he'd been a magical creature, they might have cared. But those had all gone to ground. After I'd seen them once as a little girl, I'd never seen the pod of dragons again, or any other uncanny beast.

Ordinary animals like the hart limping deeper into the woods were all we had left.

"Should we chase it?" the soldier called to his mates, voice coming harsh down the ridge.

No, I thought, *you shouldn't.*

"Cadno," I hissed. "Rocks. Hurry."

Wales favored a hedge to mark a boundary. But a wall would do.

"A wall, a wall, a wall," I chanted under my breath, panting a little, pushing tangled red hair out of my eyes. *"A wall, a wall, a wall."*

As Cadno darted away, quick and neat from his pointed fox's nose to his well-groomed red tail, I dropped to my knees just inside the tree line, scratching a ditch in the dirt with my nails. When Cadno returned with a mouthful of stones, I scraped them hurriedly into the trench.

And then I began to sing.

Ravens and crowns, sweeties and gowns
Are out of my reach, are out of my reach
Treetops and roof thatch and castle walls high
Are out of my reach, are out of my reach
Thistles and nettles and beetles and stones
Are under my feet, are under my feet
But you, o my true love, lady so fair
Raven of hair, who moves on the air,
Are out of my reach, are out of my reach

A line of crocuses popped out of the ground alongside the trench.

Boots pounded closer down the hill, one soldier trampling a patch of gorse and swearing when it snagged his trousers, another laughing at him.

They didn't hear me singing. They didn't notice anything about their surroundings. In fairness to the soldiers, most people didn't.

Sleeping beneath hedges and surviving off the gifts of the forest, having left my mother's home behind—I'd learned to notice.

I scrambled backward on my hands and knees behind a tree, pushing all my magic and my song about untouchable things toward the little trench I'd dug directly in their path.

"It can't have gotten far," said the soldier who'd fired the shot. The toe of his boot nudged a stone on the trench's edge, sending it clattering inside.

I held my breath, clinging to Cadno. My magic was always stronger when he was close.

"Leave it," another said suddenly. "We need to get back to the watchtower. Don't have time to chase some beast into the woods because you can't shoot properly."

The first one drew up, offended, and made to push through the trees. "I can shoot—" He paused. "Stop. Is this the place they told us about?" He dropped his voice. "The witches' wood?"

Just one witch, actually. The Foxhall only came to the forest when they needed a grove or a meadow or a herd to sacrifice.

The soldiers were too casual as they talked over one another, overexplaining why they needed to get back and away from the forest. When they finally trooped up the ridge, I dropped my forehead into the dirt, heart hammering.

It had only been a song my mam-gu, my father's mother, had taught me, sung beneath my breath. Only a little line of stones a couple feet wide. It was nothing like Offa's Dyke, the wall of earth their watchtower guarded. Eight feet tall and three kingdoms long.

But I'd built a wall here on the edge of Foxhall Forest, and it had held.

After a moment, I hauled myself to my feet and dove into the trees,

Cadno at my heels. Twilight was coming. And I'd sent the soldiers off, but there were more where they'd come from.

The stag had left a path of broken branches and crushed bracken leading into the forest. I followed his tracks across the clearing and through the trees on the far side, toward the brook that ran a mile or so from the forest's edge. The water was edged with rocks and lichen-covered ash trees large enough to hide behind to lick your wounds; and there, beside the brook, behind a boulder taller than me, lay the stag.

Though spring had come, he had yet to shed his crown of antlers, and his coat was a rich red-brown. The arrow still jutted from his leg.

At Cadno's soft whine, the stag wheezed a cry of distress and rose—or tried to. His forelegs jerked up, but his back right leg buckled beneath him as he tried to dart away. I felt a stab of pity. "I'm here to help you," I said softly. "It's all right."

He watched through liquid brown eyes as I crossed to his side.

"I'm here to help," I said again, gentler still, and he let himself collapse.

When I reached for the arrow in his leg, the stag wheezed again. Again, I shushed him, one hand pressed to his muzzle as if he were a dog and not a king of Foxhall Forest.

Maybe he could sense that the forest trusted me. Maybe he'd just lost too much blood to fight.

The job was hideous. When I'd finally worked the arrow free of muscle and gristle and fur, the stag lay defenseless in front of me, ribs appearing and disappearing as his side heaved. But I wasn't done. I rinsed my bloody hands in the brook and reached for the pouch at my hip.

A feverfew charm, first, for the wound. I always carried my grandmother's spellbook, the one Dad had passed on to me, but I didn't need it for this any more than I had for the wall I'd built. I held the stag's leg firmly; but when I began to sing, he fell still and silent.

It was a different song than the one I'd sung earlier. This was the song I'd sung to the forest the day we'd come to our understanding.

Foxhall Forest was more my home than the town had ever been. It was where I'd taken Mam-gu's spellbook the day I'd found out Mam was expecting my little brother Hywel, and I was five years old and jealous and miserable right down to my guts.

I was a curmudgeonly little thing, even then. So when Arianrhod and Gareth, my older sister and brother, had told me to find a friend in town, I'd asked the woods for a friend instead.

The spell had called for a poppet—a little doll to represent the person being summoned—alongside a few of the person's belongings. My mother was a Foxhall covenwitch, and therefore able to read and write; but I was five, only slightly literate, and not at all attentive to detail. I'd twisted together a clumsy poppet of twigs and grass and offered alongside it a pair of mushrooms and a fistful of foxfire I had found on a log.

The foxgloves had grown thick and tall that summer, so I had offered a bouquet of them, too. I hadn't known any better.

In later years, I would realize that the summoning charm I had performed that day, with the poppet and the childish little song I made up on the spot, might have—*should* have—gone horribly, desperately wrong.

Anything could have happened. But the forest had been gentle with me.

A fox kit had come trotting out of the bracken toward me, nose down, tail up.

He had followed me home. He'd been with me ever since.

As I sang the panting stag the song that had summoned Cadno so many years ago, a butterfly began to push out of its cocoon on a branch beside me.

My mam-gu had always sung as she worked. Foxhall witches like my mam and sister never did; they didn't need to. But singing lent rhythm to my work, helped me gather my focus and make the best use of my lean resources.

Besides. I was alone so much, it was good to hear a voice, even if it was my own.

The hart stayed calm as I circled his wound with amber to encourage it to seal itself, then wrapped his leg in felt and linen smeared with the white of a lifeless egg I found beside the brook. When my work was done, he laid his head against my knee with another weary huff. Cadno watched with mildly jealous eyes as I stroked the stag's neck, humming and murmuring words of comfort.

Finally, I got to my feet. It was almost full dark, and my stomach felt as empty as my pouch.

I had more work to do.

2

TAL

Mathrafal Castle, Powys

Dafydd hadn't even bothered to change his clothes. That was my first thought the afternoon my brother and I really became rivals.

I'd changed my shirt, washed my face and hands, and changed my shirt again when I got our father's summons. Presentation was vital. But Dafydd showed up in his leather blacksmith's apron, nails and palms seamed with soot.

Dafydd never worried about what side of himself to present to Mathrafal Castle as he greeted high men and the help alike. He actually seemed to think he had more in common with the latter than the former, even as the elder prince of Powys.

Absurd.

From behind the throne room doors came the blunted sound of bickering. "They're fighting about something in there," Dafydd said dully.

"Just another day," I said under my breath, nodding at one of my father's high men as he slipped into the throne room past us. The sounds of argument grew louder as the doors opened.

But before I could follow, Dafydd caught me by the sleeve. "Are you friendly with Elgan?" he asked, frowning.

"Keep your voice down," I hissed. "And yes, I'd like to be. I'm hoping he'll invite to me to his hunt this summer. Father doubled his holdings last year."

My brother snorted. "Of course. And now you have to court his favor, court his daughter—"

"Maybe. If Elgan doesn't get overeager and deplete the new fields, she might end up rich enough to be worth my time." Inside the throne room, the squabbling turned into shouting. "What was her name aga—?"

Dafydd shook his head and pushed through the iron-studded doors.

He had no patience. He had no discretion. It didn't matter.

Unlike me, Dafydd wanted nothing my father had to offer.

Unlike Dafydd, I wasn't our father's favorite. I wasn't even legitimate. But in Powys, a bastard prince could become king, if he was clever about it.

So I was clever about it.

I found the throne as empty as the rest of the bannered red-stone hall. My father, King Cadell, paced the length of the high table. He was blond, like Dafydd, with braids in his hair and a scar running through his right eyebrow and a gold hoop in his right ear. His eyes were bloodshot from drinking the night before with the chieftains who now sat around the huge yew table.

"My king," said one, "we should press the Foxhall into service."

"No need to bring the hags into it," said another—Elgan. "We should levy a tax."

"We can afford to recall troops from the southern border!" said a burly chieftain. "Powys has cowed Brycheiniog. King Meirion poses no threat to us; is his nephew not imprisoned beneath our very feet? We—"

My father interrupted him. "Prince Dafydd. Prince Taliesin. You're here—no, stand." He held up a hand when I started to sit next to Elgan. "Neither of you will be here long." Face heating, I backed away.

Ordinarily, this room would've been crowded—peasants paying taxes and making petitions, kitchen varlets tending fires, soldiers delivering reports and taking orders. Men of little stature trying to attain more.

Ordinarily, my father's men didn't look like children waiting to be punished.

Maybe today wasn't just another day.

Either Dafydd didn't notice the tension in the room, or he didn't care enough to be delicate about it. "Dad, what's happened?"

"An attack," Dad bit out. "And one that is apparently bound to kill me."

"An attack?" I straightened. "Who? Where?"

Beside my father's empty throne sat his magician, Osian. Cross-legged, half naked as always, he was studying a spread of bones carved like the phases of the moon. "From Mercia," he said. "But I don't know where. The attack has not yet fallen."

I'd always been wary of the magician. With thinning light hair and strange light eyes, he looked almost elderly, though he was actually younger than Dad. His tattoos had always unnerved me, too, his white, ropy-muscled stomach and thighs and neck and arms inked in red and green with Welsh dragons—the afanc and gwiber, the ceiliog neidr and draig goch. Wings, scales, nostrils, curling tongues bursting flame.

Osian never wore more than a loincloth, the better to show them off. The better to remind everyone at Mathrafal of his power, even when he wasn't lighting fields on fire or butchering flocks of sheep to fuel his magic.

"One day last week, I performed my nightly sacrifice. A raven—an unsighted one," Osian clarified unnecessarily, as if all the magical monsters hadn't been missing from our kingdom for a decade. "I wrung its neck, and in its broken bones, I foresaw an attack from the east, beyond Offa's Dyke. In my vision, I saw your father dead on an enemy spear."

Dafydd and I gaped.

Osian always did this, made pronouncements without seeming to watch how they landed. Though, given his connection with my father—the connection that let them sense the other's feelings, see or speak to or even speak *through* one another—maybe he'd decided tact was pointless.

More than his tattoos or his near nudity or even his magic, that brutal honesty was why I'd always avoided him. Not that I didn't hate the magic as well. It stank like earth and the air before a storm, sounded like a pot on the boil. I looked forward to his twice-yearly departures, when he presumably left to search for long-gone unicorns or take naked forest walks.

"Did you see when this would happen?" Dafydd asked.

"The leaves were green," said Osian. "It was spring, or a very wet summer. There was no moon."

"This spring?" I asked. "Next spring? Five springs from now?"

"This year."

"How do you know?" I asked.

"I cannot say." Osian shifted, glancing significantly at Dafydd.

But Dafydd didn't acknowledge the look. "Could you ask the forest to show you more?" he suggested. I frowned, unsure what he meant.

Osian cracked the knuckle of his left thumb, then his right. His left hand was tattooed all over with gwiberod in green ink; the right was covered in dreigiau goch in red.

"I cannot," he said simply. "My magic is gone."

Silence.

Without thinking, I met Dafydd's eyes.

When we were young, Dafydd's white skin had had an almost bluish cast to it. The past few years at the forge had left his arms and face tanned, sometimes burned.

Just now, my brother looked bloodless. Gray, like a corpse. But despite everything, for my part, I felt almost relieved.

I knew the loss of Osian's magic was a blow to the throne. I was still planning to dance at its funeral.

I understood now why today wasn't just another day.

But why had my father called us here?

"Gone?" Dafydd seemed to choke on the word. "Magic is Powys's only sure defense. What do you mean, it's gone?"

The chieftains murmured angrily. One rose, face purpling. "Our *only sure—?*"

"Do you know why?" I interrupted.

"Prince Taliesin." Osian turned his odd light eyes on me. "You've been a sharp one since you were just young. Do you know whence my magic comes?"

I shrugged. "I assumed it came from your sacrifices. That missing nail of yours. The animals you kill every day to be sure my father won't be joining them." Osian rubbed idly at the empty spot at the end of his right index finger; last month, he'd sacrificed the nail for a spell.

"The beasts are fuel for the fire, so to speak," he said. "But my magic is tied to Pendwmpian Forest. It is the source of my seeing and working."

Pendwmpian. I bothered with very little outside Mathrafal, but I knew I'd heard the name before, and recently.

"According to our scouts, Mercia has felled Pendwmpian. The last tree was cut two weeks ago," Osian said. "My vision was fragmented, cloudy—I suspect it was the forest's last effort to reach me before its spirit departed."

"Wait." Suddenly, I remembered where I'd heard the name. "Didn't we grant the Mercians logging rights to Pendwmpian? Because of its proximity to the dyke?"

Dad's jaw worked. "Only to the northeast quadrant."

Meaning: We had extended Mercia a concession.

Meaning: They had ignored it and taken what they wanted, as they always did, and the loss of Osian's magic was the consequence.

My boots suddenly became extremely interesting to me.

"Do neither of you have anything to say?" Dad burst out, beginning to pace again. "Welsh magic is already on the wane because of their cursed dyke, and now my magician, who has aided me since before you two whelps were born, is useless on the eve of an attack during which I am apparently fated to die. All because the Mercians could not keep to their agreement."

I tried to look nonchalant, like I wasn't imagining a spear piercing my father's chest.

I didn't want him to die. I especially didn't want him to die before he'd named me heir.

A cold thought. But I had more than one parent to worry about.

"We did debate the matter at length, my king," said one chieftain. *We did warn you,* he didn't say.

There had been discussion here in this room, he meant. Among my father's men.

Because there was no negotiating with the Mercians. It was true now, and it had been true ten years ago.

About a decade earlier, their King Offa had redrawn the border between Mercia and Wales with an earthwork running from sea to sea. The dyke became the new eastern boundary of the Welsh Marches—our kingdom of Powys, Gwynedd to the north, and Brycheiniog to the south—and it had severed more than a few Welsh villages, forests, moors, lakes, and rivers from the eastern edges of the petty kingdoms. Upon its completion, all our magical creatures had gone to ground. My father also believed the dyke was responsible for the loss of our magic.

Offa mocked us with what amounted to a wall running from one end of Wales to the other. And we had "agreed" to the new boundary, as if we'd had any other choice.

It was an eight-foot-tall, 180-mile-long insult.

"I'm listening, Father." I didn't know what he wanted me to say.

"Taliesin, always listening. Always planning." But Dad wasn't looking at me. He was looking at the burns on Dafydd's arms, the soot lining his palms and brow. "And Dafydd, always somewhere else, hard at work on something that does not matter."

My father's expression was all bitter disappointment. Dafydd watched him, silent and stolid as a cow.

"What angers me most is that Mercia thought itself safe to do this—felling one of our magical forests, cheerfully violating an agreement not one year old." Father thrust a hand at us, speaking now to his men as they picked their teeth or dug their knives into the table. "My two sons are our future. And when Mercia looks at our future, they feel no fear."

"Father." I spoke carefully, sensing his mood shift toward something precarious. "What are you going to do?"

"I am not going to do anything. This attack is a threat to my life. But the two of *you*—" He broke off, eyes glinting, shaking his head at Dafydd and me.

My heart hit the pit of my stomach.

"Tradition mandates that when a king dies, his lands are divided evenly among his sons, though only one is chosen as heir. I have not yet named my successor. But the promise of that tradition has made you too comfortable," my father said. "So I am going to break it."

"What do you mean?" Dafydd's voice was steady, but there was dread in his eyes.

"I mean that you and Taliesin will solve our problem," Father said.

"The Mercians' constant incursions, the slow leaching of magic from our land. I have had enough of concessions and agreements that do not profit Powys. So whichever of you can destroy King Offa's miserable dyke and restore magic to Wales will accede to my throne and inherit all of Powys when I die. The one who fails will be his candler."

The high table exploded.

Frantic whispers filled the space between shouts of confusion and complaint. This changed everything for my father's men. Everything they expected about the future.

It could completely upend mine.

Candling was done to purify places so used-up or polluted magic couldn't inhabit them—salted fields, fouled wells, and the like. Some said it was a trick that magicians had learned from housewives, who lit flames to burn dust and filth out of the air. Others said candling was an homage to dragon fire, which scorched a place to ruin so it could come back to life. The king's candler spent his life traveling from one damaged place to another, where his job was simple: to light a candle and wait as it burned down, at which point magic could return.

A candler's job meant leaving everything behind. Home. Friends. Family.

My heart was pounding. I couldn't be candler. I *couldn't*.

I had to think. Quickly.

"But we already have a candler. Your cousin—" I racked my brain. "Bronfraith." It was such a minor role, I could hardly remember his name.

"Old, and likewise in need of a successor," Dad bit out.

"You could just recall our forces from the north and south," Dafydd said, challenging. "You could withdraw troops from our borders with Gwynedd and Brycheiniog. They aren't a threat. We'd have the numbers to defend ourselves, whenever the Mercian attack fell."

"I could," Father agreed, eyes glittering, mouth a grimace. "I could do that, if I wanted to. Because I am king. And if you were king, you could make that decision."

Dad crossed the room and stood nose to nose with Dafydd, the son with his eyes and his hair and his shoulders.

I might as well not have been there at all.

"But you don't want to be king, do you, Dafydd?" Father said, so quietly only the three of us could hear. "Tal wants to be king. You want to play at peasant in your forge and pretend that you don't sleep in a feather bed and that laundresses don't wash your clothes. You simply want to inherit a parcel of land when I'm gone and not be bothered with any of this."

Dafydd didn't deny or confirm what he said, didn't apologize or defy. He just stood there.

"Well, son," Father breathed. "How about now?"

And that was when I knew that Dad's plan had nothing to do with me.

He only wanted to force Dafydd's hand. It didn't matter what happened to me, or anyone else, if Dafydd would agree to be his successor.

"Nothing?" Dad asked, his whisper growing loud. "Tal has a plan, I'll wager," he said, finally turning to look at me. My thoughts raced.

I hated that his attention made my chin lift, my spine straighten.

I hated that the slightest bit of effort on Dafydd's part would be welcomed the way all my trying never, ever had.

"I'll speak to you in private very soon," I said. I had to be discreet. I had to be patient.

Patience. Discretion. They were foreign concepts to Dafydd, but essential to an effective scheme.

I'd learned this from my father. But my mother was why I'd absorbed the lesson.

Dad huffed a laugh, seeming to approve for just a moment. And then, as quickly as it had landed on me, his attention was gone.

Briefly, I dared a look at my father's men. I'd spent years politicking for their favor. I'd wanted it even when I'd only *hoped* to become king and failing meant being a prince forever until I became lord of some nowhere patch of ground.

I would need their favor now. Because now, becoming king was the only acceptable outcome.

The throne. My father's respect. My mam's safety.

Everything hung on my next move.

"Go," Father said. "Go, Dafydd and Taliesin, and prove that our enemies should be afraid."

3

DAFYDD

When six o'clock comes, then up fellows rise
And into the forge, where the embers do fly
Where bellows and hammers and anvils resound
Go fellows who live by the sweat of their brow.
—"The Workaday Song"

Tal had left to go spin his spiderwebs the moment Dad dismissed us. But I'd wanted to be back in the forge as soon as I'd answered his summons. Gruffudd lifted his shaggy dark head off his paws and yawned as I stumped back inside the smithy and attacked the bellows.

I wanted to be so tired I couldn't feel anything else.

As the flames rose, I asked them what my father wanted from me. No matter that I already knew the answer.

Dad wanted me to be king. I could only guess what my mother would have wanted; she'd passed away a long time ago.

I didn't want to become king any more than I wanted my father to die in battle. I'd thought for years that Tal should take the throne. He was the sharp one, the one who could keep our father's high men and chieftains in check. The quest Dad had put to us—it was exactly Tal's kind of challenge.

Heat built in the forge. Again and again, I forced Farmer Gerwyn's bent harrow into the fire, heated the mangled tines, beat them straight on the anvil until they cooled and had to be heated again. When I yanked off my tunic, I ignored the shrieks and whispers from the goose girls in the courtyard outside. They were easier to ignore than the unsighted ravens that circled the forge roof, nested in its eaves, hopped around the edges of the packed-dirt floor. The birds croaked and cawed, sounding like ornery old men, like so many advisors offering me opinions I did not want.

I focused on the burn in my arms that told me I had done a good day's work. That I had done only good, and no harm to anyone.

Skin dirty, hands clean. Just like she'd taught me.

Harrow into the fire. Harrow onto the anvil. Beat the tines. Harrow into the fire.

"Prince Dafydd!" Alfie, an errand boy of about eight, tore through the forge. "Prince Dafydd, have you seen the steward of the armory?" I shook my head. "How about the jailer?"

"No." He started to dash away, but I caught him by the scruff and drew him back. "Alfie, it's nearly suppertime. Your mam will be expecting you home. What on earth do you need the jailer for?"

"Prince Taliesin," he said. "He's outfitting his guard."

I shoved the harrow in a bucket of water. "Why does he need to get into the prison?"

Alfie's eyes lit. "He's releasing Prince Angws of Brycheiniog. He's going to ransom him back to his uncle, King Meirion, and raise an army."

King Meirion poses no threat to us; is his nephew not imprisoned beneath our very feet? One of my father's men had just said so.

They called Meirion the Sighted Raven, able to see through any deception. I wondered how Tal would fare against that.

Still. He'd plotted this even faster than I'd expected. "And Taliesin told you this?" I asked. Alfie flushed. "You were listening at the keyhole?" I tried again.

"He called me to run an errand, and then I heard him talking with his mam. Don't tell him I told you," he pleaded.

I stiffened. "Would Tal punish you?"

"Oh, no. But the prince spends silver for favors and information, and I . . ." Alfie looked sheepish.

"Fair enough." I ruffled his hair, fished a coin out of my pocket, and tossed it to him. "Go home to your mam. I'll see Tal gets what he needs."

As he dashed away, I thought again of my father's challenge, and felt my own smile fading.

Wales was poorer without magic; I believed that. Serving as candler, spending my days burning away the pollution in fouled or depleted places so magic could return—the work sounded satisfying. Dad clearly didn't understand me at all, to imagine that I'd consider it a punishment.

Except.

My brother was clever. But cleverness wasn't all a king needed. Sometimes, I felt I hardly recognized Tal anymore.

His scheme was bound to work. I couldn't let him try it.

I banked the fire and left the forge, dragging myself back to the castle proper. I filled a bag from the kitchens first, then found the jailer. And then—

Prince Angws of Brycheiniog was waiting in one of the dungeon's three cells. He leapt to his feet when I came down the stairs. "Prince Dafydd!"

Angws was fourteen at the outside, pale and dark-haired, legs long as a colt's, face pimpled as . . . well. As a fourteen-year-old's. He was skinny, too, though not from captivity at Mathrafal; he'd been like this three months ago when a guard dragged him stinking like dung from the garderobe near my father's rooms, where he'd crawled inside through the waste line.

"Is he finally going to talk to me?" Angws white-knuckled the bars. "Am I going to—"

I slid the key into the cell door. "We're not talking."

The prince's expression was a mix of confusion and disappointment. But whatever he'd come for, I couldn't talk to him.

"Come on." Quickly, quietly, I hauled Angws toward the stairs, down the corridor, out into the courtyard where the day was dimming. As we bypassed the stables, I shoved the bag of food at him, glancing around the courtyard. "Hold this."

I didn't do this sort of thing. I couldn't believe I was doing it now. But I wasn't backing down.

Angws held the satchel away from his body like I'd handed him a bag of snakes. "I need to speak with King Cadell."

"Mm. This way." I hauled him past the forge, in the direction of the village. Toward the city walls.

"Where are you taking me?" His voice was worried, almost whining.

Past a row of huts, past the well, past the village green. The gates were in sight.

"Home," I said. "Now stop talking."

4

FFION

Foxhall, Powys

When I'd gathered enough feverfew to replace what I'd used on the stag, I made my way back along the hedges to Foxhall, toward the back door of one of the finer houses in town. The well-dressed housekeeper eyed me skeptically but let me in when I offered to charm out the mice I could hear in the walls in exchange for my supper.

My mother would be humiliated, I knew. But I hadn't eaten in three days.

I did my work, shared the bowl of cawl with Cadno, and left for Olwen's. As I walked, the covre fou chimed, the bell that meant all fires were to be put out and guilds were to finish working. Smiths stopped hammering at their forges; food sellers stopped cooking and trading; a weaver unhooked a length of wool from its tenter frame as a guild leader inspected it for overstretching.

Winding around the public toilet and the gutter that ran down the center of the street, past the communal oven where women retrieved their loaves for supper, I wondered if I was imagining the tension on the air. Were people hurrying into their homes a little more quickly than usual? Or was it only the sight of Mercian soldiers not two miles from the village that had left me feeling strained?

Maybe the day had worn me out. Maybe it was just that everywhere I went, people stared. I pretended not to see them cut their eyes at my tangled hair and torn clothes, pretended not to hear them whisper about how I smelled.

They knew that I was a witch by my loose hair. They knew that I was the hedgewitch because I was alone but for Cadno beside me.

Beside the village green, I jerked to a halt.

A rowan tree that had stood tall for eighty years had been cut to a stump. A chalk circle and charms surrounded it and a wilted foxglove lay on top, the symbol of the Foxhall's requisition.

They'd probably claimed the tree to put another enchantment on their doors. Couldn't have the rabble getting beneath the hill.

This sort of thing was happening more and more lately.

I had always thought it counterproductive to fuel my spells by using up the very things that kept magic alive in our land. When I could, I gleaned what I needed, choosing to gather downed branches rather than cut wood, search for fallen fruit or flowers rather than pick them. But it was more work to do things my way, and it took more time.

The Foxhall wasn't inclined to waste time. Just everything else.

Blood simmering, I walked past the crowded doors of the Dead Man's Bells. Some were only there for a meal, but plenty of travelers who'd come to seek the coven's help would stay the night, because tomorrow was a Penny Day.

And then I rounded a corner, and there was the dugout, waiting at the end of the lane.

The dugout door was a perfect circle painted the color of a fox's ears. Were it an ordinary place, in summer, brilliant pink foxgloves would crown its roof of earth; in autumn, it would wear a thatch of red and gold leaves. Once winter had passed, dark earth and ivy and thorns would give way to crocuses and tender green grass.

But this was no ordinary house. This was the home of the coven under the hill, where extravagant and extortionate magic was worked.

And so here, all seasons—and foxgloves, and gold leaves, and crocuses, and thorns—existed at once. By day, ravens tended to hover around it; by night, owls hooted from its lintel.

There were larger and finer buildings in our village than the one that belonged to the coven under the hill. There was the Dead Man's Bells, for one, and two rows of half-timbered houses like the one where I'd begged my supper. There was our market and our mill. But the Foxhall was the rotten core of the town.

Tomorrow, there would be a line outside for me to push through. But for now, I could hurry past easily. A good thing, because I could already hear the baby coughing.

I knocked on the door of the hovel, and after a few more barking coughs, Olwen answered. "Oh, Ffion. It got so late, I was afraid you might not come." Her pale face was carved sharply with hunger and exhaustion, brittle hair straggling from her modest crown of braids. Rhodri, innkeeper at the Dead Man's Bells and best friend to Olwen's deceased husband, kept her in firewood and well water. But Rhodri wasn't a healer.

"I said I would." My voice came out mulish as I crossed the threshold and bent to touch the coughing baby's back. "Hello, cariad bach."

I built up the fire beneath a kettle of water to ease his cough with steam. Then I set to work, Cadno lending me his strength as I sang health into Deri with a nonsense song about a gloriously chubby baby.

As I was out in Foxhall one lovely summer morn,
I saw the finest babe, ma'am, that e'er had been born.
This lad was fat of trunk, ma'am, this child was fat of limb;
At three feet high and three stone large, none could well carry him.
This babe, he could drain four breasts dry and finish thirsty, still,
Eat a cauldron of cawl, could this little lad, and yet have room to fill,

A mouth full of teeth and rosy of cheek and he never once was ill,
And the finest head of hair, ma'am, that I'd seen e'er or still!

Before I left, I gave Olwen all the elder cordial I had. "Dose him with that twice a day," I said, uprooting the little cluster of mushrooms that had popped up by the hearth as I worked.

But I didn't have much cordial, and I wouldn't be able to make more, either. Unless I found some sporadically produced by spellwork—not something to be counted on—elder wouldn't bloom until later in the spring, and it wouldn't fruit until summer. And I couldn't afford the apothecary's prices.

The Foxhall paid for its witches' access to her stores. The apothecary and I had no such arrangement.

"Diolch, Ffion," said Olwen. "I promise, I'll pay you as soon as I can. I know you—"

"Don't worry about me," I interrupted. "You're nursing, and you don't have enough to spare."

She winced at my tone but didn't argue. "I've asked the Foxhall for help since Alec died. But no one answers the notes I send, and I can't wait in line on Penny Day. You can spend hours and not even get in the door."

I kept my face placid. But it was hard to ignore the anger bubbling beneath my skin.

The Foxhall called the days they deigned to open their doors to outsiders Petitioners' Days. Most people called them Penny Days, though, because of the penny they had to pay even to wait in line.

To the Foxhall coven, there were those few worth their time, and there were those beneath their notice. Most of Foxhall fell beneath their notice. Including me, the hedgewitch on its fringes, the town's last magical resort, a small, sharp thorn in the coven's side.

But it was harder every Penny Day to stomach the length of the line outside and the number of petitioners who went away empty-handed.

I turned to go. "Let me know if he gets any worse, will you?"

"Yes." Olwen rubbed her tired eyes. "Please let me know if there's some way I can repay you."

She was just another Foxhall widow. Just another person I wished I could do more to help.

"I don't need repaying." I turned back into the lane. "Come on, Cadno."

Olwen couldn't afford to pay.

But others could.

I needed to visit my mother's house, anyway.

Our family home was a whitewashed three-room cottage near the center of town. With a thatched roof, a vegetable patch sprouting onions and leeks, and a few chickens out back, it was like the other houses on the lane—though ours was the only one with a rowan tree outside whose leaves were perpetually orange.

I'd lived here contentedly enough until two years earlier, around the time the twins were born and Mam and Dad had split. Dad had been off fighting one pointless battle or another for King Cadell most of the time anyway, but after that, their separation—informal, Mam being unable to divorce Dad, since he'd never been unfaithful—was deliberate, and not a matter of circumstance.

That left seven of us. Gareth was a cooper, and Arianrhod sat on the Foxhall with Mam, and then there was Hywel and the twins and me.

After listening a moment at the cottage's back door, I decided my younger siblings were the only ones home; I could hear Tegan and Taffy babbling in the front room and Hywel protesting, aggrieved. If I hurried, I could be in and out before anyone realized I was there.

As stealthily as I'd approached the wounded stag, I let myself and Cadno in the back door.

Lavender and thyme and onions dangled from the ceiling. Ducking to avoid them, I didn't notice the painted wood chest to the left of the back door. I knocked into its corner and clutched my upper thigh, hissing a curse.

Mam had moved the chest since I'd been by at the end of last year—a few other things, too. The room looked different.

A dull ache throbbed in my chest.

"Stand by the door," I told Cadno, cutting my eyes toward where I could hear my siblings playing. "And keep an ear out." Then I set to hunting.

The top drawer of my mam's cabinet was stuffed with dried marjoram and dried stinging nettle leaf by the bagful, huge chunks of amber and tiny garnets and quartz the color of a sunrise. Grains of paradise filled a soft silk pouch. A fistful of glittering turquoise feathers as long as my arm curled along the drawer's edge.

Though it was packed to the brim with supplies, Mam's cabinet was never locked. Why would she bother, when the apothecary's whole shop was hers for the taking?

It was no matter to the Foxhall what they used up, as long as their magic was quick and strong.

I opened the next drawer, and the next—there. In the bottom drawer was a bottle of elder cordial too big to clutch in my palm. And then Cadno was at my ankle, snuffling frantically.

Looking up from my crouch, I saw what I hadn't noticed when I first entered the room.

Wool cloaks hung by the back door, boots lining the wall below them. The smallest were Tegan's and Taffy's and the next biggest was Hywel's, the pair that had been mine only a few years ago. And the next pair—*the next pair.*

There shouldn't have been another pair of boots by the back door. I'd thought only Hywel and Tegan and Taffy were home.

But there were Arianrhod's boots beside theirs.

I snatched up the bottle of elder cordial, yanking at the tie on my hip pouch as my heart pounded. Why was she home, *why was she—*

"Ffion."

I tensed. Slowly, I turned, rising from my crouch.

"Arianrhod." I met my older sister's eyes. "I thought you'd still be under the hill."

"I finished early tonight. I thought I heard something back here." Arianrhod took in the bottle in my hand, the open cabinet at my back. The tangles in my hair and my filthy bare feet. I forced myself not to flinch.

My older sister stood a full six inches taller than me, even leaning on the cane she sometimes used when she was tired. Her pink-and-white complexion and strawberry-blond hair were smooth, and her eyes were gray, like mine. Unlike mine, her gaze was calm and clear.

Arianrhod was four years older than me, and if she'd ever been as messy and stupid as I felt most of the time, she never showed it.

Her steady expression made everything worse when she spoke. "Are you stealing from Mam now, Ffion?"

"No." I swallowed. "I came to see her. But she's not here." An obvious lie. An *obvious* lie.

"She's not usually here until after supper the night before a Petitioners' Day," Arianrhod said, as if I didn't know this. Behind her, Taffy raced across the aperture of the front room door, waving a rag doll.

"Right," I said. "Well."

I'd known Mam wouldn't be home. Arianrhod shouldn't have been around, either, but luck had failed me.

"You could wait for her," she said suddenly. "You could wait. There's plenty to eat."

I said nothing. Arianrhod adjusted her grip on her cane, voice growing almost urgent. "You know, Gareth's been talking about moving into the cooperage. If he moved there, you could come back. You could have the front room all to yourself—"

"I can't," I cut in.

"Why not?" Arianrhod's voice grew less steady now, more frustrated. "You're not staying at the monastery, I know you're not staying somewhere in town, because I've asked—"

"You *asked?*"

"I didn't know if you'd—found someone." Arianrhod stumbled over the last words, as if unsure how to broach the subject of my imagined romance.

"Well, I haven't."

"So nothing's changed. You just prefer sleeping beneath hedges to living in your family home." Arianrhod's jaw worked, and her gray eyes grew a little distant, as if she wished she were somewhere else. I knew I did.

"Plenty of people my age leave their family homes," I said. "Plenty of people younger than me do it."

"Yes, because work calls them away," she said. "Or because they get married. But you aren't doing either of those things. And now you're *stealing* from Mam?"

"It's not like she can't get more," I ground out. "Arianrhod, nothing's changed since I left. There are too many people in this house. I couldn't do it anymore."

It was a lie. But Arianrhod wouldn't understand the truth.

After all, Mam hadn't.

"I have to go to Olwen's," I said, pretending to rummage through my pouch. Another lie. "Deri is sick."

"Tegan and Taffy aren't much older than Deri," Arianrhod said. "They hardly know you."

The words landed where she'd hoped they would. I gripped the elder bottle, not speaking, not trusting my own voice.

"Why, Ffion?" she asked quietly. "Why do you always have to go?"

A beat. I turned for the door. "Don't tell Mam I was here."

I let Cadno out first, then followed him.

I needed to go. I needed to sleep. But I had another job first.

Stuffing my hand into the satchel at my hip, I drew out the small pouch I'd fashioned the moment I'd seen the Mercians on the ridge, before the soldier had ever drawn his bow and shot the stag. The bag held mint leaves for wholesome air, a sliver of parsnip for a sturdy foundation, a leaf from the tallest oak I could climb for a firm roof, and a tiny bead of amber for prosperity and strong walls. It was nearly ready.

Glancing around to be sure I was alone, I dug a tiny chunk of daub from the back wall of the house with my knife, then swiped a pinch of thatch from the eaves. I added both to the pouch. Then I began my ritual.

"*Safe, safe, safe,*" I chanted quietly. "*Safe, safe, safe.*"

I crawled sunwise on my hands and knees along the cottage wall, running the pouch over the foundation, singing once more about unreachable things—quietly, so my siblings wouldn't hear. At the front door, I rubbed the bag over the lintel and posts.

After I'd turned the next corner, and the next, I dug a hole at the back of the house. I dropped this latest charm beside the last one, and brushed the dirt back over them all.

A foxglove popped up where I finished my work. I ripped it up by the roots and tossed it away.

My magic was sturdy. But my fears remained.

The Mercians were getting bolder every day. The Foxhall was more concerned with itself than anything around it, cutting down acres of timber and sacrificing beasts to work its spells. Destroying that which was magical to make shallow, heartless magic.

It was why I had refused to join them.

It was why I had left home.

There, where no one could see me, I leaned my head against the side of the house where I'd been born and felt the walls rattle with Tegan and Taffy's roughhousing, the twins roaring like bears over Hywel's protests and Arianrhod's chiding, their laughter sounding like a bubbling cauldron. Cadno licked my hand, and I clutched him against my ribs as I tried not to cry.

I wished that I could tell my sister the truth.

I wished, more than anything, that I could stay.

5

TAL

Mathrafal Castle, Powys

It was only an hour or two after I left the throne room that I made for Meirion's nephew's cell in the dungeons. I'd needed every interceding minute to throw up in the nearest garderobe and ready my personal guard.

But by the time I reached his cell, he was already gone.

In nearly a hundred nights in the Mathrafal dungeons, the prince had never once attempted to escape. Yet somehow, tonight, he'd gotten out.

I paced the empty cell, seething, as the courtyard guard explained what he'd seen. Angws, released. Dafydd, walking with him toward the castle walls. The guard hadn't thought to question my brother.

Dafydd shouldn't try to sneak. He wasn't built for it.

I didn't know how he'd found out about my plan to ransom Angws for an army. But of course he'd stolen it. He certainly wasn't capable of producing one himself.

Cold anger built inside me as I tore through the castle looking for Dad. I jutted a finger at an errand boy. "My father. Have you seen him?" He shook his head, and I raced on.

Could I catch up to my brother and Angws on the road? Would Dad punish Dafydd for cheating? Would he care?

Finally, a pantler told me he'd seen my father in my brother's forge. I didn't know why he'd be there, with Dafydd gone. But when I came in sight of it, I drew up short.

There was my father, like I'd been told. And there was my brother, hard at work as always.

Not on the road. Not absconded with Prince Angws. I didn't understand.

Dafydd lifted his work from the fire and placed it on the anvil. Dad stood beside him, talking and talking, hands outstretched. My face felt hot.

I'd told Dad I would obey; Dafydd had ignored him. And yet here my father was, still begging Dafydd to get in line.

I strode from the courtyard into the forge, rounding Dafydd's worktable and shoving his shoulder. "Where is Prince Angws?" The iron he'd been heating clattered to the ground in a spray of sparks.

"Tal!" Dad exclaimed. But Dafydd wouldn't look at me.

"Where is he?" I pressed. "Tell me where he is!"

"Where do you think he is?" Dafydd asked carefully. I was so angry I could hear my own heartbeat in my ears.

I seized the front of Dafydd's apron and swung for his jaw.

We hit the floor together, pushing and shoving as we rolled. I punched Dafydd in the ribs; he elbowed me in the cheek, trying to shake me off. Wood and metal groaned and shrieked as the table slid one way and tools fell the other.

"Tal!" My father dragged me off him, shook me by the shoulders. "Tal, what do you think you're doing?"

I pointed at Dafydd. "He sabotaged me!"

"What do you mean?" Dad asked.

"He cheated! I thought at first he'd stolen my plan, but he didn't. He just released Meirion's nephew so my plan would fail," I said, panting. "Deny it, I dare you."

Dafydd dabbed at his bleeding lip. "I didn't sabotage you," he said. "I was trying to protect you—"

"Then you admit it?" I surged toward him. Dad grabbed my arm, holding me back.

"—from yourself!" Dafydd finished, dark but earnest. "I was trying to keep you from doing something you would regret, trying to win this stupid pissing match, which I refuse to participate in." This, he directed at my father. Dad's face darkened.

"We don't have to meet this attack in Mercian fashion," Dafydd said. "Arawn—I know the dragons disappeared, but there were sightings of him near Pendwmpian, once. Some said he might've survived. And the Marches still hold the llafnau, don't they?"

"Dafydd." Dad widened his eyes and looked nervously around. "Yes. Our llafn remains . . . well guarded."

"So Powys isn't completely without magic," Dafydd said. "We could weather an attack."

I had never heard of the llafnau—*blades*, the word meant, so they must be weapons. But clearly, Dad and Dafydd had talked all about them.

Why, *why* was the throne so tied up with magic? Wasn't a strong will and a clever head enough?

"Arawn hasn't been seen in ten years. Even felling Pendwmpian hasn't produced him," I spat. "The dragons are gone, Dafydd. We need a plan, not fairy tales."

Wales had been rife with monsters before the dyke was built. But it was the dragons whose memory everyone seemed to pine after. Arawn, and the others.

The blue-gray afancs who lived in the water. The horned ceiliogau neidr, crested and feathered like birds of prey, dwelling in cliffs and caves. The green-winged gwiberod that lived coiled in trees, and the dreigiau goch, the red dragons that had ruled the wild places of Powys and beyond. Arawn was one of these, thought to be the oldest and most powerful in Wales—thought, perhaps, to have remained, when the others had left. But he had disappeared, too.

I understood regretting the loss of magic as a defense. I *didn't* understand how the extinction of monsters capable of incredible destruction churned up such tender yearning.

"I know you don't mourn their disappearance, Tal," said Dafydd. "But I do."

"So restore them," my father urged. He was almost pleading. "Return magic to Powys, and bring them back."

"I will," Dafydd said, and my heart dropped until he continued. "As candler. I'll heal one meadow or forest or lake at a time."

Dad turned away. "No."

"Let him!" My eye roll was probably visible from the nearest Mercian guard tower; why wouldn't Dad just *let him*? "Precious, sanctimonious, self-martyring—"

"You can't make me compete!" Dafydd burst out, pointing at Dad. "You can't make me become you!"

And this was Dafydd's mistake.

"I can," our father said. His eyes were incandescent.

"How? What can you possibly take from me?" Dafydd held out his arms. "This is all I want."

"Are you certain of that?" Dad's voice was cold iron. He was no longer pleading.

He stepped close to Dafydd, now speaking so softly I couldn't hear his words. Dafydd stared at my father, then glanced at me before muttering a reply.

In the seconds I waited, I thought my heart would burst.

"Fine," Dafydd finally said. "I'll do it."

"You'll—" My anger was choking me. "You'll do it? You don't even want it!"

"Things change," Dafydd said, sounding choked himself.

"That quickly?" I demanded. "Then again, I'd thought I could count on you four years ago, and then one day you just walked away and left me to the wolves."

It hadn't always been this way between us—between Dafydd and me. We'd been true friends once. True brothers.

I hadn't understood that the very nature of our relationship was rivalry. That we were born to be competitors, that for me to succeed was for him to fail. That there was one throne, and only one of us could hold it.

Letting Angws go was just Dafydd's latest betrayal. I ought to have been used to him doing what he wanted and letting the chips fall where they would. Letting me swing in the breeze, alone.

"Enough." My father's voice was hard. "Dafydd, you will go north. Tal, you will go south. I don't care what you do, just don't go near one another."

My brother started to protest. "But—"

"Dafydd, do not think to deceive me. Tal—" Father glanced at me, weary, almost dismissive. "Go do what you do best."

He spoke like he was pronouncing a tynged—a doom, a divination. The words were an order and they were our fate, shrouded in darkness, impossible to see, impossible to avoid.

"Suits me fine. I'm going south," I said, making for the forge's exit. "I have a prisoner to catch."

I gave the laundress a coin to pack my things and spent another on a second errand boy to find the steward of the armory, since the first one had disappeared. I had a visit to make, and no time to waste.

"Mam?" I knocked on her door, nodding at her guards. "Mam, are you there?"

After a moment's wait, the door cracked open, and a memory flashed through my mind—another night at another door, my mother peering out. A memory of snow on the ground and horrible empty eyes.

Tonight, and oh, the longest night,
The longest night, the longest night,
Tonight, and oh, the longest night,
Come we now to your door.

No. Tonight was different. It was springtime, not Midwinter. We were safe in Mathrafal Castle, not out on our own in the town.

And besides. Magic in Powys was nearly dead. I wrapped the fact around me like a blanket.

"Gods' candles!" My mother, Gwanwyn, called me back to myself, eyes wide at the sight of my scrapes and torn clothes. "Taliesin, bach. Look at the state of you!"

"Dafydd started it." I crossed the threshold, wincing. "And Dad, I guess."

My mother set down the wool she'd been carding and reached for my split knuckles. Her own were stained blue with woad dye. "I heard you swung first, and Dafydd finished it," she said, arching an eyebrow.

Looking at Mam was like catching sight of my reflection in the water, or maybe seeing my own future. I'd inherited her light brown eyes, her narrow jaw, her white skin that tanned easily and her brown hair that bleached in sunshine. Once, when Father was feeling kind, or possibly just drunk, he'd said I had her smile.

Mam's features had drowned out the obvious good looks Dad would have passed along to me, all the traits Dafydd had inherited as easily as if he'd never had a mother at all—the broad frame and straw-blond hair, the blue eyes.

I'd only gotten my height from Dad. Dafydd had gotten that, and everything else.

"What else did you hear?" I asked.

"Enough. I spoke to Cadfan, Elgan, some others." Mam sounded worried. "Offa's Dyke, Tal? Are you sure you know what you're about?"

No. "Of course."

Her expression shifted. "Then your plan remains intact?" she asked ironically. "The report I heard of you and Dafydd fighting in the forge like piglets in a pen doesn't mean things have gone, in any way, awry?"

"Slightly awry. Maybe." I crossed my arms and looked away. "But I'll be on horseback," I said firmly. "And he'll be on foot."

Mam already knew about the prisoner I'd be chasing. Mam always knew everything.

"And you will travel with guards," she said sternly. "And you will be *careful*."

"Always," I promised. And I meant it.

Mam turned away for a moment, pouring herself a cup of water and taking a drink.

I took advantage of her distraction to scan the room. The laundresses and scullery maids had done their jobs—the bed was made, the water basin full, the floor swept and covered with a mat of fresh rushes.

It was no surprise to see the room sparkling clean. It was what I bribed them for.

I hoped they would keep up their end of that bargain while I was gone. Not that it mattered all that much to Mam. But it mattered to me.

It mattered to *me* that I had her here, behind walls and locked doors and the crossed pikes of armed guards. That we lived in Mathrafal Castle, where I could keep her safe.

I hugged her tightly and was on the road within twenty minutes.

The sooner I left, the sooner I could be back, and the sooner I could be back to watching over her.

6

DAFYDD

When eight o'clock comes, then up the town rises
And out comes the market, to tempt with its prizes
To purchase it later, or perchance buy it now?
Ask good folk who live by the sweat of their brow.
—"The Workaday Song"

I met Osian on the roof. He was ghostly white beneath the moon, his tattoos looking like so many scars, his hair like dandelion fluff. I leaned beside him on a parapet, close, but not too close.

Osian's presence could be off-putting. But I'd never mistrusted him the way Tal did. Before it had disappeared, Osian's magic could determine if it was safe for us to travel, or what day was best for us to take up a new task. And though his magic had always been a little extravagant for my liking, it was at least gentler than Foxhall working.

About a foot from where I stood, Osian had spread out his bone shards again on the castle wall, thirty white pieces and one small black rock for the new moon, when the attack would come. He picked it up now, studying it.

Below us, Offa's Dyke wrapped Mathrafal's eastern wall in a one-sided embrace.

What would happen if it were broken? What consequences would we face, meeting violence with violence?

"Did you know he was going to do this?" I asked him. "Pit Tal and me against each other?"

"He told me nothing."

"That's not what I asked you."

"Your father's mind is not a ledger for me to peruse. His thoughts are not open to me when he does not wish to share them. You should know that by now." Osian shot me a significant glance. I snorted.

"He's sending me north," I said. "So I'm going to Bleddyn's court. Though he'll probably send me away the second I arrive. We've been skirmishing with them for as long as I can remember."

"If it's so futile, why are you going?" Osian asked. "Not to Bleddyn. I mean, why obey Cadell at all?"

I hesitated, thinking over the past hour.

One minute, Dad and Tal and I had been talking. And the next, Dad had been pretending my brother wasn't even there.

Are you certain there's nothing I can take from you? he'd asked.

And I'd been certain there wasn't. I'd been almost cocky.

I'd lost my mother as a baby. I'd learned long ago my father wasn't the man I'd believed he was. What else could he take from me?

If Tal takes victory over you—not simply receives your forfeiture—I will make him king and you candler, just as you wish. His voice had been cold, fury barely contained. *But if you refuse to participate, I will send Gwanwyn away, and you will not be king, but Tal will still get nothing. I have cousins. I can find another heir.*

I'd been stunned. *You'd rather a cousin be king than Tal? You'd rather punish Gwanwyn and Tal than see me pull out of the running?*

A bitter shrug. *You're more concerned for Gwanwyn's happiness than you are for my life. You'd rather be a mere candler than a king. Apparently, we're both disappointments.*

"Thinking of her again?" Osian asked.

Her. The girl, he meant. For once, the answer was no.

I shook my head. "Dad threatened Tal," I finally said. "Gwanwyn, too. So I have to try." Gwanwyn—Tal's mother—was the only person who mattered to Tal. Being separated from her would destroy him.

"Does Tal know?"

"No," I said. "And he can't find out." He was so self-sufficient in so many ways. Tal couldn't know that I'd had to underwrite his place in this fight.

"You take good care of him, Dafydd," Osian said. "But who takes care of you? Who is looking after your future?"

"My future's been decided for a long time."

Osian waved a tattooed hand. "We didn't anticipate this," he said. "Who knows what else may lie ahead, good or ill?" I smiled tightly.

I had little enough future to look after. Little enough to hope for. I turned toward the door downstairs.

"Goodbye, Dafydd," said Osian. "I hope you succeed."

For years, I'd done my best to sidestep the throne. Tal would be king, and I would oversee the land to which I was entitled. I would make it a good place to live.

But now the crown and the land were all bound up together, and I'd begun to have real doubts about Tal.

Now I had to try for the crown, knowing I'd have to fail to attain what I'd always hoped for. I didn't even know what succeeding meant anymore.

"Goodbye, Osian," I said. "Take care of Dad. Keep trying to find your magic again."

Osian nodded, not looking up, back to piecing through the bone shards.

He was such a strange character. But Osian had become for me what my father had failed to be. Someone to talk to. Someone to respect.

We had secrets from my father, Osian and I.

Interlude

Ffion dreamt of water.

It was no place close to her town of Foxhall. It was no place she'd ever seen.

A flat of gray-brown sand. Water and sky and standing stones colored silver and pale blue.

The ocean bubbled like a cauldron. The sky raged.

Salt air tore at the skin of her face and her hair, and her heart beat like she was running.

She *was* running, she realized. Into the water, up to her knees, bitingly cold, salty waves stinging the cuts on her feet.

There was terror. There was hope. There was no time left.

From behind her came splashing.

From behind her came an unearthly sound.

Ffion woke beneath the hedge.

7

FFION

Foxhall, Powys

The dream unnerved me. When I woke, I wanted to stare up at the bottom of the hedge and muse over what it could have meant with Cadno.

Where was that beach? Why had I run into the water? And what was that *sound?*

But the coven beneath the hill wasn't going to help my neighbors, and I couldn't just lie around woolgathering. As I made my way to Olwen's just after sunrise, the line outside the Foxhall was already thirty people deep.

Another day had dawned, and I had more work to do.

I'd intended to get back to the stag early in the day. But the hours rushed past me in a blur of errands and appointments.

First, there was the visit to Olwen's, where I found myself too cowardly to knock on her door. I slunk over to the Dead Man's Bells to give the elder cordial to Rhodri. "Are you sure you don't want to give it to her yourself?" he asked. "She'll be grateful for it."

"No time." I brushed him off, brisk to the point of rudeness. The thought of Olwen's gratitude made my stomach twist.

I didn't feel guilty, stealing from the Foxhall. But I'd needed their wealth to help Olwen, and today, looking at the line, I hated that.

After I left the pub, I visited a young woman whose house needed protecting from a vicious former suitor, and a forgetful older widow who'd asked for help remembering where she'd mislaid a priceless bit of woodwork made by her deceased husband. Midafternoon, Cadno went ahead of me to visit the stag. My magic would be weaker without him, but he would be able to scent any foulness in the arrow wound and let me know if I needed to come sooner than evening.

I crossed the town once, twice, three times, stopping where the bakers' guild had blocked a lane to parade a dishonest member with one of his moldy loaves hung around his neck, then stopping again at the well to get water for the memory charm.

As I waited, bucket in hand, a pair of women my mother's age talked about seeing Mercians outside the village that morning—even nearer than the ones I'd seen the day before.

With every slosh of the water in my pail, I thought again of the dream. And every time I crossed town, the line outside the Foxhall was longer and more hopeless-looking.

Parents waiting with sick children. Farmers towing injured animals. Folk who'd lost their homes or their jobs or one of their five precious senses. The hopeful ones were even harder to look at. Because I knew no one beyond the orange door would deign to help them today.

The sight pushed me to keep working, despite my weariness.

I had stolen from the Foxhall. I ached for those who actually had to darken their doorstep.

I didn't care how dire my circumstances became. I would never, ever be one of them.

Around the time the light began to grow long, it was a relief to put the town behind me and make for the forest. I could have walked with my eyes closed down the lane and through the hedges, around Farmer Cefin's field and across the meadow beyond.

I relaxed as the tree line came into view. Where the watching eyes of town brought pressure, the forest had only ever brought me peace. In sunlit winter mornings hunting for truffles with Cadno; in summer afternoons washing my kirtle in the brook while he chased his tail; in autumn evenings spent poring over Mam-gu's spellbook, an apple in my hand and Cadno batting his own around; we'd been happy. Foxhall Forest had not stopped its gifts the day it sent me Cadno in exchange for my poppet and song.

I am a witch of Foxhall
And I've come to beg a boon
My house it is quite lonely
Yet we're also out of room
I'm come to Foxhall Forest
And I hope not to offend
I offer you this poppet
And I ask of you a friend

I belonged to Foxhall Forest, and it belonged to me. I *was* a witch of Foxhall, even if I would never sit with the coven under the hill.

As I hurried around the edge of Cefin's field, careful not to trample his rye seedlings, I wondered how Cadno and the stag were faring. It was only when I reached the meadow that I noticed the smell of smoke.

Something was wrong.

I tore across the meadow, into the trees. My heart almost burst with relief when I saw the stag limping through the haze. "You're walking?"

I could hardly believe it. I'd saved him. At the sound of my voice, though, he broke away through the brush.

I wanted to follow him, but I kept searching for the source of the smoke. I had to stop long before I ever reached the water's edge.

The ground should have been too damp to burn, but it smoldered in the afternoon air. All around me, inside a chalk circle dotted with charms, trees were scorched to ruin. Fire crackled along the branches of a willow beside the brook, sparks and embers still swaying in its leaves.

The stag had somehow escaped the chalk circle.

But at its edge lay Cadno, beside an afterthought fistful of foxgloves.

I couldn't breathe. My chest rose and fell like a bellows, working faster and faster. I hadn't realized I had fallen until I was on my knees, crawling to him. My friend was unrecognizable, blackened from smoke and flame.

I couldn't breathe. I had—I had to—

I ripped my spellbook open.

How to find water. How to ease a cough. How to ward a house. I screamed and threw the book aside.

Useless. Nothing I could use to bring him back. Nothing but the summoning spell I'd used to call him when he'd first come to me.

The summoning spell. I froze, my heart seizing with hope and fear.

Would it—could it—work?

I crawled back over to my spellbook, found the spell, dumped out my pouch. Some dried stinging nettle leaf and half a dried apple fell out. It wasn't enough.

I scrabbled around, looking on the ground and in the river for anything else I could offer, anything I could use for the spell. I found only burned leaves and burned ground. Nothing powerful enough. Not with the magic in the land so weak and thin.

There was nothing.

I had nothing.

I buried my face in Cadno's scruff and screamed. Tears rolled down my nose and onto his body, curled up tightly from pain I hadn't been able to soothe.

He did not wake. I had failed Foxhall Forest, and Cadno.

I was alone. And now I always would be.

Dew would gather that night and soothe the scorched earth. I hoped it would comfort Cadno's spirit, as the ghost of him lingered until the new moon.

But my rage only billowed as I sobbed. I scooped up Cadno's small body and got to my feet.

I was going to bury my familiar. And then I was going to go back to town.

A Mercian had shot the stag. But the Foxhall had killed my friend.

I wasn't going to ask the coven under the hill for help. But I was going to darken their doorstep.

I would darken it like night falling.

8

TAL

Powys, en route to Brycheiniog

I jumped down from my horse and began to pace.

Angws had escaped us. I had failed.

We had tracked Meirion's nephew through the long night and morning, all the way to Powys's border with Brycheiniog, following his progress through tracks in the mud and bracken and the eyes of villagers who had noticed a stranger on the road. But in the filmy hours around dawn, with the rising sun in our eyes, he'd slipped through my fingers and across the border.

As my guards conferred in low voices, I fought to control my temper. I only had so much silver. I could only ensure their loyalty so far.

It wasn't their fault that the nephew had eluded me, anyway. It was Dafydd's.

Wherever the road north had taken my brother, I hoped his luck was as bad as mine.

Heart still racing from our gallop, I leaned against my horse, Derog, and stared at the dyke opposite the hilltop.

The earthwork dominated the landscape, stretching from horizon to horizon, flanked by a deep ditch on the Welsh side and grown over with a hedge. It afforded Mercia a perfect view of our kingdoms and an ideal ground for attack.

There was no going around the dyke. It was over, or nothing. And anyone trying to climb it would be in view of the Mercian watchtowers that rose every five or six miles, some surrounded by entire camps of soldiers.

The dyke and the watchtowers were the reason my father and the other kings of the Marches had hurriedly built their border castles just over a decade ago. My father owned more comfortable palaces deeper within Powys, but in general, he remained at Mathrafal. If he had to leave, Osian remained, to act as his eyes and mouth.

My men's conversation behind me was beginning to sound like gossip *about* me. I turned back to them, trying to form another plan. "Where's the nearest town?" My voice was hoarse from the long chase.

"Foxhall is like to be the nearest town with a pub and beds," said one. "Five miles west."

Another snorted wearily. "Perhaps the hags under the hill can find the Sighted Raven's nephew."

They laughed, but I didn't join them.

Foxhall. It was like I'd slipped on a sheet of ice and hit my head. First the sense of falling, and then the solid cold of dread at my back.

I scanned the dyke again, like it might offer me alternatives. They came thick and fast and impossible—and all more appealing than my men's suggestion.

We could cross the dyke into Mercia, infiltrate the guard tower looming three miles away, and spy out Offa's plan of assault. We could keep pursuing Prince Angws into Brycheiniog, all the way to Black Darren. We could ride north and west from village to village, handing out silver to gather men and mount an army against the attack.

Or I could just go home, admit failure, and lose my last chance at becoming king.

I turned back to my men, bracing myself.

We couldn't go south into Brycheiniog, not on the tail of this chase. We couldn't go east into Mercia. It was west, or north. And the road north was the road home.

I couldn't go home. I couldn't.

Maybe I really had cracked my skull.

"West to Foxhall," I said numbly. "Lead the way."

Magic is Powys's only sure defense, Dafydd had said.

Dafydd had sabotaged my plan. Surely he wouldn't mind if I borrowed a little strategy from him.

Sometimes, when entering enemy territory, traveling incognito was wisest. The ride into Foxhall, I decided, was not one of those times.

Sunset was only an hour or two away when we rode into its bustling high street. Like many Welsh towns, Foxhall had been built on the site of a former Roman garrison, so its inhabitants were descendants of any number of peoples and places, just like the legion stationed there had been.

But the town also drew travelers. Petitioners traveled from all over Wales and much farther to beg help from the powerful coven beneath the hill.

Unfortunately, they would all have to wait till I was finished.

We found ourselves at a pub called the Dead Man's Bells. My guards announced me, and the owner, a full-bearded, barrel-chested Black man named Rhodri, called a groom to stable Derog and the other horses and a varlet to lock up our more valuable possessions. He was an efficient man, self-possessed, and while I doubted the Dead Man's Bells saw royalty every day, he was clearly not awed by our arrival.

"Do you need anything else before supper, Your Highness?" Rhodri asked, handing me a key.

"The Foxhall," I said, nails digging into my palms. "I'm on an errand from my father and need to speak with them."

Curiosity lit behind his eyes. "You're in luck, but only just," he said frankly. "It's a Penny Day, but they'll stop seeing petitioners after sunset."

"Petitioners?" My voice was affronted. I'd seen the supplicants outside the Foxhall—but I wasn't *one of them*. Still, Rhodri didn't correct himself.

Something about his polite nod told me he'd seen men like me come and go before.

Something about his eyes as he went about his business made me wonder what he knew and I didn't.

The Foxhall was a stone's throw from the Dead Man's Bells.

A long line straggled outside the dugout's deep orange door, nervously eyeing the bizarre unseasonal growth around it and the unsighted ravens that circled above. A market swarmed in the surrounding streets, vendors selling firewood and preserves, cheap dyes and the first of the spring's wool.

We pushed to the head of the line, and one of my men pounded on the door. "Open," he called, "in the name of Prince Taliesin of Powys." Gasps sounded behind us.

It was a minute or two—longer than I'd ever waited to be acknowledged by anyone besides my father—before the door opened on a pale-skinned witch with red-gold hair and a cane in one hand. Another woman squeezed past her out the door.

Distinguishing witch from petitioner was easy. One had loose hair, and one was openly sobbing.

"Prince Taliesin." The witch smiled grimly. "You will notice the line to your right."

"Ah," I said winningly. "But I am not a petitioner. I'm a prince."

"Everyone seeking help from the Foxhall is a petitioner, whether chieftain or charwoman." She lowered her voice, expression growing pained. "And all of these people have been here for hours."

"Do they all have a purse full of silver to offer the Foxhall for its help?"

"No. But I imagine a few of them have pocketknives ready to cut your purse strings. I'd advertise your wealth less widely."

Heat crept up my neck.

I put a silver penny in the collection box beside the door. And then, for the first time in my life, I made my way to the back of the line and prepared to wait.

I kept my eyes forward as the next two hours passed. Ahead of me, petitioners nursed injuries and steered friends or family members or animals and recited their pleas below their breath like prayers. I found myself doing the same.

I could ask the Foxhall for help retrieving Angws, I supposed. But as long as I was bothering to consult the hags, I might as well do the thing thoroughly and just ask for help breaking the dyke and dealing with the attack.

One by one, my fellow petitioners passed through the Foxhall door. Some left in tears. Some didn't. None left looking as though their hopes had been answered.

As daylight faded, I began to wonder with gathering horror if mine would be heard at all.

Twilight had fallen by the time the strawberry-blond witch came to the door again, looking more exhausted than before. "Rhiannon has declared the day at an end," she called, and frustrated murmurs went up from the still-long line. "The next Petitioners' Day will be in one week."

She moved to close the door, but I raced forward. "No," I said firmly, careful not to throw her off-balance as I kept her from shutting me out.

I'd waited. I'd let the Foxhall demonstrate its power and precedence in front of the town. I wouldn't be put off indefinitely.

"Don't let her—Rhiannon?—don't let her make you do her dirty work," I said. "If she wants to throw me out, let her do it herself."

I set my face, and she held her ground. But only for a moment.

"Your funeral." She stepped aside.

Then I crossed the threshold and closed the door, shutting the village out behind me.

It was cold under the hill, the deep dark broken only by rush-lights on the bare earthen walls. Ropes of ivy and thorny vines hung in clumps from the dugout's ceiling; a parliament of owls dozed in a niche in one corner. Beneath my feet, the wooden floorboards were painted the disorienting blue of a starry night sky.

A raised dais stood to one side of the hall, where nine women sat at a high table. Each of them wore their hair unbound and uncovered.

Loose, uncovered hair was the domain of children and wantons. But there wasn't a veil or a wimple or a neat braid in sight. Only the witch at the center of the table, an elderly woman with white skin and hair and reticent dark eyes, wore any kind of headpiece: twin fox ears, pinned to either side of her head. Their orange fur was matted and shabby, like she'd worn them every day for many years.

Dozens more witches sat on the room's perimeter. All of them watched the fox-eared witch.

I didn't trust crowds. But I had studied them extensively.

It was time to work.

"Well met, Foxhall," I said, executing a court bow. "I am Prince Taliesin ap Cadell, and I come to beg a favor." I caught murmurs of interest, but none from the high table.

"I am Rhiannon." The fox-eared witch considered me. Her shoulders were very narrow, and she seemed to frown without ever wrinkling her forehead. "What sort of favor do you seek, Prince Taliesin? And what do you offer this most eminent coven in exchange?"

"The coven beneath the hill cannot have failed to notice Mercia's increasing boldness," I began. I pitched my voice like I was tuning an instrument, trying to concentrate on my job of swaying them and not on the magic that hung thick on the air. "Offa's guards attack border villages without cause. His dyke he built without regard to existing boundary lines and largely under cover of night. He has pressed advantage wherever he could find it, wherever he thought we might not be able to retaliate—most lately, by the leveling of Pendwmpian Forest."

A gasp rose from the witch with the red-gold hair. Young as she was, she sat directly next to Rhiannon. "And the dragon—Arawn? Was he in hiding, as some had hoped?"

"Nowhere to be found," I said.

The young witch whispered something to Rhiannon, who again somehow frowned without moving her face. Pleasure sparked in the back of my mind, smoother than triumph, more satisfied than joy.

I was winning them over. I could feel it, their reactions coming in time to my words as though I were a storyteller or a musician and not a mere petitioner in their hall.

"And this is only their most recent affront," I continued. "My father is convinced that the dyke is the reason for magic's diminishment across Wales."

"What do you know of diminished magic?" Rhiannon asked.

"I know Pendwmpian's felling has caused our magician Osian's magic to disappear."

Murmurs rose again. Rhiannon's eyes sharpened on me, and I tried not to squirm.

I'd been too eager to sling back an answer. The Foxhall didn't need to know that it currently held more magic than the king of Powys.

Patience. Discretion. I'd forgotten.

It was time to make my point. "My father wants Offa's Dyke destroyed and our magic restored," I said. "I call on the coven under the hill to aid me. In exchange, I offer wealth, position at Mathrafal—" I broke off before I could offer the coven its own larger parcel of land. A more independent Foxhall was the last thing the throne needed.

I paused, trying on a smirk I didn't feel. "So, which of you will help me?" I asked. "Which of you will become rich beyond your imaginings and become my court magician when I'm king of Powys?" A few of the witches leaned forward, eyes narrowing, minds visibly churning with visions of futures that could be.

I knew what it looked like to persuade people. I could feel them bending to my cause.

"No," said Rhiannon.

I blinked, startled out of my thoughts. "What?"

"No, Prince Taliesin." She spoke simply, shaking her head. "We will not help you."

"But—" I fought to get my bearings. I caught sight of my feet on the star-painted floorboards and again felt that horrible sense of falling. "But one of you would be my court magician. Anything you want—it would be yours."

"What we want," Rhiannon said, "is to be left out of the affairs of kings and princes."

"Can you bear to see Powys trampled by Mercia?" My hands were shaking. "Can you bear to know that Arawn was the last of his kind, and now he's lost, too?"

I had had them. I had *had* them, and—

"Speak not to me of the lost creatures." Rhiannon's voice was hard. "I have watched Welsh magic wane my entire life, and I was born long before Offa completed his infernal dyke."

I stood in front of the coven, my chest heaving. I was sweating with anxiety and anger, I could *smell* the magic of the place, like rain and earth and—

The door to the Foxhall flew open with a crash. A ginger-haired witch more goblin than girl burst through the orange-painted door, stalked to the dais, and slammed her hands down on the high table.

"You," she raged. Her kirtle was covered in mud, and tears ran down her cheeks. Her face was red, from running or from weeping. "You killed him."

9

DAFYDD

Powys, en route to Gwynedd

When ten o'clock comes, the day stretches long,
Our hammers grow heavy, our faces grow drawn.
We wish but to rest, but time does not allow
There's work to be done, by the sweat of our brow.
—"The Workaday Song"

The rain was endless.

I was cold to my bones. My clothes clung to my body, my legs chafing against the saddle. Gruffudd kept close to my horse, but even Terrwyn's frame couldn't block the storm.

Tal had assembled a guard and a plan before he struck out. When I left Mathrafal, I hadn't bothered with either.

I'd ridden through the night; that morning, a silver halfpenny I'd found in my pocket had bought Gruffudd and me breakfast at a farmer's table. Sometime during the day, the road through Powys, a muddy, beech-lined drover's track, had turned into the road through Gwynedd.

The day had a smeared, unreal quality to it, the storm so heavy I was nearly upon the town before I spotted it. But when I saw the shepherd's hut, I dismounted and ducked inside the open door so quickly I almost hit my head on the lintel.

If the owner took issue with a large dog under his roof and a larger horse under his eaves, I would apologize and go. But the place was dark and seemed empty, so I shucked off my cloak and waited for the feeling to come back into my hands.

Suddenly, I felt a twinge in my side, an echo of pain that wasn't mine. I laid a hand over the tattoo on my ribs and grimaced.

"In a bit, I'll find us something to eat," I said. Gruffudd shook water out of his dense black fur. "Find us somewhere to sleep. Maybe . . ."

As my eyes adjusted, I lifted a boot, frowning at the filth caked on the floor. But then I heard the rustle of wings, and I looked up.

Black-winged, black-eyed, nesting in niches or hunched on pegs, a score of unsighted ravens stared down at me like a sky full of unforgiving suns.

I was not in a shepherd's hut.

I was in a columbarium.

My breath rasped in and out of my chest. I could see nothing, feel nothing, but the pitiless black eyes trained on me.

The columbaria had been built all over the Marches as resting places for sighted ravens, but they had all disappeared. Only unsighted ravens and other birds remained to fill them now.

These were not sighted ravens. They had no magic. They could not see to the heart of me and tell me the truth about myself I most feared.

But some were, once. Some could, years ago.

I had been living in dread of them half my life.

And by the poor light of the storm and my terror, they all looked the same.

I was on my mount and out in the storm as quick as Gruffudd could follow me. And I felt far safer out in the rain than I had sheltering beneath their gaze.

10

FFION

Foxhall, Powys

"You will have to be more specific, Ffion vch Catrin."

I hated when she called me that.

Rhiannon's expression was all mild irritation, shuttered calm. The coven under the hill was closed to outsiders; didn't I know?

And I'd never felt more like an outsider.

Rushlights, owls, inky-blue floors, packed-dirt walls. At the very back of the hall, consigned there as punishment for separating from my father, my mother sat looking horrified. My sister watched me steadily from Mam's old spot on the dais beside Rhiannon.

"Who are you?" someone—a boy—demanded, crossing the dugout floor.

Brown eyes. Beauty mark just right of his upper lip. Jewels on his fingers, gold on his boots, red coat made with expensive madder dye.

Rich. Pretty. I bit back a snarl. "Who are *you?*"

"Prince Taliesin ap Cadell."

"A prince? So it was for you, then," I seethed.

The prince took a startled step back. "What was for me?"

"They sacrificed a full acre of Foxhall Forest. Scorched it without even clearing the area." I turned again to the dais, my voice breaking. "You killed my fox."

Cadno was dead. I couldn't make the fact stick in my brain.

Dead, he would haunt the land of the living until the new moon in twenty-two days. Then, when the veil between our world and the Otherworld was thinnest, Cadno would leave me forever.

The prince frowned. "Burned a forest?"

"And killed my familiar," I said. "I hope it was worth it, peacock." At the back of the room, my mother's face went scarlet.

I waited for Rhiannon to react. But Foxhall witches didn't bother with familiars. She wouldn't know what it meant to lose one. "The sacrifice was not for Prince Taliesin," she said coldly.

I turned to the boy in the elaborate coat. Prince Taliesin. "Do you know what this place is?" I asked him in a mock whisper. "It's not a coven. Covens were never meant to be forty or fifty witches strong. It's a court, Prince Taliesin. It's an empire.

"There used to be a few dozen hedgewitches in every one of the petty kingdoms. It used to be that a mother, an aunt, their daughters, and a familiar or two"—I scrubbed my sleeve over my eyes again, *don't cry, don't cry*—"made a coven, and worked hard to make a little magic for the people who needed their help, and that was all anyone wanted. But that's not fast enough or strong enough for the Foxhall. So they lure every hedgewitch in Wales here with offers they can't refuse."

"Lies." Rhiannon's voice was dangerous.

I ignored her, eyes on the prince. "And now you have to come to Foxhall to beg for a spell or a charm."

"Every petitioner I saw left empty-handed," Prince Taliesin said keenly.

"So the brain inside your pretty head *does* work!" I snapped my fingers. "And there you have the rest of it. Travelers come to petition the coven under the hill. They pay their penny to wait in line. But the Foxhall only helps those it deems worth their attention. It appears you were not, for the record," I added, grimacing. "I should have realized they didn't burn the forest for you—no one who's anyone comes on Penny Day. The requests they actually honor are generally made privately." The prince's eyes widened in obvious offense. I didn't care.

I swallowed bile, looking from Rhiannon to my sister to my mother. "And whatever the magic costs, sacrifices are made."

"Catrin!" Rhiannon snapped. "Is *all* of your household beyond your control?"

"Don't you know by now?" I laughed bitterly. "I'm beyond anyone's control."

"Come on, Ffion. We can discuss this at home." Mam came to my side, head ducked, blushing. She was the image of Arianrhod in twenty years, the same pale skin, the same red-gold hair.

"I don't live at home, remember?" I bit out.

"Then—outside." Mam seized me by the shoulders. "This is humiliating. You have to go."

"And to think, I was worried what you'd think of me begging my supper last night." I laughed again, now in desperate, humorless gasps as she pushed me toward the dugout door; my chest didn't seem to be working properly. Tears pricked my eyes. "What was the sacrifice for, Mam? An old horse some nobleman wanted to breed past its years? A beauty charm?"

The sky above was dark. The lane was quiet, though light spilled from the open pub door.

My mother looked away. "A high man in Ceredigion. He wanted an invisibility spell for his mistress's house."

I was going to burn to death on my own anger. When I swung my fist, chunks of earth flew from the dugout wall.

"Ffion, if you were on the Foxhall, you could change things," my mother said, imploring. "If you don't like the way things are done, then join us, and make your case, and—"

"And in the meantime, what? Be party to this squander? This ruin?" Rage ate me up, flesh and bone. "Rhiannon doesn't listen, Mam. I've been saying for years that the Foxhall cares too much about money and power."

Now my mother threw up her hands, lined and red from years of changing nappies and preparing charms. "And is having power so terrible? Ffion, I know you stole from my chest, and I don't care. Because the world is dangerous, and you are working with scraps when you could have abundance instead. Why do you oppose power simply to be perverse?" she pleaded. "Why do you make everything so difficult?"

"Why do you make everything sound so simple? 'Come to the Foxhall, where we'll burn all the magic out of Wales to work spells that no one really needs!'"

"Then you won't come home?" she asked. "Your father doesn't like you living on your own, either."

"Dad's gone. He doesn't get a say. And you were the one who made me leave."

"I did *not* force you to leave. You decided you wanted to be alone."

"Dad never pushed me, but you did. I didn't want to join the Foxhall, and you wouldn't leave me in peace. And I wasn't alone until I lost Cadno." I pointed down the corridor. "And it's *their* fault."

Mam's voice was dark. "Your dad doesn't try to convince. He just *does,* and you find out what it cost you later." She paused, and when she spoke again, her voice was softer. "Ffion, I know a familiar is precious, but—"

"You don't know anything," I said. "Mam-gu would've understood. But you could never." Mam's blue eyes grew wet.

I'd aimed for a sore spot, and I'd found one.

Good.

"If you wanted to be like your mam-gu so much, you could've chosen to live with your father," she said quietly.

"You know I couldn't. Foxhall is my home," I said. "Besides, if I leave, I expect I'd come back to find Rhiannon's turned you into a decoration. Not like you're much more than that these days anyway."

With that, I stomped back into the coven's receiving hall, where Prince Taliesin waited.

Arianrhod and I had heard of Prince Taliesin, of course. He was a schemer who tended to land on his feet. Rhiannon would regret not helping him later, when he got whatever it was he wanted.

That, I wanted to see. If I was going to drown in loneliness, I wanted to watch Rhiannon drowning in regret alongside me.

"I will see this place finished," I said, and it was more than a promise. It was a tynged pronounced over them.

I stamped my foot, and a single vine of poison ivy pushed its way between two floorboards, curling like a venomous snake against the night-blue wood.

Unmistakable. Irrevocable.

I turned to the prince.

"Prince Taliesin, I have the unfortunate habit of helping people the Foxhall ignores. And tonight, I'm feeling particularly helpful." I watched Rhiannon as I spoke. "If you want to talk, I'll be at the Dead Man's Bells."

The pub was busy when I arrived, folk eating and drinking at its long, low tables, enjoying the big fire in the hearth. Two maids served honey- and cinnamon-scented bragawd from casks and carried sausages and cawl and caws pobi out from the kitchen, all of it just enough to mask the stink of the tallow candles.

I propped myself against the bar and proceeded to wait.

How many times had I been here with Cadno? *I have to keep this place clean, Ffion!* Rhodri would exclaim, and I'd say, *I bathed three weeks ago!* and he'd try to feed us both without letting me pay.

But Cadno was dead. I had nothing powerful enough to raise him, and unless I stole my mam's chest and the apothecary's entire supply, that wasn't likely to change.

When I'd buried him on the forest's edge, I'd sung a lullaby over his grave.

The hunters now are gone to bed,
Reynard, in your coat of red,
Sleep, little fox, sleep.
The doe her spotted fawns has fed,
Bruin rests his heavy head,
Sleep, little fox, sleep.
Badger's ceased his burrowing tread,
Night the sun's last light has bled,
Sleep, little fox, sleep.

The night of the new moon, in twenty-two days, he would cross from our world to the Otherworld, Annwn. But for now, at least, he could hear me.

I wondered if I was imagining that I felt him close by. I hoped the song had brought him comfort.

I wiped my eyes and crossed my arms and dared anyone to bother me.

Rhodri appeared at my side, brow cocked. "Ffion. What brings you here twice in one—are you all right?" His face changed when he caught sight of mine.

I looked away. "Cadno was caught in one of the Foxhall's sacrifices. He's—" I cleared my throat. "He's gone."

His big shoulders sagged. "Ffion."

"I don't want to talk about it."

"All right." He nodded, turned away for a moment to pour ale for a patron. "What brings you here, then?"

"Waiting for a customer. You may have seen him," I said. "I can't decide if I'm more excited to annoy the Foxhall or to bilk a prince out of his pocket money."

"Prince Taliesin?" Rhodri poured another ale.

I nodded. "Did you see the coat he was wearing? What a peacock."

"You already called me that," a voice said behind me. "I'd consider a new insult. Spendthrift, maybe. This coat *did* cost me eighteen ceiniogau."

Prince Taliesin ap Cadell. He'd come after all.

"You could hire a knight for four days for that much money. You could pay a cooper for a month. You could buy—" I buried my face in my hands, exhausted. "So much grain."

"But I didn't want grain or a knight or a cooper. I wanted an impressive coat."

I dropped my hands, turning to stare at him over my shoulder.

Prince Taliesin was as tall and lean as when I'd left him ten minutes earlier. Same golden-brown eyes and hair, beauty mark in the same spot.

But his face was different. Almost sorry.

For a long moment, I couldn't look at anyone else in the pub.

He cleared his throat. "My condolences on the loss of your familiar."

"Diolch." I turned back to the bar. "We should talk over dinner. You're buying. Oh," I added to Rhodri, "and I haven't eaten since yesterday, so keep it coming." Rhodri rolled his eyes.

I made my way to an empty bench.

"Ffion?" I looked up. Arianrhod.

"What are you doing here?" I asked as she sat.

"You don't even know what he wants," she said without preamble. "You don't even know what he asked the Foxhall."

I laughed bitterly. "Are you opposed to me taking your leavings?

Aren't sisters supposed to share things?"

"It's dangerous, Ffion," Arianrhod bit out. She never spoke to me this sharply. "No one will be able to protect you if you go with him."

"Cadno died two miles from the edge of town." I slammed a hand on the table. "What protection do I have here?"

"Don't pretend this is only about Cadno. I just don't understand what we did to make you prefer being alone to anything else in the world. I don't understand what I did wrong."

Guilt surged through me, and then anger. "It's not about you. It's about them. And you're with them."

My sister had been frustrated when I refused to join the Foxhall at fourteen. And though she hadn't hounded me like Mam, her heart had slowly broken as it became clearer I'd never change my mind.

"I am," she agreed. "Magic has a cost, Ffion. I do the best I can. But I'm just one person. This is the way the world works."

"I don't accept that." I shook my head. "If this is how their world works, then I'm going to find another one."

"You can't just leave!" she said. "Mam—"

"Mam's got you."

"Like Dad always had you." Arianrhod's expression tightened. "Ffion, don't act like I'm the only one who's someone's favorite."

"Maybe, but I didn't pick a side. Dad's gone, and I'm alone. Mam's here, and you're around to comfort her while Rhiannon tosses her scraps," I said. "So what does she need me for?"

Arianrhod hadn't spoken up for me earlier at the Foxhall. And I didn't take back my words as she picked up her cane and left.

The prince arrived with two tankards of bragawd and settled himself across the table. "Your sister?" he asked. I nodded. "Bit harsh."

I *had* been harsh. I'd been cruel to Arianrhod, and Mam, and I hated myself for it. But I was too wrung out for guilt.

"The world's a harsh place," I said. "And the first thing you should know about me is that I'm not a nice person, Prince Taliesin."

"It's Tal," he said. "And neither am I."

"Excellent. Self-awareness is a rare and beautiful quality." I took a brief drink; I hadn't eaten, and I didn't want to be too loose to work.

Taliesin—Tal—sipped delicately from his own cup, brow furrowing. "What do you mean?"

"I mean that lots of people think that they're nice because their lives are nice," I said. "It's nothing to be pleasant if you sleep in a warm bed, always have a full stomach, and spend your days among other pleasant people. That's not goodness. That's good living."

The prince seemed to consider this. "That may be true. It's just not true of my life." From his faintly wistful faraway expression, it was clear I was meant to pursue the point with a question.

It was clear, generally, that Tal enjoyed (and was used to getting) questions about himself and other kinds of attention. It was just bad luck for him that a barmaid appeared then with an armload of plates, because never in my life had I paid attention to a boy when there was food to see to.

Two bowls of cawl—stew made with salted bacon, swedes, and carrots—hit the table first, followed by a platter of caws pobi and a plate of sausages and root vegetables. I picked up a sausage automatically and made to pass it to Cadno.

When I remembered he wasn't there, I had to brace myself until the moment stopped stinging.

"So if you're a witch," Tal began, "why don't you sit on the Foxhall like your mother and sister?"

I put the sausage down and dragged a bowl of cawl toward myself. "When I was seven, I saw them sacrifice a brace of hawks by fire. Burned them alive," I said around a mouthful. Tal cringed. "That's their way. I always knew I'd never join them after that."

"You could always stage a coup. Seize power from underneath Rhiannon and do things differently."

"Ha! Spoken like the Prince Taliesin I've always heard of," I said. "Anyway, I work alone, in a fashion too small for the coven under the hill."

"I'm not sure *small* is what I'm looking for." Tal retrieved an ornate knife from his belt and cut into a sausage. I reached for a slice of caws pobi, the toasted cheese burning my fingers as it dripped off the bread.

"Maybe you should tell me what that is, then," I said irritably.

Taliesin glanced around the pub before he spoke, and when he did, his story was almost too fantastic to be believed: a magician whose magic had left him; a forest felled; a dragon lost; an attack forthcoming; our king fated to die and his sons sent out to stop it, the victor to be king and the loser to be candler, once Offa's Dyke was broken and magic restored.

When he was done, I let out a long whistle. "I'm not surprised the Foxhall turned you down. No letter from your father. No guarantee of payment. Just a risky job. Too bad for you that the Foxhall would rather not make enemies when they could make money instead."

Tal pulled a face.

"And Osian is powerless now?" I asked. "I'm sure Rhiannon found that interesting." I certainly did.

"I shouldn't have told her," Tal muttered.

"No, you shouldn't have." I thought for a moment. "Where has Prince Dafydd gone?"

"I don't know. He went north, I went south," he said. "And I don't know why he agreed to do it. He doesn't even want to be king—or he didn't before, anyway." He took a bite of cawl, wincing at its temperature.

He had a frivolously pretty mouth, I thought; his teeth were straight, his lips with their beauty mark as extravagant as his clothes. Apart from the red coat embroidered with gold, his shirt and hose were of impossibly fine wool. Bronze glinted on his fingers and around his neck.

"I don't know exactly what I need from you," he finally admitted. "What I know is that King Offa has limitless forces at his disposal. Knights on horseback, soldiers on foot. Powys will never match him for numbers."

"But?"

"But Mercia does not have magic," said Tal, bending his head toward me. "Offa has never brought a magician to battle. We've never heard of his keeping one at his seat at Tamworth Castle. We *have* heard gossip that his Mercian soldiers are mistrustful of witchcraft." He drained his bragawd. "I won't bother trying to match him where it's impossible to do so. I want to press what advantage we have."

He was as clever as I'd heard. "And what do you know about magic, Prince Taliesin?"

The wash of expressions over his face was too quick for me to follow. It was doubt, it was mistrust, it was schooled into something careful before I could properly read it. "Only that even weak Welsh magic is terrible to behold."

"And your father wants us to destroy Offa's Dyke to restore it," I said. "Before Offa's attack, which could be as soon as the next new moon."

Tal nodded. "Osian said it was a new moon. So I think we've at least got a month."

"Twenty-two days."

He blinked. "Pardon?"

"There are twenty-two days until the new moon," I said, feeling a zip of nerves.

Could it be a coincidence that the attack was due the day Cadno would leave me?

I thought of Mercians felling our forests and encamped on our moors, of magic leached from our land like color from winter grass. Of the pod of dragons I had seen once as a child and never again, and of all the other creatures that had once roamed our land but no more.

Could magic really be restored with Offa's Dyke destroyed?

Was that really all it would take?

Before all our magical beasts had gone to ground, every year, a creature called the Mari Lwyd went walking. She was the temporary revival—the incomplete resurrection—of a unicorn who'd recently died, one who hadn't yet crossed over to Annwn. But she hadn't returned in years, and it was widely assumed that this was because there'd been too little magic left in the land to raise her.

But if magic returned to Wales—

My heart began to pound.

If a lack of magic in the land was to blame for the Mari Lwyd's absence, then magic's return might be her return, too.

And if the Mari Lwyd could return—what else could I bring back?

A hard look crossed the prince's face. "There would be payment, of course. Whatever you thought was fair."

I didn't think it merited telling him money hadn't even crossed my mind. "I would think many, many times the cost of your coat a fair price," I cautioned him, hiding my hands so he wouldn't see them shake.

"Unsurprising." He rolled his eyes. Then he sobered.

Plenty of men in Foxhall were sturdier built than the prince, with rougher hands and harder faces. But I'd never seen eyes as sharp as his in someone who lived so comfortably.

Eyes that sharp usually belonged to the mildly criminal, the somewhat street-bred, the hedge-dwelling. Those who'd been intimate friends with desperation.

I could hardly believe it of a rich pretty boy like Prince Taliesin, but it seemed possible we might understand one another.

So it wasn't warmth, exactly, that spread through me as I stuck out my hand and Tal shook it.

It was more like a warming fury. A righteous rage. A dark kind of hope that eased through my veins and made me smile.

The Foxhall was not going to take my familiar from me. I was going to take back what they'd stolen.

I was going to restore magic to Wales, and I was going to resurrect Cadno before he crossed over to Annwn.

"As hedgewitch of Foxhall," I said, "and for a price, I offer you my services."

"As prince of Powys," said Tal, "I accept."

11

TAL

The fire crackled; Rhodri took orders at the bar; two men at the far end of our table argued over a game of knucklebones. Nothing had changed, but suddenly everything had.

"Have you done this sort of thing before?" I asked.

"Eaten more than my fair share of a meal?" Across the table, Ffion studied me as if I were a lock she was picking. But two could play that game. I studied her right back.

Ffion had come to the Foxhall to brawl, and she looked like it, with her snarl of ginger hair and stained dress snagged with leaves and grass. Where Arianrhod was tall, with smooth hair and a round face, her younger sister only came to my shoulder and was thin to the point of ill health. Freckles like daisies in a field covered her from forehead to bare feet, and there was a gap between her two front teeth, and her skin was as pale as the milk peasants used to leave out for the bwbachod.

Ffion's face was fey, curious, almost foxlike. But beneath her assertiveness and wit, her gray eyes were hollow with loss. And though she was hard to look away from, she was too thin, too hard-edged—too wild—to be properly beautiful.

"You know what I mean," I said. "Magic. On this scale."

Ffion made a face, pulling a piece of gristle from her teeth. "Has *anyone* worked this sort of destruction before? The dyke runs the length of three kingdoms."

She had a point. "Maybe the Foxhall, or Osian?" I'd done my best to ignore Osian's work through the years, but I vaguely recalled him once bursting a massive dam. Still, even that hardly compared.

"Osian, whose magic has left him." Ffion scratched at a ragged cuticle. "I wonder what he'll do with himself now."

"Hopefully leave court forever—well, why would he stay?" I asked, almost defensive, when Ffion eyed me curiously. "What good is a magician who can't do magic?"

"What good are half the ones who can? So much forest destroyed," she muttered into her tankard. "And for what?"

"Are you talking about the Mercians or the Foxhall?" I asked. We stared at one another for a long moment, both of us sobering.

"I'm not sure how I'd bring down the dyke, Tal," Ffion finally said. "My magic isn't given to destruction. I help sick children and old women and animals. But maybe . . ." She chewed the inside of her cheek. "My grandmother told me when I was little that a branch of the mine near Coed Croes collapsed and the men inside had to be rescued."

"What did they do?"

"She had to blow the whole thing open." Ffion reached into the bag at her hip and produced a book.

"You can read?" The words were out before I could stop myself.

She shot me a poisonous glare. "No! Maybe you could teach me? I'm sharp enough, it should only set our quest back by a few months."

"I beg your pardon. My mistake," I said, smooth as I would have to any high man's daughter. Ffion acknowledged the apology with barely a lift of her eyebrows as she began flipping through the pages. Farther down the table, one of the men playing knucklebones spilled his bragawd and cackled.

"Ha!" She thumped a page covered in writing. "Here. The spell Mam-gu used to break into the mine. It calls for a fragment of what needs to be broken, and fuel for the breaking."

"That's all?" I cocked an eyebrow, reaching for the book, but Ffion snatched it back.

"Of course that's not all." Her voice was defensive. "If this spell is like the others I've worked on houses and buildings—spells I've worked to strengthen them, I mean—I have to keep close to it. When I'm charming my mam's house, I touch every wall. I touch the roof, the daub, the doorframe. And I bury the charm near the foundation."

I nodded. My food was forming a lump in my stomach from all this talk of magic. "And—what kind of fuel?"

"I use things I've gleaned, generally. Most witches would use wood or animal entrails or some such. But a charm like this . . ." Ffion took a bite of cawl, swallowed. "Here's what you have to understand, Tal. The Foxhall would sacrifice a whole forest. Honestly, I bet they'd sacrifice a magical creature, if they could find one."

A thrill of horror. "Do they exist here?"

"Not anymore. There used to be gwyllgwn in these parts," Ffion said. "Mam-gu said there were ceffylau dŵr in the lakes to the west, and a llamhigyn y dŵr in the brook in Foxhall Forest." The gwyllgi was a terrible black dog that haunted roads and graveyards, and the ceffyl dŵr and the llamhigyn y dŵr—a water horse and a winged, froglike water leaper—harassed anyone who came near their lakes and rivers.

"They say my great-great-grandfather and his magician rode an aderyn llwch gwin into battle. Dad said he had a whole stable of them and the floor was covered in shed feathers and talons. There used to be bwbachod in the castle, too," I added, stifling a shudder at the idea of finding a house fairy by my hearth or bedside.

Untold numbers of creatures had gone missing a decade ago, some more common, some rarer. Some were unique beasts that had kept their rampaging to particular regions, like the Cath Palug, a huge, horrible cat in Anglesey, and the Twrch Trwyth, a prince who'd been cursed to become a wild boar. And then, of course, there was the Mari Lwyd, who appeared many places, but always at Midwinter.

I couldn't fathom how the dyke could be responsible for the creatures going missing. In any case—good riddance, I said.

"Anyway." Ffion swallowed. "That's not how I work. I don't need a sacrifice of that size or rarity."

"No?"

"No," she said firmly, almost vehemently. "If I travel the entire length of the dyke, a smaller sacrifice will be enough. That's the difference in how the Foxhall and I work. Their methods are quicker and easier, but they use more fuel, or richer ingredients. I put in more work, so my gleaned materials can do big jobs," she said. "My labor—the contact, all the walking—makes my materials more potent."

"Wouldn't it be faster and surer to do it their way?" I asked.

"It would. And I want to see the job done, because I want magic restored as much as anyone," she said. "But their way—I think it's a mistake."

Ffion didn't know how much I wanted magic's return. Meaning, I didn't want it at all.

My first plan had been to ally with Brycheiniog and solve the imminent problem of Offa's attack. That done, surely Father would've had to hand me the throne, with or without magic restored—especially if Dafydd had done what he usually did, which was absolutely nothing. But things were different now. That plan couldn't work, because Dafydd was a true player in our game, and I couldn't expect to succeed while ignoring half of our father's challenge.

The idea of bringing magic back still made me feel ill. But then I remembered something.

When I'd been below the hill, Rhiannon had said that magic had been waning since well before the dyke was even built. Could that be true?

It made sense to me. After all, how could walling off some of our land—land I assumed wasn't any more magical than the rest—have killed magic?

So maybe it didn't matter. Ffion would destroy the dyke—still necessary, since it gave Mercia an advantage in battle—and surely Dad wouldn't fault *me* if it didn't effect a supernatural change in our land.

But even with the dyke destroyed, there was still the attack to be reckoned with. We needed to be able to stand against the Mercian armies and their weapons, and—

My thoughts snagged. *Weapons.*

"Have you ever heard of the Marches' blades? The llafnau?" I asked suddenly. "I wonder how Mercia would fare against them in battle."

She frowned. "I've heard of them, but I don't know anything about them."

Neither did I, really. But I remembered clearly what little my father and brother had said.

Weapons. The Marches. *Powys isn't completely without magic.*

"They have magical properties, I think," I said. "They protect the Marches—so Gwynedd and Brycheiniog must have some, too. One is housed at Mathrafal, but I don't know where."

"They have magical properties, but they're weapons?" Ffion's frown deepened with confusion.

"I'm not sure what kind of weapons," I admitted. "Probably swords, but they could be daggers or pikes or glaives or—"

Ffion held up a hand. "You don't have to list every weapon you can think of. You don't know anything else about them?"

"We can ask at Black Darren and Prestatyn Castle."

"You don't want to ask Osian?" Ffion cocked an eyebrow.

"No." I wished I'd asked about the blades before, but I hadn't. And given the nature of Dad and Osian's connection, I wasn't going to do it now. I'd seen Osian's eyes glaze over and my father's voice come out of his mouth too many times. I didn't even know if their thoughts could be kept secret from one another.

I wasn't letting my father in on my plan until it had succeeded.

"Anyway," I pushed on, "I can use them. If you break the dyke, I can collect the blades to fight the Mercian army."

Ffion shook her head, and for the first time she looked unsure of herself. "Merthyr-Tewdrig to Prestatyn. It's so far."

"You were the one who proposed walking the length of the dyke," I said. "If you don't think you can do it—"

Her expression shuttered. "I can do it," she snapped. "I've just never been farther than a few miles from Foxhall, is all. It's harder to travel without fancy boots and a fine horse," she added, eyeing my shoes significantly.

"As it happens, I haven't spent much time away from Mathrafal," I said, gesturing around the pub. "What is there out *here* to lure me away from court?"

Ffion gave a sharp laugh, more animal than human. "You're a snob." She paused. "I don't know, Tal. The llafnau—if they're part of our defense against Mercia, shouldn't they stay where they are? What if we need them more in the future?"

"Carry that logic through to its end, we'd never use them," I said. Head bent toward her bowl, Ffion's brow furrowed meaningfully, as if to say, *exactly*.

"I assume you have a plan for how we're going to obtain these magic blades from King Bleddyn and King Meirion? Seeing as how we've been harassing their borders for the better part of—well, forever," she said. "Knowledgeable about court affairs as you are, I'm sure you've considered that."

I did my best to turn my wince into a smirk. Ffion didn't know the half of it. I'd have to tell her about my attempt to ransom Prince Angws eventually, but for the moment, I'd rather keep looking clever.

"Lucky for us, I've made something of an art out of salvaging sour political situations."

"Even in a court where the king can supposedly always tell the truth from a lie?" Her expression was pointed.

"Look. I'll figure out how to get the blades," I said impatiently. "Can you be ready to leave in the morning? We'll need to outfit ourselves, and I'll need to summon a company of soldiers to meet us at—"

"No companies of soldiers," Ffion cut in. "No soldiers at all."

"I'm not spending a hundred and eighty bickering miles alone with you, Ffion vch Catrin. You'd slit my throat with a smile in two days."

"'Vch Catrin'?" Ffion asked, frowning again, and I did, too. "Daughter of Catrin"—wasn't that what Rhiannon had called her? She shook her head, moving on. "Believe me, if I'm going to kill you, I'll do it in your sleep. Less bother."

She was absurd. "So. Soldiers?" I prompted. "A company of them."

"No more than half a dozen."

"A dozen."

"Ten," she countered. "Any more, and you can find yourself another hedgewitch."

"So—just my personal guard." I rolled my eyes. "Fine."

Ffion took a swig of her ale, thinking, staring into the fire. "Why did you accept my help, Tal?"

I blinked at her. "Are you reconsidering?"

"No, no." She shifted, hunching like a bwbach as she drew her bare feet up beneath her. "Just curious. After all, the coven under the hill are notorious, and I'm a hedgewitch nobody's heard of."

"Because you're my last resort," I finally said. "The maneuver I attempted failed, and then I was denied by the Foxhall, and then you made a very compelling case."

Everything about Ffion made me suspect she might ruin all my plans. But as my plans had already been ruined three times over, I'd gone ahead and followed her to the pub.

"I highly doubt that I'm your *last* resort." Ffion flicked the signet ring on my thumb. I yanked my hand back and gave her knuckle a thump to see how she liked it. "People like you have net after net underneath them—chances upon chances. You act like you've danced with desperation, Tal, but I'm finding it hard to believe."

"Believe what you want," I said, no bitterness, all rue. "I wish you were right."

"You're a prince of Mathrafal. What else is there to know?" She paused. "Maybe I should have asked this before I agreed to travel with you."

I scowled. "I don't have any bizarre secret vices, if that's what you're asking."

"Tell me why I should pity you, then," she asked, a smile tugging at the corner of her mouth. "I think you want it, a little bit. To be petted and cooed over, to be the sad, charming bastard in the fine red coat sulking attractively in the corner."

"Pity me for that, if you want," I offered with a grin. "Because I am a sad, charming bastard. Because despite Dafydd's disinterest, King Cadell has made it clear that he wants Dafydd to be king; I am, at best, his second choice."

"Only second choice for king?" Ffion grinned, not sharply enough to hurt. "Truly, a tale of woe."

"Truly." I paused, thinking. "I will give you one thing, Ffion. I have not danced with desperation, to use your words, but desperation has certainly appeared at my door. And I've had to set the bar and draw the latch to keep her out."

Tonight, and oh, the coldest night,
The coldest night, the coldest night,

Tonight, and oh, the coldest night,
Come we now to your fire.

Ffion watched me. Her gray eyes were like river stones, like cold water, like low clouds promising rain. "Interesting."

At the end of the table, one of the men swept the knucklebones into a pouch at his hip, muttering insinuations. The other began to raise his voice, until Rhodri called to both of them to settle down or settle it outside, he didn't care which.

"You said we needed outfitting," Ffion said. "Can I take care of that for you?"

"That would be helpful." I shoved a hand through my hair, thinking. "My men are armed and outfitted, and their horses have been tended to. But we'll need food, and you'll need clothes fit to be seen in." Ffion crossed her arms. "No offense."

"None taken." Ffion looked thoughtful. "What did you say that coat cost you?"

I thought. "Seventeen ceiniogau. No, eighteen."

"Right, right." She counted on her fingers. "I'd say twenty-five ought to cover it?"

"That much?" I had more than that in my purse, but still.

"It's still early spring. Stores are short." Then she nodded at my bowl of cawl. "Are you going to eat the rest of that?"

I frowned at the almost empty bowl. "It's not good manners to clean your plate."

"Ha!" She dragged the bowl over, using a piece of caws pobi she'd apparently squirreled away to sop up what remained. "Your courtly manners won't serve you so well away from Mathrafal, Taliesin. You're out in the wilds now." She grinned up at me, a bit of dried parsley stuck in her front teeth. Somehow, I knew she knew it was there and didn't care.

"Clearly." But as I counted out coins and watched her go, I felt my spirits lift for the first time all day.

With Ffion and her feral grin in my arsenal, I could destroy the dyke and earn the throne.

Rhiannon must be right. And Ffion was only one hedgewitch. And I knew what she didn't.

Sometimes we couldn't make things better; we could only keep them from getting worse. Sometimes offense was impossible, and all we could hope to do was defend the thing we loved the most.

One girl might be able to keep Wales from destruction. But magic in our kingdom had died.

And no one could bring back the dead.

12

DAFYDD

On the Dyke, Gwynedd

The sweat of our brow, the sweat of our brow
In the smithy, the mines, at the back of the plow,
An honest day's work for an honest endowt,
We labor and live by the sweat of our brow.
—"The Workaday Song"

The pub was called the Bwbach and Board, and since I'd forgotten to bring a purse, I had to pay for my supper and bed with my undershirt. The landlord said it would fit him nicely once it had dried out.

I dripped all the way across the floor to a bench by the hearth, Gruffudd at my heels. The landlady had offered me a blanket, which I had thought was kind. After I'd begun to dry my face and Gruffudd's fur with it, she told me the blanket was my bedsheet, and it was mine to do as I liked with, and very welcome I was.

"Humbler surroundings than you're used to," said the woman at the end of the bench. "Aren't they?"

The blanket was a lost cause; I chafed Gruffudd's fur with it, not looking up. "What makes you say that?"

"There's copper chasing on your knife handle," she said. "Yet you don't travel with coin. You're used to being anticipated. Welcomed." *You're inexperienced*, she didn't say, but she didn't have to. I glanced up just long enough to be polite.

She was in her early thirties, pale face a little lined, light brown hair in a knot. But beneath the ordinariness was a composure I recognized. Gwanwyn had it, too.

The girls my age who lingered outside my forge whispering made me nervous enough. I turned back to Gruffudd, trying to look busy.

I was relieved when a man with hair and eyes the same color as hers came and sat down opposite, two bowls of cawl in hand. "She agrees with you," he announced, nodding back at the landlady. "She says you feed the child and let the adults die."

"You're heartless, sir!" the landlady called.

He threw out his arms. "Who's going to take care of the child if the adults have died?"

"Iorweth." The woman cut her eyes at me.

"I—what?" The man glanced over, catching my expression. "Oh, I'm sorry. It's just a riddle. Well, not a riddle, exactly."

"We're philosophizing," the woman explained. "I'm Canaid. This is my brother Iorweth."

"Dafydd," I said.

"Hm. Nos da, Dafydd." Canaid nodded briskly. "The question is: If you and another adult and a child were starving and had no more hope of getting food, who would starve, and who would eat?"

My stomach twisted, and I glanced at the door. "Dark philosophy."

"Maybe." She studied me, from the gleaming copper in my knife grip to the soot under my nails. "Iorweth says that everyone should eat until stores run out. We"—Canaid gestured at the woman behind the bar—"say that the adults should starve and give the child a better chance of surviving. I've heard some say one adult and the child should eat, so if the child lives, he'll have a guardian."

The barmaid put a plate of caws pobi and a hunk of lamb at my place. I stared at the plates, my mouth bone-dry.

"I would search out more food," I finally said. Gruffudd pressed against my leg; I pressed back against him.

Iorweth grinned jovially, gesturing at me with his tankard. "That's not one of the choices. You have to choose."

"No. I would search for supplies and not come home until I found them." My voice was too loud; across the pub, people were turning to stare.

Iorweth frowned. "No, that's not how—"

"It should be," I interrupted, louder still, and suddenly, I wasn't arguing with Iorweth and Canaid anymore. "How can you choose who starves and who survives? You're not a god, and you shouldn't have that power!"

Canaid spoke calmly. "Dafydd, it's just a game."

"It's *not* a game. You don't know anything." My voice was shaking now. I got to my feet.

If I ate now, I'd throw up. I stuffed the bread in my pocket and tossed the lamb to Gruffudd, then pushed through the door.

Starvation or survival. Adult or child.

Candler or king.

Some questions were too hard to answer. Some burdens were too heavy to bear.

Crown a sighted raven, I cursed the night sky. *Crown a dragon. Crown a god. Leave us mere mortals to our work.*

Sitting against the pub's outer wall, I reached out to the girl in my thoughts, wishing she were here.

She was the girl of my daydreams. The girl I was destined for.

She and my work were the only things that had ever brought me peace.

The problem was, we'd never spoken. We only knew each other from afar. But she'd still taught me everything I'd ever learned that mattered. I touched the tattoo on my side and leaned against the stones.

I sat in the rain until my teeth were chattering, Gruffudd barking worriedly at me from under the eaves. Then I went upstairs to my narrow room, peeled off my clothes, and slept.

Gruffudd whined uneasily in his dreams. And I would've given away every last stitch of my clothing if it would've kept the questions out of mine.

13

FFION

Foxhall, Powys

The prince was an idiot. The knowledge gave me no small degree of satisfaction as I left the Dead Man's Bells with a full belly and absurdly heavy pockets.

Twenty-five ceiniogau to feed our company for a couple of weeks. I could've fed Foxhall for an entire season with so much money. He was a fool. As I bedded down alone that night beneath the hedge, I tried to be comforted by this.

No matter how clever the prince seemed, he knew nothing about the world outside Mathrafal. I could work toward my own ends while I worked for him, and he would never know.

I had the dream again that night. Water and standing stones, the sea and the sky and the sand all silver and gray, and a blazing burst of wind.

There was anger in the dream—true anger that I felt deep in my bones. But there was power, too. And freedom.

I let its memory warm me as I set out into the chilly morning, starting my first day without Cadno since I was five years old.

It was another market day, so after a rummage in the forest and a visit to the mill, I bought the rest of our supplies. At the butcher's stall and Cefin's farm stand, three silver pennies bought enough to feed our company for a month. Two more ceiniogau and a visit to the seamstress's stall later, I was in possession of two clean kirtles—one undyed, one black—and a cloak. Secondhand, as many of the clothes at Adara's stall were. "This was Rhiannon's, as it happens," she said around a mouthful of pins, fitting the black garment closer to my shift and hose underneath.

I had spent my life in Arianrhod's, and occasionally Gareth's, old clothes. But wearing something of Rhiannon's gave me the shivers.

The cloak nearly made up for it, though. It was thick and warm, weld-dyed the color of an autumn leaf before it fell and embroidered with a pattern of mushrooms and acorns.

I saved the worst errand for last.

When my mother answered my knock at the cottage door, the hopeful look on her face was enough to make me feel sick.

"Ffion!" she exclaimed, turning to look over her shoulder. "Tegan! Taffy! Look who's come to see you!"

Taffy took her thumb out of her mouth and raced over on fat little legs, beaming. "Fee?"

"Ffion's here?" Gareth appeared in the back doorway, dirt on his trousers. He and Hywel must have been in the vegetable patch. The hearth looked as if they'd rebricked it, and the front room walls looked freshly whitewashed. I hadn't noticed when I'd been here the night before last.

The house looked wonderful. They all looked wonderful.

Everyone that belonged was here, except for Cadno.

"We're glad to see you," Mam said warmly. "Please, sit. Will you take something to drink? After last night, I—"

"Mam!" I cut in. "I can't stay."

"Can't stay?" She repeated my words as if I'd spoken them in another language. "But you just got here."

"I know." I swallowed hard; a lump had formed in my throat. "I didn't come to sit or have anything to drink or to—to see the twins."

Arianrhod's voice was quiet. Her eyes were red. "Then why did you come, Ffion?"

Guilt sat like spoiled food in my stomach.

Wordlessly, I dumped the twenty remaining silver ceiniogau into my mother's hand. Tegan scrambled over when one slipped from my fingers to the packed earth floor. "Shiny!" he hollered up to Arianrhod, who took the coin before he could put it in his mouth, then scooped him up as he began to wail.

"Ffion." Mam's voice was uncertain. The coins sang in her palm; two more fell to the ground. "Ffion, what is this? Where did you get it?"

"Where do you think I got it?" I looked away from her. "It's to pay for the elder cordial I took."

"Ffion." She hesitated. "Did you steal this?"

"Did I—?" I scoffed. "Maybe I did. But when I come back, I'll have more. Lots more."

This wasn't even my payment. This was just what Tal had had lying around for expenses.

But for the moment, at least I was square with the Foxhall. I owed them nothing. And soon, I would have something to show for my work, for all Mam doubted my methods.

When I reached for the door, she stopped me with a hand on my arm. "Where are you going?"

"She's going with Prince Taliesin." Arianrhod didn't look away from me, even as Tegan squirmed in her arms. "She's going to destroy Offa's Dyke."

My mother gasped. "Ffion, no. It's too dangerous. And even if you can manage the magic, it's going to start a war."

"It's not going to start a war, Mam. War's already coming, and it has to be met." Mam had never confronted a fact when she could sidestep it altogether.

"But the doings of the powerful, so far from home—they aren't our affair." She shook her head. "This is why Rhiannon—"

"Rhiannon didn't turn Tal down because of the risk, and you know it," I said vehemently. My throat felt thick. "Cadno was my home. And he's gone now. But Powys is my home, too, and someone—someone who loves it more than money or power—has to protect it."

"*This* is your home!" my mother shouted, and I nearly stumbled back in my surprise. I'd never heard Mam raise her voice. Not at any of us. Not at my father, even when they'd parted ways for good.

I'd also never truly seen her cry. But she did now, turning away from me, burying her face in her hands. Arianrhod caught at her shoulder, holding Mam even as she held my littlest brother.

I hated it. But tears pricked my eyes as well.

"You're right," I said, my voice breaking. "This is my home. But I can't stay here. And you know why."

Arianrhod frowned. "What do you mean?"

My mother said nothing. In the harsh midday light streaming in from outside, she looked drained. As stripped as a scorched forest or a hacked-down tree.

"Mam knows what I mean," I said. "But for the first time, I can do more than poke charms in the earth outside the foundation. I can help protect our kingdom and the people I love."

"Our kingdom." Mam's lips thinned. "Leave that to people like your father. That's what he left us for."

"He left us because you forced him out," I ground out, frustrated. "The same way you forced me out. And the irony is that the two of you are exactly the same. You both tried to control me. You're both spendthrifts, just with different patrons. But you're still missing the point, Mam."

"And that is?"

"Whether our home will still be here if Mercia gets its way. And even if it doesn't—if the Foxhall is going to go a step too far one day and destroy something it can't get back." I wiped my nose on my sleeve and looked again at the place where Cadno used to sleep beside me, back when our lives were simpler and smaller. "Maybe it already has."

"Ffion." Mam's face didn't soften. Her eyes only grew wistful. "You'll never make it on your own."

My voice was ragged. "I shouldn't have to."

Arianrhod said nothing. She just looked between my mother and me, confused, trying to understand what had been said and what hadn't.

I hugged Gareth and Hywel and Taffy. I kissed Tegan's cheek and then squeezed him and Arianrhod.

I hugged my mam the tightest, blinking furiously, refusing to release the tears in my eyes.

"I shouldn't have to make it on my own," I said again as I let them all go. "But I certainly will."

Before I left, I looked around one more time, at the house and the lives that had gone on so perfectly without me.

Outside, I charmed the walls and the roof and the door. I saw them watching me through the window, sensed them listening as I sang. *Out of my reach, out of my reach.*

Then I left my mother's house.

14

TAL

Merthyr-Tewdrig, Brycheiniog

The day we set out from the Dead Man's Bells didn't feel like the start of a great and noble quest. Not that anyone had ever called me great, or noble.

Though she insisted on walking the length of the dyke, Ffion had agreed to ride to its southernmost end. She'd met us at the pub at midday, dressed in a clean kirtle and a gold wool cloak, carrying a heavy black cauldron by its handle. Her eyes had been red.

Unlike Rhodri, I had a sense of self-preservation, so I didn't ask if she'd been crying.

Unlike me, Rhodri was someone Ffion actually seemed to like, so she didn't bite his head off, just said she'd be back soon.

For the next four days, we rode south over the Welsh Marches, traveling well west of the dyke. Across Powys and Brycheiniog, we kept a low profile—hoods raised, weapons hidden.

Surrounded by my guard, Ffion and I spoke little. She studied her spellbook as we traveled; I got a letter from my mother informing me that Dafydd had left on his own the same night I did. She'd had no other news of him, but she wished us both well.

I didn't want anything too terrible to happen to Dafydd on the road north. But I wanted him to fail. I wanted him to fail grandly, publicly, profoundly.

I wanted him to fail so spectacularly that he would see he'd been right all along.

It was late morning on the fifth day when we arrived at the dyke's southernmost point beside the sea at Merthyr-Tewdrig. Though it was only early spring, the day was hot; the sun glared off the water, and birds screamed overhead. Just east of the dyke, a little way from where it began, Mercia's southernmost border tower loomed. Guards leaned on their elbows against its crenellations, not taking much notice of us. Not yet, anyway.

As my own guards began to pass around a flask, Ffion stared at the dyke, shoulders stiff, dismay in her expression.

The look passed from her face as quickly as I'd seen it. But it was seared into my mind.

I'd spent the morning feeling vague and flat from the heat. But now, watching Ffion poke and putter around the beach, lugging her cauldron, I felt afraid—both of the magic she was about to work, and of the possibility that she had taken on a task too large for her talents.

All too soon, she was leaving the water's edge, crossing the beach to the very start of the dyke, where the flat ground began sloping upward to its eight-foot height. "It's time," she said.

As Ffion buried a pouch in the earthwork, beneath the hedge, the Mercian soldiers in the tower joined my own guard in staring at her, craning their necks as she wrapped two lengths of ivy torn from the dyke's side around her ankles.

Ffion had already told me what she would do. The ivy was the fragment of the dyke she'd carry with her for her spell, she'd said; then she'd shown me the pouch, explaining the ingredients inside. "Jimson-weed picked by moonlight, while its blooms were blown open. I was lucky to find any at all so early in the year. An empty egg. A pine cone ready to shed its seeds, a hollow bit of bark."

"What will it do?" I'd asked her.

Ffion hadn't answered aloud. Only shown me her shut fists and mimed them opening.

I'd wanted to roll my eyes. *Witches.*

She could've just explained. It was clear enough, though, that the charm was meant to help coax the earthwork open.

But though I already knew her plan, fear spiked again in my thoughts as she clambered down into the ditch. I remembered my father's high table smeared with feathers and blood, the scent of salt and copper everywhere, and Osian's palms stained sacrificial red. I'd heard the birds' panicked screeching in my dreams for weeks after.

Every last Mercian soldier in the tower angled his bow toward Ffion as she coated her feet with mud.

But they never loosed their arrows. Because Ffion simply climbed out of the ditch and began to walk north alongside it, singing as her path carried her toward the tower.

Singing.

Fear crashed in my thoughts like a gong.

I was too far away to hear what Ffion was saying. But where magic was involved, I only ever heard one song. Ignoring the soldiers' raised bows, I staggered toward her in a horrified trance until I could make out her words.

Leaven a-bubble, leaven a-bubble, water and sour leaven a-bubble

I stilled, listening.

The sun warmed my neck and shoulders. Something loosened in my stomach.

There was no blood. No death. It was just a breadmaking song, something her mam or mam-gu might have taught her.

I listened to her throaty voice, and for a moment, I let myself forget.

A moment later, though, the Mercian soldiers understood Ffion's song. And the relief that came over their faces was not the relief I'd felt.

The guards' laughter came loud and harsh from the watchtower. One even began a mocking imitation of Ffion's walk—hunching his shoulders like she did, pretending to hold skirts out at his sides, exaggerating the fairylike toe-heel of her step.

His men found it hilarious. Mine looked from me to Ffion and back to me again, torn between humor and humiliation on my behalf at her woman's song and simple magic.

My stomach tightened again. But Ffion didn't even seem to notice.

I could understand soldiering on through mockery. I had ignored scorn for years, until the smirks had turned into invitations. Ffion truly seemed not to mind the soldiers' contempt, though, walking along the dyke, singing and squinting at the relentless blue horizon.

Didn't she know what it would mean for Powys for the rumor of my absurdity to travel far and wide? Didn't she know what it would mean for me? Was I doomed to be candler after all?

I wondered how Dafydd was faring, wherever he was. No one ever laughed at Dafydd.

Ffion walked until the Mercian soldiers were well behind us, a few crying out in disappointed derision, most having obviously grown bored. I caught up and walked beside her as our guards trailed us, subdued with embarrassment.

Miles passed beneath my boots, my feet growing leaden as they carried me up hills and down, past copses of trees, past views of the sea, past fields full of sheep with heavy coats and some with heavy bellies. The lambing would begin soon, Ffion told me.

Every now and again, she would glance over at the dyke, and I knew I hadn't imagined the doubt on her face.

On and on she sang, first about breadmaking, next about ravens and crowns. I got tired of walking well before she called for a rest.

When I climbed into the wagon beside a few of the men, they wouldn't look at me.

My guards were still avoiding my eyes when we stopped that night on the outskirts of a small village just west of the dyke and the Afon Gwy. I didn't follow them as they made for the Ring and Raven, a pub on the town's high street. Instead, I moved near Ffion, who stood—she was still standing somehow, though her bare feet had carried her the whole distance we'd traveled—staring at the dyke and the ditch.

"They find us ridiculous," I said quietly. "The Mercians, and our own men."

I had expected more of the unconcern she had worn all day. But Ffion's sidelong look was sly. "And so much the better for us."

I frowned, confused. "What do you think this will do to my reputation? Do you want Offa and my father to think I'm a fool?"

"Do you want to be dignified?" Her freckled brow wrinkled. "Or do you want to be king?"

"I want—" I shook my head. "Both. I want both. What do you mean?"

Ffion looked away from me, still smiling, obviously pleased with herself. "They find us ridiculous, Tal. I saw it as soon as I saw them watching me. And as long as they do, we'll be left to our own devices. We might be laughed at, but we won't be stopped, as long as they believe we're harmless." She glanced back to me. I couldn't look away from her. "And it's not for them to know that we aren't."

A chill prickled my skin.

For hours, she'd been cooing at lambs and singing her soft, homely songs; for days, she'd been blunt with me to the point of rudeness. But now her eyes were wily as a fox's.

She'd kept this part of herself a secret. She'd kept her thinking from me all day.

What else was she holding back?

"I'm going to dismiss the men," I said. "I'll drive the wagon from here onward."

"Good." Ffion dropped her cauldron with a *thunk*. Nimble as a cat, she jumped into the wagon bed and rummaged around, producing a loaf of bread, a jar of currant preserves, and a blanket. "I told you we didn't need them."

"I hadn't wanted to put myself entirely at your mercy," I muttered, looking away.

"Oh, Tal." Ffion gave a dry laugh and hopped down, drawing nearer. By twilight, she was more goblin than girl, just as she had been the night I met her. "You are entirely at my mercy. There was never any question of that."

15

DAFYDD

Prestatyn Castle, Gwynedd

When two o'clock comes, our fires are they roaring
Our hammers are busy and patrons imploring
Work faster! Work cheaper! they cry; aye, but how?
We only survive by the sweat of our brow.
—"The Workaday Song"

Prestatyn Castle was a fortress by the sea. Blue-gray afancs flew on banners from silver-gray towers; the gently rounded moon hung high overhead like a silver ceiniog.

I could picture it by day—the sky a perfect blue, the sea dotted with fishing boats, gulls circling and crying above. In my imagination, flesh-and-blood afancs perched on battlements and glided along the seabed like they might have decades ago, protecting the castle and the fishermen alike.

Gruffudd and I made our way to the gates. I stated our business, and under the watchful eyes of the gatekeeper and the moon, we made our way into the fortress.

But the next morning, I was told King Bleddyn was unavoidably detained. There was nothing to do but wait and pace the grounds with Gruffudd; I wouldn't leave for fear of being unable to return, but I couldn't stay indoors indefinitely, either.

The castle proper was an enormous stone labyrinth. Silver paint gleamed from embellished carvings on its walls, on the teeth of more afancs and the edges of twisting shells. When Bleddyn finally summoned me, two full days after I'd arrived, I found its throne room was the same—towering, silver, with sea air drifting through the grilles over its windows.

"Prince Dafydd," the king said. "My thanks for your patience." He was younger than my father, about thirty, neat and trim, with a withdrawn smile.

I bowed, suddenly nervous. The throne room was crowded, which didn't bother me, but also strangely quiet. The king and his retainers were dressed formally, in embroidered clothes that reminded me of Tal's best coat.

Tal would've felt right at home. But I felt myself squirming.

"Thank you for seeing me," I said. "Like Powys, Gwynedd is a large kingdom. My father's days are consumed with attending to his subjects' welfare, so I understand you have many demands on your time." Then I paused. "I've come because Powys's magician has foreseen an attack from Mercia. We seek an alliance with Gwynedd to help us weather it."

I didn't have a plan yet for destroying the dyke. But for now, surely, Dad would honor this effort.

Still, I knew my proposal had been too blunt. Tal was the persuasive one. It was just a shame that he and I were on opposite sides of this horrible game.

I waited anxiously for Bleddyn to offer the obvious response.

Yes, I'm sure your father is busy, given how much time he spends pushing your border north.

Yes, Powys is a large and powerful kingdom. Why does it need our help?

Yes, but wouldn't we be free from your harassment if Mercia crushed you?

"Disquieting news." Bleddyn frowned slightly. When he shifted on his throne, the silver threads in his tunic caught the afternoon light. "Gwynedd will certainly come to Powys's aid."

I searched for words a moment before I found them, and they were few enough when I did. "You have my thanks, Your Majesty," I finally said. I didn't know if my heart was jumping, or sinking, or bursting between my lungs.

"Oh—" King Bleddyn raised a hand. It was cleaner than mine, soft-looking, and he wore a thin silver bracelet set with a red gemstone. "But in exchange, I do have one request."

16

FFION

On the Dyke, Brycheiniog

Tal went into the pub to rest himself. Riding primly in a wagon was evidently very hard work.

It couldn't possibly have been as difficult as what I'd been doing.

I'd heard it all my life: Prince Taliesin of Powys was a talented schemer. But Ffion of Foxhall was not. And I'd been lying to our company all day.

I threw myself into the ditch, breathing hard. "How?" I whispered, pressing my forehead into the dirt. "How, how, how?"

Everyone knew of the Foxhall; everyone knew Osian worked magic for King Cadell. But everyone also knew the Mercians had no magician on their side.

So why was King Offa's Dyke absolutely stinking of magic?

I'd grown up barely five miles from the dyke, but I'd never gotten close to it. No one who valued their life did, what with the watchtowers and the guards.

But I'd sensed the magic rolling off the dyke the moment I'd climbed down from the wagon that morning. I'd had to stop and gather myself on the beach before I could face the prince and his company again.

And then the fun had really gotten started.

Leaven a-bubble, leaven a-bubble, water and sour leaven a-bubble
Out of the old cometh the new, start with the sour leaven a-bubble

Hey-dilly, hey-dally, hey-dally-do, water and sour leaven a-bubble

Flour and salt, flour and salt, sift you together the flour and salt
Sticks to your fingers and stings in your cuts, first with the flour, then with the salt
Hey-dilly, hey-dally, hey-dally-do, sift you together the flour and salt

Dough on the block, dough on the block, thumpety-thump, dough on the block
Under your hands, work as you talk, knead you together the dough on the block
Hey-dilly, hey-dally, hey-dally-do, thumpety-thump, dough on the block

With my heart threatening to climb out of my throat and tell the whole world what apparently only I had ever noticed, my mam-gu's breadmaking song had been the only one I could think of. Tal had spent the whole day staring at his boots because of it.

The charms, the songs, the ivy, the walking. I'd been sure they'd be enough. But my plan was absolutely nothing compared with the power in the dyke.

I crouched in the ditch and fought down the panic that had been rising in me since midday. *How, how, how?*

We would need more power. More potent ingredients. But what could stand against magic like that?

Before long, I got to my feet again. While there was light left, I had to search the ditch for materials to raise Cadno. I didn't know how I'd do it, with this new wrinkle in my plan to break the dyke and restore the land's lost magic, but I hadn't left home to quit on my first day of trying.

I'd begun searching that morning at Merthyr-Tewdrig, where I'd found a cut sea sponge on the beach; later, I'd found an uprooted fistful of stinging nettle. As I searched that evening, I came across an interesting mushroom, an empty bird's nest, and some early crocuses that had died with the frost. They all went into the cauldron.

I wanted to take more. I wanted to pull every leaf from the hedge, uproot every herb, dig with bare hands till my nails struck silver. I wanted all of it to help me bring Cadno back, once there was enough magic in the land to do it. But I wouldn't cause harm to get what I needed.

I would show the Foxhall and Osian what could be done with hard work and little else.

I could do this. I had seventeen days until the new moon.

The stars began to come out as I lay beside the ditch, covering myself in my cloak. I scratched at my ankles beneath the ivy until I finally took it off; it wouldn't last me 180 miles if I tore it up in my sleep.

Not that sleep felt imminent. Not with magic surging out of the dyke, so powerful I felt like I was sleeping beside a bonfire.

Could I write to my mother about it, I wondered? No.

Would Dad and Mam-gu have ever noticed, or talked about it? Maybe.

Most of all, I couldn't let Tal learn the truth. Neither he nor his men seemed to sense the magic—in fact, Tal had hired me because he believed the Mercians *had* no magic.

I could still do this: destroy the dyke, restore magic, resurrect Cadno. I would find something stronger to work with. But I couldn't let Tal find out things had gotten more complicated. Because if he chose to change his plan, it could completely ruin mine.

The next morning, Tal dismissed our company. I didn't need their doubt, and we didn't need them hanging around while we tried to be inconspicuous. Rather than return to Mathrafal immediately, the soldiers stayed in town, apparently needing a respite after a day (a whole day!) of riding and being mocked by Mercian sentries.

"The gods be thanked for such fierce warriors," I said as Tal paid the last of his men.

He laughed grimly and climbed onto the wagon, pulled by a stolid mare and his own chestnut gelding, though Derog clearly viewed this as beneath his dignity.

Very little was beneath my dignity. As the miles passed, I was just relieved not to have to perform for a crowd.

"Aren't you tired?" Tal demanded sometime before noon. We had passed through beech woods and a lime wood, the latter forest floor blooming white with early garlic where it wasn't recklessly scarred by the ditch and the dyke. I gathered fallen blooms, keeping between the wagon and the ditch. Not far off, another watchtower loomed. "Because I'm tired."

"We've hardly walked six miles, Tal." I *was* tired, not that I'd ever admit it to him. My eyes were playing tricks on me. Twice that morning, I'd thought I'd seen Cadno peering out from behind a tree.

Aside from that, I'd had the dream about the sea again last night. But the dream had been clearer this time, every sound and color sharper and fiercer. It made me want to sleep so I could see it again.

"Well, I'm dying in this wagon." His voice was irritable. "I feel like a baby's rattle."

"And no rattle ever looked so fine," I crooned, reaching up to tweak his elbow. Tal hissed and swatted my hand away. "Lucky the child whose rattle is wrapped in such an expensive coat."

"You're unbearable."

I dropped a curtsy.

"How much farther do we have to go today?" he asked.

"At least another nine miles, if you're hoping to make Prestatyn by summer."

Tal sulked. "I bet Arianrhod wouldn't have punished me like this."

"And Tegan and Taffy aren't even three years old," I said, "but I bet they wouldn't complain like you."

Tal paused, seeming to count on his fingers. "Remind me how many there are of you?"

"Gareth and Arianrhod are older. I'm in the middle. And then there are Hywel and the twins."

"And your mam and dad," Tal added.

I shook my head. "My parents are separated."

"Really?" Tal looked interested. And then I remembered, of course, that his mother and father didn't keep company anymore, either.

I wondered why they'd parted ways. If they'd started out in love like my parents had, and let their loyalties and jealousies get in between them. If they'd tried to make Tal pick sides, too.

"What does your dad think of all this?" Tal asked, waving a hand at me.

"We've had fewer occasions to talk about *this* than you'd think." I waved a hand right back at him. "My father's always off fighting for yours."

I made my way ahead of him, going down the hill, and didn't look back.

17

TAL

The trouble with the country was that everything smelled like magic—like earth, and animals, and moisture on the air. As Ffion walked and I rode past villages and farms, the stink of it was everywhere, just like it always seemed to be when I left Mathrafal—which was why I so rarely did.

I doubted there was anything special about the hamlets we were passing or the roads we traveled. Likelier that my encounter years ago had left a mark on me—had left the stink of magic up my nose, the way a rotten smell sometimes stays with you. The feel of it twisted my guts. I wanted cobblestones and castle walls more than I wanted a meal that wasn't stew.

No one else had ever seemed to notice, and Ffion didn't, either, as we carried on alongside the dyke. "Do you think the fey ever lived in these woods?" she asked, switching her cauldron from her right hand to her left.

"I'd rather not think about it."

"Fair," she said. "Though I don't think they were always terrible. They could be tricky and cruel, but—so are humans."

Cleverness and cruelty, I could manage. But I had no desire to meet human-looking things whose logic was nothing like human logic, whose schemes couldn't be unpicked like human schemes. "Where did they go?"

"The same place as the dragons and bwbachod and ceffylau dŵr,

I guess." She clambered down into the ditch to pick up something that might've been a leaf and added it to her small pile of garbage. "Did I ever tell you I once saw a pod of dragons?"

"No. No, you didn't." My voice came out too sharp. "When was this?"

"About ten years ago. I was seven. I must have been one of the last people to see them."

I tried not to let Ffion see my whole body relax as I searched for the kind of question I ought to ask. The sort of thing I might say if I weren't myself at all. "What were they like?"

Ffion was quiet so long, I thought she might not answer me. "Indescribably beautiful." She looked at me sadly. "Have you ever seen one? A dragon, or a unicorn, or a water horse, or—not in a painting, I mean. A real, live creature."

My stomach rolled, and for once it wasn't from the jostling of the wagon beneath me. "No," I said shortly. "I've seen one. But it was already dead."

We spent the night in Llandeilo Gresynni—me in a farmhouse, Ffion outside in the mud—and midmorning the next day we came to the village of Llangatwg Lingoed. It was a desolate little hamlet beneath Brycheiniog's Black Mountains, nothing but a green and Saint Cadoc's Church and a pub called the Dithering Crow, where we stopped to water our horses. To my surprise, the arms of King Meirion himself—a black wing on a yellow field, crowned with three black mountains—swung over the door. "A toast to our lord and sovereign," said a man sitting on a bench outside, raising his tankard to the crest as his friend laughed.

"Seems strange to call your pub the *Dithering* Crow and then give it your king's arms," I whispered to Ffion.

Before she could answer, one of the men spoke. "That's a very fine coat, young sir. Where are you headed, dressed so well?"

"Llanfihangel Crucornau," said Ffion, naming a town west of the mountains. "To take plague clothes to be burned—but don't worry, we don't think the man who gave him the coat died of it." Ffion hid a smirk as both men paled and began inching away from us down the bench.

"Well, you can follow the dyke north awhile longer and then take the drover's path west, as I'm sure you know," the first said hurriedly. "Though if you cross the lime forest, you've gone too far, and you're nearly at Black Darren."

"Is King Meirion's castle so close?" she asked.

"Twelve miles or so."

Ffion and I exchanged a dismayed look. We'd never make it by nightfall.

"Though perhaps a plague at the castle is just what we need," said the second man, looking sour. "You two are too young to remember. But things used to be different in Brycheiniog. Dragons in the skies, sighted ravens in the trees. They could look you in the eye and tell you a terrible truth about yourself."

"And we had a real king on the throne," the first agreed. "Not a dithering crow."

The Dithering Crow.

What were we going to find at Black Darren?

"Anyhow, you'd best be off." The first man eyed us nervously. "Your errand and all."

As I climbed into the wagon, I took mercy on him. "We're not burning plague clothes," I said, nodding to Ffion, who was pulling some bread out of our bags. "I'm returning my wife to her family in Llanfihangel Crucornau before she drives me mad."

Ffion choked. "Your wi—?"

I snapped the reins and the horses took off. She could only chase me out of town, barefoot, ivy around her ankles and murder in her eyes, while the men outside the pub laughed and laughed.

"You! Are horrible!" Ffion shouted as I bounced up the slope, the wagon rattling over the rough ground.

"Come on, wife," I called. "Can't delay returning you to your mother. I was promised a biddable woman, and you are not she."

"I will bid you right into that ditch, you overly embroidered ass!"

"Why do you hate this coat so much?" I demanded. "Are you truly so offended by wealth? Because my wealth is what will be paying you so handsomely at the end of our quest."

With no warning, Ffion seized Derog's bridle. He drew up short, and I nearly fell into her.

"To begin with," she said in a low, pleasant, dangerous voice, "it's not your wealth. It's your father's wealth."

I rolled my eyes. "For all intents and—"

"But yes, I am offended by it. Not by honestly gotten comfort, but by bread taken out of the mouths of children and physick denied to babies who might live more gently if their king weren't constantly levying taxes and sending his men off to fight in pointless wars."

"As far as I can tell, only the Foxhall is denying care to babies in your village," I said, "so save your words for them."

"I haven't spared the Foxhall. Be assured of that." Ffion let go of Derog's bridle and kept walking.

"Then what do you want from me?" I asked, exasperated. "Do you want me to hide the coat?"

"I want the coat to never have existed."

"You're the witch," I retorted. "Undo the past, if you want. Cast a spell that can turn back time and make me leave Mathrafal in something else. I honestly hadn't thought I was so conspicuous when I left."

"You'd be less conspicuous naked."

I considered this. "I doubt it. You haven't seen me naked."

"You're a pig." Ffion flung the heel of her loaf at my head; I only narrowly dodged it.

"And now you're wasting food." I shook a finger at her.

"As if you care!"

"You're impossibly rude," I called. "You'll have to contain that when you get to court."

"You need someone to be rude to you, Tal. You need trials beyond deciding what to wear to dinner and who to flirt with when you get there."

"Why are you so convinced that I lack substance?" I demanded.

"Why are you so unable to convince me otherwise?"

We were going to kill each other before we ever made it to Black Darren. If I managed not to poison her, she was going to shove me down a mountainside.

"Will everyone at court be like you?" Ffion suddenly asked, arms crossed over her chest.

"What, recently washed?"

She bared her teeth at me. "No, a useless priss."

I fought to control myself. "I can't answer you if I don't know what you mean, Ffion."

"Refined," she ground out. "Educated in dancing, dressing, dining, diplomacy."

"I'm actually not much of a dancer."

"Tal."

"Only joking. I'm an excellent dancer."

"Tal!" she nearly shouted. "I'm serious. How will I know how to act if you won't tell me what to expect? And if I don't know how to act, how can I convince Meirion to give us the blade?" Ffion clenched her hands together, but not before I noticed they were shaking a little.

I stopped the wagon.

I'd noticed Ffion eyeing the dyke nervously. But I hadn't considered how she'd feel about court—the place I felt most at home.

I jumped down, taking Derog's reins in my left hand and holding out my right arm.

Watching Ffion decide whether to trust me was like watching a horse decide whether to throw its rider. Her gray eyes seemed to take my full measure in one long, slow look. I pressed my lips together and hoped I wasn't blushing.

Slowly, she slid her arm through the crook of my elbow.

"So. Dressing, dining—what were the others? Dancing, diplomacy," I began as we walked. "What you're wearing right now is all right for anything that isn't an *occasion*. Were you able to buy anything finer? I know Foxhall's a backwater, but—ow!" She elbowed me in the ribs. I nudged her back irritably.

"I found a black wool dress. It's a little frightening. One of Rhiannon's castoffs, actually."

"Hm. Well, *frightening* might not hurt our cause," I said. "As for dining, you'll have to learn to eat like you're not starving."

"Easy for you to say."

I winced. "You're right. That wasn't fair." Ffion was tough as old boots, sinewy as a stray cat—but I could feel her ribs when her torso brushed against my arm. She'd been hungry for years, and I was awful, just like she'd said.

"And dancing?" she asked.

"You've been to dances before, surely."

"It's been years."

I shrugged. "Foxhall is probably behind, but the fashions don't change that quickly."

"That's not what I mean. I was a child at my last dance." She stared at me meaningfully. But I still didn't understand.

Ffion sighed. "I used to tag after Arianrhod and Olwen and the other girls old enough to be pretty—old enough to be asked to dance," she said, looking away from me. "Sometimes I sat with Arianrhod when she got too tired. Sometimes I danced around the edges of the room with Cadno." She smiled. "Once, when my father was actually home, I danced with him and Mam all night. I fell asleep while he carried me home to bed." Her smile tensed as she met my eyes again. "But I was a child. I have no practice being a girl—a woman—in society."

I was so surprised to find Ffion turning red and looking away from me that I didn't even have the heart to rib her about the idea of *society* in Foxhall. I was so suddenly aware of her arm against my side and her hip bumping against my leg I doubted I could've come up with anything, anyway.

I swallowed hard. "Should we practice?"

"Practice—dancing, you mean?" Ffion frowned. "How?"

I pretended to glance around the hill we'd finally crested. "Well, we'll have to ask everyone to make room."

When I grinned at her this time, she didn't scowl or ask me to be serious.

Maybe she didn't have the energy. Or maybe she just felt like rolling her eyes and laughing instead.

"Do you know the jac y do?" I asked—the jackdaw.

"Of course."

"Good. What about the ring dance?"

She shook her head.

"All right. Well, it's easy, really." I released Ffion's arm and stood in front of her. "We circle each other one way, and then the other. And then we sashay as a circle of dancers. So—" I took her hand in mine, showing her the first steps.

There was dirt under her nails, and her palm was rough, but it was warm.

I cleared my throat. I was being an idiot.

I taught her the first two steps. Then, of course, everything fell apart. Ffion couldn't seem to picture where the other dancers would be, or grasp our positioning for the next step, and confusion made her pricklier than ever.

"Here," I said, fighting my aggravation. "My right hand holds your right, and my left hand holds your left." Our right hands were joined in front of my torso, and my left hand snaked around her shoulder to take hers. This sequence pulled us close, fitting her against my chest and beneath my arm.

"Yes, but how did I *get* here?" Ffion demanded.

I tried to answer normally. But my tongue felt thick and stupid and all I could think of was the delicate line of her neck, the way her head fit just below my chin.

Your body's so much smaller than the rest of you, I nearly said.

Abruptly, Ffion stiffened and pulled away from me. "Good enough. I've got it."

Had she read my thoughts on my face? "What's wrong now?" I asked, too sharply.

"Nothing."

"Not *nothing.*" My guilt made me defensive. "We were practicing, and then we weren't."

"Maybe I just don't like being pressed up against you. Being rejected by women is probably a fresh experience for you, Tal, but you'll have to get used to it."

She might as well have slapped me. "Pressed up—we were *dancing,* Ffion!" I threw up my hands. "Maybe you do need more practice, if you can't even stand next to a man without running away like a wild animal."

My face felt hot. I hoped Ffion thought it was from anger and not embarrassment.

Of course I wasn't used to being rejected. I hadn't spent my life learning how to charm and impress people for nothing.

"Anyway, I'm not the one in dire need of a bath," I added. "Honestly, I should be the one running away."

"Oh, of course not." Her tone was mocking. "Who needs to bathe, anyway, when you sleep on a cloud and burn your worn clothes every night. Except for madder-red coats that cost eighteen ceiniogau—"

"Not the coat again!" I shouted. "I swear by every god I've ever heard of, if you bring up my coat again, I'm going to bury you alive in it, so it's the last thing you see before the sweet release of death!"

"Still a better fate than being your dance partner!" Ffion stomped across the hilltop.

I dropped the reins and ran after her. "You are impossible."

She whirled. "How about this for a strategy, Tal? You keep to your ways, and I'll keep to mine. I'll arrive smelling like filth, I'll eat and dance like a wild animal, and then I'll sack Black Darren like a raider until I find something that leads us to Brycheiniog's blade."

"Don't play the fool, Ffion, because you can't fool me." I shook my head, seething. "Your problem is that you've convinced yourself you can't win. You're so used to hiding out in hedges and sleeping on the road that you're certain you could never thrive anywhere else."

Ffion scoffed. "You yourself went to the Foxhall first," she said. "I *am* apprehensive about Meirion's court, and it's not because I've *convinced* myself of anything."

I stalked close to Ffion and stabbed a finger at her chest. She grabbed it, trapping it in her fist. "You may be a thorn in my side, Ffion vch Catrin, but you don't miss a single trick. It's the reason you've survived in the hedges and the woods and in a town that never took care of you."

My breath was coming too fast. Her own chest rose and fell, her face turned up toward mine. This close, I could see the freckles on her eyelids.

"How do you know?" Her voice wavered.

"The same way I know you're keeping something from me. The same way you'd better hope it's buried deep by the time we reach the Sighted Raven's court." Satisfaction rose up in me as her face paled. "Because we're the same."

"We are *not* the same," she said vehemently. "And I'm not keeping—"

"You know how to do this, Ffion. All you have to do is enter a room and watch it for a moment or two, and you get the trick of it," I said. "You see who's got something to hide, who's got something to trade, who wants something. Pretend you're a green girl all you like, but you're more than ready for Meirion's court. Watch and learn for a moment before you open your mouth, tell careful truths that might as well be lies, and no one will be any the wiser that you've lived like a wild thing these past few years."

Ffion stepped closer to me. She still clutched my finger in her hand, her fist pressed just over my heart.

"Is that what you do?" she asked. "Tell truths so winding they might as well be false?"

"It's the only way to survive at court," I said. "And it's what you're going to do as well."

"You can't just order it and make it so," she said.

We were almost chest to chest.

"I can." I held her gaze and watched her blush one last time, feeling something more than satisfaction. "I'm a prince."

18

DAFYDD

Mathrafal Castle, Powys

When four o'clock comes, our fires are a-fading
Our embers are dark'ning, our woodpiles are waning
So we add to our woodpiles! The bellows, we pound!
The fires only burn by the sweat of our brow.
—"The Workaday Song"

I was fifteen the day I lost faith in my father. All of fifteen years old the day I realized the man was capable of absolutely anything, and that if I followed his example, I could end up just like him. That was the day I decided I would be like her instead.

I was nineteen the day I had to prove it.

An hour after my audience with King Bleddyn, I rode away from Prestatyn Castle.

My hands were empty, but my conscience was clear. I wondered if Tal would've made the same choice I had.

I thought of the girl again—the one I'd watched for years from a distance, the one I'd only seen in my thoughts. She'd showed me who and how to be when my father had failed me. In a way, the forge had been her suggestion.

She would've shown me how to be king one day. But that wasn't my future anymore.

I wondered what she thought of me now. We'd never met, so I didn't know.

And now we never would.

19

FFION

On the Dyke, Brycheiniog

Tal and I trundled down the hill and past the drover's track where the man outside the pub had told us to turn for Llanfihangel Crucornau. I fished a shard of clay pot and a snail shell out of the ditch, trying to carry on normally.

When I'd heard Meirion called the Sighted Raven in the past, I'd always assumed it meant he was intuitive. Insightful. I hadn't thought about him actually sifting through my secrets. I hadn't thought I would have anything secret to keep from him—only from Tal.

The idea unsettled me almost as much as our dance had.

I saw little of my father, but there were other men and boys in my life—Hywel, Gareth, Rhodri. But Tal was neither family nor old friend, and the solidity of his chest against my shoulders had caught me off guard. As we crossed into the lime forest, I felt myself faltering, and not only because I was tired.

"Maybe we should stop," Tal said, looking a little concerned. It only annoyed me.

"If we stop every time you suggest it, it'll be our ghosts reaching the northern end of the dyke."

"I beg your pardon," Tal grumbled. "It's just that not all of us are martyrs."

"Moving for twenty minutes at a time doesn't make me a martyr."

"It's a steep climb!"

"I'm the only one climbing!" I was trying to prepare for an attack and save Cadno, and Tal thought we were on a picnic.

"*And* you refuse to wear shoes."

"Because my magic demands it!" I was pretty certain this was true, anyway. I went barefoot for the same reason we were traveling the dyke from end to end in the first place. *You are working with scraps when you could have abundance instead,* Mam had said.

Abundance. Mam had been working with Rhiannon's foot on her neck for years. If that was abundance, she could keep it.

Tal let out a growl, snapped the reins, and rode ahead of me. But near the far edge of the woods, he stopped short.

"What is it?" I called. He held up a hand, silencing me as he drew back into the trees.

Instantly, I grew alert. "What is it?" I asked again quietly. Tal climbed down shakily from the wagon, and I came to his side.

"Soldiers," he said just over his breath. Fear spiked through me.

"Brycheinig? Mercian?"

"Can't tell. They're on both sides of the dyke, but they're mostly crowded around a lake," he said. "They could all be Mercian, or they could be both."

I nodded.

"Think. I have to think." Tal stepped away from me, hands on his hips, one leg bouncing. Abruptly, he straightened, yanking off his coat and stuffing it into one of our bags. Underneath, he wore a plain but delicately woven linen tunic. "If you say a word about my coat, I'm going to tie you up and toss you in the back of the wagon," he added.

"Wouldn't dare." I swallowed hard. "What are you doing?" I'd seen men wearing fewer clothes, doing farm work or other labor. But suddenly Tal looked less than fully dressed.

"Making myself inconspicuous." He unclasped the chain around his neck and slid the rings from his fingers. Then he paused and studied me, eyes wandering from my hair to my bare feet and back again.

"See something you like?" I demanded, heat climbing up my neck.

Tal seemed to contain himself with effort. "I—no, that's not—"

"Don't hurt yourself, Tal."

"You are conspicuous," he said tightly.

"I apologize." My voice dripped with sarcasm. "When I am dead, I will raise my complaint to the gods and ask for duller hair and fewer freckles, should they send me on a return journey."

He turned away from me, pressing his palms into his eyes. "How are we bickering right now?"

"I don't know," I groaned. "I know you're trying to help. I—I can braid my hair."

"Good," he agreed. "Yes, braid it."

I ran my hands through my hair, wincing as it snarled around my fingers. Tal watched desperately as I tied it with a piece of twine and tucked it inside my cloak.

"Still that bad?" I asked.

He shook his head and turned away. "I shouldn't have dismissed our company. I don't like these odds."

"I'm glad you dismissed the soldiers. The soldiers are the problem."

He jutted a finger toward the edge of the woods. "No, *those* soldiers are our problem."

"You—" I squeezed my eyes shut. "Nobody sees. How does nobody see?"

"See what?" he hissed. "See that we're two against two hundred if those men decide to murder us?"

"See that this is how the magic dies," I said, seizing Tal by the shoulder and forcing his gaze to mine. "I'm a witch descended from witches, Tal, and if they've taught me anything, it's that magic requires respect. Humility. Space. You can't stare at it and expect it not to run.

You can't tramp through forests and over moors like they mean nothing. You can't drain bogs because you don't like them and redirect rivers to move borders and cut into mountains to carve roads so that yet *more* people, companies of soldiers twenty men wide, can tramp across them." I heaved a sigh, suddenly drained. "This is why the magic is leaving us, Tal."

I was exhausted. The night before had been unusually damp, and my throat hurt more than ever. But I would explain this again and again and again until someone who could do something about it understood.

Tal ran a hand along his jaw. "I don't like this, either, Ffion. But I need you to trust me. Can you do that?"

"It's only you and me out here," I said. "I trust you about as far as I can throw you, but I haven't got anyone else."

"Inspiring," said Tal, and we made for the edge of the woods.

With my eyes on the ditch, I felt, rather than saw, the soldiers notice us. And even with my hair braided and my head down, I knew how men tended to behave in groups.

The hooting and whistling started as we drew near the lake. Its waters were amber-colored, shallow enough to show gray-brown stones and weeds at the bottom; more of the same straggled along its shores. The birds and animals who lived on the lake's edge had fled—except, of course, for the soldiers acting like pigs. I rolled my eyes.

My dad had taught me how to deal with large groups of men. With any group that made me uncomfortable, really. *Go about your business,* he always said. *They'll mock you—until they see your work.*

Up in the wagon, Tal's knuckles grew white around the reins.

"Climb up here," he said stiffly. "Now."

"It'll only draw more attention. Besides, I want to see what's wrong with the lake."

Up close, it was clear the soldiers belonged to two separate camps. The first group, only twenty men or so, was clustered on the western shore. The other group—a few hundred soldiers, with tents and cookfires and latrines far too close to the water—was camped on the lake's eastern side, against the dyke and beyond it. The two groups seemed to have met on the south bank, amid shovels and wagons, piles of trash, and more latrines.

As for the water itself—it smelled foul, and it *felt* foul.

I didn't quite hear the men's calls getting louder. But I certainly noticed the one who strode up to me and demanded that I state my business.

Older. White. Bald and broad, with a pike in hand. He spoke Welsh like a Mercian.

Tal was behind me in a moment. "Your pardon, sir. My sister is easily distracted."

The man scowled. "And your *sister* has disturbed my men at a moment I need them settled. What is your business in these parts?"

"I was under the impression I was traveling in Brycheiniog, not Mercia," said Tal.

"I was under the same impression," said a boy of about fifteen, stomping toward the Mercian. "And I wasn't finished speaking to you!"

The boy was thin and pale, with acne around his mouth and jaw. He would probably grow into his features someday—huge eyes, a prominent nose, and a froglike mouth—but at the moment, he seemed to be nothing *but* features.

I felt a stab of pity. What was he doing facing off against a crowd of Mercian soldiers?

But when the boy spotted Tal, his entire expression changed. "*You,*" he snarled.

"Him?" I turned to Tal.

The boy changed direction, making for our wagon. "Wasn't it

enough that you chased me from Mathrafal clear across Powys?" he asked. "What are you doing here?"

Horror flashed across Tal's face. But he was in control of himself in an instant. "I'm so sorry," he said. "Should I know you?"

The boy reddened. "I am Prince Angws, nephew to King Meirion of Brycheiniog. I was held prisoner at Mathrafal Castle for months. And when I was released by Prince Dafydd, you—Prince Taliesin—chased me for a night and a day!"

My stomach was going to fall out of my body.

Would Tal really have done such a thing? What had he said when he first arrived in Foxhall? *The maneuver I attempted failed.*

I whipped around to face Tal again; but he only shook his head, politely chagrined, glancing past the boy at the Mercian guard. "I'm sorry. My name is Owain. Do you know this young man?"

Gods' candles. He *had* done it.

I tried to catch Tal's eye, but he wouldn't look at me.

"I am Wystan. I serve King Offa of Mercia," said the guard. "And Prince Angws seems to have forgotten that Mercia has an agreement with Brycheiniog permitting our use of this lake."

"To *use* Llyn Glas, not to foul it!" Angws exclaimed. "Your men have made the water undrinkable! And you—" He turned to Tal again, his already thin voice pitching itself higher. "Why are you acting like you don't know who I am?" Angws's men exchanged unreadable glances.

He was humiliated. And Tal didn't care.

"Enough!" Wystan barked. "Princeling, back to your uncle's castle like a good boy. You two, state your business."

"I've told you," Angws interrupted. "He's Prince Taliesin, he's here to—"

"And he's said he's never met you before," said Wystan. "And you two are alone, and I am backed by an army," he added to us.

Angws was pale and raging at Tal. Wystan was annoyed at Angws and glowering at Tal. Tal looked like butter wouldn't melt in his mouth, but sweat had begun to gather under his arms.

Let him sweat. This was at least half his fault.

"Can we help somehow?" I asked. Without intending to, I took another step toward the lake.

"Unless you can unfoul a lake and un-idiot my men, probably not," Wystan said flatly. "They've been looking for the hedgewitch up the side of this mountain half the afternoon, but nobody can seem to find her hut."

I cleared my throat, peering at the water. I could sense the filth even more clearly now—the discomfort of the trout in the water, the swans' refusal to get close. If Cadno were with me now, he'd probably do the same; he'd always had refined sensibilities. "Actually—"

"Don't you dare," Tal muttered in my ear.

I shook him off. "We'll discuss your contributions to this mess later," I hissed.

The whistling began all over again as I shucked off my cloak and made my way to the lake's edge, cauldron in hand. I hadn't actually known Tal spoke Mercian, but he seemed to demonstrate an impressive range of vocabulary as he shouted back to the soldiers.

"Ta— Owain!" I said. "Calm down."

Tal was not calm. But as I'd known it would, his response had only made things worse. The men continued to taunt me, and I continued to ignore them.

I sat down beside the lake and began picking through my cauldron, thinking of Osian's power tied to Pendwmpian Forest. Was some witch tied to this lake? What had become of her magic when the Mercian soldiers dug their latrines too close to its shore and began polluting it? And what would become of the little magic left in our land as the story repeated itself?

"What are you going to do?" Angws rushed over, his wide mouth set in a worried frown. "This lake belongs to my uncle. If you damage it further, I can have you imprisoned!"

I didn't put a hand on Angws's shoulder. But I wanted to. He was already a child doing an adult's work, and now Tal had made him feel like a fool in front of his men and the Mercian camp.

I'd heard once—years ago, before my parents separated—that Tal was clever, and that his cleverness could be cruel.

It was interesting to hear as a story. It was disappointing to see in a friend.

"I'm going to help you," I said firmly. "Now be quiet and let me think." Angws flopped back and snapped his mouth shut.

The lake needed to be candled, but I didn't have any candles. And did I even have a song for water? I knew my mam-gu had taught me one, but I couldn't remember it. Not with hundreds of soldiers and Angws, Wystan, and Tal watching me.

But I remembered one for ale.

Reluctantly, I took a sprig of lavender and the sea sponge I'd gathered in Merthyr-Tewdrig from my cauldron and dunked them in the lake, cringing as my skin touched the foamy amber water.

"Close enough," I muttered to myself.

O Bronwyn loves her bragawd,
And Brin and Branwen too,
And Bethan loves her bragawd,
Loves Betrys well her brew!
And Buddug Bregus Brynmor
Keeps bar at Blackbird Pub
And loves she only bragawd strong,
She has no need for grub!

Bragawd sweet, bragawd strong, billy-gilly-go,
Bragawd cheap, bragawd dear, billy-gilly-go!

It was a song I'd picked up at the Dead Man's Bells, and Mam and Mam-gu both would've been horrified. But I focused on the sponge and the foul water before me as I sang the lyrics again and again. By the third round, Wystan's soldiers had joined in, and the water had begun to change from amber to brown. The smell grew worse, and my stomach churned.

"What are you doing?" Angws asked again, distressed. "Are you turning the lake to bragawd? Take it out!"

Brown to green. The stench was unbearable.

"Don't be a fool, boy." Wystan rolled his eyes. "The song isn't a spell. Some of them just sing. The last Powysian king's magician used to as well, if my memory serves."

Before Tal could speak up and ruin everything, I lifted the sponge from the water.

The response was immediate. Angws recoiled, pinching his nostrils shut. Tal drew his tunic over his nose and Wystan buried his own in the crook of his elbow, still holding his pike in one hand.

Luckily, the other hand was free.

When I dumped the sponge in Wystan's open palm, full of all the filth that had tainted the lake, he retched and dropped it at once.

"Dig your latrines at a proper distance, and bury that somewhere far, far away from water," I said flatly. Then I turned to Angws. "Your job now is to protect this lake," I said, keeping my voice gentle. "Speak to your uncle. Don't let them do this again." He nodded silently.

Behind us, swans had begun to settle down on the water. A willow sapling sprouted on the bank.

The soldiers were still braying like donkeys as I wiped my filthy hands on the grass and cut away from the lakeside through their ranks. I'd lost a valuable bit of fuel, but the water looked and smelled clean, and it felt less troubled.

But as Tal hurried into the wagon and its rattle picked up behind me, I told myself—no more.

With more power in the dyke than I knew how to reckon with, I needed to be about finding more fuel to destroy it, not spending what little I had.

Polluted lakes and princes in distress would have to be someone else's problem.

20

TAL

I was eleven years old when I got into my first real fight.

The cause of it was simple enough: Dad had brought his latest mistress to a formal dinner, and a chieftain's son had sneered at my mam. *A discard,* he'd called her.

After dinner, I waited for the boy outside the hall.

Dad had said later that a brave man would have demanded satisfaction then and there at the table, instead of lying in wait like a sneak thief. Dafydd would have done it that way, he'd said.

The difference between Dafydd and me, of course, was that Dafydd was a year older and three stone heavier, and he had more than one friend. (I had exactly one friend: Dafydd.)

It would be many years before our brotherhood soured into competition. But now I wondered if the beginnings of what was to come were already there.

The boy beat me up, of course, and then Dad whipped me again later. He'd told me he was going to teach me a lesson about how to treat the sons of men whose loyalty he needed.

The lesson I learned, of course, was that the only person who would take care of Mam and me was myself.

Sometimes I wondered if I'd hit that boy because I couldn't hit my father.

Either way, the whipping had driven home what I already knew: other people couldn't be trusted.

I'd thought Ffion understood this, but evidently, she didn't. Evidently, she thought she was invincible, as a witch. Or maybe she just didn't know how to back down from a challenge. But I was seething, sick with imagining what could've happened as we put Llyn Glas behind us.

When we were well up the hill and out of earshot, I jumped down from the wagon and stalked toward her, feeling like I'd been holding my tongue for a year. "Inconspicuous," I said. "You were going to be inconspicuous. And then you *carved yourself* into the memory of an entire Mercian camp and a Brycheinig prince!"

Ffion's face was livid. "Yes, let's talk about that Brycheinig prince. Was he your *maneuver that failed,* Tal? A skinny little boy you chased from Mathrafal to his uncle's border—that was your plan?"

"The enemy prince who invaded my father's chambers?" I said. "Yes. I was going to take him to Black Darren and extract an alliance while keeping him safe and comfortable."

"And when that failed, you hounded a child across two kingdoms!"

She was unbelievable. "He was old enough to devise a plan to infiltrate Mathrafal! Prince Angws was the reason we had to install grilles below all the garderobes!"

"Still a child!"

"I was fourteen!" I exploded. "I was fourteen when it happened!"

Didn't she understand what could have happened by the lake if the crowd's mood had changed? Didn't she know what she'd risked?

I was fourteen the night I saw them all outside our house.

Dafydd hadn't been there to help me that night, either.

Tonight, and oh, the darkest night,
The darkest night, the darkest night,
Tonight, and oh, the darkest night,
Come we now to your lamps.

"Fourteen?" Ffion's anger shifted into confusion. "This happened a week ago."

"Not that." I ground my teeth. "I asked you to trust me. To be inconspicuous. Because crowds—" I had to pause to catch my breath. My heart felt like it was going to burst. "Crowds can't be trusted. They can turn in an instant."

"It was just a bunch of boys acting stupid, Tal." Her voice was frustrated. "Just talk. And I've heard much worse."

"No," I said. "It's only talk—*until* it's worse." Ffion frowned, reaching for the tie at the end of her hair.

I told myself that I could look away as she unplaited the ginger length of her braid, working it between her pale fingers. I could have looked away at any time. But I didn't.

Suddenly, I was exhausted. "Should we stop here?" I asked. "Or should we keep looking for a village?" We were surrounded by trees, the dyke to our right, fine green moss growing underfoot; twilight was settling.

Ffion's frown deepened. "A village?"

"Yes. A village." I couldn't sleep out here, in this place reeking of magic and the monsters who had once lived here. "I require it."

"You—require?"

"Will you stop repeating everything I say?" I flung out my arms. "Yes. I'm going to sleep this day off in a bed, and you can sleep among the gorse, or whatever it is you prefer to being indoors where it's safe."

"We're not going to *find* a village, Tal!" Ffion's laugh was acid, the loudest thing on the mountainside. "We're still climbing. If there were a village close enough for us to reach before nightfall, we'd have seen it already. It would be rising up ahead of us."

She said it like it was obvious. Because it *was* obvious.

"Take the reins," I said suddenly, thrusting them in her direction.

"What?"

"Just *take* them." I stuffed the reins in Ffion's hand and stomped twenty yards or so along the ditch.

"What are you doing?" she demanded.

I didn't answer. I just threw back my head and cursed as loudly as I could, shouting into the night until I didn't want to tear my own hair out anymore.

"Gods' candles, young man," a creaky old voice said beside me. "I think Offa can hear you all the way from his seat at Tamworth."

I jumped. A small woman—skinnier and shorter than Ffion, and that was saying something—stood beside me, leaning on a stick. Her white skin was wrinkled and sunbrowned, like she was just another shrub that had grown up on this ridge; her arms were covered in grizzled hair, and her joints crackled like twigs as she moved. She wore an extraordinarily ugly old hat with a black-and-green feather tucked into the brim.

"Where did you come from?" I demanded. *The ground?* I wanted to add.

She gestured to a thicket west of the dyke. "My hut. Where did *you* come from?"

"Lately, from Llyn Glas," Ffion said, the cart rattling up behind her. "And before that, from . . . farther."

I wondered if the woman would ask more questions. But at Ffion's appearance, she seemed to lose interest in me entirely. "Well, well," she said. "I wondered if we'd ever meet."

Ffion looked uneasy. "Did you?"

The woman nodded. "You look just like her, you know. Not the hair, but the eyes. Your nose and mouth, too."

Ffion hesitated. "She was blond when she was young, like Dad," she finally said. "But yes, that's what they tell me."

Whatever they were speaking about in code, I was getting

impatient with it, but I was beginning to suspect we'd found the hedgewitch the Mercian army had been looking for.

"I will pay you to shelter us for the night," I said. "Whatever you require."

"Not much to offer," she said, mouth pinched. "But I'm happy enough to take your pennies. Come, girl."

The hut wasn't much more than a single room with bunches of herbs hanging from its poorly thatched roof. Marks from the woman's walking stick dotted the dirt floor. A pallet lay in the corner, a few shelves lined one wall, and a cauldron hung over the cook fire.

I didn't ask what was in it.

When I put a silver ceiniog down on the woman's hearth, Ffion elbowed me, and I set down another beside it.

"For your hospitality and your trouble," I said. The old woman laughed, throwing me a look over her shoulder as she stirred her pot—just cawl, I realized, thank the gods. Her laugh turned into a cackle of satisfaction as Ffion produced salt pork and bread she'd brought from our supplies; the pork went immediately into the soup, and the bread she tore up and passed around.

"She recognized you," I said to Ffion in a low voice as she returned to my side.

"Of course I recognized her," said the woman. "Everyone knew Sioned. And my hearing is excellent," she added, glancing at me sharply.

"My mam-gu was a witch. Everyone always tells me I look just like her," Ffion explained, a little sheepish.

I thought I remembered her telling me the first bit. Ffion had certainly mentioned her grandmother before. "Was she on the Foxhall?"

"No, not Sioned. It wasn't her way," said the old hedgewitch, chewing meditatively. She nodded to a shelf lined with stoppered bottles and kitchen things. "Someone hand me those two bowls. You young people will have to share, as I have no intention of doing so." I brought them to her obediently, though she swatted me away when I tried to help her to her stool by the fire. "Don't be silly," she said waspishly. "If I don't make use of these old bones, they'll stop being any use at all. Sit down, you're making me nervous."

"Yes, ma'am." I settled down meekly onto the floor beside the fire and passed the bowl to Ffion. "You first."

"Diolch." Ffion cupped the bowl and took a drink, then returned it to me, her fingers brushing mine. It was strangely intimate, sharing it.

"Now," said the old hedgewitch. "Why don't you tell me what you're out here doing?"

Ffion glanced to me, and for whatever reason, I nodded. "We're on a mission to break King Offa's Dyke," she said. "I'm walking from Merthyr-Tewdrig to Prestatyn to do it."

The old witch whistled. "Gods' candles, that's a long way."

"We're also looking for something called the llafnau," I added, quickly explaining the Mercian attack coming, and how we hoped to meet it with the blades. "Have you heard of them?"

"Well, yes." She frowned. "They were kept secret from most, so they'd stay a secret from Mercia. But the witches knew, and the kings knew." She nodded at Ffion. "I'd have thought you would, as well."

"Me?" Ffion drew back. "Why?"

The old witch looked nonplussed. "Well, because Sioned favored you so. She always said you were her boy's favorite, too."

Ffion looked at me uneasily, and I remembered what Arianrhod had said to her before she left the Dead Man's Bells. *Don't act like I'm the only one who's someone's favorite.*

Ffion shook her head. "Why would that matter, though?"

"You asked about the llafnau," said the old witch irritably. "It matters, little witch, because Sioned made them."

21

DAFYDD

Mathrafal Castle, Powys

Come six o'clock hour, our fires do we bank
And make for the pub and cry for a tankard
We purchase each draft with pennies laid down
The silver is ours, by the sweat of our brow
—"The Workaday Song"

"Right. Now, Una, you help Caradoc restack the woodpile," I called over my shoulder.

"I don't want to stack the woodpile," Una whined. "I want to play with Gruffudd. Can that be my job today?" Gruffudd lay pitifully on his side, looking as if he'd never known human affection.

Caradoc threw out a hand. "No, I want that to be *my* job." Unsurprising. At the age of six, identical twins Una and Caradoc shared liquid brown eyes, olive skin, and absolutely all tasks, possessions, and interests. Unless they happened to be fighting over them.

"It can be both your jobs," I said, working the bellows. "I always need help taking good care of Gruffudd." Years ago, when I opened my forge, I'd let it be known I required regular assistance. This sometimes consisted of fetching and carrying, cleaning tools, or sweeping the forge floor, though with Una and Caradoc and other children their age, it most often involved petting Gruffudd.

Still. A few of the older children, I'd been able to teach actual smithwork, and some had even left me to go work for the big forge in town. That had pleased me.

I'd had to abandon Farmer Gerwyn's harrow when I went north. But I was nearly finished repairing it when someone else—not Una or Caradoc—spoke at my back.

"So," he said, "you've come home again."

My father's voice was quietly furious. I didn't turn away from the fire.

"I have."

"I told you that there would be consequences if you chose to defy me."

I laid the harrow on the anvil, hammering one glowing prong until it ran straight, only curving downward at the end. Only six prongs to go. First, though, I needed to go split more wood for the fire, draw more water from the well.

"Una, Caradoc," I called, glancing back at them. "Can you come back tomorrow? Your pay's on the bench."

Even Gruffudd wasn't enough to keep them at work once I said they were free to go. The twins snatched their coins with a whoop and ran outside without a backward glance.

When they were gone, I faced my father. "I didn't defy you. I rode north. All the way to Prestatyn, in fact."

"Prestatyn?" he asked, surprised. I nodded. "And?" Dad jerked his gaze toward the courtyard, like Bleddyn's troops might be amassing at our gates even as we spoke.

"And—nothing. The king refused. Flatly." I watched my hands begin to sweep iron shavings into a little pile like they weren't even mine.

"So the northern Marches have abandoned us, then," my father said bitterly. "Perhaps we look south. Perhaps we look west."

With his gold braids and the gold ring in his ear and his giant arms crossed over his broad chest, my father looked like some kind of god in the forge light. That was how I'd seen him when I was young, when I'd wondered if I'd ever grow to be as big as him.

Now I was. And I was old enough to see that my father wasn't a god, or anything close to one.

"And Tal?" I asked. Would my father punish him and Gwanwyn? Or had I done enough?

He glanced at me, distracted. "What about Tal?"

"What about—?" My words snagged, hurt for my brother mingling with confusion and relief in my blood. But Dad saw none of it.

He shook his head. "I'm disappointed, Dafydd," he said. "This isn't over."

He left me then, dread soaking into my skin.

Of course it wasn't over. I'd been an idiot to think my father would leave me be after one attempt.

But when *would* it be over? When would I know my fate, so I could begin to accept it?

When could I finally relax, knowing the worst was behind me?

My wants and fears were an unsettled sea. I didn't want to be king. Did I want Tal to be king? And though my father wasn't a great king, I didn't want him to die.

So much was wrong in our kingdom. Mercia took advantage, and my father took more than he should from our people. But I was afraid of the changes coming. Surely a strained peace was better than open war.

I knew I couldn't hope for better. But I couldn't help hoping I could cling to what I had.

I'd taken up a new project that night when he came to me.

"When you left for Prestatyn, you told me you would try," he said.

"And you told me the next time you came to the forge, you would wear more clothes."

Elin's sickle needed reshaping; I pulled it from the fire and laid it on the anvil. But ignoring Osian's stare was impossible.

"Do you know how I knew the attack would be this spring?" he asked. "It was because of her. I saw her, and she was unchanged."

Startled, I missed my mark and burned my arm. I hissed, cursing. "That's not possible."

"All sorts of things are possible," Osian said. "But not your success, if you continue to hide here."

"My success is imminent," I said flatly. "Soon enough, I'll be candler."

"You are meant to be king," Osian said. "You are meant to be king, and she is meant to work beside you."

Her.

No matter what we were talking about, we were really always talking about the girl.

"But I can't be king. Because I'm trying to do what's right," I said. "She understands that, doesn't she? She knows that if things were different and I could take the throne, I'd never choose anyone else."

"You admire her very much, and I'm sure she'd say the same about you," Osian said.

That comforted me. "Soon enough, I'll be candler," I finally said again. "And for now, I'm doing good work."

If Osian had been anyone else, he might have nodded politely, whatever he really thought. Instead, he shrugged, frowning. "You're also taking business from the other forge in town."

I stopped short. "I am not. I don't charge anything. I only take work from people who can't afford to pay him."

"And how do you think that's affecting his custom?" Osian asked. "He did work for free sometimes, too. Sometimes, later, when his customers could pay him, they did. It was a dignified arrangement between people who understood one another." He pulled himself cross-legged onto my stool. "When you set up shop and began working for free, you interfered with those relationships. Did you think people were proud to come to you for charity?" he asked. "And now you're taking work away from a man with a family to feed, employees and apprentices and suppliers to pay."

I gripped the edge of the bench, the old anxiety rising in my chest. I'd never thought of any of that. "Why haven't you told me this before?"

I'd thought I was doing good. Helping in a way that couldn't possibly cause harm.

Osian shrugged again. "You didn't need to know before. Now you do."

"This is all irrelevant," I finally said. I picked up the broom Una had been pretending was a pike and began to sweep up. "I did what Father said. I went to Prestatyn and failed; I will be candler. Tal is still in play, so I am, too."

"Do you want Tal to be king, Dafydd?" Osian asked.

"I don't know," I said. "I don't know. I've done everything I can."

"You are capable of more."

I swallowed hard.

That was precisely what I was afraid of.

"Ah, well." Osian twisted his back, joints popping. "I can see you need to think. I only came to tell you that the Foxhall has sent word to your father."

I stopped sweeping, but didn't turn.

"They're coming to Mathrafal," he said. "I thought you'd like to know."

22

FFION

On the Dyke, Brycheiniog

I gaped at the old hedgewitch. "My grandmother made the llafnau?"

"I'd have thought you knew," she said again.

I hadn't. Even keeping secrets from Tal, I wouldn't have kept that back.

The memory of my mam-gu was precious to me. It was an unspeakable gift to learn something new about her so many years after she'd passed. "Will you tell us about them?" I asked eagerly.

The hedgewitch rubbed at her grizzled old arms. "For a price."

Tal—who looked intrigued for reasons very different from mine—reached for his purse. "How much more?"

"Put your money away, silly boy." The hedgewitch pointed an arthritic finger at me. "I want a bit of magic."

"Oh. All right." I was surprised, given the sense of power already permeating the hut. "What can I do for you?"

She held out her liver-spotted hands. Some of her fingers were twisted, and every knuckle was painfully swollen. I wondered if her arthritis had eaten into her ability to work. "Can you help with the pain?"

"Of course," I said. "Just give me a minute."

It was quick work to dash outside and collect a fistful of twigs, but a bit slower to scrape the bark off each with my knife. When I was done, I laid them in the hedgewitch's palms in line with her fingers, smearing them with a little grease from the salt pork's wrapper. The fat was smooth, like the movement her hands had lost. But it wouldn't be enough.

I looked into my cauldron, at the pitiful pile of materials I'd gathered to resurrect Cadno.

I wanted to be frugal. But my plan to destroy the dyke and restore magic was already in doubt. And without the llafnau, Tal had no strategy for meeting the Mercian attack. We needed information.

Reluctantly, I took the stinging nettle I'd gleaned and swatted it at the underside of her hands against her swollen joints.

Then I began to sing.

O daughter, daughter, newborn girl, o running gleeful child
You wish to grow as tall as trees, to climb like ivy wild
But I did wish for pale, dry flesh, did wish for wrinkled skin,
I dreamt of walking with a stick, I dreamt of walking bent

O maiden fair, o maiden fair, o dancing charming youth
You wish for comely figure, bright and laughing eyes, but sooth
I wished to be as thin as thin, o, whittled to the rind
I dreamt by day of rheumy eyes, by night of going blind

O woman grown, o woman grown, o mother, gentl' and warm
You wish for swollen belly, breast, and softly rounded form
I wished for fallen breasts and empty crib, as cold as stone
I dreamt of children at my side, not wee but fully grown

A crone I am, a woman old, a silver-hairèd queen
I wished for crooked fingers, aching back, and wrinkled mien
I wished for fallen breasts and children grown and wed and wived
Care not for maiden fairness, only that I have survived.

The song had been one of Mam-gu's favorites. *It is only men, Ffion bach, who want women to be young,* she'd told me once. *An old woman is free.*

I'd been confused. *Free from what?*

Not free from. *My youth is gone, and now I'm free to be what I wish,* she'd said. *I have years of love to be grateful for, a lifetime of work to be proud of, and no fear of the opinions of others. No need to be beautiful or young.*

But you are beautiful, I had protested. For years, I'd told Mam I didn't want my hair to be red; I wanted it to be silver, like Mam-gu's.

But I don't have *to be,* Mam-gu had insisted, smiling down at me. *Someday you will understand what a gift it is, to be free to be a little bit strange, or ugly, or old.*

When I finished singing, the old hedgewitch lifted her hands, turning them this way and that. I hadn't been able to unbend her fingers entirely, but the twist in her right ring finger was less pronounced, and the joints were less swollen. A lily had sprouted from the ground beside her stool, and I left it for her to enjoy.

"Little witch!" she exclaimed. "I hadn't hoped for so much. Your power is very like to Sioned's."

"Impressive," Tal said quietly, expression unreadable, and I felt myself blushing.

"Well," the old hedgewitch said with a sigh. "One good turn deserves another. Let me tell you a bit about the llafnau.

"We all know there used to be uncanny creatures about. Used to be gwiberod in these woods, actually. You'd see them lying in the sun in the morning like grass snakes. Always after my chickens, they were," she said with a chuckle.

"But you also know that about ten years ago, they all began to disappear. One day, there were creatures about, and magic could be relied upon. Then it was as if someone had built a dam, and the river started drying up. A pod of gwiberod wouldn't be in the nest they'd occupied for years, or a ceffyl dŵr would disappear from its lake. There was one in Llyn Glas, and it was gone one morning, just like that." She snapped her fingers and gave a surprised laugh. "Haven't done that in ages," she said, looking pleased. Then she sobered. "Anyhow, it happened slowly at first. But Sioned saw what was happening from the very beginning.

"Sometimes, when a creature disappeared, it left something behind. A hair from a ceffyl dŵr's tail, a gwiber's tooth, suchlike." She adjusted her hat and cleared her throat. "For the last year of her life, Sioned collected the few she could find. And whatever power was left in those pieces, she tended and amplified—it was a long, complicated spell, one far beyond me," she added. "And they became the llafnau, gifts to the kings of Gwynedd, Powys, and Brycheiniog, to repel and defend against the Mercians who had endangered their magic."

Tal looked chagrined. But an idea glimmered at the back of my mind.

"I don't understand," he said. "They're called blades. They're meant to be weapons."

The hedgewitch's brow knitted. "I'm sorry they won't be much use in soldiers' hands, but did you think Wales's strength lay in arms? Our power is in our magic, boy. Our land, our creatures, our people." She paused, looking ruffled. "Besides, who would bother to enchant a pike? A weapon is already a weapon, why would it need magic?"

Tal's expression shuttered.

I knew why he was looking resentful. We couldn't fight off the Mercian army with an enchanted water horse hair.

But I thought I might have another purpose for such powerful sources of magic.

"And so." The old witch nodded. "If you still seek the llafnau, nearest place to start is Black Darren. Ask King Meirion if he's willing to deal."

"Understood," I said. I wanted to talk to the old hedgewitch more—mostly to ask if she'd ever sensed the magic in the dyke. But I couldn't raise that question in front of Tal.

He rose abruptly then, still looking sulky. "I need to sleep. Ffion, I'll see you out to the dyke."

The old woman blinked up at him. "My, but you're a handsome young man," she said, as though confused by the fact. "Such lovely brown eyes."

". . . Thank you." Tal looked equally bemused. "I'll be back momentarily."

I thanked the old witch, and she nodded farewell. But she was mostly focused on opening and closing her hands again and again.

"Why didn't you heal your hands yourself?" I asked, pausing in her doorway. I could feel the power in her hut; asking me to do it didn't make any sense.

"I don't practice anymore. Those are just relics," she added, the feather in her hideous hat bobbing as she nodded at the bottles on her shelves. "My magic died with my familiar a few years ago. A gwyllgi." Her wrinkled face fell a little. "I found him curled up in a thicket with a Mercian arrow in his side. Broke my old heart, it did."

"I'm so sorry." I felt a pang like an arrow in my own chest. Osian losing Pendwmpian, the old hedgewitch losing her gwyllgi—I'd heard so many stories of lost anchors lately.

My own loss was all-consuming.

But suddenly, a terrible feeling began to simmer low in my gut.

"Bran was my friend for fifty-five years. Had the loveliest black coat you'd ever seen. That's why when the Mercians came looking for me today, I was nowhere to be found," she added. "Wouldn't have helped them even if I could have."

"I understand." I spoke the words, but they sounded distant in my ears.

Realization came to me slowly, inexorable as spreading mold.

How had I not—

"Wait." Tal straightened, sharpening. "Wait. Ffion's familiar died a week ago. But Ffion still has magic."

"Gods candle his soul." The old hedgewitch frowned.

I couldn't speak.

My heart was crashing through the floor.

"Yes, of course," Tal said impatiently, starting to count on his fingers, awareness dawning in his expression. "But—Bran died, and your magic disappeared. The Mercians cut down Pendwmpian Forest, and Osian's magic disappeared. So why does Ffion still have magic, even though Cadno's died?"

His logic was relentless. My ears were ringing. The old hedgewitch put a gentle hand on my arm.

Don't say it. Don't—

"When an anchor's spirit leaves our plane, that's the end of its witch's magic," she said. I couldn't stop shaking my head.

How had I not realized what else would come of Cadno's death?

"Well, when does that happen?" Tal demanded, turning to me. "How long before your magic runs out?"

My hands shook. "Cadno will cross over to Annwn at the new moon," I said. "He'll be lost to me then."

"Yes," she said. "And your magic will be, too."

I couldn't breathe.

My grief had been so complete, I hadn't thought of anything but how to undo its cause. I hadn't thought the consequences of losing

Cadno could be any deeper or sharper than my own pain.

I'd known that soon Cadno would go away forever if I couldn't bring him back. I hadn't realized my magic—the thing that made me who I was—would go with him.

"What are we going to do if you don't have magic?" Tal looked affronted. "How can we complete our quest if—"

I couldn't think. I couldn't breathe.

"Thank you," I said to the hedgewitch, and lurched toward the door.

"Sleep well, little witch," she said, but her eyes looked troubled.

I had to get away. I had to *think*. I staggered back through the dark, hardly knowing where I was going.

"Ffion, wait."

A lime branch grasped for me; I ducked beneath it, pressing back down the path we'd followed to the witch's hut. Already I could feel the magic of the dyke more strongly, distinct from the magic I'd felt in the cottage.

Back on the day I'd burst into the Foxhall, I remembered thinking Rhiannon didn't understand what it meant to lose a familiar.

Apparently, I hadn't understood, either.

"Ffion, wait," Tal said again, and I whirled.

"What?" I demanded.

"What do you mean, *what?* What are you going to do?" he asked. "Your magic is going to disappear when the new moon comes!"

We both glanced up. The moon was nearly full.

"So you have—"

"Fifteen days," I finished.

"Did you know?" he asked me. I shook my head. Tal pushed his hands through his hair, chest heaving.

"First I find out the blades are useless relics, and then I find out—" Tal broke off.

He didn't say *you are, too.* But I heard it. I felt it.

"How can you destroy the dyke if you don't have magic?" he asked.

My heart was going to burst.

If Tal ended our contract, I couldn't be sure he'd see the dyke destroyed. And then Cadno and my magic and Wales's magic *would* be gone for good.

"Stop. Stop." I held up a hand. I forced myself to look calm, though I felt anything but. "Listen. I have a plan. We are still going to destroy the dyke and meet Offa's attack when it falls."

Tal grimaced. "Do I get to know about this plan?"

He got to know some of it. "We need the blades," I said. "I can use them to fuel the destruction of the dyke."

If I had the blades, the power in the dyke wouldn't matter. With them, my spell could overcome it—even if they also had to compensate for whatever magic *I* might lose in the next fifteen days.

Would my magic burn out slowly, like a dying fire? Or would it disappear as quickly as a snuffed candle?

It didn't have to matter. With the blades, our plan could still work, and Tal would never need to know what we were really up against.

"I thought you had that managed," he said. "With your death march and your pouches."

"I do," I said, hoping I sounded so offended he wouldn't question whether I was telling the truth. "But you of all people understand hedging your bets. Preparing for all eventualities."

"Fine. We'll stick to our plan to get the blades, then," he said, sounding grimly determined. But there was uncertainty in Tal's eyes when he looked back at me. "Is there something else you're not telling me?" he asked.

I wasn't telling him that I was falling apart. I wasn't telling him that I was scrambling to contain our situation as my plans continued to collapse.

"Unlike you, Tal, I'm not convinced that my every thought is interesting enough to share," I said flatly. "I'm *not telling you* plenty."

I spoke irritably. But as I walked back to the dyke alone, I was trying not to cry.

I couldn't fall apart. No matter what happened now, I had to have the blades to match the power in the dyke. And it would take all my will to get them.

As long as I could destroy the dyke, magic would return.

As long as enough magic lived in the land, I could resurrect Cadno.

As long as I could resurrect Cadno, my magic would survive.

I'd held my life together with twigs and twine for years now. I could do the same until my magic was secure.

I ignored the part of myself that sometimes longed for something just a little bit sturdier.

23

TAL

The next morning, we climbed the rest of the way to Black Darren in the rain.

I'd lain awake for hours on the floor of the hedgewitch's hut the night before, wondering why Ffion was lying to me about *hedging our bets*. She wasn't simply forming a contingency plan—that, I knew.

She didn't think she could destroy the dyke.

Had she been lying to me all along? Was it because her magic was due to leave her? Or had something else suddenly caused her to doubt?

Whatever it was, the dyke was—if nothing else—an advantage to Mercia in battle, and their attack was due to fall in two weeks. We had to destroy it.

Whatever margin I'd thought I had, it was gone. We *had* to have the blades.

Hunched beneath the oilcloth, an uneasy quiet between us and the smell of earth and rain up my nose, I thought there seemed something ironic in desperately hoping Ffion's magic wouldn't disappear while wishing Wales's magic wouldn't return.

About a mile from the castle, Ffion reached into her cauldron. "Here," she called softly. "I'll do it here."

I glanced toward either horizon. The guard tower to the south was too far away and at a poor angle to see our position. To the north, guards paced on the tower parapet, but their attention was fixed on Black Darren.

"Fine." I pulled up the wagon to shield her as she dropped into the ditch and buried another pouch in the earthwork's side. Then she hauled herself out, singing just like always, and we made for the city gates.

The streets on the edge of the town surrounding King Meirion's seat were little more than muddy paths in the rain; water ran down roofs and walls and the awnings of market booths. Masses of damp-clothed townsfolk crowded our wagon, buying and selling and shouting.

At the center of so much disorder and grime, Black Darren was an unambiguously welcome sight. It was a black-stoned keep shaped like a columbarium, crenellations flanking its domed roof, narrow windows in its walls. Outbuildings—stables, and an actual columbarium—dotted the rest of the grounds.

I felt my whole body relax with relief at the sight of so much stone and civilization. It would keep the smell of earth and magic out; I was sure of that.

After stabling the horses and wagon, we straggled into a yellow-painted entry hall lit with beeswax candles. Errand boys and serving girls gaped at Ffion, at her loose hair and her ankles wrapped in ivy and her feet covered in mud. But a discreet word to the steward had him off to King Meirion and us off to a guest chamber.

I wondered how long it would take Prince Angws to find out we'd arrived.

In the manner of a columbarium, the few spare rooms at Black Darren were fitted like niches into the three-story keep's top two floors. Our room was narrow, with a large wooden bed, a bureau with a basin, and a small table holding a few candles.

"Turn around," Ffion ordered, and I obeyed and began peeling off my wet clothes. For a few minutes, there was nothing but the sound of us shivering and drying off.

"I'm trying to decide if I should wear your favorite coat, or go to court naked like we discussed," I said as I pulled on clean clothes. "You know, really make an impression."

It wasn't a good joke, but we only had so many between us to choose from just yet. I waited for her to groan or elbow me blindly in the ribs or call me a pig again. But she didn't answer.

Well.

"Ffion?" I asked.

I wondered what she was wearing.

I fought a growl of frustration. Last night had ruined everything. I found myself wishing she would say something about my stupid coat, if only to make the moment feel more normal.

"What if they don't listen?" she whispered.

"What do you mean?" I half glanced over my shoulder, then remembered— "Are you dressed?"

"What do I know about kings or wars?" Her voice was faint. "Why would Meirion listen to me when the coven in my own town won't take me seriously? What if I accidentally lie to him somehow, and he throws us out?"

A knock came at the door. "Prince Taliesin, the king will see you."

"How would you *accidentally* lie to—Ffion, are you dressed?" I asked.

A choking sound. "Oh—yes."

I turned.

Rhiannon's old black kirtle drowned her. Her skin was sallow against the fabric, and her eyes looked hollow and worried.

She'd put on a convincing face when we were arguing last night. But her doubt was unmistakable now. My mind raced as I washed my hands and face and Ffion wiped her feet.

Things weren't as I'd hoped. Ffion's magic was at risk, and something about our task daunted her, and she was lying to me about it.

Still. Managing a trifling king like Meirion—that, she could do.

Squaring my shoulders, I crossed the room and hauled her firmly to her feet. "Fee, you know what to do. We need the blade to do our job. Think of the money, if you have to."

Ffion didn't care about money, I knew. She cared about getting Cadno back. But some things I couldn't give her.

"I already took twenty ceiniogau from you," she said desperately. "Maybe I don't need any more."

I frowned. "You took—"

"Did you really think it would cost twenty-five ceiniogau to outfit us? Tal, honestly. I could've cleaned out every stall in the market." She pinched the bridge of her nose.

Well. I hadn't been expecting that.

"Ffion." Abruptly, I put my palm to her cheek, rested the other hand on her shoulder.

For half a moment, I wasn't sure if I wanted to shake her or kiss her. For half a moment, I knew she was wondering the same.

Her eyes were so close to mine; the pale plane of her forehead, the ginger lines of her brows, her pointed chin and the gap between her teeth.

Ffion shut her eyes. "What are you doing?" she whispered.

The knock came from the hall again.

"What did you feel when you saw the dragons, when you were a girl?" I asked her. I could feel her breath against my cheek.

"Tal, I'm not sorry about the money—"

"Forget the money, you imp," I hissed. "Tell me what you felt."

Ffion's throat worked. "I felt wonder," she said softly. "Wonder, and a wish to protect."

I felt an unexpected wave of jealousy at her words.

What would my life have been if magic had made me feel that way? If I had met wonder instead of horror? If I had felt the desire to guard the magic, not guard *against* it?

But I didn't have time for those questions. I already had to contend with knowing Angws was likely somewhere in this castle, and his presence and my own actions were going to complicate our efforts here.

I leaned closer to Ffion.

"Imagine a world with that sort of wonder around every corner," I said. She opened her eyes, and her breath seemed to catch. "Imagine the return of unicorns and sighted ravens and dragons. Imagine every hearth tended by a bwbach and ceffylau dŵr in the rivers and waterfalls." I raised my eyebrows. "Your love for them is all truth, Ffion, and no lies. If you can't think of the money, then think of that."

"Prince Taliesin!" The knock came again from the hall, this time less patient.

"We're coming," Ffion called out. Her voice was stronger now—strong enough, anyway.

"Stay close, Ffion," I said, making for the door. "They may call Meirion the Dithering Crow farther down the mountain, but we're in his court now, and I'm taking no chances."

The messenger led us down the stairs to King Meirion's throne room, a room not unlike my father's, which sat at the center of the columbarium. Built of the same black rock as the rest of the castle, its walls were painted honey-yellow and covered with hangings—black wings on banners and mountains on cloth-of-gold fields, enough embroidery and painted silk to blunt the cold. Unlike my father's throne room on the last day I was at Mathrafal, the hall where we met King Meirion was full.

A crowd, and a king who could tell truth from lies. My nerves began to buzz.

At least Angws was absent; if I was lucky, I'd be spared talking about him at all.

"King Meirion." I bowed, low but not too low. "I thank you for your warm welcome."

Truth.

King Meirion sat on a throne made of black wood at the center of a close circle of retainers. Even seated, he was obviously unusually tall; his posture was froglike, his feet together and his knees splayed, and his eyes and mouth were wide like his nephew's. He was probably around forty, white-skinned and dark-eyed.

Did he already know who I was? Was he reading my thoughts even as I stood in the middle of his throne room?

But the king's brow furrowed. "Who are you," he asked in an unexpectedly deep voice, "and who is your friend?"

"I am Prince Taliesin ap Cadell, second son of the king of Powys," I said. *Truth.*

"The bastard?" he asked. A few startled gasps. Meirion blinked. "I beg your pardon," he added immediately.

How polite. "Yes. I come seeking a favor," I said—*truth*—not waiting for him to ask *and why are you here?* in that disturbingly low voice of his. "Your help, in fact, in defending Wales against the Mercian threat." *Truth.*

The court stirred worriedly around us, responding just as I'd known they would, just as if we were mummers in a play—though I'd been careful to speak in perfect honesty.

Meirion looked concerned for a moment as well. He leaned close to one of his retainers, whispering something.

Then a smirk crossed his face, and my stomach lurched.

"Defending *Wales*," he said thoughtfully. "How interesting."

"Yes." I swallowed. "My father's magician—"

"No, stop," he said. When he continued, his tone was as cheerful as his words were sharp. "I'm still thinking of how your father must have been defending *Wales* when his high men moved the boundary markers on our northern border. And clearly, Cadell was only thinking of *Wales* when he refused to stop his soldiers from sacking border villages from Bryncoch to Mynydd-bach!" Abruptly, the king sat forward, his expression avid, almost friendly. "And you were only defending Wales when you chased my nephew across Powys to my border."

The crowd stirred again, but there was malice in the sound now.

For a moment, I wondered which I hated more: crowds, or magic.

Because I wasn't sure I could rebut his claims without lying.

"We've settled matters with your nephew," I said. *Truth*. I pushed down the thoughts that had troubled me all night in the hedgewitch's hut—thoughts of Ffion telling me I'd been cruel.

"Can the matter be settled, until you have settled it with me?" Meirion shook his head, exchanging glances with his men. "I ask again: Who is your friend?"

"My name is Ffion." In her funeral shroud of a dress, surrounded by the court, she looked smaller and paler than ever. "I'm the hedgewitch of Foxhall."

"Of the Foxhall?" Meirion frowned. "A hedgewitch, one of their number?"

"Hedgewitch to the town, not the coven," Ffion said. "I am traveling with Prince Taliesin to help him address the Mercian threat."

Another advisor leaned close to the king, whispering in his ear. King Meirion straightened. "And were you addressing the Mercian threat when you cleaned Llyn Glas for their soldiers?" he asked.

"I unfouled a Brycheinig lake for Brycheiniog," Ffion said. "We're speaking of a greater threat than a camp of soldiers on your border." She hesitated, then glanced over, prompting me.

"We mean to destroy Offa's Dyke," I said. "To do so, we require one of the blades you hold here at Black Darren."

Meirion held up a hand, eyes darting nervously around the hall, as if I might say too much. "You've lost your senses. I will not cede our remaining blade, not even to a prince of Powys. The gift of Sioned vch Blodwen is ours to keep."

Perfect. I'd been waiting for him to mention her name.

"Not even to Sioned's—?"

But Ffion cut me off. "Not even to counteract a Mercian attack foretold by Osian, King Cadell's own magician?"

I frowned at her interruption. Meirion did, too. "An attack?" he asked. "Upon Brycheiniog?"

Ffion hesitated.

"We cannot say for certain where the attack will fall, or when," I admitted. "But we know the attack will come from Mercia, and we expect it to fall on the next new moon."

When King Meirion didn't ask for evidence, I was grateful. But then he shot a grin at the advisor to his right and flopped a little in his seat.

"So let me see if I understand," he said. "A Powysian magician foretells an attack—sometime. Somewhere in the Welsh Marches. Presumably in Powys, if his magic is bound to his own kingdom, as one might expect." Meirion tapped a finger to his lips in a show of thoughtfulness. "What about this story, Prince Taliesin, is meant to compel me to lend Powys the blade that keeps Brycheiniog safe? Is it the threat to our bullying northern neighbor? Or the pitifully short sight of its magician?" Snickers rose through the room. Meirion seemed to draw strength from the sound.

I hated crowds.

Ffion drew herself up. "You mock Powys's guardians at your peril."

It ought to have inspired more laughter—the ragged girl in the too-large dress, unpolished voice piercing the throne room. But Ffion lifted her chin and opened her palms, and the room stilled. Meirion seemed to shrink back in his chair.

I thought I had seen her angry. But I hadn't seen her like this.

She was a goddess carved in alabaster and wreathed in copper. No—not a goddess. Ffion belonged to a time before goddesses.

Standing beside me, absolutely furious, she was an eldritch power. A primeval force, more fox or fey or dragon than human. I was so amazed, I forgot to be afraid.

Again, the king's eyes darted around nervously. "I have no wish to offend the Foxhall."

"Offend the Foxhall all you want." Ffion's voice was flat. "But do not offend me."

A lull. Meirion sat lacing and unlacing his fingers, not looking at the advisors hovering behind him. "Will you prove it?" he finally asked. "I might forgive your prince's sins and consider your request if you would demonstrate your skill for Black Darren."

I exchanged a confused glance with Ffion. Hadn't he just told us he already knew what had happened at Llyn Glas? "Demonstrate how?" Ffion asked.

"However you choose." Meirion hesitated. "A feast tonight, I think. No—tomorrow afternoon," he corrected himself.

Magic for a favor; watching Ffion make this exchange had become almost routine. Even knowing what we'd learned from the hedgewitch last night, I hadn't expected to see worry behind her eyes.

"Very well," she said.

Ffion had claimed ignorance of court politics. But even she would have known what she looked like as she swept from the room with her hair and skirts swirling.

"If you want a display," she intoned, not breaking her stride, "then I will give you one."

24

DAFYDD

Mathrafal Castle, Powys

The sweat of our brow, the sweat of our brow
In the smithy, the mines, at the back of the plow,
An honest day's work for an honest endowt,
We labor and live by the sweat of our brow.
—"The Workaday Song"

Around sunset the next day, the witches appeared.

It felt like half of Mathrafal Castle was pressed against the windows to watch the six covenwitches ride in on their blue roans, their loose hair and black dresses blowing behind them. An extremely compact old woman led their number, followed by a familiar-looking girl with pinkish pale skin and strawberry-blond hair.

My father and his men called the Foxhall witches hags. And now he was welcoming them to Mathrafal.

I stepped away from the window and pushed back through the other watchers. Gruffudd trotted after.

"The Foxhall at Mathrafal. Certainly unexpected." Gwanwyn's voice came from where she stood farther down the hall, leaning against another window.

I cleared my throat. I hadn't spoken to Tal's mother since he and I had fought in the forge. "Osian told me they'd sent word ahead of them."

"That isn't what I meant." Gwanwyn grinned and bent to scratch Gruffudd. "Though you're lucky to have Osian on your side."

"Well. We don't all have mothers looking out for us," I said.

My own mother was nothing but a hallowed, untouchable story to me; she'd died before I was even a year old, and my father had taken up with Gwanwyn what some people considered indecently soon after.

But the gossip had meant nothing to me. Tal and I had grown up together, played together, been tutored together. So for years, I had counted his mother as mine, too. Where Dad had always made it clear he was interested in me and ambitious on my behalf, Gwanwyn's affection had been simple.

We had been family. Now we were nothing to each other.

Now Gwanwyn lived to keep an ear and an eye out for Tal. They were all the other had, since Tal had made it clear they wouldn't count on me for anything anymore.

I wondered what—if—she thought of me now.

And not all sons can be counted on, I thought she might say. I would've deserved it.

"Are you attending their audience with your father?" she asked instead.

"I wasn't invited."

"He'd probably be pleased if you did." She glanced at me sidelong. Gruffudd bumped his head against her leg. "He would probably give you another chance if you asked for one."

The trouble wasn't that I was out of chances with my father. The trouble was that Gwanwyn was right, and every chance was another opportunity to make the wrong choice.

"I don't want another chance," I said quietly. "You know I don't. I don't want to be—"

She watched me, brown eyes and narrow jaw set unsettlingly like Tal's. "I know, Dafydd bach" was all she said. Then she nodded at the staircase.

The witches were waiting, and so was my father.

I wasn't sure which I dreaded meeting with more.

They held the meeting on the roof of the keep. Evidently, the Foxhall had no interest in appearing as petitioners in my father's throne room.

The wind blew strong in the witches' hair and my father's braids as I crossed the roof toward them, hands in the pockets of my leather apron, Gruffudd loping after me.

"Dafydd." My father stared in surprise.

"Pardon my lateness," I said. "Please, continue."

"We've nearly finished, Prince Dafydd." The Foxhall's leader, a woman with white skin and dark eyes who wore what looked like old fox ears pinned into her gray hair, gave me a gracious nod. "Your father has made his case already. We have but to reply."

The meeting had been too brief; that couldn't mean anything good. And though the old witch's words were courteous, her voice was cold enough to set me on edge.

"King Cadell, we oppose your aim to destroy the dyke," she said, turning to my father, "but we have no objection to assisting you with your Mercian problem."

Osian looked concerned. A tattooed afanc on his neck leapt as he leaned forward. "Rhiannon, without the destruction of the dyke, magic will not return."

She shrugged elegantly. "Surely with no viable alternative, you can agree to these terms."

No viable alternative to giving up Welsh magic, with Tal still in play? Unacceptable.

But before I could protest, Dad spoke. "And you say that Taliesin has recruited a hedgewitch?"

"An unpredictable chit with little magic and less dignity." For the first time, Rhiannon's composure slipped. "Believe me, if your task is left to them, the Marches will be crushed."

The strawberry-blond witch white-knuckled the cane in her hand

and pressed her lips together. Osian eyed her and Rhiannon, expression unreadable.

"It's true that my first concern was to put down Offa's assault." My father fingered the end of a braid, thinking. "Though I can't think why you would prefer the dyke remain."

"Your answer, Cadell," said Rhiannon.

He was actually considering this.

I wasn't like my brother; I trusted magic. But standing on that roof, I began to have real doubts about the Foxhall.

"Father, the vision promised your death," I reminded him, unable to keep the dread from my voice.

"I will avoid battle. But as matters stand, my son, I am left with no choice." Dad's jaw hardened. "Dafydd, you will hold Mathrafal in my absence. You understand why you will do this without complaint."

I thought of Gwanwyn downstairs and nodded.

My father's game continued to evolve. All I could do was try to keep playing and hope he'd end things before someone got hurt.

Dad gestured roughly to Rhiannon and the other Foxhall witches, returning to the keep to start their preparations. "It seems the only way to ensure Powys is defended is to defend it myself."

When Osian left the roof, I followed him inside.

"Did you know they were going to propose that?" I hissed, tracking him down the stairs, Gruffudd lumbering behind me. "Leave Offa's Dyke right where it is? Keep magic from coming back?"

Osian popped a series of bones in his spine. "I should have," he said. "I know Rhiannon."

I'd never heard of Rhiannon before, and I'd have been very happy for that to have remained the case. "Who is she?"

He sighed. "She's a very powerful witch—by which I mean, she is immensely powerful, and intimidating, and wealthy, and she is also a witch. She has connections and resources even *she* couldn't have imagined a decade ago."

"What does that mean?"

"It means she doesn't want magic restored to the land," Osian said. "In magic's current state, enchantment is very costly to work. Only the coven under the hill can afford to pay those costs."

"There are hedgewitches," I said. "Like the one Tal hired. Like—" I eyed Osian meaningfully.

"There are," he agreed. "But none with a purse as deep as the Foxhall's. So magic's scarcity makes the Foxhall powerful."

Osian began to descend again, and I followed. "So why are they here?" I asked. "My father's always hated the Foxhall."

"They sent word because Tal tried to recruit them," he said wearily. "He was a kitten walking into a hawk's nest. I know you think my methods of working magic are excessive, but you haven't seen theirs."

I cleared my throat and looked away; I hadn't thought Osian had noticed my squeamishness over the years.

"And they don't want Welsh magic to return," I finally said. "Even if that means we never see another creature again, and my father might die." I couldn't believe he'd adopted such a toothless strategy so readily.

No, *toothless* was the wrong word. Their proposal was *all* teeth. It was focused entirely on the attack, and completely neglected the intent of the quest: to strengthen Wales, to bring our magic and our creatures back to us.

"He must avoid the battle," Osian agreed. Then, to my surprise, he laughed. "There's nothing they can do to stop magic returning, though."

I stopped short. "What do you mean?"

Osian's eyes crinkled at the corners. "Have you visited the

columbarium lately? I don't know what she and Tal have been up to, but she's done something."

She.

Doubt crept up my spine. My stomach plummeted.

No matter what we were talking about, we were really always talking about the girl.

But I didn't know why Osian had brought up the columbarium. Or why he would mention her in the same breath as Tal.

My mouth was dry. "Do you mean—"

But I couldn't finish.

"I mean she is the hedgewitch he has hired. I mean the girl your visions have shown you now travels with him. I mean this, Dafydd: you can choose to become candler and let Tal claim the throne," Osian said, fixing me with his unearthly stare. "And if you do, he will claim her as well."

Tal. Tal, and the girl. It was as impossible as a columbarium with its sight restored.

I turned my back on Osian and ran.

I fled the dank air of the keep, running through the courtyard, past the forge, stopping just short of the columbarium.

I panted, hands on my knees, and forced myself to look skyward.

Emerald-and-black wings, flashing golden eyes.

Sighted ravens circled the roof of the columbarium, croaking and cawing.

They'd returned.

25

FFION

Black Darren, Brycheiniog

After my dramatic exit from the throne room, I couldn't remember where our room was. Tal had to remind me where to go.

There was sweat on his forehead from our audience, I noticed. So much careful truth-telling had evidently worn him out.

Up in our room, we talked over other ways to find out more about the blade. "The serving girls might know something," he said, eyeing the meal they'd left on our table. "I doubt they know what it is. But I'd bet they know where treasure tends to be kept. I'll spend the day poking around."

"Mm." I bit into a bun. "Why would they tell you, though?"

Another grin from Tal. Crooked smile, perfect teeth, beauty mark, eyes shining. "Why *wouldn't* they?"

I threw the bun at his head. "Handsome or not, those girls are too busy for you to waste their time flirting. At least, not for free. If they tell you something, pay them."

"True. I heard one say earlier that they have to walk outside the city walls to draw water."

"With Mercians just down the ridge? That's hardly safe."

"It really isn't," Tal agreed. He cocked an eyebrow. "You think I'm handsome?"

I groaned, stuffing more bread into my pockets, then yanked a blanket off the bed. "You're the worst kind of handsome, Tal. Handsome, aware of it, and pretending you're not. But don't worry." I patted his cheek a little too hard. "The serving girls and I will do our best not to cry ourselves to sleep pining over you."

"Where are you taking my blanket?" he asked. "I need that!"

I hated that Meirion was wasting a day unnecessarily. But since I had the time, I needed to think. I needed to wander.

I needed to listen.

"Whining is unattractive, Tal," I called over my shoulder. "I'll see you later."

"Remember—truth, no matter how careful. Remember to stand up straight when you speak. You'll look taller, and your voice will carry farther. Oh, and make sure your nails are clean before you serve yourself. And don't drink too quickly, the bragawd will probably be stronger than what you're used to." On the way downstairs to King Meirion's banquet, Tal muttered instructions almost more quickly than I could listen. "And what kind of magic are you going to work?"

"Did I give you my nerves from yesterday?" I hissed. "You're talking too much, and I'm fine."

"And I'm glad of that," he said, expression insistent that *I am also fine*. "But you also didn't come back to our room until half an hour ago. And working magic isn't the same as convincing a court. You can see why I might have questions."

"I've been busy."

"Osian—"

"Is a master of performance," I interrupted. "I know."

Osian or the Foxhall would have spent the past day requisitioning expensive or exotic materials from the apothecary or nearby farms. Or, worse yet, scouting forests or meadows or moors to be sacrificed. Rhiannon and her covenwitches would have argued over what spell would be most impressive to their customer.

For all that Tal had spent a week watching me work, when he

thought of magic, he still thought of this sort. Flashy, expensive, get-rich-quick.

But the Foxhall had their ways, and I had mine.

I had spent the past day or so exploring the keep, the grounds, and the town. Amid folk musing over what the mysterious blade could be, I'd found kitchen varlets hauling water from outside the city walls, because the well had indeed run dry the year the castle was built. And in the kitchen and around the castle, I'd seen charms and wards years old, their magic weak and thready.

Brycheiniog had no court magician. And I imagined it was for the same reason half the kingdoms in Wales didn't have a single hedge-witch: because the Foxhall had poached them.

Tal had told me Black Darren was positioned securely on a ridge. But there was more to safety than position.

He walked down the steps until he was at my eye level. He was wearing his red coat again, and his chain, and two glittering rings—one set with amber, the other a bronze signet.

"So what are you going to do?" he asked again. "Do you have what you need?"

"I have myself, Tal." I held out my arms. "Do I pass inspection?"

I hadn't expected him to actually run his eyes over me. My cheeks burned.

"You need something," he said. "Turn."

"They're waiting for us," I protested.

"Then hurry."

I obeyed, but I jumped when I felt him brush my hair to one side. "A little display of wealth never hurt anyone's cause," he said in my ear, clasping the chain around my neck.

My nerves were tingling. I crossed my arms mulishly. "I don't need it."

"Maybe not," he said, "but this is going to be hard." His tone was all gentle condescension. I turned.

"Do you know the wonderful thing about working with mold and mushrooms and animal bones, Tal?" I waved my fingers in his face, and was delighted when he reared back. "You always have grimy hands. And you're never afraid of getting them a little dirtier."

"You have a gift for mysterious pronouncements, Ffion," he said, grimacing. "I just hope this one means something."

At the banquet, I bided my time.

Meirion had placed me and Tal a third of the way down the table full of chieftains and high men and ladies. Tal told me that so much distance was rude, but not enough to cause trouble with Cadell. Prince Angws sat near his uncle, staring at us so persistently that soon I wished he'd ignore us like everyone else.

As the piper, harpist, and singer played and sang, carvers, pantlers, ewerers, and cellarers moved through the room, helping guests wash their hands and serving the meal. Lamb, salted bacon, sausages, pies, cawl, carrots and leeks, oat loaves and barley loaves served with huge scoops of butter, loaves studded with candied fruit, bragawd aplenty—Meirion was an unfriendly host, but his kitchens were more than hospitable. I ate as much as I could, watching smoke billow from the fire and trickle toward two vents in the ceiling. Not far from the hearth waited a massive woodpile.

Perfect.

"Now then," boomed the king in his abysmally deep voice. His every word felt like a cave where I might accidentally stumble and lose myself. "Hedgewitch of Foxhall. I believe you and I parted on an understanding yesterday, did we not?"

"We did, Your Majesty."

I exchanged a private glance with Tal. *Don't worry,* I tried to tell him. But he was twisting his rings around his fingers, jaw set.

As I stood and crossed the room, I moved opposite to how I had approached the stag in Foxhall Forest. I squared my shoulders, raised my voice when I spoke. Today, I had no desire to look small or unthreatening—though I imagined the effect was somewhat confused when I squatted and began to root through the woodpile, sending insects and spiders scurrying.

Many of the logs were short and fat, no longer than my thigh, and more were only broken chunks; none of these would serve. I didn't let myself be hurried as I sifted through the fuel, not as the remaining pile grew smaller, not as titters rose throughout the room.

I could imagine Tal twisting his rings, inwardly perishing.

It didn't matter. This was the part that had to be perfect.

Near the bottom of the stack, I found a long, forked branch. Setting this aside, I began to repile the wood I'd disturbed. "Leave that for the scullion," boomed King Meirion, but I didn't acknowledge this as I finished cleaning up my mess.

Finally I stood, branch in hand. "I understand, King Meirion, that you have no well inside Black Darren's city walls."

"Yes, that's correct." The king began to flush. "A well was dug when the castle was built, but it dried up more quickly than expected."

A dried-up well was a risk to everyone in this castle and town. In the event of a siege, people would die. And things like siege were coming.

"That's strange," I said. "Because I can hear water beneath your castle."

Murmurs filled the hall.

Over the past day, I had thought over how Osian would bargain for the blade. How the Foxhall would do it.

But more important to me was how my mam-gu would get what she needed, if my task were hers.

Meirion shook his head. "You are mistaken, hedgewitch. In nine years of searching, we have found no water here—not in the courtyards, not on the green, nowhere in the town."

I considered this, swishing the stick in my hand for effect. "When we spoke yesterday, King Meirion, I asked for Brycheiniog's blade, and you asked for a demonstration. But I will do better," I said. "In exchange for the blade, the loss of which will make Black Darren more vulnerable, I will give you a gift to make your fortress stronger."

Find what people need, my mam-gu would've said, *and work hard to get it for them. Take what you have to, and give what you can.*

"There is water beneath your fortress," I said. "And I am going to draw it out for you."

I gave the king my best fox's smile. Then, taking one fork of the branch in either hand, I lifted the tail in the air a little and began to walk.

Come now, I said silently to the dowsing rod. *Let's hunt.*

I had heard the water beneath Black Darren our very first day in the keep. As I'd washed my feet, I had heard the water swishing around in the basin, turning gray with campfire ash and mud.

And then I had heard more water, farther away—wilder water. Water moving deep underground.

It had reminded me of my dream. The beach, the standing stones, the sea.

It was only because of the castle's thick walls that I'd been able to hear it at all. Outdoors, nearer the dyke, all I could feel was the earthwork's power.

Suddenly, the end of the dowsing rod jerked downward.

"What's below this room?" I asked King Meirion.

He frowned. "The kitchens."

Lovely.

I heard rather than saw what happened as I left the great hall—tankards caught up in hands, curious whispers and benches scraping over the stone floor. I felt the crowd behind me as I followed the dowsing rod down the stairs into the kitchen.

The room was hot and cramped, full of burly men moving massive pots of the belowstairs dinner off the fire, kitchen varlets scrubbing dishes in a basin, laundresses up to their elbows in lye soap. They stared at me as the dowsing rod led me into a corner and half the banquet into their midst.

I hoped I would make their lives easier and not harder with what I was about to do.

When the dowsing rod stopped leading me, I set it aside and reached for a ladle.

"What is she doing?" demanded King Meirion.

Behind him, Angws looked confused. Tal just looked pained.

"Watch," I finally said. "And fetch a shovel, if you like." Gasps rose around me. A kitchen varlet traded me a little spade from a basket full of leeks for the ladle.

I began to dig. And I began to sing.

A shovel is the miner's friend
Away, a-way!
Your hands to the handle, your back to bend,
A shovel is the miner's friend.

A lamp, it is the miner's friend
Away, a-way!
In with the light, the dark to fend,
A lamp is the miner's friend.

I crouched and sang and dug with the little spade, my back sore from days of walking as if I were a miner from the song. It was one I'd heard as a child, out by one of the mines near Foxhall. Thinking of my grandmother had put me in mind of the time she had rescued the men from the collapsed shaft.

At the front of the crowd that filled the kitchen, Angws watched me breathlessly. Tal stood beside him, silently forming contingency plans.

The varlet traded my spade for a shovel.

A pick, it is the miner's friend
Away, a-way!
Into the earth, the rocks to rend,
Oh, a pick is the miner's friend.

Unbidden, I thought how much faster the work would go if Cadno were there. When Gareth had taught me how to garden when I was little, Cadno had picked up the work so enthusiastically that he'd dug a hole two feet deep in the middle of a patch of beans.

I wiped my eyes with the sleeve of my dress and kept digging.

I was up to my hips in the hole. I was up to my chest. I was up to my neck. Again, the kitchen was full of gasps.

And suddenly—there was water.

I was filthy, I was sweaty, my black gown was covered in earth and the small creeping creatures that live beneath the ground. Water gushed around my feet, lifting my hem.

I searched for King Meirion. "How do you think, my lord?" I asked, panting. "Have I performed to your satisfaction?"

Black Darren would be more secure now than ever. Surely, I had earned us its blade.

But Meirion didn't speak.

The king's pale eyes moved to the advisors who usually hung around him. But the men only looked startled—almost accusatory—as they glanced from me and the well I'd dug to Meirion.

The silence tugged more words out of me. "I've made a display, as you asked, and I've strengthened your keep, as I promised," I said, speaking more and more quickly, my anxiety mounting. "I have proven to you that there is truth in my magic, and that I am to be trusted, and—"

King Meirion held up a hand, jaw wobbling, and came to the lip of the well.

"You have performed a cheap trick," he said. "You are no more a witch than the hucksters playing dice outside the walls of the keep."

Silence. Then muttering. Meirion's court stared, confused.

"You cheat," said Tal. "Everyone here can see she's done magic. She's done you a great service."

"She has dug a hole in the ground like a common laborer," he said. "There is no truth in her or her magic. How are we to know this is not merely another trick of Cadell's to take what is ours?" Meirion glanced around the kitchen, searching the faces of his varlets and scullions and chieftains as if looking for agreement or answers.

He'd wanted a demonstration, and I'd given him one. He'd gone back on his word, and even that choice he clearly doubted.

I hated to agree with the men outside the pub. But their king was, indeed, a dithering crow.

Prince Angws looked confused. "Uncle—"

It was enough. I hauled myself out of the well, and King Meirion scrambled back.

He was never going to give me the blade. I was only grateful I hadn't used any of my stock to help him.

"You won't accept this as proof, then?" Tal asked.

"I—no. I will not." King Meirion's voice wavered. Outside the keep, rain began to fall in torrents.

"Brycheiniog's fate is on your head, then." I crossed the kitchen and handed the shovel to one of Meirion's chieftains. "Dig the well as deep as you can. The water will be cleaner."

On my way to our room, I shook the dirt off my dress.

If this place was eager to see the back of me, I was every inch as eager to leave it behind.

26

TAL

It was unthinkable.

Once again, Ffion had done real magic. Real, tangible magic that would make Black Darren safer and its inhabitants' lives better. And with our time running ever shorter, King Meirion had looked us in the face and said it hadn't happened.

I'd been told the king could distinguish lies from truth. But he wouldn't even acknowledge what he'd seen with his own eyes. Apparently, no one at Black Darren could lie but King Meirion himself.

Ffion went back to our room, seething, after the king had made his decision. But I couldn't follow her upstairs.

As the crowd cleared out of the kitchen, I made my way back to the dungeons—empty, as Brycheiniog was currently keeping no prisoners. My blanket from the night before lay folded on a bench where I'd left it. Beside it sat Prince Angws.

"They tell me you slept here," he said.

Sprawled on the bench, Angws looked a little like his uncle. I sat down beside him, trying to chew and swallow my own anger and digest it into something different. Something diplomatic, or at least something easier to hide.

I nodded. "Only seemed fair. You spent more than a few nights in our dungeons. After what I did, I wondered if I ought to spend just one."

I had refused to concede to Ffion that I regretted chasing Angws.

But I understood now that I'd behaved cruelly, even if my intent wasn't cruel.

Intent wasn't all that mattered. Watching Mercia and the Foxhall destroy our land in the same way for different reasons had convinced me of that.

"Why did you do it?" Angws asked. "When your brother let me go, why did you run me down?"

"Because I needed a way to make your uncle listen to me," I said. "Why did you infiltrate Mathrafal?"

Angws's laugh was hollow. "My uncle doesn't listen to anyone. Neither, apparently, does your father." He wasn't wrong.

"My mam told me she heard you asked for an audience several times before you broke in through the waste line," I said. "Is that true?"

Angws nodded. "Powysian soldiers sacked my parents' manor. Hurt our tenants. I just wanted King Cadell to make it stop."

A pang. Another parallel I couldn't bear to think about. "Badly enough to break in through a stinking privy?"

He shuddered. "It was disgusting. But I thought that if I broke in, he wouldn't be able to ignore me." Then Angws finally met my eyes. "When Cadell wouldn't speak with me, I hoped you or your brother might. But neither of you ever came."

"Dafydd did," I pointed out.

He shook his head. "He didn't want to talk, though. He looked nervous every time I opened my mouth."

I imagined Dafydd, trying to protect me from myself, but too cowardly to talk to Angws.

I wondered what he would've thought of me sleeping here last night. Taking a page from his book, martyring myself for a moment. Except—I wasn't really martyring myself. Just trying to make amends.

"Do you know the word *hiraeth*?" Angws asked, unexpectedly. "Have you ever felt it?"

"Of course," I said. "It means homesickness."

Not that I'd spent much time away from home. But Mam was as good as home, and I was never settled when I was apart from her.

"It does and it doesn't," he said. "It means aching for someplace, or sometime. One that can't come back."

I thought of the cranky old men outside the pub in Llangatwg Lingoed, going on about how different things used to be in Brycheiniog. "Isn't that just nostalgia?"

"Maybe," Angws said. "But for me, it's also doubt."

"Doubt?" I frowned. "About what?"

"About whether the Brycheiniog I remember from my childhood has actually gone, or if it ever existed to begin with. If the world was ever really like I thought it was," he said. "If people talk so much about the magic that used to be because it was just that wonderful, or because they like fairy tales better than reality. If the peace I remember is a false memory, or if there really is more war in the Marches today." Angws looked at me keenly.

I'd never known peace. Not in my earliest years, when Mam and I had lived alone, and not since.

"I think people have always been at war with their neighbors," I said frankly. "I think everyone wants what someone else has. I think that's just the way of things."

His mouth folded unhappily. "I can't accept that. I have to believe things can be better. That whatever we're missing from the past, we can build it in the years ahead. At the very least, that some sort of agreement can be reached."

I shrugged, uncertain. "I think you just have to protect the people you're responsible for and hope everyone else can do the same."

Up in the great hall, the music struck up again, accompanied now by the sound of dancing. Apparently, the crowd had settled after Ffion's performance.

"Work on Black Darren started when I was only four," Angws said. "My uncle moved here from a palace on the western edge of the kingdom."

"My father did the same. He wanted to keep an eye on the Mercian border."

Angws sighed. "So did my uncle. But he's misunderstood at every step."

"How do you mean?"

"My uncle used to be able to tell truth from lies. It wasn't just a rumor," he said, glancing at me seriously. "About a decade ago, he rooted out two or three traitors from his court. He was the most trusted judge in Brycheiniog. They called him the Sighted Raven. But then he punished someone no one could believe had actually committed a crime—even though my uncle was *sure* it was him." Angws shook his head.

"After that, the truth he couldn't stop seeing was that his people didn't always like his decisions. He could see the truth—but that didn't mean others could. And now they've questioned him for so long, he refuses to make a decision without others' agreement. He really *has* begun to dither. And so that's what they call him."

"The Dithering Crow." My voice was somber. I was ashamed to say it.

I understood panicking beneath the weight of a crowd.

"So that's why I broke into Mathrafal," he said. "Because I wanted to *do* something."

"You did," I admitted. "And when you came back, you kept on. You dealt with the Mercians at Llyn Glas."

"Ffion dealt with them," he corrected me, grinning slightly. Then he cocked an eyebrow. "Are you two—?"

"No," I said shortly. I cleared my throat. "And Ffion did what she said she was going to do tonight, and your uncle still denied her."

Angws's face fell. "He felt like a fool," he said. "My uncle's been promising to find water for years. You saw the way his men looked at him, like somehow it was his fault Ffion had found water when he couldn't. What Ffion did was good. Uncle Meirion's pride is just stung."

I leaned my head against the wall behind me, staring at nothing.

I didn't know why I wanted to help Angws. He was nobody to me. Nobody I could afford to worry about. But I did.

For a long moment, we both sat there, listening to the thump of dancing footsteps overhead.

"What if there was a way to preserve his pride," I asked, "that let him keep our bargain?"

"What do you mean?"

"What if he agreed to give us the blade, but didn't tell anyone?" I sat forward, thoughts churning. "Or—what if there was a way to do it that publicly strengthened his position?" I hesitated. "Something that made him look wise and powerful, even if it made me look like a fool?"

Angws blinked at me. "But why would you want that?"

I expected my father would've asked the same thing.

Apart from the risk to his life, Dad had sent Dafydd and me out in the first place because he said Mercia didn't take us seriously. Would making a fool of myself undermine Powys's safety? Would I just be giving Mercia occasion to laugh at me, to doubt us even more?

Or was the calculus as simple as I hoped and feared it might be: a little of my ego in exchange for what it would take to help Ffion break the dyke and protect Powys?

Do you want to be dignified? she had asked me only a few days ago. *Or do you want to be king?*

"Because Offa is coming, and the Marches are in danger," I finally said, a little sharply. "And I have pride to spare."

Angws spoke to King Meirion in private. And then I knelt at his feet in the great hall, and made my plea, again, in front of his people.

I talked at length about my youth and inexperience. I said that I had slept in the dungeons as recompense for what had been done to Angws. What *I* had done to him.

I told the court at large that Ffion and I hadn't found the well at all, but that King Meirion had been searching diligently for water, and we had overheard his latest findings before he could inform his court. I told them that Angws had gotten the truth out of me, and that it was their own king who was to be credited for protecting the castle.

Ffion wouldn't care, I knew. Image, reputation—they were nothing to her. But I grew redder with every word I spoke.

With Angws's encouragement, the king had agreed to pretend that his refusal in the kitchens had simply been the opening of our negotiations. When I was done speaking, he graciously—and loudly—agreed to give us the blade.

"I always intended to do so, of course," he said magnanimously. "But Powys had to know its place."

"Of course," I agreed.

I could see he was relieved to withdraw his unpopular refusal of Ffion, to offer a response that earned pleased murmurs from his retainers and his court instead. I could see he was more than a little gratified to see me humbled.

But I was determined to choke down the shame and live with the taste in my mouth.

As I got to my feet, King Meirion pulled Angws and me near. His voice was deep as a pit when he muttered, "Take him to the witch."

Though I threw an oilcloth over my head as I rode after Angws from Black Darren, I only needed it for a moment. The rain poured only over the keep—not even in the town beyond.

In hindsight, I should have known the first time Ffion and I visited her. Upon my second visit to her hut, though, there was no mistaking the blade's presence.

"Nos da, Enid," Angws said, bowing to her. "I looked for you when I went to sort out the Mercians, but I couldn't find you."

"Nos da, Angws bach," said the hedgewitch, smiling at him from beneath her hideous feathered hat. "I did not want to be found."

Angws grinned a little and left us alone.

"So," said Enid, eyeing me curiously. She was spinning, her spindle and healed fingers flying. "You convinced Meirion. How did you do that?"

"Ffion dug a well," I said. "And I publicly disgraced myself."

She nodded. "A small price to pay for a bit of legendary magic."

"I agree." *But not for magic's sake,* I wanted to say. *For Powys, and my throne.*

"And you aren't really a hedgewitch," I said. "You were King Meirion's court magician before your magic disappeared, weren't you?"

"I was both. I was a hedgewitch all my young life, and I became his court magician when my predecessor died. It isn't a hereditary matter in Brycheiniog," she added.

"Ah." I nodded, not sure what she meant.

"Anyhow. The blade, the blade. Where—ah." Without ceremony, Enid plucked the feather from her ugly hat and held it out to me. "Here. I suppose this is yours."

I blinked at her, then at the feather. Black, shot through with iridescent green.

We'd been looking right at it without realizing.

"Interesting properties attached to this llafn," she said casually as I took it. "It belonged to a sighted raven. Predisposes folk to truth-telling in its presence. Lends the bearer a bit of insight. Not that you're lacking in that," she added.

"It does?" I asked.

"You didn't think to question why you told me all your plans the other evening? Or why I blurted out that you were a handsome young man?" Enid looked mildly incredulous.

"I *am* a handsome young man."

She threw her head back and laughed. "Not lacking in confidence, either."

"If I have this, will Ffion still be able to keep secrets from me?" I asked. *Will I still be able to keep secrets from her?* I didn't add.

"I said the feather had *belonged* to a sighted raven, not that it turned you into one," said Enid. "She can still choose to keep things from you. And you can still choose to keep things from her. Though you might consider why you're doing so, since it's clear you'd rather tell her. Did you sort out the matter of her disappearing magic?" Her voice was sharp.

I said nothing. Ffion had told me she had a plan, but she hadn't trusted me with the details.

Enid sighed. "The problem with secrets is that people do have their reasons, princeling. And most of them are fear." She looked away, eyes suddenly disappointed. "Sioned gave Meirion the gift of the truth, and he was too fearful of others' doubts to bear it. So I keep this blade, and it does its work repelling the Mercians from here."

"I understand," I said. "But you're wrong about Ffion. She's not afraid."

"She is. Worse still, Ffion believes she is alone, and that is a feeling worse than fear. That is fear realized," Enid said decisively, eyeing me as she leaned heavily on her cane. "Perhaps if you can show her that she is not alone, you two might find yourselves sharing secrets instead of carrying them on your own."

I expected Ffion to already be asleep on the dyke. But when I returned to our room in the castle, it wasn't empty.

Ffion's black dress hung over a screen. Behind it, I heard water splashing in a tub. When she gave an unexpected hiss, I wondered if the soap stung the cuts on her feet, and wished she would wear shoes.

The hallway behind me was quiet. I wasn't sure why I didn't announce myself. Instead I stood in the doorway to our room, leaning against the wall and listening as Ffion began to sing.

I once loved a boy, a tall, handsome boy,
With a laugh just as broad as the sky,
Oh, hair like the sun and eyes like the stars
Had my darling annwyl Cai.

I met him in town—no, I met him afield—
No, the lane, as he rode his horse by,
It matters not where, it matters not how,
For I fell for my annwyl Cai.

My mam and my dad, they liked him at once,
His rough hands and his shoulders so wide,
"A strong boy like that can take care of you, girl,"
So I trusted my annwyl Cai.

Oh, I trusted his hands, and I trusted his eyes,
And the arms that I slept in at night,
So it hurt all the more when he gave them to her,
My wandering annwyl Cai.

My mam and my dad, oh, they asked what I did,
If you kept the boy's bed warm, then why?
Yet I fault not that girl and I fault not myself,
But my faithless annwyl Cai.

Ffion's voice echoed through the room, the candle flames seeming to flicker as it rose and fell. With the stone walls multiplying the sound, I could hear her better than I ever had out in the open.

She was nothing like the high, sweet-voiced singer who accompanied my father's favorite piper; her voice was rough, raw, prone to break occasionally.

Ffion's voice was fey, primordial as the mountains and moors. Elemental as she was.

When I heard the unmistakable sound of her rising from the tub, I knew I had to declare myself. I cleared my throat, shutting the door behind me noisily.

"Hello?" Ffion's voice was startled. "Tal?"

"It's only me." I stood twisting my rings around my fingers as fabric rustled and Ffion's black dress disappeared behind the screen.

"How long have you been standing there?" Ffion asked as she emerged. Her hair was dripping, and she looked suspicious.

"Not very long." There was so much to say, but my tongue felt clumsy. Clearly, the raven's feather only encouraged truth, not eloquence.

Ffion turned her back to me, wringing out her hair and rubbing it with a towel. Her hair seemed to hold so much water I wondered if she wouldn't be damp all over again, but I assumed she'd done this a few times before, and decided for once not to ask stupid questions.

I had plenty of other stupid things to say instead, such as "Who is that song about?"

Ffion glanced at me over her shoulder. "It's not about anyone."

"It's about someone."

"Well, I suppose all songs were about someone once," she said. "Now they're not about anyone. Or they're about everyone."

"Right." I ventured cautiously into the room, toeing a loose flagstone. My boots desperately needed oiling.

"You're being strange, Tal. What's the matter?" she asked, still drying her hair. Already the finest bits were beginning to corkscrew around her face. Her cheeks glowed from the bath.

"Meirion was horrible to you," I said. "He dismissed you in front of his entire court."

"I think you forget that I'm used to being dismissed," she said. "I just don't know what to do next." I sat beside her, looking at her closely. Her eyes were swollen, and her nose was red. Had she been crying?

I reached into my coat pocket and passed Ffion the feather without looking at her. "I got it. The blade."

Ffion gaped at me, at the feather in her hand. "How?"

"I talked to Angws. He helped me think of a way to allow Meirion to give it to me while still looking like he had the upper hand. I paid for this with my dignity. And yours, I'm afraid. I told the court we didn't really find the well by magic."

The words were hardly out my mouth when Ffion almost knocked me off my feet.

"You did it," she whispered. Suddenly, her arms were tight around my neck, her torso pressed to mine. "You did it. Tal, you're amazing."

Somehow, my arms wound around her back.

Her hair was everywhere, damp and sweet-smelling against my neck, dripping on my shirt. My heart galloped in my chest.

For a moment, I let myself forget everything else.

When Ffion's hands fisted at my collar, I shifted, making to draw her closer. But she gave three or four small sobs before she collected herself and pulled away. "This is good," she said, smiling and wiping her eyes. "This is good. We can—Tal, we're a third of the way to bringing it back."

Suddenly, even despite her smile—even though I could still feel her hair against my neck and her cheek against my collarbone—I was cold.

I wanted so badly to think of Ffion's songs when I thought of magic. To think of annwyl Cai, of breadmaking and bragawd and miners.

But when I thought of magic, I still—would likely always—only ever hear one song.

So open up your door tonight,
Make room beside your fire tonight,
Give houseroom at your lamps tonight,
No more than is your due.

I jerked to my feet and crossed the room, away from the feather. Suddenly, I could *feel* it, feel power pouring off it, even when I wasn't touching it.

Ffion's voice was uncertain. "Tal, what's wrong?"

"Nothing. Nothing is wrong." I kept pacing.

"*Tal.*" The candles backlit Ffion's hair, turning it ginger and gold and flame-colored, shadowing her fine-boned face. "I don't understand. You wanted this. What's the matter?"

My jaw locked. But somehow, I couldn't keep the words down. I couldn't look away from the feather in her hand. "I don't trust that."

"The blade?" Her eyes grew wide. "This blade is one-third of what is going to save our kingdom."

"No," I said emphatically. "That is fuel for the breaking. You said it yourself. *You* are what is going to save our kingdom."

"I am not a what. I am a who. And how is my magic any different than the blade's magic?"

How was it different? *Was* it different? "It just is. That blade can inspire truth. It gives perception. It's different when you do it."

"Different how?" Ffion demanded. "Different, less powerful? Different, ineffective?"

"It just feels different!" I exploded. "That thing feels raw and strange, and so do you. But you are—you feel—safer?" I faltered on the word; it wasn't exactly what I wanted to say, but it felt close.

Ffion was not mollified. "Safer?" she bit out. "I have magic that could kill you, Tal. I could break your bones. I could give you a wound that would never stop bleeding, not until you died of it. I may not inspire truth, but I could steal your very mind."

"I know!" I held my hands up, somehow not backing away from her but stepping nearer, as if I were trying to tame her. "I know, Ffion. What I mean is—you wouldn't."

"I wouldn't?" She said it like a threat.

"What I mean is, I know you have power. I know it's at risk—but your magic is real." I spoke quickly, getting closer and closer, lowering and softening my voice. "What I mean is that there is no—no good will or bad, no sense of intention or limit with the blade. But with you, even though I know you could do all of those things, I know you wouldn't."

Ffion crossed her arms. "How do you know I haven't?"

"Maybe you have," I said. "Have you?"

She looked away. "No."

"Exactly. Because your magic is good. Your magic is bent toward help. Toward healing." I thought for a moment before it came to me. "When I first asked you for help destroying the dyke, you had to think through whether you even had that kind of spell. You said your magic isn't given to destruction."

I still didn't trust magic. I hated it, and I didn't want it to come back to Wales in full force. But somehow, I still meant what I was saying.

"Why do you have spells to break bones and create wounds?" I asked.

Ffion scowled. "Sometimes you have to break a bone to reset it," she muttered. "And sometimes blood needs to be thinned." She lifted her chin. "And to steal your mind—"

"You've already made me lose my mind," I ground out. We were only a foot apart now, close enough that I could hear her breath hitch and quicken. Close enough that Ffion's hair brushed against my arm when she turned away from me, rolling her eyes.

Even through my shirt, through the red coat she hated so much, I felt it like a bolt of lightning across my skin.

I didn't ask. I didn't speak. I just reached out and ran a hand over her hair. Over curls the color of candle flames, dancing my fingers through the tangles, catching and rubbing the snarled ends between my fingertips.

Ffion did not move a muscle.

"You are driving me out of my mind," I said in a low voice. "I never know what absurd thing you are going to say to irritate me. I never know what ridiculous hill you are going to choose to die on next."

"And I never know what shape your arrogance will take," Ffion said. Her voice sounded strangled. "If you think you're near to losing your senses, Taliesin—I'm nearer."

She looked back at me over her shoulder then, piercing me with her fox's gaze. Neither of us spoke.

"Are you going to stay," I asked, "or are you going to go?"

"Go," Ffion said. One small word, so quiet, from her barely parted lips. "And tomorrow, we keep going."

27

DAFYDD

Mathrafal Castle, Powys

No matter what we were talking about, we were really always talking about the girl.

She was the girl of my visions, the girl I had been bound to. She would have been my court magician, if I'd become my father's heir.

When I decided at fifteen that I didn't want to be king, she was my only regret.

I had been only six when Osian asked me if I wanted to meet my best friend. It was a strange question, and I'd told him so. Anyway, Tal was my best friend, and I'd told him that, too.

Osian had said this was something different, that she was a new friend who would help me when I was king someday.

I had been dubious about that *she*. But one day Tal and I had a fight over whose pony was faster, and in my sulk, I'd gone to Osian.

The girl's name was Ffion, he told me, and she lived in a town called Foxhall, a town dominated by the voracious coven under the hill. And someday, we would share everything in the world that mattered.

Osian tattooed my right side with the image of her fox familiar, and we began to see one another after that. Not often, and never with any warning, but I would suddenly be inundated by a vision of thick red hair and freckles like sparks off an anvil. Busy in the forest, busy with the fox, gleaning, creating charms. And singing—always singing.

I asked Osian if he had made me like one of the sighted ravens in the columbarium, able to see the truth of her.

Not yet, he had laughed.

She couldn't see me in my visions of her. But Osian said soon enough she'd have her own visions. And someday, we would be able to share one another's feelings, read one another's thoughts, and speak out of one another's mouths, as he and my father could.

I grew up waiting for Ffion to arrive and fix everything with her magic. Once she joined me at Mathrafal, there would be no more starvation in Powys, no more death by the elements, no more destruction of our wild places. Our people would be safe from their enemies.

But I wasn't supposed to tell my father, Osian always reminded me. He wanted to me to know my someday-magician, but Dad wouldn't understand.

It was our secret.

In later years, I became self-conscious about our bond. I'd never seen Ffion in a private moment, or at anything less than her best, but what had *she* seen? Later still, I developed more doubts about what Osian had done—and not only about his asking a child to keep secrets from a parent. As I hadn't officially been named heir, I worried over what our bond meant for Tal's chances. I wondered what Osian had against him.

Osian never gave me direct answers to my questions. I would've asked Ffion, but she never came to Mathrafal.

She changed, too, as the years passed. As I waited for her to arrive, I saw her refuse to join the Foxhall and move out of her family home, choosing instead to do good alone on the fringes of her village, helping the ones the coven had forgotten.

Ffion's work never hurt anyone. Her efforts were bloodless. Her hands were always dirty, but her hands were always clean. I wanted to be the same.

So when my father broke my heart, and I decided never, ever to become him, I had decided to become like her, instead. To work in my forge until I had the land that was due to me. To work that land alongside our people and make it a safe place to live and let live.

Even when I worried about the day our connection might be broken—even when I'd had to set the dream of her aside—Ffion had been my inspiration.

And now she rode with Tal.

I'd known Ffion would never become my magician, because I didn't want to be king. But somehow, it had simply never occurred to me that she would become someone else's.

I'd been foolish, oblivious. But knowing now—I couldn't bear for Tal to take the throne.

And I couldn't bear to share the vision of Ffion with my brother.

28

FFION

Black Darren, Brycheiniog

Something felt different between Tal and me when we set out the next morning. Something hung between us, half-said, raw and unfinished.

I hauled my cauldron along, trailing my ragged ivy anklets and stealing glances at him as he drove beside me. He'd grown deft after a few days at the reins, his posture somehow both easier and more powerful, his hands relaxed, and he'd tanned a little in the weak spring sun. Every now and again, he would climb down from the wagon and join me to stretch his legs.

In his plain wool shirt, with his rings hidden around his neck on the chain I'd awkwardly returned that morning, he could have been the son of any comfortable farmer taking me for a walk.

I berated myself for even letting myself imagine it. Things like that didn't happen to me.

I told myself I was glad when he climbed back up into the wagon to drive again. The better for me to forage, and sing, and keep my mind on my business.

I once loved a boy, a tall, handsome boy,
With a mind just as keen as a knife,
Oh, hair like the earth and eyes like the night
Had my darling annwyl Cai.

I met him in town—no, I met him afield—
No, the lane, as he rode his horse by,
It matters not where, it matters not how,
For I fell for my annwyl Cai.

So I didn't mind the quiet. I busied myself reckoning with Cadno's return and the disappearance of my magic. With the dream so real I could nearly taste the salt on my lips, and the new moon drawing closer with every passing minute. With the power radiating from the llafn in my cauldron and from the dyke.

And then there were the Mercian guard towers that loomed above us, no matter where we went.

From a hilltop above Haya, we saw a tower surrounded by a camp of soldiers, a blazing bonfire at its center, carelessly close to tents and a nearby stand of trees. We coughed through its smoke until we reached the valley below. Near Pencoed, a group of soldiers repairing a tower base stopped us for no reason. I gripped Tal's arm so hard it must have bruised.

Somehow, he kept cool. When they asked where we were going, he put his hand on my back and told the guards we were going north to his father's house, in some town I hadn't heard of.

The next day, we crossed from Brycheiniog into Powys without even realizing we had returned to our own kingdom.

The weather had been clear enough for most of our journey. But halfway to Betws-y-Maes, our luck on that score finally gave out.

We traveled uphill, rain pelting us from all directions. My hair was heavy with water; my gold cloak and kirtle were sodden, and my feet were like ice. Despite the oilcloth wrapped around him, Tal was no drier, his dark hair clinging to his temples and his clothes clinging to his skin. Even the horses were miserable. But with ten days left to reach the dyke's northern end—only ten days before my magic disappeared and Offa's attack fell—we couldn't afford to take cover every time we met damp weather.

By the time we reached the village, I'd begun to sneeze uncontrollably. I hurried to help Tal get the horses into the barn outside the Ivyside Inn, then turned wearily back toward the dyke. When I sneezed again, my feet slipped in the mud, and I cursed furiously.

"Where did you learn that?" Tal demanded in surprise.

"Gareth," I said. "My mam-gu taught me witchcraft and my brother taught me to garden and swear. Good night."

Tal caught my arm. "You can't sleep out there tonight."

The rain was still bucketing down. Even the guards in the nearby Mercian watchtower had abandoned the ramparts to shelter indoors.

But my dreams had become vivid, sharp as glass, cold as the water I stood in. I wanted to see them again. And for that, I knew I had to be near the dyke.

"I can," I said. "In fact, I need to."

"Ffion, it is *pissing* rain, quite a lot of which you are already wearing."

"You *are* from Powys, aren't you, Tal?" I asked. "It rains here. It's uncomfortable, not dangerous. Anyway, not all of us sleep in palaces."

"No, but even peasants make an attempt at shelter, as I understand it."

"I'm not a peasant. I'm a—"

"You're the bane of my existence," Tal growled. "Will you stop staring at the ditch and look at me? You need to be in dry clothes, near a fire. You're going to get sick."

"I'll be fine."

But Tal didn't give up. He stalked after me as I returned to the wagon and fished out the first food I laid hands on.

"Why?" he asked, suddenly out of breath. "Why do you always have to do things the hard way?"

He hadn't meant to. But I found myself cornered, trapped between Tal and the barn wall. He towered over me, hair plastered to his forehead, chest rising and falling, frustration in every line of him. A single bead of water clung to his lip beside his beauty mark.

He was hard to look at.

No—not hard to look at. Hard to look at casually. Hard to look at without thinking about last night.

If I didn't look away, I'd never stop staring at his mouth.

But everywhere I looked, there he was.

I pushed past him. Away from Tal, back to the work that demanded my focus.

The Mercian magic. My magic. Cadno.

"No need for dramatics, princeling." I picked up my cauldron and my blanket and moved back out into the rain. Water poured down my hair, down my back. "It's simple. Because life is hard."

I wished I could go inside where it was dry. I wished I didn't have to be alone.

But wishing wouldn't help. Nothing would, except the will to do what was needed.

The ditch was so muddy I could hardly walk in it, let alone find anything useful. I hung my cloak over the branch of a yew tree beside the dyke and lay down beneath it, its arms spreading above me as if in apology. I was at least out of the mud where the grass grew thick between two of the roots.

Somehow, the sound of rain lulled me to sleep. But it was another noise that woke me.

I sat up inside long shadows cast by a broad, bright moon. The world looked distorted, the grass dark and the sky light. Off to my right ran a stream.

That was where it must have come from. The splash that woke me.

"Cadno?" I called. My hands shook.

I didn't know why I thought it was him. But I felt him. I felt—something.

The slow-moving water was like a run of night sky tied to the earth. My toes squelched in the mud on the riverbank; I watched my feet, careful of my balance.

Suddenly, I stopped. My foot had fallen inside another footprint, fresh, made since the rain had stopped falling.

Heart pounding, I crouched. But it wasn't a fox's paw print, or a human footprint.

I had seen frog prints in mud a hundred times before, and these were like them. Toes splayed, smeared from jumping.

Except they were the size of my palm.

I slipped and nearly fell into the river.

They were the tracks of a llamhigyn y dŵr. Only the water leaper left marks like these.

I dropped to my hands and knees, scrambling around after the tracks. No sign of a dragged tail—an adult, then. And the tracks led away from the stream, not toward it.

Had that been what had woken me? The llamhigyn y dŵr bursting from the river?

I could imagine it. The water leaper hopping onto the bank, its slick green-brown back glistening, its waxy amber wings filtering moonlight and dripping water. Giant froglike eyes searching for fish—or something larger.

The llamhigyn might lack the romance of other creatures. But it was made of magic, just like all the rest. And it had been *here*.

Something in me thrilled, even as pain squeezed between my ribs.

Of course it hadn't been Cadno. Cadno was gone, waiting in the place between.

Most of the streambed was lined with smooth stones. But down at its bottom, I thought I could see something. Without thinking, I peeled off my dress and my smallclothes and slipped under the water.

Beneath the surface of the stream, the night was quieter, and the freezing water steadied me and cleared my thoughts. My fingers and toes met the riverbed quickly.

And there, between the rocks that covered its sandy floor, was a round hollow as wide as my arm was long.

I burst into the night air and climbed back onto the bank, as the llamhigyn y dŵr must have done. My hands shook as I dressed again, and not only from the chill.

I'd found the resting place of one of our lost creatures.

And more important, I'd heard it come back to us.

29

TAL

On the Dyke, Powys

Ffion paced beside the ditch. "Tell me again what you saw," I said. "And slowly, this time."

Back and forth, back and forth. Her feet were wearing a track in the mud, her freckled, stubby-fingered hands gesticulating as she spoke about the splash, the hollow in the river, the tracks on the bank.

A llamhigyn y dŵr.

"We'll have to keep our eyes open from now on." Her voice was avid; she was too excited to smile. "We have to see what else might have emerged, or woken up, or—or come back to life."

Anxiety zipped up my spine.

I climbed into the wagon, and Ffion took up her cauldron with renewed energy, and on we went. "You do know what sort of damage these creatures can do," I said.

Ffion gave a snort, which promptly turned into a cough. "Yes, the destruction left in the wake of the water leaper is legend. Woe to the fish and birds in its domain."

"I don't mean the llamhigyn y dŵr," I said irritably. All this focus on what used to be, Angws's talk of hiraeth, had left me rattled. "Enid, the old hedgewitch—she said herself that the gwiberod used to go after her chickens. I've heard bigger dragons would go after cows and sheep. I've heard of gwyllgwn destroying cemeteries, gwiberod nesting in orchards and wrecking them—the Cath Palug laid waste to whole fields before it was dealt with—"

"Tal, most of these creatures are only dangerous if you get between them and their young, or if you trouble them during mating season."

"And what if you do have the bad fortune to run into their whelps or trouble them when they're—feeling romantic?" I stumbled over the words.

"Feeling romantic." She rolled her eyes at me, and I felt myself turning red. "The problem is usually with fools who can't give them space, or who destroy their homes."

"And then they go wandering into *our* homes, or our fields, and cause problems. Or even kill people, Ffion."

"So do bears, sometimes! So do wolves!" Ffion wiped her dripping nose with a handkerchief, eyes incredulous. "I caught Cadno near our own henhouse once. Do you suggest we do away with every animal who has to be approached with care?"

"Can bears and wolves and foxes set towns and woods on fire with their breath?" I shot back. "Anyway, wouldn't we all be safer without those beasts, too?"

"Is safety the most important thing? Is it more important than beauty, or wonder?" She spoke flippantly, but her expression was serious, and then curious. "Tal, this is what we've been working for. What's changed, that suddenly you're so worried?"

Nothing had changed. Nothing had changed, except that I'd slipped and said too much.

I was getting too comfortable with Ffion.

I shook my head, searching for a change of subject. "Your cauldron is getting full. What are you gathering all those—did you just pick up a dead beetle?"

She smiled placidly. "I've found some excellent patches of mold and lichen growing along the ditch today, too." From what I could see, she'd also found a large chunk of amber and two tidy-capped mushrooms.

"But we have one of the blades now," I said. "Why bother?"

"In case you've attempted to ransom someone else's nephew and I have to cleanse another lake to make peace."

"Testy." I tutted at her. "Someone should've slept in a bed last night."

"My mam-gu taught me how to forage. That's what I'm doing," she ground out.

My mother had taught me how to patch up a coat so no one could see it was worn out, how to turn one ceiniog into two; Ffion's grandmother had taught her how to pick through rubbish. I wondered which of us had the more practical skill set.

"Besides—" Ffion stopped to sneeze, lurching a little in the mud. When she recovered, she scowled at me like it was my fault. "Besides. If I'd stayed indoors last night, you'd only have told the innkeeper some elaborate lie. That I was your mother or your daughter or something. It's too strange."

"My mother?" I demanded in horror. "My daughter? What's wrong with you?"

"You've already told different people I'm your wife and your sister. Not as if those are easier lies to believe."

"Sister's easier to believe than wife," I scoffed.

Ffion snorted right back. "We don't look alike."

"We also never stop bickering," I said, gesturing exasperatedly between us. "This is why no one would believe we were married."

"Well, you don't make it easy to not want to kill you, and my husband won't be allowed to die young. I'm not going spend years alone the way my mother has," she said, voice dropping into a mutter. "He's expected to grow old and gray and strange right alongside me. Whoever he is, there will be no escape."

"I can just imagine it," I said dryly. "Some poor man beaten into submission by your pigheaded temper, forced to live on leaves and twigs until he's as thin as one himself." I was blushing; *why* was I blushing?

Ffion gaped, affronted. "Well, I'll expect him to be sturdy enough to handle it."

"Well, I'll expect my wife to increase my position, not diminish it. So there, we both have expectations." I said the words in a rush, and Ffion gave an incredulous laugh.

"How romantic of you."

It shouldn't have, but something about that laugh—too loud, unpolished, unguarded—hit me like a punch.

"Prior claims, Ffion," I finally said. "I've got more to consider than merely what I want."

She paused. "What do you want, Tal? Besides to be king?"

For my father to look at me, for once, instead of at Dafydd.

For my mam to be safe and respected.

To touch Ffion's hair again.

I wanted more things than I could possibly tell her.

I cleared my throat. "There's nothing else, Ffion. Being king will get me everything I need. Power, that's all I require."

"Fair enough," Ffion said.

But even as she walked ahead of me, following the ditch and the dyke and its hedge with her cauldron at her side, I didn't think she believed me.

I knew I didn't.

30

DAFYDD

Mathrafal Castle, Powys

There were sighted ravens in the columbarium. And Ffion rode with Tal.

I couldn't escape my thoughts. I could only avoid the columbarium and pour out sweat beside the fire.

Elin's sickle, another harrow, a rake, an auger. I tore through job after job, singing as I worked, as I'd seen Ffion do so many times.

When six o'clock comes, then up fellows rise
And into the forge, where the embers do fly
Where bellows and hammers and anvils resound
Go fellows who live by the sweat of their brow.

When eight o'clock comes, then up the town rises
And out comes the market, to tempt with its prizes
To purchase it later, or perchance buy it now?
Ask good folk who live by the sweat of their brow.

When ten o'clock comes, the day stretches long,
Our hammers grow heavy, our faces grow drawn.
We wish but to rest, but time does not allow
There's work to be done, by the sweat of our brow.

The sweat of our brow, the sweat of our brow
In the smithy, the mines, at the back of the plow,
An honest day's work for an honest endowt,
We labor and live by the sweat of our brow.

When two o'clock comes, our fires are they roaring
Our hammers are busy and patrons imploring
Work faster! Work cheaper! they cry; aye, but how?
We only survive by the sweat of our brow.

When four o'clock comes, our fires are a-fading
Our embers are dark'ning, our woodpiles are waning
So we add to our woodpiles! The bellows, we pound!
The fires only burn by the sweat of our brow.

Come six o'clock hour, our fires do we bank
And make for the pub and cry for a tankard
We purchase each draft with pennies laid down
The silver is ours, by the sweat of our brow

The sweat of our brow, the sweat of our brow
In the smithy, the mines, at the back of the plow,
An honest day's work for an honest endowt,
We labor and live by the sweat of our brow.

I was trapped at Mathrafal, forced to do my father's bidding, kept from the girl I wanted by a role I couldn't accept.

Even in the forge, I didn't know if I was doing more good than harm anymore.

But I had nowhere else to go.

Interlude

Ffion dreamt of earth.

She was suffocating. Everywhere was dirt and mud and stones and creeping creatures. Earthworms moved blindly through the soil; moles and badgers and rabbits burrowed homes and slept softly in small furry piles with their fellows.

The earth breathed; but Ffion could not. There were chains at her throat, chains on her arms and legs.

She had been buried alive. She dreamt of clawing her way out.

She gasped. Choked. Her throat burned.

Ffion woke beside the ditch.

31

FFION

On the Dyke, Powys

We were twenty miles from Mathrafal when we left Betws-y-Maes that morning. By late afternoon, my cough was a bark that seemed to carry for miles. Through Trefaldwyn and Ffordun and past a massive Mercian camp just on the far side of the dyke, I could feel myself making an enormous, noisy spectacle, and I couldn't even care. Why shouldn't the shepherds on a drover's track stare at the damp, coughing girl as she went up the road? Why shouldn't the brown-robed monks in the road sign concernedly to one another with deft, rapid hands? Why shouldn't Tal look annoyed and slightly mortified all at once? "This is my punishment for teasing those men outside the Dithering Crow," I grumbled into a handkerchief, and Tal didn't argue. "I pretended we had plague, and now I've got it."

"You need rest," Tal insisted. He wanted to stop for the night when his oilcloth blew away outside Trelystan early evening. But it simply wasn't possible. So Tal went up and down the village, offering any price for another so we could make it the last four miles to Mathrafal.

I didn't like the look of the man who finally sold him an oilcloth, or the way he leered at me and the contents of our wagon. But we'd found what we needed. So we pushed on.

In the end, though, Tal had been right.

"Are you pushing?" I called from the front of the wagon.

Tal's shoulder was thrown against the back right wheel. "What do you think, Ffion?"

"I think the wheel is stuck and you're not even trying."

Tal grunted. Rain soaked my shoulders and hair, and my feet skidded in the mud as he shoved and I pulled. A moon wearing a crescent of shadow lit the woods. "I think you're lucky murder is a hanging offense." He paused. "Though perhaps my father would be lenient given the circumst—"

"Are you pushing?" I called again, stifling a laugh.

Tal cursed the rain, the mud, the wagon and whoever had built it.

I couldn't help it. He was too easy to rile.

Then I sobered, my own dismay rising again. We were nearly to the hilltop. The ruins of Caer Digoll, the fort at the summit, were visible barely a quarter of a mile ahead. Gently, I put my hand on Derog's nose and tried again to coax him forward.

"That's it." Tal stomped to the front of the wagon. "We're stopping here. The wagon can't go any farther, and neither can I."

"What are you talking about?" I asked. "Mathrafal is just down the other side of the hill. We're two miles away. We can be there in an hour."

"Can you charm this wheel out of the mud?" he demanded.

I said nothing. I couldn't afford the magic.

"Didn't think so." Tal's voice was flat. "Come on. We'll sleep in the back under the oilcloth."

I felt an irrational wave of panic. "I'm not sleeping next to you!"

But he was already in the bed of the wagon, rearranging our provisions and bracing the fabric around them to create a shelter. "Done. It's barely enough space for us to lie down in, and the cloth will be about a sneeze away from our faces, but it'll be more or less dry."

"I have to sleep on the—"

But Tal didn't even let me get the words out. "We're *on* the dyke,

Ffion. Don't tell me you won't be close enough unless you're sleeping in the mud."

I didn't know what to say to that. He was right. The dreams would almost certainly come even if I wasn't sleeping on the ground.

I'd had a new dream the night before. A dream of earth, not of water. It had been dark, close, terrifying. It had left me with a thousand questions.

Was it a vision of the future—of a cave, or some other place I'd be going? Why had I been trapped?

And why, when I woke, did I have the sense that I was being watched?

Exhaustion from that wary feeling pressed at my eyelids, radiated through my back and legs after hours of climbing. I wanted to sleep.

Though I could still feel the restraints at my throat, I wanted to dream again.

So I made Tal turn around as I changed into my dry kirtle and slid beneath the oilcloth, curling up on my side, careful not to kick the cauldron at my feet. A moment later, Tal climbed in beside me.

He smelled like rain; maybe we both did. Stretched out on his side just a few inches away, his shirt hung open around his throat, exposing his collarbone and the shine of his necklace. A faint tan line stretched in the shape of a V between his clavicles.

I had the strangest urge to touch it. I clenched my fist instead.

"So." Tal grinned smugly. "Is this so unbearable? Or is it better than trying to sleep in the mud?"

"Vainglory is unbecoming."

"You're not going to tell me it *isn't* better."

"And so is meekness requiring constant reassurance."

"Ffion!"

"Tal!"

"Why do you have to be so stubborn all the time?" he demanded, incredulous.

I sneezed into my elbow, turning away from him just in time. "One of my many charms," I croaked.

Outside the wagon, the rain had become a softly falling mist; badgers and foxes began to creep about softly, and owls hooted gently from their perches in the trees. I shut my eyes, listening. "How do you sleep without this at night?" I asked.

"Without . . . this?"

"Night music." I smiled. "There's something safe about the woods at night. Nocturnal animals getting their food, digging their little homes, moving through the trees. Cadno and I used to forage at night, with nothing but the leaves and the stars watching."

He hesitated a moment, watching me. "You miss Cadno, don't you?"

I missed my friend more than I knew how to explain. Sometimes, right before I fell asleep or woke up, I imagined I could feel him there beside me. I saw him around every tree, just behind every stone.

Finding the water leaper's tracks last night had been a victory. But some part of me still wanted them to be Cadno's.

"I'm still not used to being alone—not *alone*, I mean," I corrected myself quickly, as Tal's smile slipped a little and I wondered for a strange moment if I'd hurt his feelings. "Just—without him."

"Of course."

The cauldron at my feet wasn't full. But another nine days of gleaning like the two weeks I'd had, and the summoning spell would work to raise him. I knew it.

As long as I had the other two blades and there was enough magic in the land to perform the spell at all, of course.

"You're an odd one, Ffion," Tal said with a grin. "Most people don't find the woods particularly comfortable at night. They'd rather be in their homes, or their villages."

"Or their castles, if they have the option?" I asked, teasing. "Villages and houses are nice, and you were right this morning—creatures can cause harm, or damage. But you can always trust an animal's motives. People are harder." I sighed, thinking again of the llamhigyn y dŵr tracks. "Did I ever tell you that when I saw the dragons when I was little, people didn't believe me?"

He frowned. "Why not?"

"Well, they'd mostly gone to ground by then," I said. "Mam told me not to tell anyone—trying to protect me, I guess. Because years later, when I did tell some of the Foxhall witches, they were cruel. They asked why dragons would have shown themselves to me instead of one of them."

"Because you're practically fey," Tal said quietly, twisting the signet ring on his pinkie. He flicked his gaze up to mine. "They were probably as fascinated by you as you were by them."

"I don't know about fey. A wild animal, sure." I laughed weakly. "You know, I saw the Mari Lwyd once, too."

Tal stiffened. "You did?"

The Mari Lwyd had been resurrected near Foxhall one Midwinter. I had vague memories of bells, of holly branches lashing the night air, of the strong scent of bragawd and slurred singing from her crowd of wassailers. "Well, I saw her through a window," I said sheepishly. "Mam wouldn't let me out of my room."

"Seems reasonable." Tal's voice was ominous. "She hasn't been raised in years. You couldn't have been more than thirteen."

"I was seven," I said. The Mari Lwyd had been the last of the magical creatures to disappear, but she was gone, just like all the others. It was possible she'd only persisted so long because she was deceased to begin with. But thinking of Cadno had made me think of her again, and of the twilight place where all things waited until the moon was gone and the veil was thin.

"Speaking again of Cadno—" Tal shifted, stretching uncomfortably as he changed the subject. "Why don't the Foxhall witches have familiars? I'd wondered, but never had the chance to ask."

"Well, there's more than one kind of anchor. Not only animal familiars. It's an easy enough spell to bind your magic to a place. My grandmother's power was tied to a lake, Llyn Goch," I said. "Anyway, the Foxhall just thinks that kind of thing is a bother. Animals, you have to feed them. Lakes and meadows and things, you have to look after them, too. And as we both found out recently, your magic being tied to a creature, or even a forest or a lake—it's a risk." I cleared my throat and looked away.

"Then why do it?"

"Because when I charm my mam's house, Cadno works the magic with me, and the earth trusts him more than it does me. When I go looking for feverfew or meadowsweet, the forest shows him where to find it. When I sleep beneath the hedge, I don't sleep alone," I said, my throat feeling thick. "Mam-gu always said having Cadno was part of what made me special. An anchor deepens your magic. And magic, adventure, beauty—they have a cost. But they're more than worth it."

"You miss her, too," Tal said, considering. "Fee, I'm wondering if you should speak to Enid again, after all this."

"Enid?" I asked. "Really?"

He nodded. "Do you have a mentor? Do you have anyone to teach you?"

"No one since my mam-gu died. Only thing of Arianrhod's I've ever coveted, much as I'd never accept guidance from the Foxhall."

"Well, everyone needs counsel. In magic, rulership, trade, what have you. My father's magician learned from his predecessor, who learned from her predecessor. Though some people depart from their training. I think Osian certainly has."

I squirmed. "Will you 'depart from your training,' too?" I asked carefully. I could only guess what kind of rulership Tal would've learned from his father.

"Ah. Well." Tal's smile was sad. "It remains to be seen whether I'll be inheriting the post or not."

Nerves twinged suddenly in my gut. "What's your father like, Tal? What should I know?" I asked. "How are we going to convince him to give us Mathrafal's blade?"

"I think he'll be pleased that we managed the situation at Black Darren, and at how far we've come without any help." Tal thought for a moment. "My father is emotional. Unpredictable. We'll have to tread carefully. But my mother will help us."

I shifted, curious. "What's *she* like?"

"The best," Tal said immediately. "My mother—I rely on her so much." He paused. "You know, I think you're my only friend whose parents are also separated."

I bit my lip, fighting a smile. "Tal, I think that just means neither of us has many friends."

He stared at me for a moment, looking offended. Then he sputtered a laugh, and I snorted, and the two of us lay there, giggling like idiots, watching one another.

The feeling was like being trapped in a bubble, floating up, and up, and up.

When we settled back down, Tal was somehow closer than he had been before.

"Anyway, I've met your mother," Tal said, shaking off the remnants of a laugh. "What's your father like?"

"Distracted. In another world, really." I twisted uncomfortably again; I didn't want to talk about Dad. "Even before he and my mother separated, he was only home a few times year. Always off serving your father, like I said. In the end, that's what came between them. Dad said she might as well be married to the Foxhall. Mam said he might as well be married to Mathrafal." I sighed. "Is your father kind to your mother?"

"He doesn't look after her anymore. He's made it clear that's not his job." Tal cleared his throat and looked away. "Some things it was impossible to keep from him. Some things he refused to see."

"You're clever enough to be king, with or without his guidance," I said. "Clever enough, strong enough. You could hold the throne."

He hesitated, eyes lingering on my face. "Would you be my magician if I became king?"

I went rigid.

I was dreading even going to Mathrafal. Things had shifted between Tal and me at Black Darren, and I knew the same would happen again at his father's castle.

"The Foxhall is my home," I said. "I have no desire to live at court, or to take up the magician's mantle."

"He doesn't so much wear a mantle as a loincloth."

"That's very distressing."

"You could live anywhere you wanted," Tal said. "At Mathrafal, with me. In Foxhall. Anywhere."

I gave a breathy, humorless laugh. But Tal wasn't laughing.

At Mathrafal. With me.

He tugged the signet ring off his finger. "Give me your hand."

I did.

Past my ragged nails, over the dirt seamed into my skin, Tal pushed his ring onto my left middle finger. The bronze gleamed warm on my hand, a perfect fit.

"At Mathrafal, that ring will open any door except the one to my father's chambers," he said.

Tal didn't let go of my hand. I didn't move. I could hardly breathe.

"Generally, I don't wait for people to open doors for me. I just burst in, like I did at the Foxhall." My voice wavered. "Or I climb a tree, or a wall, or I—"

"I'd rather you didn't have to climb walls or trees," he interrupted.

"I'd rather you be able to get safely inside, if it comes to that."

"It's not so bad outside, Tal." My voice was quiet.

"It can be," he said baldly. "I don't like sleeping out in the open, Ffion. I like fortresses, and walls, and locked doors. And I don't like people."

What had happened to him?

Tal pursed his lips. I wanted to touch them so badly I might have stretched out a hand, if my fingers weren't locked in his.

"I know you don't." My voice was airless. "You don't like anyone."

"No one," he agreed, eyes never leaving mine.

When the twig snapped and I woke up, my first thought was whether I would ever sleep through the night again.

At first, I couldn't remember where I was. My nose was running and my throat was sore, and I wasn't on the ground. And then I felt Tal's back pressed to mine.

His shoulders rose and fell, the long muscles along his spine expanding and contracting with his breath. My bare feet were tucked between his calves.

Another twig snapped. I shut my eyes. Tal was so warm behind me.

I was nearly asleep again when I heard the voices.

I stiffened, untangling my ankles from Tal's. He gave an incoherent grunt and turned toward me. "Fee?" His voice was in my ear, thick with sleep.

"Shh. Tal, I think there's someone out there."

"What?" He was too loud. I rolled to face him and pressed a hand to his mouth.

Voices, and footsteps.

They didn't sound extremely close. And they could've just been other travelers, like us.

Except they sounded like they were trying to keep quiet.

Beneath my fingers, Tal's lips were as soft as I'd imagined.

"I think there's someone sneaking around outside," I said.

"I tell you, they're not out here," said a man's voice.

Tal's eyes went wide. We both froze.

He took my hand in his. "They're speaking Welsh, so they're not Mercian." My blood sped as he leaned nearer to my ear, his free hand pushing my hair back. "I want you to go. I want you to climb out of here and untie Derog—leave the other horse—and ride to Mathrafal. Tell them where I am. I'll follow you as soon as I can."

I jerked back. "I won't leave you, Tal."

"They can't have gotten far in all this mud," said another voice. "The boy let it be known they were making for the castle. Had a purse full of silver and a wagon full of goods. And they didn't leave town by the road."

Panic pulsed through me like blood gushing from a wound.

Trelystan. The oilcloth.

We'd been followed.

"You have to go." Tal's hand was still in my hair, chafing my curls between his fingertips. "You have to. You'll have to ride without a saddle, but—"

"No!" I gasped again. "Tal, Mathrafal is just over that hill. You are a *prince*. If we tell them who you are, surely they won't risk hurting you."

"Ffion." Tal's voice was severe now. "Listen to me. I can talk myself out of a lot. But I don't think they'll believe me if I tell them who I am. It might actually make things worse for us. And I cannot watch you—" He cleared his throat. "I can't—"

"Tal." His name broke over my lips.

"Go," he said softly, looking as though it hurt.

I put my palm to his cheek, and he leaned into it. Just a little.

And then—I couldn't help it.

I turned away from Tal just in time not to sneeze in his face.

"There!" A man's voice, not twenty feet away.

"Go, now!" Tal shoved at me, and I ripped my way from beneath the oilcloth. I didn't bother trying to untie his horse; too late, I remembered the fancy knots he'd tied, the animal's impossible height. I'd never be quick enough.

Three men in dirty clothes pulled knives from their belts, leering and laughing.

These weren't puppyish soldiers acting like fools. These were men who wanted to do us harm.

Suddenly, my blood wasn't pounding in panic. Suddenly, I was furious.

I reached for my own knife where it hung at my belt and leapt down from the wagon, ignoring their laughter as I hacked lengths of dead wood from a thornbush.

Tal started talking to the men, but I wasn't listening. As the thieves drew near, I strewed the thorny branches across the ground around the wagon. And I began to sing.

One night did I go riding, a-riding I did go
The moon was in the sky-oh, the moon was on the snow
With pockets full and heart alight, I rode out through the snow

Upon the empty highway a lone man I did see
I slowed to bid him evening, and yea, he greeted me
With comrades and a length of rope, the man he greeted me

Fair mistress! he did cry out. We wish you none of harm
Alight from your fine gelding, and do stretch out your arm
Cease to ride and pray come down and do stretch out your arm

Your purse, miss, is it heavy? Or, mistress, is it light?
My men and I are bound to pick your pockets on this night
Pray empty out your pockets to my good men on this night

My pockets they are heavy, sir, I pray you gentle be
I am a maiden ruthful, off to offer charity
But all I carry is now yours, I render it to thee

I got down and I there unlade my pockets jingling, rife,
My gold and then my copper and a shining silver knife
"My pockets to your bowels, sir," and there I drove the knife.

32

TAL

She was supposed to run. She was supposed to be safe.

Panic bubbled in my skull.

Some people, I knew, froze when they panicked. Some people retreated; others put up a fight.

Fear had left me frozen once. But after what had happened to Mam and me, I had trained myself. I would never let anyone threaten us again.

Now fear made me fluent.

"Good morning." I hopped down off the wagon, eyes on the men and their blades, putting myself in front of Ffion as she went to work on a thornbush with her knife. "Anything I can share with you gentlemen for your refreshment?"

Sometimes, it worked to offer something before it could be ripped away. Sometimes, it was just surprising enough to keep the peace.

But their leader only laughed and pushed past me. I felt an irrational pang of loss as he ripped the oilcloth away from where we'd been sleeping, tearing through our things and giving a cry of pleasure when he came across my purse. "What have we got in here?"

I couldn't care less about the money. If I'd thought it would've saved us, I would've told them there was a whole treasury full of silver at Mathrafal just down the hill.

"Very well. You've got what you wanted," I said sharply. "Take your coin and go."

But I'd chosen my moment badly. Just then, Ffion had begun throwing bracken on the ground, singing, crawling on her hands and knees. The man cocked an eyebrow.

"No," he said. "I don't think I will."

It was too much, they were too much, it was a spring morning and I was here and it was now but it was also four years ago, and here I had no door to keep them out.

Mam wasn't here. But I had Ffion to protect.

"You're all from Trelystan." My own voice was changed in my ears, harsh and loud. "You—you and your elderly parents live in the wooden farmhouse east of the village. You and your mother live in the third hut on the lane off the high street. And you live with a wife and three small children next to the mill." I pointed sharply from man to man, telling them what I remembered from my errand in town the day before, and they recoiled, surprised. "That's right. I remember every one of you."

"Dead men remember nothing," said the one with the children. But he sounded uncertain.

I shrugged. "Maybe you succeed. Maybe you kill me, and you get away with that pouch—which I'm glad to give you anyway." My jaw hardened. "But say you don't. Say you fail to kill me. Say, worst of all for you, you hurt her and you leave me alive," I snarled. "I know where you live. I know your faces and your families' faces. And I'm not a good man."

I'd been indiscreet in Trelystan. That was my mistake.

But I never forgot a face. And I never let go of a grudge.

Ffion jumped up, her song finished. Her gray eyes were wild on me, on the thornbush bits she'd scattered across the ground, on the three men and their three shining knives.

The first one lunged, and Ffion's magic came to life.

A thornbush sprang up around him, climbing over his body,

digging into his skin and drawing blood. Close by, a tree crashed to the forest floor, and a sapling burst out of the earth beside it.

I gave a wild laugh. "What do you say, men? Care to test my hedge-witch?"

Fear still beat through my blood. But for once, magic wasn't the reason. I pulled Ffion close to my side, and she pressed her cheek to my shoulder.

The thieves snarled. "Tricks are no match for a sharpened blade," said one of the men, beginning to cut his companion free. A second cage of thorns leapt up to trap him.

But then my stomach dropped.

Though the earth had answered Ffion's magic, her spell seemed to falter; the second snare rose barely to the thief's knees. The vines of the first snare drooped and struggled. With the help of their accomplice, the two men quickly pulled free.

Horror crashed over me in a wave. I couldn't understand. And then—

No.

My gaze shot up to the sky, searching out the moon. It was broad, well over half full, still days from disappearing.

Could Ffion's magic be slipping away from her already?

"Tal." Ffion was pale beside me. "Tal, we have to—"

I knew what she wanted to say. I had to tell them who I was.

It was our last hope.

"I'm Prince Taliesin of Powys," I finally ground out. "My father's castle, Mathrafal, is just down this hill."

I held my breath. I shouldn't have bothered.

"'*My father's castle is just down this hill,*'" one of the men mimicked. "We know who King Cadell is. And if you're his bastard princeling, then I'm the highest of his high men."

"What are you going to do?" Ffion asked. The knife was beginning to shake in her fingers, so she gripped it with two hands.

I'd never seen Ffion use a weapon. Why would she, when she had magic?

I wondered how much longer that would be true.

"Whatever we want." The man across from me bared his teeth in a grin.

He lunged, and I pulled out my own blade, ready to fight for Ffion's life and mine.

"Stop!"

A voice boomed from the top of the hill. A figure, backlit by the gold beginning to tint the sky to the east. A dagger filled his left hand; a hatchet filled his right.

He carried them with a confidence I'd envied all my life.

"Or what?" asked one of the thieves.

Ffion gaped, and for a brief moment, I saw our rescuer through her eyes. Horse as golden as his hair, skin smudged with soot. He wore a white shirt and a leather apron, and even in the dark, it was clear he was bigger than me, broader than me, stronger than me.

"Or," he said slowly, "I will gut each of you, cart you each back to Mathrafal in my brother's wagon, and give your bodies to my father's magician to use however he pleases."

Ffion stopped breathing.

So did the thieves.

"In the name of your king and both your princes," said Dafydd, "I suggest you run."

The men didn't wait. Dafydd's guards gave chase as the thieves ran down the hill; Dafydd himself got down from his horse and hurried toward Ffion.

"Your Highness." She curtsied, panting. "Thank you for coming to our rescue."

"I had to," he said. "Didn't you know that I had to?"

I wasn't expecting Dafydd's answer. I wasn't expecting his voice to be so fervent.

"Dafydd." Finally, I caught my breath. "How did you know we were here?"

He hadn't helped me when I needed him four years ago. I didn't know how to feel now that he had ridden to our rescue. But I seemed to almost catch him off guard.

"Tal!" His voice was pleased, but not overly so. "I actually—well. I knew she was here." He gestured at Ffion.

Ffion, but not me. Or—Ffion, and me by association.

Again came that horrible feeling of falling.

"How?" I asked.

Ffion bit her lip. Dafydd stepped toward her, putting his back to me. I suddenly felt entirely irrelevant.

"Ffion." My brother's voice was almost reverent. "Ffion, it's you. After all this time."

"How do you know her?" My own words seemed to be coming from far away.

"Because." Osian jumped down from the saddle of a blue roan, nearly naked as always despite the cold. "She's destined to be his magician. As her grandmother was to your grandfather. As her father is to yours."

My heart sank, my blood froze, my pulse stuttered, I *did not understand.*

"Hello, Ffion," said my father's magician, his strange, light gray eyes dancing.

She avoided my eyes. But looking between them—I saw it. I saw now.

"Hello, Dad," said my hedgewitch.

33

DAFYDD

Caer Digoll, Powys

She doesn't know me.

It was the only thought in my head as we rode out of the forest.

All the way to Caer Digoll, I had been afraid I would be too late. When the vision had come—greedy-eyed men with knives creeping toward their wagon—I was shaking Osian awake in under a minute. I was on Terrwyn's back in under three. I hadn't even waited for Gruffudd.

And when I'd burst into the woods, guards in the distance behind me, there they were. The three thieves, and my brother.

And her.

Hair like fire, freckles like sparks. Her hands were bleeding.

But when I stepped forward and said her name—

Ffion knew me by sight and title, I could see that. She certainly knew who Osian was to my father. Who her grandmother Sioned had been to my grandfather Brochfael. She might even have known the role her father wanted her to take, someday. But she didn't know me.

Not the way she seemed to know Tal.

"We should carry on to Mathrafal," Ffion said, instinctively turning to him. "There could be more of them." Tal nodded.

For so many years, I'd watched Ffion's life, overwhelmed by longing. I'd ached for the freedom she'd enjoyed since she was young. I'd wished to be as relentlessly generous as she was as she served her village. I'd thought I understood envy the year I caught a vision of her the day after Pasg, when boys go house to house, looking for girls amenable to being stolen and carried out on their shoulders. A fifteen-year-old Ffion and a girl I thought might be her sister had laughed from behind their door, telling the boys to go away and tossing them a coin.

It would've taken more than a coin to send me off. I would've waited all afternoon, if I'd thought she wanted me there.

But the grudge I'd held against the boys of Foxhall was nothing to my jealousy as Tal put a hand on Ffion's elbow, talking quietly with her before he climbed up into the wagon.

There was strain in her face, and frustration in his. But Ffion and I were strangers. And she and Tal were not.

We freed their wagon from where it was stuck in the mud. Then I took Terrwyn by the reins and walked alongside Ffion toward the top of the hill. "What brings you to Mathrafal, Mistress Ffion?"

"Just Ffion." She gave me a wry look, adjusting her grip on her cauldron. "You already know what Tal is up to, and if you know who I am, I expect you know I'm working with him."

I hoped Ffion would miss my frown. But she was too quick. "What? What's that face for?"

"That's not how I know you." I looked away from her, staring after Osian's back.

What did you do? I wanted to shout at him.

"No, I guess not." Ffion's brow furrowed. "'After all this time'—that's what you said."

I felt myself redden. I hadn't meant to blurt that out.

My insides were churning.

"This is harder than I thought it would be. Because I—I thought you would know," I said.

"Know what?"

I hesitated. "Your father didn't tell you?"

"Tell me *what*, Dafydd?" She sounded frustrated.

"You never had visions?" I asked. "Or dreams?"

"I've had strange dreams lately," she admitted, and I must have looked hopeful, because she let me down gently. "They don't make any sense, though. They're about places I've never been. They're the same images, over and over."

"And—" My heart hesitated on a knifepoint; misery waited over the edge. "And I'm not in them?"

"You?" Her eyes widened. "No, of course not."

She must have seen the wan smile I directed at the ground. I must have looked as lost and foolish as I felt.

"Have I been in your dreams, Dafydd?" she asked quietly.

I felt winded. It took me a moment to catch my breath.

I'd suspected, but now I knew. To Ffion, we were strangers.

"Visions," I corrected her. "In my visions. Since you were four and I was six."

"Since I was—" Ffion stopped short, her cheeks bloodless beneath their freckles. "You've been having visions of me for twelve years?"

"Your father told me you would be my court magician someday," I said. "He bound us together when we were only children."

Ffion stared at me, completely stunned. "Did you ever see me bathing?" she demanded after a moment. "Or undressed?"

"What?" I was horrified. "Of course not!"

"Relieving myself?"

"No!"

Ffion paused, looking small and uncertain. "Did you ever see me crying?"

I wanted to lie, but I couldn't. I hesitated too long, and she grimaced and looked away. "Only once," I said. "But Ffion, the visions—Osian told me you would have them, too." I sounded panicked. I *felt* panicked.

Because—hadn't he?

Had Osian ever explicitly said Ffion had visions of me as well?

Had he ever answered me directly about when she would come to Mathrafal? Or had he just said it would happen *someday, in due course, when the time was right?*

Up ahead, Tal crested the hill in the wagon, riding through the stones of what was left of Caer Digoll. Osian sang idly to himself, sitting on his blue roan.

My face heated with humiliation as Ffion stared at her father, mounting horror in her eyes to match the nausea growing in my stomach.

I hadn't grown to know Ffion over the years. I had *watched* her, unbeknownst to her; I'd learned about her habits and likes; I'd seen her become beautiful and strong and resourceful. But I didn't *know* her, because she didn't know me.

Throughout my life, I'd seen my father's bond with Osian in action. I'd seen Dad speaking out of Osian's mouth, seen Osian speaking directly into my father's mind. With the trust that lived between them, it was a fierce, fail-safe bond. No one knew them better. No one could be closer. But without it—it was a bizarre invasion of Ffion's privacy, and just as bizarre a betrayal of my trust.

I felt like a voyeur. I felt sick to my stomach.

"He always had an explanation for where you were," I said haltingly. "He never said—"

"I know. I believe you," Ffion interrupted, voice gentler now. "But Dafydd, I don't want to be court magician. Foxhall is my home. Tal told me you don't even want to be king."

I knew what choices I'd already made. But her words were a blow.

"I'm not willing to pay the price to hold the throne," I said after a moment. "But before I decided that, I waited for you for a long, long time."

It didn't matter that I wouldn't be king. She wouldn't have chosen to be my magician, anyway.

I couldn't look at her. I was so embarrassed, I doubted I'd be able to look in the mirror later.

Suddenly, though, I realized something was missing. "Ffion, where's Cadno?" I glanced around our feet—wherever Ffion was, the fox was never far.

"You knew Cadno?" She glanced at me swiftly.

"I knew of him—wait. *Knew?*" I asked. But then I caught her expression.

Oh, Ffion.

"How?" I asked. "How did it happen?"

"The Foxhall didn't watch where they were stepping." Her voice was grim.

Cadno had been by her side every time I'd seen her—foraging, working spells, playing in the woods. He'd been her best friend for more than ten years, and now he was gone. "Ffion, I'm so sorry. He was so smart and such a funny little thing. And he loved you."

"Thank you, Dafydd." She sounded sad, and almost surprised. "That's very kind."

We came to the ruined fort at the top of the hill. Only a few heaps of broken reddish stone remained; my father had cannibalized its walls when he built Mathrafal. Across the hilltop, Osian and Tal rode behind the guards and the thieves.

Every few moments, my brother glanced back at us over his shoulder.

He will claim her, Osian had warned me. Because I wasn't willing to pay what the throne cost, and Tal was.

As things stood now, Tal wouldn't have to take Ffion from me. She wasn't mine.

Hair like fire, freckles like sparks. Gray eyes iron-sharp and heavy as a hammer. I could hardly bear to look at her. I could hardly bear to look away.

As I walked alongside Ffion back toward Mathrafal, I knew that I wouldn't let Osian's interference tarnish what I'd waited for all these years.

I would fix things with Ffion. She would know who I really was—or at least, she would have a chance to know.

I would make sure we had a chance.

I didn't know if I wanted Tal to be king. I didn't know if I would fight him for the throne.

But I knew without a doubt that I would fight him for her.

"Dafydd. Ffion. Are you two coming?" said Tal. "I have a favor to ask Dad, and I don't want to be delayed."

I glanced up at Tal. For the moment, he was as much a mystery as Ffion. What had happened since he left? Was he still angry that I'd freed Prince Angws?

It didn't matter. We'd never lacked cause to argue. We certainly wouldn't now.

"A favor?" I asked.

"I'll explain to him at home," Tal said shortly.

Oh. "Dad's gone. Ceredigion, he said before he left." A kingdom to the west. I didn't mention the Foxhall, though I wasn't sure why.

"Didn't you just return from Ceredigion?" Tal sounded irritable.

"Gwynedd. I returned a few days ago. Dad went then."

"Why?"

Ffion spoke at the same time. "So who's going to make decisions while your father is gone?"

It was an understandable question. It wouldn't have set me off, had the two of them not exchanged a meaningful glance. They didn't speak; they didn't need to.

It was all wrong.

"I am." My voice was crisp. I climbed onto Terrwyn's back, nodding significantly at my brother. "Sounds like you have a favor to ask me, Tal."

34

FFION

Mathrafal Castle, Powys

King Cadell's fortress was pressed against the dyke, the border between Powys and Mercia nothing more than the line where stone met earth.

The castle's towers and walls were made of dusty red stone, and Cadell's green-and-gold standard rose above them in the breeze. Around the castle lay the effects of my father's magic: a field full of daffodils that never stopped blooming, and a stand of oaks whose leaves never turned. The town that butted up against the keep stirred beneath the sunrise.

The four of us rode downhill, all of us but Dad tense and uncertain.

I'd kept so much from Tal. And my father had done the unthinkable. And—Dafydd.

I couldn't believe what he knew about me. I couldn't believe how much he'd seen.

Twelve years. Twelve *years* of visions. My childhood, my life at home, my life since.

He'd seen me cry. Had he seen me sick? Had he seen me arguing with my mother?

I felt exposed. But somehow, Dafydd was the only one I could stand to look at.

As he walked beside me, obviously crushed but trying to contain himself—trying not to make his feelings another burden for me, I could see—I couldn't properly work up the unease or resentment

I thought I should feel toward him. I was furious at my father, but Dafydd wasn't to blame.

And beneath my shyness and anger and confusion, I felt worry creeping in.

The new moon was still eight days away. What had happened to my spell in the woods shouldn't have happened.

"I should plant another pouch here," I said when we were out of view of the nearest Mercian guard tower, about a mile from the castle, and climbed down into the ditch.

I chose a planting song I'd always liked, and tried to concentrate.

Root, little seed, root, little seed
There in the dark, dig in your feet
Root, little seed

Leaf, little seed, leaf, little seed,
Out in the air, breathe and be free
Leaf, little seed

Bloom, little seed, bloom, little seed
Soft, tender petals, beds for the bees
Bloom, little seed

Fruit, little seed, fruit, little seed
Summer has come, sunshine and sweet
Fruit, little seed

Magic had never left me tired. But burying the charm took something from me, just as the spell in the woods had before it fizzled. I shuddered, thinking of the thornbushes springing up and then faltering.

The spells I worked always cost me effort. But that slip back in the forest had almost cost me everything.

And my magic *was* slipping.

You'll never make it on your own, Mam had fretted.

I refused to let her be right.

I needed to speak to Dad. We had to talk about the power in the dyke. And I needed to know what on earth he had been thinking, to bind Dafydd and me and never say a word. Did King Cadell know? Clearly Tal hadn't.

When I was done, I brushed off my hands and made to climb out of the ditch. But when I looked up, there was Dafydd, his hand outstretched, his blue eyes earnest on mine.

I thought you would know.

I hadn't. But should I have?

Who wouldn't have felt such attention and curiosity, across the years and miles?

Dafydd was exactly as Dad had always described him. He had none of Tal's angles; his chest and shoulders were broad, and beneath his shirt and leather apron, his arms were bigger than my thighs. His skin was burned in places, and there was soot in his thick gold hair.

He had a broad, inescapable kind of presence, unaffected and friendly, warm as the sun.

And my face had been in his mind for twelve years. That was all I could think as he hoisted me gently and easily out of the ditch and we started down the hill again.

Despite my father's endless coaxing, I'd never been to Mathrafal, so I watched the town with curiosity as the sky brightened over its lanes and houses and the red stone walls of the busy castle courtyard. Inside, scullions slopped the pigs and fed the chickens, and a kitchen boy hauled water.

"Taliesin!"

A woman hurried across the gravel toward us. With Tal's light brown eyes and a narrow jaw exactly like his, she could only have been his mother.

"Mam." Tal hugged her tightly, pulling apart only to exchange hushed, rapid words.

The chickens pecking around my feet darted away when a giant dog with thick black fur lumbered over, looking accusingly at Dafydd.

"Who's this?" I asked, crouching to scrub at his side.

"That's Gruffudd."

"Well, Gruffudd is a very good dog." I scratched behind his ears, missing Cadno again down to my guts.

When I glanced up, Dafydd's smile was heartbreaking, broad and brilliant, if a little tight around the edges. Something heavy waited behind his eyes, and his throat bobbed as he reached down to rub Gruffudd's head.

He was so disappointed. He was trying so hard not to show it.

"I have to go," he said. "I'm due to hold court soon. But I hope we can speak more later."

"Of course," I said, and to my surprise, I meant it. "Later."

I had to speak to my father, anyway. *Later* wasn't soon enough to deal with what he'd done.

"Dad—Dad." I jogged after him toward a columbarium on the far side of the courtyard, and he turned, looking surprised to see me following him.

"Yes? What is it, Ffion?" His light eyes were blank.

Distracted. In another world. That was how I'd described my father to Tal. Even now—even after everything I'd just found out and everything that had happened in the forest—he looked surprised that I wanted to speak.

I pushed past my frustration and focused. "I have so much to tell you," I began, and my words bubbled out in an incoherent rush.

"There's magic in the dyke. Did you know there was magic in the dyke?" I asked. "And Cadno is dead, just like Pendwmpian, and my magic is going to disappear just like yours. I have to bring him back, so I can bring my magic back. So I have to destroy the dyke, so we have to figure out why there is magic in the dyke!"

Dad blinked at me. I cleared my throat.

"Magic in the dyke?" My father frowned at the horizon like I'd told him he couldn't have a picnic because it was going to rain.

"Yes," I said hurriedly, my exasperation building. "Did Mam or Mam-gu ever say anything about it? I don't know how it got there. The Mercians have never had a magician, have they?"

"No, they never said anything," Dad said. Disappointing, but unsurprising; we'd always avoided the dyke because of how heavily fortified it was. "Brycheiniog had a magician until recent years. Gwynedd, occasionally. But Mercia, never." He paused. "Obviously, Powys is short of a magician at the moment as well." For the first time, his eyes lit on me with purpose.

"Yes. About that." I crossed my arms, struggling to speak.

I thought again of Dafydd and his blue eyes, Dafydd helping me out of the ditch.

"Dad, how could you do it?" I finally asked. "How could you bind Dafydd and me? How could you do it and not tell me?"

"It was necessary. And sometimes telling the whole truth will only lead to unnecessary fuss." Dad glanced significantly at Tal. "You understand that."

"Me not telling Tal that you're my father is *not the same* as you tying me to Dafydd without my knowledge," I hissed. "What does this mean for when Tal becomes king? Because he's the only one of the two of them who wants the throne!"

"You are meant to be court magician, Ffion. Dafydd will change his mind. And Taliesin is unsuited for the throne. He cannot be king."

"Tal has a mind like a knife," I said vehemently. "Tal would keep Powys safe."

"Tal would build walls a mile high."

"Offa's already done that," I snapped. I was almost breathless with anger at his calm. "I don't know how to forgive this, Dad. You did wrong, and you lied about it for over a decade."

"I don't require your forgiveness," he said evenly, baldly. "I will study the dyke. And, oh—" He paused. "How's your mother?"

I stared at him. "Too thin," I said. "Worried about me, per usual."

"Mm." Dad made a face, and walked away.

In another world. Just like always.

Just like always, my parents had acted without thinking about how I'd feel, and I was dealing with the fallout on my own.

"Ffion!" I glanced up to find Tal beckoning me. Dread rang through me like a gong.

I crossed the courtyard, avoiding his eyes. "Bore da, mistress," I greeted the woman beside him.

"Mam, this is Ffion vch Catrin. Ffion, this is my mother, Gwanwyn."

"Vch Osian," I corrected him. Carrying my father's name was hard, but it was easier than my mother's. I hated that Rhiannon always called me Ffion vch Catrin. But when I met Gwanwyn's eyes, I could see she didn't care what he called me.

Tal was close to his mother, and he was convinced she'd help us. But she was looking at me with obvious suspicion. "It's a pleasure to meet you, Ffion," she said.

It wasn't. And I had no idea why.

35

TAL

I thought nothing could've distracted me from how angry I was at Ffion. But then we reached the door to my mother's rooms, and I found it standing unguarded.

When Mam and I had first moved to Mathrafal, guards had been the first expense I'd deducted from my allowance. I'd organized soldiers to guard her door before I'd even bought her furniture, or linens, or gowns.

I'd bought all those things as well, of course. But the trio of armed guards never, ever left her door.

"Mam." My jaw dropped in horror. "Mam, where are—?"

But my mother shook her head, shoving Ffion and me through her door. "Now," she said, "tell me where you've been. Tell me everything."

I wanted to ask her again, and finish my sentence this time. But I could see from the furrow of Mam's brow how she'd reply. Probably the same way she had when I came back a few weeks ago reeking of the ale Dad had been guzzling with his men. *I birthed you into this world, Taliesin. When I ask you where you've been, I expect an answer.*

Anyway, it was a relief to finally tell her everything. Though it was less a relief to hear what she had to say when I was done.

"They were here," Mam said. "The Foxhall."

"The Foxhall?" Ffion echoed. "Why?"

"I don't know. Perhaps you could speak to Dafydd about that," my mother said, eyeing her significantly.

I felt ill.

No one could've missed the way Dafydd had looked at Ffion when he'd rescued us in the forest. As he'd walked beside her, helped her out of the ditch.

When I glanced at Ffion, she looked away, just like she had all morning. But she couldn't dodge me forever.

"Well, we'll need to speak to him," I said. "If Dad's left Dafydd keeper of Mathrafal, we'll need his permission to take—well." Quickly, I explained the nature of the llafnau, how I'd gotten Brycheiniog's blade from Enid with Angws's help.

"Clever of you." Mam squeezed my shoulder, and I felt a rush of comfort. "I don't know anything about the blades. But I'll see what I can find out."

"Please. The fewer favors I have to beg of Dafydd, the better." I sighed. "Now, Mam, please. Where are your guards?"

She sighed. "It's Luned. Your father's new . . . companion."

I was on feet before I realized I was moving. "Dad's new mistress requisitioned your guards?"

"Not exactly. She asked your father why they were paying for three guards outside my room—"

"Why *they* were paying?" I demanded. "Luned isn't queen, so there is no *they*. And *I* pay the guards' wages."

"Luned convinced your father that my having them was self-important, and he had them dismissed."

"She had no right!" I started pacing. This was unacceptable.

"Critical thinking isn't Luned's strong suit," Mam said, placating. "Please calm down, bach. I don't want to make a fuss."

"Then I'll make it for you," I said.

Two weeks. I had been gone two weeks, and the guards I'd had outside my mother's door for four years had been removed. And two weeks was nothing compared to the ten or so months of the year that my father's candler spent traveling.

The guards, the walls, and me as someday-king—this was the whole point. I would reign at Mathrafal, and she would be safe and respected here.

If I'd ever had any doubts, I was certain now: I could never, ever be candler.

"You worry too much, Taliesin."

"I worry for a reason."

"I should go." Ffion got to her feet and began edging toward the door. "I'm sure you two want to spend some time together."

"Ffion, wait." I stopped her with a look. "Let's go for a walk."

She'd lied to me. And I was going to find out why.

We left Mam's rooms with me hauling Ffion by her sleeve. "Where are we going?" she asked. I didn't answer, just led her away until we reached a quiet corner.

"How could you?" I breathed. "Ffion, how could you?"

It was all I could say. I'd been holding it in for hours.

I'd never seen Ffion look ashamed. Not after she'd raged at the Foxhall, not after the Mercians had mocked her on the dyke, not after King Meirion had denied her at Black Darren. But she did now.

"You told me your father was in the army," I said quietly. "Why did you lie to me?"

"I said he was always off serving your father." Ffion looked away. "And he was. Just maybe not the way you assumed."

She was unbelievable. I ducked my head, forced her to meet my eyes again. "Are you really saying I'm to blame for not realizing Osian is your father? You had two weeks to explain, and you chose not to. After everything—"

A pair of errand boys dashed down the hall, tailed by a serving girl with her arms full. I broke off, pressing my lips together.

I thought of Ffion asleep beside me in the wagon, of Ffion in the dawn light with her fingers on my lips.

And then I thought of Dafydd's eyes on her. *Ffion, it's you. After all this time.*

The last time I'd seen Dafydd, he'd released Angws and wrecked my plans. And now—

"My parents separated for their own reasons. But the aftermath was terrible for all of us," she said. "The Foxhall punished Mam for leaving Dad. They demoted her, because they considered it a lost connection for the whole coven. Arianrhod took Mam's side in the split. I refused to do the same.

"But I told you last night, I don't want to follow in my father's footsteps any more than I wanted to follow in my mother's. So to have Mam suffering and still pushing me, and Dad still writing me letters, telling me I could always come to Mathrafal—" Ffion set her jaw, looking mulish. "So no, I don't talk about it. I did tell you what was relevant, though, which is that I don't work magic the way he does, and I don't want to be court magician."

She was right. She had told me that much.

"I didn't even know Osian had a family," I said. "I didn't even know his role was hereditary."

"You didn't know because you don't like my father, and you avoid him." She paused. "The loincloth is, admittedly, off-putting."

"He cultivates an off-putting presence. And you're right, it isn't your fault I didn't know those things." I swallowed hard. "But you let me be caught off guard today, Ffion. You knew what Osian was to you, and Osian knew, and Dafydd knew, and I was the only one who didn't. And I felt so, so stupid."

"Your entire reputation is built around your scheming," she mumbled. "You lie to everyone."

"Not to you." I took a step toward her, forced her eyes to mine again. "Lying to the rest of the world isn't the same as us lying to each other."

It was a struggle to speak the half-truth with the raven's feather in her cauldron; unpracticed as she was, Ffion probably couldn't have managed it at all. It was a lie of omission, but it cost me effort.

I should've told her I didn't want magic to come back. I should have. But that conversation would have opened the door for another, one I simply couldn't have.

Ffion's gaze darted to my mouth, and my pulse jumped.

"I'm sorry, Tal," she said, and I could hear in her voice that she meant it. "I never wanted you to feel foolish. My intent wasn't to hurt you."

I nodded silently, swallowing hard.

The truth was, now that the shock had worn off, I didn't care much that Osian was her father.

I cared very, very much that Dafydd seemed to think he had some kind of claim on her.

"And you had no idea that my brother—" I hesitated. That he knew her? That he loved her? How could that be, when Ffion and I had only just met?

"Dafydd said Dad bound us years ago, the way my father and yours are bound. But I swear, I didn't know," she said, holding up her hands. "He's had visions of me—I never did."

The admission took my breath away. But I had to believe her. If I couldn't trust the way Ffion looked at me now, knife-sharp and deadly serious, I couldn't trust anything about her.

As ready as I had been to reach Mathrafal, I suddenly couldn't wait for us to be gone.

I shook my head. "And now Dafydd is holding my father's throne."

"And the Foxhall's been here," she added. "Why? What are we going to do, Tal?" Ffion stepped even closer to me, and suddenly our corner of the corridor felt small.

After she'd fallen asleep the night before, I'd lain awake for what felt like hours, listening to her talk in her sleep. Once she'd hummed a snatch of a song before rolling over, pressing her back to my chest.

I'd wanted to hold her. To slide my hands around her waist and spend the night with her hair pressed to my cheek.

But I didn't want Ffion in my arms by accident. And I told myself again now that I had no space to be impulsive. Not with the throne and Mam's position at Mathrafal on the line, and Dafydd holding the power to wreck everything.

And yet: Ffion's face was tilted up toward mine. She still smelled like rain.

Impulsive.

I took her fingers between mine and began to count.

Ffion went very still.

"First, we are going to bring your father to our meeting with Dafydd when we make our request," I said, tapping my forefinger against hers.

"Second, my mother is going to pursue intelligence about what Mathrafal's blade might be." My forefinger against the tip of the middle finger that wore my signet, and then her ring finger. "Third, whatever the Foxhall was doing here, we are going to find a way to undermine them."

Ffion's fingers trembled in mine. I bent my head to whisper in her ear as I had earlier, when we'd been almost alone.

I'd never spent much time with girls, but this felt as natural as Ffion's voice in her sleep.

It was a heady thing, to hold her and know she wanted me there.

"But most of all, you are going to trust me," I said, my cheek pressed against her hair, one hand resting against her neck. "Because you know you can trust me, and because we're at Mathrafal. And here, I know what I'm doing."

I hadn't told her everything. I was still avoiding the whole truth.

But court was dangerous. Despite everything, I was still Ffion's best bet.

It was nearly nightfall before Dafydd would deign to see Ffion and me. Gruffudd snored at his feet in the throne room; Osian sat as he always did, cross-legged, almost naked. At the moment, he was cutting his fingernails with a knife at the high table. *I always keep them short,* he'd told me once. *The blood cakes underneath if I don't.*

For once, Dafydd looked as uncertain of Osian as I always felt.

"Powys has something we need," Ffion explained to my brother. "Something I need to perform the magic that will break the dyke. I don't know if it's here at Mathrafal or elsewhere, but I'm hoping you can help us."

"What is it?" Dafydd leaned toward her. I could tell he was trying to contain himself. But he was still so eager—so *obvious*—that I wanted to leave the room and drag Ffion out with me.

I'd told her I knew what I was doing here at Mathrafal. But I'd walked into this meeting with a chip on my shoulder.

"To destroy the dyke is a massive undertaking," said Ffion. "Which is why I've walked all the way from its southern end. But to break it will require real power—a heavy sacrifice." She glanced at her father. "We need the blades Mam-gu created."

"Oh." Dafydd sat back, disappointed. "Ffion, I'm so sorry. I wish I could, but I can't give you that."

"We already have Brycheiniog's," I countered, picking the raven's feather out of Ffion's cauldron with the tips of my fingers and setting it on the table. "Actually, a mutual friend helped get it for us. Prince Angws." I raised my eyebrows at Dafydd.

Osian cocked his head. "I heard Ffion dowsed and dug a well as part of the deal."

"The *official* story is that Meirion had already found the water," I said.

But Dafydd ignored us both. "I'm not Dad. I can't give away the llafn. I don't even know where it is."

"Do you know *what* it is?" Ffion asked. Dafydd shifted uncomfortably. But his glance to Osian answered the question for me.

"I told him years ago, before it was lost," said Osian.

I scoffed. "Of course you did."

Dafydd blinked at me. "What's that supposed to mean?"

"It means it's clear that Dad's not the only one who had favorites." I gestured at Osian, hands shaking. "Did Dad know you bound the two of them?"

"It was unnecessary that he know," Osian said evenly.

Unnecessary to tell Dad—or Ffion, apparently. But necessary to give Dafydd a mark of kingship when we were only children.

I had always known I was my father's second choice. I hadn't known Osian considered me entirely irrelevant, too.

What had I ever done to him? With Osian's chosen two connected, did I even have a chance at the future I'd worked for?

Ffion knitted her pale fingers together. On the knuckle of her right pinkie, I noticed a star-shaped freckle.

She'd cupped my face with that hand only this morning. Before I knew she'd never been meant for me.

"Look." Dafydd made an obvious effort to collect himself. "This is irrelevant. The blade is lost."

"You could ask the ravens where it is, Dafydd," Osian said. My brother stiffened.

I was surprised Osian had spoken up to help us. But from the way he was watching Ffion, it was clear he wasn't doing it on my behalf.

"What ravens, Dad?" she asked.

"Oh. There are sighted ravens in the columbarium again," Osian said absently. "Didn't I tell you?"

"I found tracks from a llamhigyn y dŵr the day before yesterday," Ffion said. Osian's expression lit with interest.

Sighted ravens at Mathrafal. A water leaper on the dyke. My stomach felt like it had fallen through the floor.

"Could you speak to them, Dafydd?" Ffion's eyes shone.

"No." If I thought he'd looked pained before, my brother was in agony now. "Ffion, I would help you if I could. But I—the ravens . . . I just can't."

I watched him, curious.

Where I'd always loathed magic, Dafydd had welcomed it. Had something changed? Or was it only the ravens he feared?

My brother stared at his hands as she changed the subject. "Dad, Gwanwyn told us the Foxhall came calling," she said. "What did they want?"

Osian's absent eyes sharpened. "They came to offer their services to Cadell after they declined Taliesin's offer. Their aim is to crush Offa's attack without restoring magic to Wales. Your father rides with them," he added, glancing at me.

"What?" Ffion gasped. "Why?"

"It's in their interest to keep enchantment unattainable for hedge-witches and their ilk," said Osian. "And you know how little they care for the lost creatures, or wild things in general."

"Dad left with them, we think for Ceredigion," Dafydd finished. "So now—"

"So now we're competing against one another, as well as—Dad himself?" I pushed back from the table.

My mind was racing. My heart was beating hard.

Dafydd shrugged. "Evidently."

"What will he do if he's the one to succeed, not us?" I demanded.

Did I want that? If Dad succeeded in crushing the attack while keeping magic out—was that as good as a win, for me? It had been my very first plan, my very first choice. Exactly what I'd wanted from the outset.

Ffion frowned. "Didn't the vision foretell the king's death? Dad, what exactly did you see?"

"Cadell on a pike. Nothing to indicate how," Osian said. "My sight was hazy, as if clouded by smoke."

Dafydd winced. "He said he'll avoid open battle," he said dully. Guilt crossed his face. "I don't know what Dad will do if he succeeds, Tal. He was disappointed by my efforts and he seemed even less pleased with yours. After the Foxhall told him who you'd—about Ffion." He blushed.

I raised my head sharply. "Not pleased with Ffion?"

"Rhiannon hates me, remember?" Ffion said. "I'm sure she didn't come bearing flattering tales."

"Worse still, I'm afraid she's continuing to spew her poison to Cadell even as they travel together," said Osian. "She cannot be allowed to undermine your position as magician, Ffion. She cannot be allowed to keep magic out of the kingdom."

"As I have said many, many times, I don't want to be court magician, Dad," Ffion said, looking almost helpless with frustration at her father. I knew she couldn't care less about her position, that what truly worried her was her disappearing magic.

But I—I felt a bizarre combination of dread and temptation.

But if you shut your door tonight,
Make no room by your fire tonight,

No houseroom at your lamps tonight,
The same, someday, to you.

The threat had hung over me since that night years ago. But if magic never returned, the promise that had haunted me all these years would mean nothing.

"What are our next moves?" I asked. My voice was too loud; I didn't know who I was asking. For once, I couldn't spin a web out of all the threads in front of me.

Maybe I should give up. Let the Foxhall and my father take the victory.

"I still need to walk the length of the dyke through the castle," Ffion said. "It butts right up against the earthworks, so I'll need to go through the cellars."

"Fine." I nodded. "When? Now?"

"Tomorrow," she said. "I need to rest first."

"Yes, you both should rest," said Dafydd. His voice rang with concern, and I felt it like a rash on my skin.

"Save your worry for Ffion, Dafydd." I rose as well, chair screeching beneath me. "You're years too late to help me."

When I met Ffion in the cellar the next morning, Dafydd was already there, telling her a story. She sat on the floor laughing and looking almost shy, Gruffudd climbing all over her like an overgrown lap dog.

"I'm sure you're busy today, Dafydd," I said. "You don't have to join us."

"I wasn't sure if Ffion would need an escort," he said.

She held up her left hand, showing Dafydd my signet ring. "Opens any door in the castle. Isn't that what you said, Tal?"

"It is," I said, not quite smug.

"Not the prisons, not without Dad," Dafydd said. "And not the treasury."

"The prisons are empty."

Dafydd directed a significant glance at his boots, and I thought of Angws.

"Gods' candles—enough," Ffion bit out. "I'm starting."

She began in the buttery. Cauldron in hand, ivy trailing in the dust on the floor, singing as always, Ffion wove around racks of bragawd in barrels, moving from there to the pantry and the empty prisons, through the larder full of salt pork and fish and the armory full of weapons. All the while I watched for the llafn that Dafydd swore had been lost.

I couldn't help watching her, too. And watching Dafydd watch her.

"What was it like, growing up here?" she asked as she entered the treasury. "In a place like this?"

"Oh, you know." I pulled a clinking bag from a shelf and dumped a few ceiniogau into my palm. "We spent our childhoods playing knucklebones with silver. Rolling around in money."

"Put those away." Dafydd snatched the coins from my hand and stuffed them back in the bag, exasperated. "Our childhood was normal. We learned like other boys. We played like other boys. Only the setting was unusual."

"And your father's position," Ffion said lightly.

Nothing about our childhoods had been normal. Dafydd had grown up in palaces, and after Mam had passed from my father's favor, she and I had lived in a fine house nearby. I'd been just separated enough from the court to feel I didn't belong in the castle, and royal enough that I didn't belong with the children in town.

"We used to play soldiers with the sons of Father's chieftains, even before we began proper exercises with them," I said, running a finger over a row of jeweled daggers. "Dafydd taught me how to throw an axe."

Dafydd straightened. "I'm surprised you remember that."

"How could I forget?" I asked, surprised myself at his reaction. Then I felt a frown cross my face. "We stopped drilling with them when I was about fourteen, though. Someone said we were going to start training seriously, and that it would have to be alone. Why was that?"

I hadn't thought of it in years. Soon after, Dafydd had announced he didn't want to be king, and our relationship had been fundamentally changed by the rest of the world's reaction.

Dafydd's face shuttered. "We should move on."

Ffion blinked at him. "Of course. Yes." She continued across the treasury floor, feet leaving small prints in the dirt, singing. *Out of my reach, out of my reach.*

I wondered how well her magic was holding together, after the near disaster in the woods. I wondered when things would begin to fray.

"Your mam-gu taught me that song," said Osian, appearing in the doorway. All three of us jumped.

"You know, Dad," Ffion said casually, "plenty of witches and magicians work successful magic while fully clothed."

"Nudity makes people uncomfortable," Osian said.

Well. There was no denying that.

"How are you progressing?" he asked Ffion, bending to pat Gruffudd's back.

"Nearly finished."

"Good," he said. "I've come to tell the three of you I've planned a celebration for tomorrow evening."

Ffion stopped short.

"A celebration?" Dafydd's voice was flat. "Osian, we're on the brink of war." It was strange to hear Dafydd speak so coolly to the magician. But Ffion's father had lied to him, too.

Still, if Osian noticed Dafydd's aloofness, it didn't bother him. "And with the rumor spreading of my lost magic, no time could be better to celebrate our new court magician." He bit at a hangnail, gesturing with his other hand at Ffion.

"Dad." She set her teeth. "I've told you, I don't want to be—"

"This is an essential display of strength," said Osian. "Unless you'd like to see Rhiannon assume that position—because, as you know, she's traveling with Cadell at this very moment—I suggest you make it."

Ffion blanched.

Osian stepped closer. "You and I have very different means of working, Ffion. You take after my mother. And I accept that." He glanced down into her cauldron, full of odds and ends and the one blade we'd laid hands on. "If you wish to cede your rightful place to people who have no respect for your methods, by all means, remain in the shadows."

Rhiannon. The Foxhall. My father. Magic kept exactly where I wanted it. I fought to control my expression.

Ffion ground her teeth. "Fine," she said. "I'll declare my presence to Mathrafal, if you think it will keep Rhiannon at bay."

"Excellent." Osian left us, looking gleeful.

As Ffion finished, there was no more singing or banter between us.

And there was no more argument that the brink of war wasn't the perfect place for a party.

36

DAFYDD

I sat on my father's throne with Gruffudd at my feet and sweat more than I ever had in the forge.

One by one, petitioners came forward, presenting me with disputes over property lines, over livestock lost through damaged walls, over seed sold that had failed to flourish.

Capable of anything—it was what I'd always feared becoming. But I felt completely incapable sitting in my father's place, like a paperweight, or a scarecrow. As much a pretender on the throne as I was in the forge. But I had no choice but to be there.

You will hold Mathrafal in my absence. You understand why you will do this without complaint.

Tal. Gwanwyn. Even as my brother stewed, he and his mother were the reason I couldn't walk away.

Worst of all, I sat alone, since I'd declined Osian's offer to join me. Angry as I felt toward my father, mistrusting Osian felt even worse.

For petition after petition, I reached no easy answers. Forge work was straightforward labor—or it had felt that way, before I'd learned about the other smith's lost business. But nothing felt clear in the throne room. I could feel myself taking too long; I asked for too much clarification. Uncertainty burrowed into my bones as I saw a dozen sides to every story, a dozen ways I could make the wrong judgment.

Tal and Ffion had told me King Meirion had earned the nickname the Dithering Crow for his indecision. Listening to argument after plea after explanation, I found myself sympathizing.

The job was impossible. I wished I were in the forge. I wished I were with Ffion. It had been a rush, watching her work at the dyke and in the cellar after seeing her work in visions for so many years.

Was she bucking against inheriting her father's position for the same reasons I was refusing mine, I wondered? Should I try to change her mind?

Even if I refused to become king, Ffion might take her father's place. Then she would be here, really here, and not just in my thoughts.

It could happen. I could feel her warming to me. I wasn't as smooth or sharp as Tal, but I knew I wasn't wrong.

But even if our bond could be undone, how I would feel about Ffion sharing one with my father, or my brother? I couldn't decide which I'd hate more.

Once I had seen Father's petitioners, it was time to mingle with his high men, and this was much worse. Though I'd hoped to speak with them about the threats we faced—Mercia, our dissipating magic—conversation returned inevitably to sly, ambitious talk about lands and titles they hoped to be granted by my father's successor.

I'd always known this was where Tal would thrive. He could handle these men and their politicking. He could make deals and trades and accept whatever sordidness the throne required, because he was one of them. They had their aims, and he had his own.

But more and more, I wondered if that was a good thing.

More and more, I wondered if the king should be a check on selfishness and scheming, and not a model for it.

In the dark of the forge, I held the bent rod of the auger in the fire and waited.

I was good at waiting. I always had been.

"Busy, as always," came Ffion's voice. A thrill spiked through me.

After she'd arrived at Mathrafal, I'd told her I wanted to speak more. I'd hoped she'd come find me out here—and she had.

"Lots to do," I said, watching the coals.

"I meant Gruffudd." Ffion grinned as she scratched behind his ears, and I smiled, too. "Are you too busy to talk?" she asked. "Because I have some questions."

"What about?" A ridiculous response. But I kept my voice neutral.

Ffion looked at me disbelievingly. "Well, for a start, about what you're *doing* out here," she said, holding out her arms. "I've heard a little about you from my father, and a little more from your brother. But I want to hear what you have to say. I want to hear why you're the elder prince of Powys—bound to me because I'm supposed to be your magician someday—and you're hiding in a smithy like you're doing some kind of penance."

"I'm not doing penance. I'm repairing an auger. They're for digging fence post holes."

"I know what an auger is for."

"I work for free for people who can't afford to pay the other smith in town," I said tightly. "I'm helping people who need it."

"Pity the smith whose customers you're taking."

She really was her father's daughter.

"Dafydd, it's time for you to explain yourself," she said. "The gods know you need to talk to someone. And besides that, you owe me," she added, almost irritably. "You spent twelve years watching me, and I—" She paused, pushing a pair of adzes and a hand plane out of the way to sit on my workbench. "I don't have the lay of things at Mathrafal, or with you, or with you and Tal and your father. And I need to understand."

The rod glowed red in the fire. I held my silence as I sharpened the end to a fine point on my anvil, then thrust it into the flames again when it went cold.

I felt nervous to speak. But hadn't I always wondered what Ffion saw in her visions of me, when I still believed she had them? Hadn't I always hoped they showed her the best of who I was?

She'd never had visions. But this was my chance.

"I was fifteen when I told my father I didn't want the throne. I told him right after an—incident." I paused. "The one that stopped our training with the chieftains' sons."

Ffion frowned. "What happened?"

"When we were children, Tal and I played with the sons of our father's men. We were always brave Powysian soldiers, trouncing soldiers from Gwynedd or Brycheiniog or Ceredigion or Mercia." I gave a bitter laugh. "When I was eight years old, one of my tutors had to explain to me that three of those kingdoms are Welsh.

"Years later, my father was pushing north into Gwynedd in earnest, and he'd pushed a chieftain—a friend's father—to raid border villages more aggressively. But one village gave as good as they got, and the chieftain came back with his leg missing below the knee."

I pulled the rod from the fire, cinched its end in the vise, and began to wrap the other end around a metal form with a pair of tongs, my hands beginning to shake.

Please, gods, don't let my father be killed.

I forced myself to continue. "My friend was as proud of his father as ever, and his father was as fearsome a chieftain as before. But his life was harder and more painful. And my friend blamed my father, and me, by extension."

"So what did you do?" she asked.

"I asked Dad to stop the raids. But he said that we were pushing north because Gwynedd had raided two towns at our northern border, and he asked if I'd like to explain to those people why we hadn't gotten justice for their lost homes and blood payment for their dead." I looked back to Ffion, feeling the weight of that question settle over me all over again. "And that was when I decided."

She shook her head. "I don't understand."

"I went back and forth with Dad, trying to figure out where all the fighting had begun. But I couldn't find the beginning, and I couldn't find a good answer to my father's question," I said. "There was no room for good at all. No line between black and white, just a gray fog I couldn't work through.

"'Cadell is capable of absolutely anything,' I overheard that chieftain saying to the other men, and it was exactly what I was afraid of becoming. Capable of anything." I gripped the auger handle, frustrated. "My father railed against Mercia for the same actions he took. Or—he said they weren't the same. But I couldn't see the difference."

I'd explained all of this to Dad. He'd said nothing, just as he'd said nothing the day I began building the forge. He'd thought I'd get over my *delicate conscience*.

Well. I wasn't the only one who'd had to get good at waiting.

"That sounds miserable," Ffion said quietly. "I'm sorry your father didn't understand. I've lived with parents who don't listen." She paused. "Tell me one more thing, and I'll leave you in peace."

I didn't want her to leave. I just wanted to talk to her about easier things. "What is it?"

"Why won't you give Tal the blade, Dafydd?" she asked. "You don't want to be king. So why won't you give it to him?"

"Ffion—" I couldn't work and talk to her at the same time. Not because the forge demanded so much of my attention, but because she did. I wrenched the auger off its form and shoved it into the water bucket; steam rose up with a hiss. "We talked about this."

She eyed me reproachfully. "Dafydd. Yesterday was an opening negotiation. Surely you knew we wouldn't leave it at that."

"I knew Tal wouldn't. I hoped you might." I paused. "Then again, considering the way you wore that landlord down, I should probably have known better." Last year, Ffion had traded a pair of frivolous charms to a landlord just outside Foxhall in exchange for his not raising rents on his farmers. It had obviously galled her to spend magic on spells to keep him and his wife from visibly aging, but she'd done it.

Ffion laughed. "You saw that?"

"It was amazing. You were a force, Ffion." I didn't even bother trying to keep the admiration out of my voice. She looked away then, but she was smiling.

"Do you want to know what I think, Dafydd?" she asked after a moment.

Of course I wanted to know what she thought.

She didn't wait for my answer.

Ffion pulled a feather from her pocket. The raven's feather. I took a step back from the workbench.

"It's Brycheiniog's blade," she said. "I brought it so you'd know I was telling you the truth."

I knew what it was. I would rather have gone without the reassurance.

Ffion laid the feather down next to my tools, then cleared her throat. "I think you find Tal a little bit grasping," she said slowly, keenly. "I think you find him gauche, compared to your own very appropriate modesty. You, the prince who does not want to be king, and he, the prince who wants absolutely everything."

"I don't."

"I think you do," she continued. "I think you decided years ago, for some reason, that wanting was shameful. And by extension, I think you think Tal being so eager to do your father's bidding and compete is somehow . . ." She shook her head. "Grasping."

Wanting, shameful? If only she knew. "That's not it," I said. "I just can't give it to him."

"Have you changed your mind?" she asked. "Have you decided you want to be king instead of Tal?"

No. Yes. I wasn't sure.

The job was too heavy for me. But could Tal bear it any better than I could?

"Tal continues to demonstrate terrible judgment, Ffion," I said, avoiding her question.

"Tal wants to protect Powys. That's a start."

"You think it's Powys he wants to protect?" I asked.

Ffion said nothing, just considered me, like she was trying to think of a song for her spellwork. Then she said something I didn't expect.

"Tal doesn't trust me, Dafydd. I've kept things from him, but he keeps things from me, too. Big things. Things like—" She hesitated. "I'm just not sure he trusts me. And I'm not asking you to tell me what made him this way," she added quickly.

"What are you getting at?" Frustration coursed through me. Couldn't she see how I felt? Wasn't it obvious I didn't want to talk about Tal anymore?

I wanted one thing: to have Ffion at my side. And Tal—Tal, who could only play my father's game because I'd agreed to play, too—had gotten to her first.

"I'm worried Tal still wishes he could have worked with the Foxhall instead of me," she blurted out. "He reacted so strangely when my dad told us that they had come and left with your father. And now I'm afraid—" She broke off, shaking her head. "I'm afraid I'm losing him, Dafydd. I need him on my side, to see this journey through. Magic *has* to be restored to Wales."

"I agree." But my voice was guarded.

I'd fixed things with Ffion, just as I'd intended. She wanted to know me now. She trusted me enough to ask for my help.

But she was asking me to face the ravens on Tal's behalf.

I turned back to my work, and turned my back on her. "I'm sorry, Ffion. I can't."

Once, when I was a child, I had climbed into the castle columbarium, probably hiding from a party or a throne room audience. I had regretted it immediately; the birds had made a mess, feathers and dung everywhere. But that wasn't what had driven me back down to the ground as fast as my legs could carry me.

I had never understood what folk meant by *sighted*. But there at the top of the ladder, I found myself nose to nose with an unkindness of sighted ravens—seven or eight of them that'd made their home in the little niches lining the columbarium.

At that moment, I had looked at the ravens, and the ravens had looked at me. And that look alone had cut me to the heart.

I had run away too quickly for them to speak to me. But that was what they did, if you let them: offered you the truth about yourself you were most afraid to hear, whether great or terrible or both. Sometimes, if you bared your soul to them, they would offer you another answer as well—a mystery, a well-guarded secret.

They could tell me where Powys's blade was, if I asked.

But I had Ffion here at Mathrafal now. I'd had enough of being cut to the heart.

37

FFION

Mathrafal's great hall was red stone and embroidered hangings and—tonight, at least—a truly appalling number of weasels and windbags who served Cadell.

I'd resented their presence since I arrived at the castle, the way they made Tal's edges sharper than ever, the way he became charming around them, or cold, or dignified—whatever he thought they wanted from him, whatever he thought they needed. So I wasn't overly delighted when I found him standing in a cluster of high men and chieftains with Gwanwyn and Dafydd, Tal in his red coat, Dafydd in blue, Gwanwyn standing between them.

"And so we *must* raise taxes," one man was saying. "To answer Mercia's army, we must raise taxes, press men into service, and arm them to the teeth. Pay their wives a pittance for their deaths, if we must."

Tal brushed an invisible speck of dirt off his coat. "That's certainly one solution."

"These people will do anything for a penny," another man agreed.

"Cadfan, didn't you just marry your youngest daughter to a high man my father's age?" Dafydd asked him.

"The connection was excellent, and she is my least favorite child," the man—Cadfan—said. Dafydd blinked at him, and Cadfan looked surprised himself. I put my hand into my pocket and bit my lip.

Dafydd had been upset when I left his forge. I wondered how things stood between us now.

I wonder how he'd feel if he knew what I was up to.

When Dafydd raised his eyes again, he spotted me. "Ffion!"

Another man laughed unkindly. "Has one of you brought a mistress to the magician's gathering?" he asked. "Like father, like sons, I suppose."

I felt myself redden. Dafydd contained himself with obvious effort.

Tal did slightly better, a muscle feathering in his jaw. "She is not my mistress," he said evenly. "In fact—" Tal raised his voice, expertly commanding the attention of the room. The crwth, harp, and drums quieted. "This is Ffion vch Osian. Her father has chosen her for Mathrafal's new court magician." I glanced sharply at Tal, confused. But he avoided my eye.

What was he doing?

"Prettier than Osian, to be sure," another chieftain mumbled. "More clothes, though, and more's the pity." Tal ignored this. But Dafydd couldn't help looking at me, eyes angry and sorry.

He wasn't the only one looking, either. The whole room was staring at me now, in my borrowed gold-colored gown and Tal's signet ring.

I wanted to threaten them all with bad sleep and loose bowels. But I knew to hold my tongue.

Tal began again. "You all know, of course, that our father has tasked both of us with destroying the dyke," he said smoothly. "Ffion, the architect of my plan to that end, has walked the entire length of King Offa's Dyke, from Merthyr-Tewdrig all the way here to Mathrafal." The murmurs grew surprised—impressed?

The high man who'd spoken first waved a hand. "You're a pup. Armies are the answer."

I knew to hold my tongue. But Dafydd didn't. "Of course that's your answer," he said, sounding angrier still, and my stomach twisted with guilt. "You'll never be sent away to die holding a pike you don't know how to wield, leaving a passel of hungry children at home."

"I have made prudent choices to avoid such undesirable outcomes."

"Yes, you were very wise to be born a rich man," Dafydd agreed.

Tal interrupted. "Ffion will walk the rest of the journey from Mathrafal to Prestatyn, and in six days' time, she will destroy the dyke with a spell tested by two generations of witches. That is," he added, "if my brother will consent to help her."

And there it was. Tal's next gambit.

He hadn't told the crowd what, exactly, he wanted. He also hadn't told me he was going to do this.

Cadell's men exchanged glances. "Surely Prince Dafydd will assist you."

"Of course he will," said another.

Tal turned an expectant glance Dafydd's way.

Public pressure wasn't the way to get his brother on our side. But I knew this was about more than getting the blade.

"Have we not harassed Brycheiniog and Gwynedd and our other neighbors for decades?" Dafydd blurted out. Gwanwyn crossed the circle and put a hand on his arm—to calm him? To caution him? I couldn't tell. "Is Powys the only kingdom with the right to peace and safety?"

"All men seek to increase their holdings," said one of the high men, looking confused. "All kings seek to increase their kingdoms."

Dafydd gave a bitter laugh. "And covetousness is the oldest story known to us all."

"Such is not covetousness," another chieftain said severely. "Such is destiny. And the commoners may have been pleased by how you received their petitions, but if you do not understand the right of kings as appointed by the gods, perhaps you have no right to your father's throne at all."

"I can't distribute the castle's treasures on a whim." Dafydd's face was bright red.

"This is not a whim," said Tal. "This is a plan, one backed by my court magician."

I gripped the sighted raven's feather in my pocket, feeling horrified. Tal had told me to bring the blade tonight. I just hadn't realized what he intended to do.

"Leave me out of this. Turning the court against Dafydd was not *our* plan," I said to him through my teeth. "This won't work on him."

"And you know Dafydd so well?" he asked. With the whole room watching us, he spoke quickly, quietly. But there was a challenge in his voice.

I gave the tiniest shake of my head. "Better than you do, apparently, if you think this is the way."

Mistrust of crowds was Tal's essential principle. I couldn't believe he'd weaponized one against his brother.

Another of Cadell's high men spoke up. "And yet—why should Prince Dafydd be coerced into aiding his brother in their father's quest?" he asked. "Why should Prince Taliesin lay claim to castle treasures to which he has no right?"

Though the man had interfered with Tal's play for what we needed, I was grateful Dafydd wasn't standing alone anymore—until he continued.

"After all," he said, nodding to me. "Who is Ffion vch Osian? We know her father, but we do not know her. We haven't seen her magic. Let her prove herself, if she wants Mathrafal's gifts." Murmurs of agreement joined him.

I tried to control my expression. But panic welled up inside me.

Some of it was from the difficulty I'd confronted time and again with Tal and others: these people were used to my father's sort of magic, the rich and bloody kind. What would they think of mine, in comparison?

As for the rest: Power had once been a gentle beast content to curl up in my lap, easy and familiar. Now it was a fey thing, elusive as our lost creatures, something I sensed more outside me than within me.

And I was being asked, once again, for a demonstration.

I could've strangled Tal. He'd started this. And though he was cleverly composed as always, I could see the slow swell of horror behind his eyes.

He'd been with me in the woods; he knew that my abilities might become less reliable the nearer the new moon came. And he knew another slip from me could ruin all his efforts tonight.

But it wasn't Tal who spoke up in my defense.

"She's already proven herself," Dafydd said irritably. "Everyone's heard about the well she dowsed and dug herself at Black Darren. She found water where none had been found for a decade." I glanced up at him, feeling a rush of gratitude.

Dafydd didn't know my magic was disappearing. He wasn't trying to save face. He only saw that I was uncomfortable and wanted to help.

"I heard that was King Meirion's work," sneered another man. "And anyway, how does service to *him* prove anything? Digging a well for Black Darren? What a boon to Mathrafal!" The crowd around him rumbled their agreement.

I was so tired of defending the magic I worked to petty, possessive men.

"You dishonor your princes and our long line of magicians by your mistrust," said Dafydd.

I gave him a tiny, grateful smile. But Cadell's men didn't look persuaded.

"Ffion." Tal looked nervous, apologetic. But I didn't nod my forgiveness. He'd started this.

"I work where there is need," I finally said. "What need does Mathrafal have?"

I hadn't noticed my father join us. But suddenly, he was beside me.

"Vision," he said. "Mathrafal needs vision. And you, Ffion, can provide it."

Could I?

He nodded slowly, significantly, like he'd expected this to happen, like all of this was going to plan. It made me want to throw a tantrum out of sheer spite.

Briefly, I wondered if my father meant I should *pretend* to have a vision, but he'd never suggest such a thing—mostly because I could never act the part convincingly.

Suddenly, though, I had a glimmer of an idea.

I pushed past Tal, stomping over to the sideboard to seize a cake and a beeswax candle. "Break it," I said, joining the princes' hands and shoving the cake into their palms.

Tal recoiled. "It's sticky."

"Do it."

They broke the cake, crumbs and currants falling onto the floor. Dafydd came away with the larger piece.

"A vision for Prince Dafydd, then." I held out my hand for his half, then ate it in two bites. It was delicious, sweeter than anything I'd tasted in years. "Come closer."

He obeyed, and I put my right hand on his cheek, holding the candle in my left.

"Ffion?" Tal looked confused. I could've snapped his head off.

"If this fails and I lose the trust of the court," I hissed, "it's your fault."

I was glad Dafydd had won, and not only because I was furious at his brother.

My grandmother's spellbook had little to say about visions, beyond explaining that they called for an offering and a flame or a scrying bowl. It wasn't a kind of magic Mam-gu had ordinarily performed, though Dad often had. Some witches received visions from their familiars or their anchors, as Dad had from Pendwmpian; some people, it was said, had received them from dragons; and some received them via connections like the one that existed between Dad and King Cadell, or between Dafydd and me.

Our connection was new to me. I hated the idea of exploring it in front of a crowd. And I knew that these days Dafydd felt as uncertain of our bond and of my father as I did.

But our bond was threaded with magic my father had already worked. Angry as I was at him for pushing me, he'd given me something my slippery magic and I could grasp onto.

Dafydd's jaw shifted under my palm.

"Be still," I whispered to him. I couldn't tell if he was trembling or I was.

I pulled a song from my memory, looked into the flame, and began to sing.

Carts are for rivers
And hands are for shoes
Boats are for forests
And I am for you
Wheels are for windows
And candles for keys
Stones are for blankets
And you are for me

Cakes are for anvils
And cookpots for plows
Pipes are for digging
And I am for thou

Hats are for hammers
And spindles for clubs
Bragawd for washing
And we are for us

It was a courting song I had heard at dances growing up, and—based on the crowd's blank reaction—clearly one that had not traveled the distance from Foxhall to Mathrafal. I'd heard songs about couples who suited like a needle and thread or birds of a feather, but I liked this one better.

For a long moment, nothing happened. Then, just when fear was eating me alive, when I couldn't see anything at all for staring into the fire—suddenly, I saw more than I could take in.

Dafydd walking beside me alongside the dyke, the sun in his eyes and a smile on his face. Dafydd climbing up a ladder into a columbarium, muscles straining. Dafydd across a fire from me, something between want and fear in his eyes. Dafydd in a silver-painted throne room, now looking truly horrified.

Dafydd and me alone in a room at an inn, faint moonlight on his face, and words on his lips I wished I could hear.

I couldn't blink. I stared so hard my eyes and my head ached.

Every scene was faded, distant, faltering the way my spell had faltered in the woods—the way my father had described his own vision of the attack and Cadell's death.

It was enough to explain nothing. Enough to promise all sorts of things.

I gasped and drew back, blinking away burning afterimages to find I was looking into Dafydd's face.

"What did you see?" he asked quietly.

His eyes were dark on mine. His voice was like a hand on my waist.

And the bond—working through it had felt like sewing the first stitch in a work of embroidery. Like the start of a rich and beautiful effort. Like the first small, fragile piece of something that could last forever.

Honeysuckle burst from the ground near the walls and climbed, twisting, up the rafters. The crowd gasped, delighted.

"Tell us what you saw," one of the high men demanded, pressing close. "We deserve to know."

Dafydd tried to argue. But I'd caught my breath by then and I squared to face the man, heart beating hard.

I couldn't lie to him. Not with the raven's feather in my pocket. But I could tell him exactly what else I was thinking.

"What I saw is between the prince and myself," I said. "You've had your performance. And now, you will remember your place."

More gasps—and not of delight. Gwanwyn watched me, brown eyes inscrutable.

Some of the men seemed angry at my silence. But though the flowers gently waving from the supports overhead were nothing more than a sign of my magic, not magic itself, I had proven myself.

I had proven something, anyway.

"What did you see, Ffion?" Tal asked. Both brothers looked at me, unsettled.

"I saw that I needed to go pant shallowly in a corner," I snapped. "Please, excuse me."

I found my father studying the honeysuckle vine running up the wall. "Pretty," he said absently when I stalked to his side. "Though not an overly powerful statement."

"Why did you do that?" I asked him through gritted teeth. "I told you about—" I dropped my voice. "About my magic feeling weaker. What if I hadn't been able to produce a vision? I've never even tried before!"

He shrugged. "But you did."

"But I—" I clenched my fists, wanting to beat my head against the wall. *"I might not have,"* I ground out.

"Certainly," Dad said agreeably. "In any case, I've been down to the dyke to investigate."

I straightened. "What did you find?"

He scratched his head. "Magic pouring off it, just as you said. I've never noticed it before, and I believe I would have, so it must be new. But Ffion, it's not Mercian magic," he said. "It's Welsh."

I stared at my father, not understanding. "What?"

Welsh magic. Welsh magic, in a Mercian build.

Did it mean Mercia *didn't* have magic? Did it mean a conspiracy was in play?

Across the room, Dafydd was helping some small boys fill their plates from the sideboard. Elsewhere, Tal made a joke, and group of women laughed.

I knew I should go to Tal. I should tell him everything. But I couldn't let him or Dafydd learn the truth.

"So what now?" I asked, faltering.

"I've already sent two scouts to the Mercian camp thirty miles across the dyke. If they hear anything, they'll return to tell us." I nodded, and he fell silent, still watching the flowers.

"We should rejoin the others," my father finally said. "Keep making your case to Cadell's men."

I didn't have to ask which case as he drifted away. He meant for me to keep putting myself forward for a role I'd never wanted.

It didn't matter to Dad what I wanted.

And as I thought of Rhiannon becoming court magician, I wondered if what I wanted ought to matter at all.

I spent the next hour halfheartedly obeying my father's orders. I danced with chieftains; I conversed with high men. But the more I said, the worse matters seemed to get. When I told someone named Elgan he would strip his soil if he didn't rotate the crops in his new fields, he looked offended. "And what holdings do you possess?" he asked.

"None." I bit into a hunk of leek pie, scattering crumbs all over his shirtfront. "But a traveler once told me that everyone in his homeland rotated theirs, and some Foxhall farmers tried it. Moved their barley to their wheat field, their wheat to their rye field—you understand. Never saw a better yield." I tried to brush the crumbs off his shirt, but Elgan jerked back.

"Country farmers and foreigners," he sniffed. "What people for our magician to be mixing with."

The wives and daughters I met were better company. Some drew near shyly to compliment the honeysuckle my magic had grown; others excitedly asked me for love spells, or to tell their futures—how many children they'd have, how long they would live. I decided one vision per evening was my limit, but I told a few how to put protective charms on their doors or ease difficult periods with willow bark and shepherd's purse.

"Anyway, there's no charm or spell that can force love," I said, sighing theatrically. "Unless you count bragawd as a charm, and I regret to inform you its effects are only temporary." Laughter.

And that was when I finally met the famous Luned.

I hadn't noticed her approaching with her circle of friends, and she didn't introduce herself; presumably, she didn't think she needed to. But loose-haired, elaborately gowned, and smelling of expensive olive oil soap—she couldn't have been anyone else.

"Real love doesn't need charms or spells," Luned said, authoritative. "Although—I think we all know who'd want one if they existed." She cut her eyes at Gwanwyn. The girls I'd been joking with grew quiet, exchanging uncomfortable looks.

I blinked at Luned. Surely I'd misunderstood. "No, you're right. There's no magic that can make s—"

"I can't believe she even still lives here," Luned continued, delicately selecting a fennel and anise candy from a plate. "Cadell has a new favorite now. Surely she understands that."

If *I* understood correctly, the king had had five or six favorites since he'd parted ways with Gwanwyn, but I was too busy trying not to gape at Luned to reply.

"She ought to know she's not wanted," said one of her friends. "I can't imagine staying where I wasn't wanted."

"Can't you?" Luned put her head to one side and stared at her. The other girl blinked.

When Tal had learned his mother's guards had left, I'd wondered if some kind of misunderstanding was to blame. Obviously, it was not.

And to think—when she'd walked up, I'd almost been enjoying myself.

"But really, to make such a fuss that Midwinter. Can you imagine not going away afterward?" said a third girl unkindly. "Poor Prince Taliesin, saddled with a mother like that. I can't imagine how awkward it was for the king, having her here."

"Gwanwyn is a clever woman," said one of the girls I'd been speaking to before, sounding nervous but determined. "Prince Taliesin trusts her."

"Gwanwyn." The first girl laughed. "Imagine being named 'spring,' in her time of life."

"People are named as babies, Aneira. Don't be stupid," Luned said, annoyed. "Anyway, I noticed her glaring at you during your vision," she added confidentially to me. "Don't take it personally. She's just old and sour, and she hates anyone who gets close to Tal."

Gwanwyn could glare at me all she liked, I decided then. I wanted to kick Luned down the stairs.

The Foxhall had punished my mam, too, after she had separated from my father—demoting her, cutting her out, speculating about what she might've done to drive him away. They'd been petty and cruel. Luned's gossip felt all too familiar.

And then there was the other thing they'd said. *Midwinter.*

What had happened at Midwinter?

"I am protective of Tal," agreed a voice at my back. "But only because men can be so thoughtless when they choose their companions."

I turned. Tal and Gwanwyn stood behind me.

A muscle feathered in Tal's jaw. "Excuse me," he said, and turned for the hall doors. Luned looked genuinely regretful as he walked away.

"Tal—" I started after him, but Gwanwyn caught my elbow.

"Don't follow him, Ffion."

I met her eyes, cleared my throat. "I'm sure he'll be back soon, anyway."

"With you here, certainly," she agreed. I flushed. "I hope I'm wrong about you," she added. "But Ffion—the boys' father has already pitted them against one another. They don't need another reason for resentment or rivalry."

I crossed my arms. "I don't know what you're talking about."

"You're playing the boys off one another," she said, pinning me with that gaze so like Tal's. "You're leading Tal on a merry chase across the Marches, and now you've arrived here and felled Dafydd in one blow."

"I'm not leading Tal anywhere," I said. "He employed me. I am working for him."

"Then tell me he hasn't talked about the future with you," Gwanwyn said evenly. "If you tell me he hasn't, I'll believe you."

Would you be my magician if I became king?

You could live anywhere you wanted. At Mathrafal, with me. In Foxhall. Anywhere.

I swallowed hard.

"That's what I thought," she said. "Tal doesn't make plans for the future lightly, Ffion. And Dafydd? Do you really mean to say you haven't noticed the way he watches you? Were you really being fair earlier?" She glanced significantly at the honeysuckle hanging from the rafters.

My hand on his cheek. Honey on his fingers and on my lips. I knew what she was saying.

"Dafydd is a prince of Powys," I said finally. "So is Tal. I presume nothing. And that"—I gestured at the flowers—"Osian and Tal forced my hand to that."

"Your presumptions don't matter to me," she said. "I care about their hearts."

"I care about them, too. And there's something I'm missing about Tal. Some piece of him I'm not putting together. Luned said . . ." I hesitated. "What happened at Midwinter, Gwanwyn?"

"Ah, Luned." Gwanwyn sighed at the woman's name, but her face—if anything—grew less troubled, as though Cadell's mistress caused her far less worry than his sons. "Perpetually wishing I'd go. Perpetually baffled by my indescribable cheek at staying where I make folk uncomfortable. Do you know why I stay, when leaving would be so much easier?"

"For Tal." Could there be any other reason?

"I stay because Taliesin would not stay without me," she said. "And I want him to be near the court. I want him to pursue all his ambitions without worrying about me. And I pass him gossip," she added. "Because his position is only secure as long as he knows more than anyone else. Because his father . . ."

"Cadell favors Dafydd," I finished.

"Yes. And I would do anything for Tal. Including subjecting myself to the mockery of eighteen-year-old girls who don't know that they won't be young forever, either."

"Luned is a fool," I said simply. "But you still haven't answered my question."

"If Tal hasn't trusted you with the truth, why should I?" she asked.

I gripped the raven's feather in my skirt pocket and willed her to confess.

I knew it was wrong. But I did it for the same reason I wanted her to confide in me.

"Because I only want to understand him," I said.

"Answer me this," Gwanwyn said. "Would you set your kingdom at naught to protect the ones you love the most?"

I thought of my quest with Tal. My journey to destroy the dyke and restore magic.

All to return Cadno to the land of the living.

"I don't know." I hesitated. "I might."

"That was his crime," Gwanwyn said. "The night the Mari Lwyd came walking."

Four Years Ago

TAL

It wasn't that I distrusted Midwinter magic more or less than any other kind. That just happened to be the night my luck ran out.

Mam did her best to distract me after sundown, making treacle till midnight, baking apples and cakes as the snow fell around our house near the keep. We hadn't lived in the castle proper since I was small; when the court had moved permanently to Mathrafal, Dad had suggested rather pointedly that Mam take a house in town, instead.

So it was up to me to take care of my mother. But I didn't mind. I was fourteen, and I was old enough.

But I felt afraid, still, when I heard them coming through the streets. Their feet crunched through the snow that lay thick on the cobblestones; bells jingled on the knees of the dancers; whips made of holly branches swished through the air.

Tonight, and oh, the longest night,
The longest night, the longest night,
Tonight, and oh, the longest night,
Come we now to your door.

It was Midwinter, the longest night of the year, when the Mari Lwyd went walking. No one knew where she might appear, but if she came to your threshold with her party of dancers and revelers, whether you lived in a hovel or a fine house, you were expected to open the door.

A Midwinter revel, a brush with the Mari Lwyd's chilly magic—most people found the prospect exciting.

Then again, *most people* weren't Mathrafal's pariahs. *Most people* hadn't been held responsible when Dafydd announced his disinterest in the throne a few months earlier.

But when my brother had retreated to the shadows, somehow Mathrafal had decided my mother and I were to blame.

And now it seemed half the town was on our doorstep, singing.

Tonight, and oh, the coldest night,
The coldest night, the coldest night,
Tonight, and oh, the coldest night,
Come we now to your fire.

Tonight, and oh, the darkest night,
The darkest night, the darkest night,
Tonight, and oh, the darkest night,
Come we now to your lamps.

So open up your door tonight,
Make room beside your fire tonight,
Give houseroom at your lamps tonight,
No more than is your due.

There was a crack in the door I'd been meaning to patch but hadn't yet. Dafydd was really better at that sort of thing. I put my eye to it and looked out at the crowd.

Waiting in the snow, the Mari Lwyd was a horrible sight.

She was a resurrected unicorn, all empty eye sockets and missing horn, a shawl over her head to hide its absence. Her party danced around her, the merryman on his fiddle, Pwnsh and Siwan scuffling drunkenly in the snow. Our neighbors trailed them, daring each other to get closer. One of them clutched the loop-handled wassail cup in his hands.

The custom was for the inhabitants of a house to argue good-naturedly with the Mari Lwyd before letting her in. Her song had six stanzas, after all; after each, the residents would offer their excuses, the sillier and more elaborate, the better.

But if you shut your door tonight,
Make no room by your fire tonight,
No houseroom at your lamps tonight,
The same, someday, to you.

"Tal." My mam came to my side, reaching for the latch. "Tal, we have to let them in. It will be fine."

She opened the door—just a sliver, just an inch—and snow and freezing air and the longest night swirled inside. I pulled her hand away and slammed it shut.

"It will not be fine," I said.

Tradition dictated all sorts of foolishness once the Mari Lwyd was invited in—whipping the house's women with holly branches, overeating and overdrinking and overstaying one's welcome. Ordinarily, it was all in good fun, with the whips delivered as light, teasing swats, and consumption restricted to what a family could afford to share.

But I had heard how the people in the village spoke to my mother. How they spoke about her when they thought she wasn't listening.

I knew if I let our neighbors into my house, their behavior would not be in good fun.

Once upon a time, I might have counted on Dafydd to help me. But Dafydd was too busy hiding in the shadows to be counted on anymore.

So I would have to take care of Mam alone.

The sixth stanza ended. And our door stayed shut.

Mam climbed heavily into her bed at the end of the night. I knew there would be hell to pay the next day in nasty rumors and ugly looks.

I accepted that price. And I accepted that I would pay it alone.

But when I went out back to add the evening's waste to our rubbish pile, the Mari Lwyd was waiting.

She moved like night through the lane behind our cottage, grotesquely belled and beribboned as if she were a child on Calan Mai and not an eerie bag of teeth and bones.

Taliesin bach, she greeted me. *There was no room at your fireside tonight?*

Though her jaw moved, her voice made no sound. A shudder ran through me, so violent I could not answer.

It is a cardinal sin to deny hospitality to one's neighbors, said the Mari Lwyd. *The ultimate insult, especially on the longest night of the year. We depend on one another for light.*

"I cannot depend on them," I finally said, voice shaking. "Not for friendship, not for light. Not even for safety."

And you are to be king, she mused.

"I am to be king," I agreed. I had only considered it in my heart before then. I had never spoken my plans aloud.

But I could think of no other way to keep Mam safe. No other way to be sure she would be protected by castle walls than to hold the castle itself.

And now Dafydd had withdrawn himself from consideration.

On this night, Taliesin bach, you chose your mother and your walls instead of your people. And so you shall not be king.

My knees went weak. "You can't stop me. You don't have that power."

I smelled earth. Rain began to fall, freezing and sharp. Somewhere, a kettle shrilled.

It is not a question of my power or lack thereof, princeling, she said. *Those dead in Annwn cannot see the living; the living cannot see the dead.*

But I live in a place between, and I see all.

The Mari Lwyd had not gone walking the next year, or any year after. Some people wondered if I was to blame. I knew I wasn't, of course.

But I had seen magic, the scent and sound of earth and rain and a kettle on the boil. And I wanted nothing more to do with it.

A few days later, I took my allowance from Dad and bribed one of his high men to move out of his apartments inside Mathrafal. Mam and I took them instead. Dad had never commented on the move or on the events of that night.

The Mari Lwyd could say what she liked. As if anyone could haul Dafydd out of hiding, anyway.

I chose Mam. I chose stone castle walls.

And whatever the Mari Lwyd said, someday, I would be king.

38

TAL

As I made my way upstairs to my father's chambers, I told myself I was lucky Luned was unable to resist a snide comment when she had the wit to string one together. I'd been looking for an exit from the party anyway.

But her words about my mother stung.

When Ffion had walked through the cellar the day before, I'd looked as thoroughly as I could around the storerooms and prisons for the blade, and tonight, I'd paced my father's hall, searching behind his throne for any loose stones or hiding places. Earlier in the day, I'd searched Dafydd's forge and paid an errand boy, Alfie, to check the stables for anything unusual. Alfie had asked me later if the stableboy dancing with a barn cat counted as unusual, and I'd given him a penny and sent him home.

The long and short of it was that I'd searched most of the keep, with the exception of the bedrooms, and Osian's party was my chance. Dad wasn't King Meirion; unless the blade really was lost, he wouldn't have stored it out of his reach. But after bribing four guards and tossing eight upstairs bedrooms, including my father's, I'd found nothing more precious than money.

I already had more money than anyone needed. And what I needed, no amount of money could buy.

When I reentered the hall, the tables had been shoved out of the way for dancing. Everyone, from my father's chieftains to his scullions, danced as a drummer, crwth player, and piper played boisterously.

Was I surprised to see Ffion dancing with Dafydd? I didn't think so. Not after he had come to her defense. Not after Ffion's vision.

Scowling at the honeysuckle still hanging from the rafters, I leaned against the wall as they circled together, and wondered if I'd ever be allowed to have something without my brother deciding he wanted it, too.

"Prince Taliesin." Osian came to my side. "I'm surprised to find you not dancing."

"I don't feel like dancing."

"And yet the hall is full of egos to stroke and any number of suitable daughters. Given your brother's success with the common folk earlier today, I would expect you to make the most of the occasion."

"You've made your point," I said, turning to Osian. "You have another candidate in mind for king. You have another candidate in mind for—" I broke off.

"You're not suited for it, Taliesin." His words were dispassionate, crueler for their calm.

"And you were so certain of that when I was five that you preemptively chose Dafydd."

"You were five, Dafydd was six. Ffion was four. But I could see your dispositions even then. And I saw Dafydd's doubts."

"You saw them?" I asked. "Or you *saw* them?"

Osian acknowledged my meaning with a lift of his brows. "I had a vision. I saw Dafydd at fifteen, refusing to be his father's heir. And I attempted to forestall his refusal." His eyes were trained on Ffion and my brother. "It bears mentioning that your father didn't know."

I felt a dawning horror as his words made sense of themselves. "You bound Ffion and Dafydd to push him into becoming king?"

"Ffion is suited to be court magician. And I knew she and Dafydd would be suited," he said. "In many ways."

"You have your opinions on that, and I have mine," I said. "For my part, I wonder if you know Ffion as well as you think you do."

Just then, Ffion stubbed her toe on a flagstone. Dafydd hurried forward, but she was laughing even as she winced.

"She's not a graceful dancer," Osian remarked.

I frowned. "She's still learning."

"Yes," said Osian, and suddenly, he didn't sound much like Osian at all. "Her father should have prepared her better for court."

My head snapped over to look at my father's magician.

His eyes were rolled back in his head. No one else was watching us.

But Osian was gone. And my father's voice was coming out of his mouth.

"I see Osian's favorite is a great favorite with your brother," he said. "What everyone sees in the chit, I cannot fathom." Osian's eyes were moons, paler than his tattooed body. My flesh crawled.

"You've been listening to Rhiannon," I said. "Father, what are you doing? Where are you? Why even set this competition between Dafydd and me if you were going to step in yourself?"

"Because I cannot count on the pair of you," my father said bluntly. "Though you haven't made quite the hash of your attempt that Dafydd has of his."

"My plan could succeed with Mathrafal's blade," I said. "Will you give it to me?"

"Lost." His voice was dismissive. "Osian said the blade rejected us because I lacked the purity of purpose to hold it. Supposedly, it's a guide of sorts. I imagine someone stole the cursed thing. I'm fortunate to have real magic to help me now," he added significantly.

"Father, if Osian is correct, you will die during this attack. And if *Ffion* is correct, the Foxhall will burn all the magic out of Wales to work lavish enchantments for just a few."

"You hate magic, Taliesin," said my father. "You don't fool me, and you can't trust her."

"And what about your death?" I demanded. "Are you willing to risk that?"

"Rhiannon is of the opinion that Osian is in error."

When had he stopped trusting Osian's word? "Of course she is."

I turned away from my father in the magician's body, watching Ffion and Dafydd sashay up and down their line.

My gut clenched when Dafydd took her hands. When Ffion laughed out loud because she had to stand on her tiptoes to form a bridge for the dancers with him. Ffion could have stood behind him and not even been visible.

He could protect her so well, if he chose to.

And all I could do was watch.

"I have to trust her," I said. "I have no one else to trust."

"Then you know her magic is at risk of fading, with her familiar gone?" Dad asked. Rhiannon must have informed him.

"She has a plan." Not that I knew what it was.

"Does that plan account for the magic in the dyke?" he countered.

I didn't look over. I didn't move.

His words knocked the breath out of me right as Ffion caught my eye.

"Magic in the dyke?" I asked him.

"Welsh magic, if Osian's right. He's been studying the dyke for her." Dad's voice was bitter. "Distracted fool forgot to close his thoughts to me. Rhiannon's investigating it now."

Across the room, Ffion mouthed something at me—*after,* she mimed, exaggerated. She would find me after she was done dancing with my brother.

"Are you certain Rhiannon's not tricking you?" I asked my father.

"More certain than you are," said Dad.

After, Ffion said again. But at that moment, I wasn't sure there was an *after* for us.

Magic *in* the dyke. Welsh magic. What did that mean? Who could've done it?

And had Ffion really lied to me again?

"Mind yourself," Osian-who-wasn't-Osian said as I made for the corridor. "If she can sense there's magic in that dyke, odds are it can sense her, too."

39

DAFYDD

My dance with Ffion ended, and the party began to draw to a close around us. I was always glad for the end of royal obligations, and I welcomed this one with relief.

Tonight, I just hoped that maybe, when I left, I'd be with Ffion.

I needed to know what she'd seen in her vision. If she'd felt what I felt.

So when Ffion dropped my hands and said, "I need to look for Tal," I tried not to wince.

I wasn't surprised he'd left early. But if Ffion were as eager to be around me as she was to be around him, I'd have welded myself to her side.

"Should we check the treasury first?" I asked, moving into the corridor. Though the party was nearly over, the night had only just begun for the scullions and kitchen boys we passed, whose task it would be to clean up the hall and anyone who'd overindulged.

Ffion laughed. "Tal's not in the treasury."

"But he's been searching for the blade while everyone's distracted by the party."

She didn't quite concede. But she didn't have Tal's gift for deception.

"Not as dull as I look," I said, tapping my temple and grinning at her, and I thought she might have blushed.

"I don't think you're dull," Ffion said. We were moving toward the outer doors, toward the castle courtyard. "I think you're reliable. Straightforward."

"When girls say those things, they mean *dull*."

"Not when they're talking about someone with arms like yours." Ffion flicked my shoulder playfully as we crossed the threshold, and I almost stopped short.

Did she mean she thought I was handsome?

I knew she was teasing. I knew better than to weight the moment too much. But my thoughts ran inevitably to Ffion's hand on my cheek and the sheen of honey on her mouth. To honeysuckle wrapping itself around the rafters and how things could be between us.

I'd felt it, during her vision. I couldn't be sure how the connection felt between my father and Osian, but I had sensed her gentle tread in my mind, the warmth of our bond in my tattoo.

It had felt intimate, natural. Like the breath we'd shared as she stared into the candle.

"What did you see tonight, Ffion?" I asked. I had to know.

She gave a nervous laugh. "I can't . . ." She shook her head and looked away, swallowing hard. "Dafydd, I need to tell you that I didn't know Tal was going to try to coerce you in front of the court tonight. I agreed to bring the raven's feather, though, and I'm afraid that's what made you say so many things at the party." She produced it from her pocket.

Yesterday, I would've reared back at the sight of the blade. Yesterday, I would've been angry at Tal for his plan, and disappointed with Ffion for being part of it.

Tonight, though, I didn't feel jealous of Tal. I'd shared something with Ffion he could never understand. And the feeling of her magic down the line of our bond—it overwhelmed every other sense.

I'd feared the ravens for years. But the sight of Ffion holding the blade didn't scare me anymore.

With Ffion connected to my very heart, so many prospects were less terrible.

"I said too much," I agreed. "But it wasn't the first time, and it won't be the last. And I know it wasn't your plan."

She laughed sharply. "Don't doubt that I want the blade as badly as Tal does."

"I know. But the difference between Tal and me, Ffion, is that where I see black and white, he just sees gray. Variations of light and dark, but no line between him and what he wants. But there are some things I just I can't accept. And I think you're the same."

It was why I had left Prestatyn without an alliance. Why I had refused to become king. And why, now, I couldn't give Ffion Mathrafal's blade.

And I couldn't.

Could I?

"You're better than I am, Dafydd. You're good. Unselfish." Her smile was placating now.

It was a pat on the head for a good little boy, and I didn't like it.

I looked at Ffion, her parted lips and the line of her throat and the hair that had begun to curl in the humid night, and swallowed hard. "I can be selfish."

She scoffed. "I don't believe it."

Abruptly, I stepped closer, stopping her in her tracks. My blood had begun to simmer, not with anger, but something sweeter, though just as forbidden.

Capable of anything threatened all the fears at the back of my mind. For once, it didn't feel like a threat.

Could I make her understand how I felt?

I took one, two, three steps forward, until Ffion's back hit stone—the columbarium wall. Her mouth had fallen open in surprise, and I found that I wanted to keep surprising her.

I wanted to surprise her. I wanted to be selfish.

I bent my head, spoke close to her ear. "What did you see during your vision, Ffion?" I asked again, quietly.

She blushed. Even in the shadowed courtyard, there was no mistaking it.

"I saw you walking the dyke with me," she managed. "I saw you in a silver throne room."

Prestatyn's throne room was silver. Had she seen the past, I wondered? Or the future?

And what else had she seen to make her blush that way?

Ffion didn't say anything else. But suddenly, I knew exactly what to do.

I couldn't hand the throne to Tal. Not after the way he'd acted tonight, scheming and stirring up a crowd to get what he wanted. And not after what I'd shared with Ffion.

Ffion, who seemed never to question herself. Ffion, who could take away the burden of all my indecision, my doubts about right and wrong. I wanted her beside me.

If Ffion and Tal's mission succeeded because I helped them—would my father count it as my success? And with Ffion to make the decisions I couldn't—could I bear being king, then?

"Do you want the blade, Ffion?" I asked quietly. "I can be selfish. I can give it to you."

"How—" Her voice caught. "How is that selfish?"

"Because I'm giving it to you for a price." I raked my eyes over her face, her iron-gray eyes, her freckles like sparks. "I won't brave the ravens' gaze for nothing."

It would take every ounce of courage I had to hear the truth from the sighted ravens. But would my attempt even succeed? The blade had been lost to my father right around the time I'd told him I didn't want to be heir, around the time my friend's father had been injured because Dad wouldn't relent toward Gwynedd. The blade was strength and wisdom; it wouldn't answer to the impure of heart.

Ffion seemed to grow taller in her anticipation. "I want it. Name your price. Anything."

"When you and Tal leave," I said, "you have to take me with you."

"Tal won't like—"

"I don't want to talk about Tal."

Silent, she nodded.

She'd seen me walking the dyke with her. She'd known I would ask this, and she'd known she would say yes.

"And there's one more thing." I dipped my head a little, held her eyes with mine.

"Yes?" she said, less certain now. Her pulse beat hard in her throat.

"A kiss," I said. "I will give you the blade, and you will owe me a kiss."

"A kiss," Ffion echoed, like she was just learning the word.

I nodded. "You can choose when, and where, and how."

She wet her lips, thinking, and I wondered if she would kiss me right here, right now.

I wished she wouldn't. I wished she would.

"Do it now," she said, and at first I thought she did mean the kiss. But then she raised a hand, pointing at the columbarium at her back.

The sighted ravens were just inside.

"Do it now, and the answer is yes," she said. "You can travel with us, and I'll owe you a kiss." The words came out nearly all in one breath, impulsive. But there was no regret on her face once they were out.

I hoped she wouldn't regret me.

I hoped she'd give me a fair shot against Tal.

I would bargain for something I desperately wanted with something that wasn't mine to give. And if I won—if victory and the throne were mine—I knew I could bear the weight of them, with our bond to shield me from my doubt.

I kissed Ffion's hand and stepped into the columbarium.

When it was done, I stepped out into the night. Goose bumps rose over my skin; I'd been sweating.

It was as hot as a forge inside the columbarium.

"Did they tell you where to find it?" Ffion's eyes were bright with desperation. "What did they say?"

My throat felt raw, like I'd been shouting, and my eyes stung as though I'd been staring into a flame. I shook my head. "Open your hand."

She did.

Mathrafal's blade was a unicorn's horn about eight inches long. It was clear here and cloudy there, like amber, lightly grooved and smelling faintly of resin.

The blade had left my father, but the ravens had kept it safe. And now I had it. And though I hadn't had a vision in the columbarium, I could see the future clear before me.

I would destroy the dyke with my brother and my hedgewitch. I would take my father's throne. And when I did, Ffion would sit beside me.

The blade felt heavy as a sword in my hand. I felt lighter, giving it to Ffion.

40

FFION

I had to ask two maids for directions to Tal's room. I had to knock four times to get him to let me in.

My heart was thundering.

I had the blade. And I owed Dafydd a kiss.

"Was starting to wonder if you were asleep," I said, pushing inside, when he finally unlatched the door.

"Couldn't." Tal's face was turned away from me. His rings and necklace were scattered across a table beside a washbasin and pitcher; his red coat lay abandoned on a nearby chair.

"Well, where were you? You left to go look around, and then you came back, and then you left again."

Tal glanced at me over his shoulder. "So you would rather have known what was going on."

"I'd . . ." I trailed off at Tal's flinty expression. "Yes. I thought we had a plan. Not that you stuck to it tonight when you decided to publicly attack Dafydd, but yes."

"Interesting." He nodded. "So you would have preferred I tell you what I was doing, where I was going. Because we had a plan."

Tal didn't raise his voice. But his words were clipped.

"Tal." I put a hand on his arm. "Stop. Explain what's happening."

He turned. Though he never raised his voice, his fury was palpable. "Why don't you explain why my father had to be the one to tell me there was magic in Offa's Dyke?" he said. "Why tonight, while you were dancing with my brother, I had a conversation with my father through *your* father's body, and he told me something I suspect you could have told me weeks ago?"

He might as well have punched me in the stomach.

"I—" I stared at him, trying to speak.

Tal shook me off, planting his hands on the edge of his bed. "You did know. Incredible."

"It's just something I can feel. And I've been having dreams." My voice was barely a whisper. "I don't know what they mean. I didn't know anything beyond that until we got to Mathrafal."

"Well, I didn't know anything at all, and tonight I looked like a fool in front of my father. Even worse, everything is different now. Is our plan even going to work anymore?" he demanded. "Did a Welsh witch betray us? Is it the Foxhall? Is someone else trying to destroy it?"

"I don't know. We've always assumed Mercia doesn't possess magic, and since the magic is Welsh, I think that's still true. But even if the dyke's been strengthened, or something like that—there's no reason our plan can't still work." I paused. "Because now I have Mathrafal's blade."

Tal had been staring up at the curtains over his bed, their dark red fabric the same color as his coat, but now his head whipped around to face me. I felt a surge of hope.

"Dafydd gave it to you?" he asked, inflectionless.

"Yes."

"Of course he did." Tal turned away.

My ire rose. "What are you implying?" I asked.

He shrugged. "I'm not implying anything. I'm saying, outright, that even though Dafydd's too pure to be any good to anybody, least of all himself, he'd give you absolutely anything you asked for, and you and I both know why."

"Maybe this is what he wants," I challenged him. "Maybe he changed his mind." Tal scoffed.

But I was grasping at straws. I knew Dafydd had done this for me.

Desperate, I went to Tal's side and held out the unicorn's horn. It glinted in the candlelight, warmer than the light from the waning crescent of moon outside.

Tal flinched. And there—I saw it.

Without the story his mother had told me, maybe I wouldn't have noticed. But she had, and so I did.

"*This* is why." My voice was almost wondering. "This is why I didn't tell you about the magic in the dyke."

"What do you mean?"

"Do you trust my magic, Tal?" I held up the blade. "Do you trust any magic?"

He shifted away. "That's a ridiculous question."

"I don't think it is," I countered. "You get nervous every time I work magic in your presence. You never want to be around Brycheiniog's blade—"

"Because it's a manipulative charm!"

"*You're* a manipulative charm!" I burst out, childish. "For the longest time, I couldn't figure out why I didn't want to tell you about the magic in the dyke. Part of it, of course, is that I make charms and protections for the poor and elderly. I don't accept charges from princes and kings. So I didn't know what to do when—after being promised it was my magic against no magic—I arrived to find . . . that."

"What's it like?" Tal asked, and I wondered that I'd never heard the dread in his voice before. "What does it feel like?"

"Like power," I said. "Power so much greater than mine. Like something primeval."

Tal blanched.

"I thought I kept the truth of it back because if you knew, you might find someone else to do my job, or change your plans again," I said, beginning to pace, speaking faster and faster. "But I think I sensed that if you found out, you would have panicked. You would've focused on meeting the Mercian attack and abandoned that part of the quest entirely, avoided the dyke at all costs. It's because you hate magic, Tal."

"That's not true."

"It *is* true," I said. "And you've hated it since you met the Mari Lwyd."

Tal turned.

"Who told you about the Mari Lwyd?" he asked.

"That's not the point."

"Of course it's the point!" he exploded. "Why is it you see fit to keep back essential details about our quest, about who your father is to our kingdom, but I'm not allowed to keep one terrible story to myself?"

"Because I want to understand you, and you won't let me!"

"Did you use the raven's feather on her?" he asked. "Did you use the blade on my mother?"

I looked away.

Tal scraped a hand along his jaw, disbelieving. "Ffion, this might be unforgivable."

"I had to," I said. "Tal, I had to. I've been wondering since I met you why you act and talk the way you do, and it's because you hate magic."

"You pried a story out of my mother with magic. And now you know what happened to us. Can you blame me for hating it?" Tal pinned me with a look. "Because you would, too."

"I'd never hate it," I said. "It's like saying I could come to hate stars, or trees, or the sea."

"You'd hate a star or a tree if one fell on your house and destroyed it," he said. "You'd hate the sea if your lover drowned on a voyage home."

Silence settled between us like dust over an abandoned room.

"I saw what happened to your spell in the forest, Ffion," he said. "I saw you panic when the chieftains demanded a demonstration tonight. We both know your magic is dwindling. How do you plan to keep it from disappearing completely before the attack?"

There was no space to hide anymore. There was no room for anything but the truth.

"The blades are going to help me finish the job," I said. "I knew I needed a backup plan once I found out there was magic in the dyke, and when Enid explained what the blades were, I knew I could use them." I hesitated. "But the only way to keep my magic from disappearing is to resurrect Cadno. That's why I've been gathering materials on our walk. Once we destroy the dyke and restore magic, I'm going to perform the summoning spell and bring him back." I wasn't keeping anything back anymore. Tal knew all my secrets.

"So you don't have a plan to keep your magic *so* we can destroy the dyke," he said. "Your plan to keep your magic *depends* on our destroying the dyke, which *depends* on us getting the blades." Tal ran a hand through his hair, a muscle feathering in his jaw. Frustration rolled off him in waves. "Ffion, that's not a plan. That's a wish. That's just you, hoping you can outrun what's been happening, hoping you could fix things before I found out what was going on. If you'd told me, I—"

"You would have panicked," I insisted again.

"I could have *helped* you. We could've built a stronger plan, while we still had time. And now—" He broke off, turning away from me. "You need to go. I need to go to bed. We need to make an early start." He poured water into the basin on his table, yanked his shirt over his head and reached for a clean one.

I was burning up.

He didn't care. He didn't care at all. He could wash his face and change his clothes in front of me, I could tell him everything that had been burdening me for weeks, and none of it mattered. Because he didn't care.

Dafydd cared.

"That's fine. If you're worn out, you can always stay here." I affected nonchalance, leaning against his bedpost. "Your brother had two conditions for giving me the blade, and one was that we let him travel with us. So if you're uncomfortable and you'd rather stay at Mathrafal, I can finish our journey without you. With Dafydd instead, I mean."

"Dafydd is not coming." Tal took a step toward me, yanking his nightshirt down over his stomach. The words were out of his mouth almost before I'd finished speaking. "No. Absolutely not."

"He has to."

"No."

"Which would you rather?" I asked. "Lose the blade we desperately need, or have your brother for company for a few days?"

"Neither!" he exclaimed. "I want neither. I want what I want, and I don't want Dafydd around getting underfoot."

"You're being petty."

"Probably I am, but this is mine, and he's not having it," he said.

"What's yours?" I challenged him.

Tal wet his lips and looked away. "You know."

"No, tell me what you mean." I stepped closer to him, forcing him to look at me. "Enough allusions. Enough posturing without *doing* anything."

"Ffion." Tal shook his head, his tone warning. "I—we can't do this. Even if I wanted to, I—"

"*If* you wanted to?" I lifted my chin.

Tal's expression was agony.

Slowly, I reached out the way I'd wanted to since the day I met him. I traced his lower lip, felt the sharp exhale of his breath as my thumb grazed the beauty mark beside his mouth.

Tal gathered me into his arms, fingers possessive, face nuzzling my neck.

We held there like fire in a hearth, not moving, never still, burning, burning, burning.

"Ffion," he breathed.

I kissed his clavicle. Tal breathed out sharply, head falling back, hands fisting in the fabric of my dress. Suddenly, he tensed.

"Ffion." He cleared his throat. "Stop. I can't."

Abruptly, I pulled away. "What?" I asked.

Tal shook his head. His pupils were blown wide.

My hands were trembling. "I thought you wanted—"

"I do—I did. But Ffion, we both heard Luned tonight. And if my mother told you about what happened with the Mari Lwyd, then you know what life is like for us here. What life is like for *her* here."

My face was on fire. I tried to smooth my hair back, tried to think about Tal's words and not the fact that he had pulled away. "Yes."

"I've spent the last four years protecting her. It's taken all my focus. It's what she deserves. It's why I have to become king, why I can't be candler. Because I have to be here. And I—" His voice caught. "I can't protect both of you."

It was like the world's faded magic, I thought, as Tal stepped away from me.

I could see the moment that had passed between us, just like I could see the evidence magic had left behind. All the pieces of it were still present. But it was gone before I'd truly been able to lay hands on it.

"You don't want to be king, Tal," I said. "You just want the castle with the highest walls."

"It's the same thing," he said simply.

And to him, it was. This was the difference between Tal and Dafydd.

"What was his other condition?" Tal asked.

I shook my head. "Not important," I said. "You know everything else now. You know what I'm doing. I know what you're afraid of." I noticed his hands were shaking, and looked away. "Is that enough for you? Or is the magic too much?"

"I'm coming with you," he said.

"Fine." I moved toward the door.

"You know, Dafydd had visions of you," he said, "but I've had dreams."

I stopped, my hand on the latch, and looked at him over my shoulder.

"I never had visions of you, like he did." Tal's chest rose and fell. "But the visions were just magic Osian gave him. My dreams about you—those were mine."

His. As I never could be.

My hand trembled as I lifted the latch.

"I told Dafydd we would leave at dawn," I said. "Be ready."

I walked the mile or so back to where I had buried the pouch to check it again, carrying the unicorn's horn and the raven's feather with me. My own power was fading, but I hoped the presence of theirs would lend the charm anything that I lacked.

I once loved a boy, a tall, handsome boy,
With a mind just as keen as a knife,
Oh, hair like the earth and eyes like the night
Had my darling annwyl Cai.

I met him at court—no, we met down the pub—
No, the Foxhall, as dark night drew nigh,

It matters not where, it matters not how,
For I fell for my annwyl Cai.

Oh, I trusted his words, and he trusted my lies,
And the secrets I held back besides,
So it hurt all the more when we both learned the truth,
My silver-tongued annwyl Cai.

I needed to rest. I wanted to sleep. Dreams, visions—whatever they were, I wanted one like I wanted to touch Tal's face again.

Mathrafal needed vision, my father had said. So did I.

Could the dreams tell me if I had any hope of succeeding? *Could* there be an answer in their merciless repetition, in the sight and sense of places I'd never seen before?

I didn't know. I could only beg to see them again and again, and hope I might eventually understand.

I'd nearly sung myself into dozing beside the dyke, missing Tal, missing Cadno, when I had the unmistakable sense again of something watching me, and waiting.

Was it Cadno? Or something else?

Suddenly, he was standing over me. Not Cadno.

"Ffion." Dad's voice snapped me out of drowsing. "Wake up."

41

TAL

I was going to feel Ffion's kiss on my collarbone for the rest of my life. I was absolutely certain of it.

Lying on my bed, staring up at my stupid red canopy and my stupid red bedcurtains, I wondered what it said about me that I was thinking harder about one kiss, from one girl, than about the magic currently festering in the dyke. Welsh magic that, presumably, a Welsh magician had put there.

I couldn't believe I'd pushed her away. I couldn't believe I'd brought up my *mother* while a girl—*the* girl—was kissing me.

I rolled onto my stomach and groaned into my pillow.

A knock came at the door.

I bolted upright. "Ffion?"

"It's Dafydd." An awkward pause. "Ffion's with me. And Osian."

I was going to die.

For a moment, I put my face into the pillow again and screamed silently. Then, mechanically, I rose and lifted the latch. Though Dafydd had been the one to speak, Ffion piled in first, hauling him by the wrist.

Two hours ago, she'd been kissing me. Had she gone and found my brother the moment she'd left? Except—no, she was also gripping her father's sleeve. Gruffudd lumbered in after them.

"What's wrong?" I asked.

Ffion and Dafydd turned to one another, as if there were so much to say, they weren't sure who should speak first. "There's magic in the dyke, but it's Welsh magic," Dafydd began, but Ffion put a hand on his elbow, interrupting him with something so quiet I couldn't quite hear it. "Sorry. I didn't realize you already knew."

Jealousy burned in my gut.

"Yes. Welsh magic. In the dyke. And you came up here to—what, remind me?"

"Of course not," Ffion snapped. "Tal, there's a witch in one of Offa's camps."

I felt like I'd been doused in cold water. "What?"

"My scouts witnessed it in a Mercian encampment some miles east of here," Osian said.

Magic in the dyke, and a witch traveling with Offa's armies. It was too much.

"What did they see?" I asked. Osian's eyes grew distant.

"Magic leaves evidence in the earth. They told me it was as if every season arrived at once," he said. "Snow falling over the camp while thousands of saplings and flowers burst from the earth. Leaves turning gold to orange to red to brown and then dying, falling with the snow."

I hesitated. "Is there any way to tell if it's Mercian magic or Welsh magic, the way you could tell in the dyke?"

Osian shook his head. "Not at such a distance."

"So who's responsible?" Dafydd asked. "A hedgewitch? The Foxhall?"

Ffion looked uncertain. "It's possible Mercia recruited a hedgewitch from Brycheiniog, but I got the impression Enid was something of the last of her kind. And I can tell you with some confidence that, present company excluded, the Foxhall has left no hedgewitch unturned in Powys." She grimaced. "But I don't think it's a Foxhall witch, either. Rhiannon would never let a covenwitch defect. Think of how she treated my mother when she stepped out of line," she added, avoiding her father's eyes.

"But?" I prompted her.

"But what about—" She hesitated. "What about Gwynedd?"

"What *about* Gwynedd?" I asked.

"Powys has been making war on Gwynedd for years," she said. "Gwynedd hates us. Who's to say a Gwyneddian witch hasn't sided with Mercia, as revenge, or for some other reason?"

I frowned. "But do you really think—"

"Yes." Beside me, Dafydd looked ill. "Gwynedd has every reason to hate us. For every attack on their border, every raid on their villages—they hate us, and we deserve it."

Osian put a hand on his shoulder. Dafydd shrugged it off.

"How will we find this person?" my brother asked, sounding choked.

"We'll ask as we travel," I said. "If a witch has disappeared, someone will know."

Osian had said magic left evidence in the earth. Surely it left evidence elsewhere, too—in rumor on the road, in pub gossip and word of mouth among neighbors.

Now it was up to us to track it down.

42

DAFYDD

On the Dyke, Powys

Offa's armies had moved north, and as soon as it was light, so did we. Tal rode in the wagon, Gruffudd snored in its bed, and Ffion walked beside me, her hair damp with morning dew.

I'd barely spoken to Osian when we left, except to leave him steward of Mathrafal; I assumed I could at least trust him with that. Dad would have something to say about it, but Dad always had something to say about it.

I wondered if I was being inexcusably stupid returning to Gwynedd. Would King Bleddyn even receive me a second time? Would I do Ffion and Tal more harm than good by joining them? And why hadn't I pushed my father harder to stop our attacks on Gwynedd a long time ago?

Tal had said that if a witch had disappeared, someone would know. But no one did. Not in Cei'r Trallwng, where Tal paused for a draft of bragawd, though it was hardly nine in the morning. Not in Llandysilio. Not in Llanymynech, where I stopped to help a woman whose horse had thrown a shoe.

"No, the last hedgewitch we had in town left to join the Foxhall about eight years ago," the woman said ruefully, hands fisted in her apron. "You might try there."

So we carried on. Ffion sang under her breath when we passed the Mercian guard towers that seemed to loom over every hill and valley.

Sometimes, when we passed out of sight of the towers, she climbed in and out of the ditch, retrieving odd items—a chunk of quartz, a cluster of dandelions, a mushroom. When I asked what she was doing, she quietly told me she planned to resurrect Cadno with her gleanings. Tal stared straight ahead, not speaking, as she explained.

"Did the Foxhall pay you a blood debt for his death?" I asked. "I know it wouldn't bring him back, but they ought to, all the same."

"I hadn't thought of it," Ffion said, smiling ruefully. "But thank you for saying so."

We walked for eighteen miles. When we reached a hilltop village called Cyrn y Bwch around nightfall, Ffion and Tal agreed casually—too casually—that it was as good a place as any to stop for the night. But when I gestured Ffion ahead of me toward the village, she shook her head.

"Ffion doesn't stay in town," Tal said. "She never does." He'd begun to do this right after they reached Mathrafal, I'd noticed, reminding me here and there that I was an interloper, that he had a stronger claim to her than I did. As if his two weeks of traveling alone with her could outweigh the bond that connected Ffion and me.

"I stay on the dyke," Ffion explained. "Better to keep close."

"But the night air—it's unhealthy. Miasmas . . ." I gestured vaguely around, then turned to Tal, horrified. "You sleep in a comfortable bed while she sleeps in the mud?"

Tal grinned mirthlessly. "I'd hardly call the average pub bed comfortable."

"Dafydd." Ffion put a hand on my arm. "I sleep rough back home. This is no different."

"It *is* different," I said vehemently. "Because Tal could choose not to leave you by yourself."

"She doesn't want me here," Tal said.

Ffion looked stricken. "I never said that."

"You may as well have," Tal said. "I'm going inside."

"I'm staying here," I said.

"Of course you are."

I knew what he meant. But I didn't back down as Ffion collected what she needed from the wagon, and neither did Tal as he drove up the lane and away from the dyke.

Ffion was a little subdued as I assembled a tent from branches and the oilcloth and she made stew in her cauldron. "There," I said triumphantly. "Now you'll sleep dry."

"Again, I'm used to sleeping in the open, as I'm sure you've *seen*," Ffion said, delicately stressing the word. "It doesn't bother me."

"Doesn't mean I like it."

She conceded with a sigh then, and Gruffudd lumbered over and dropped beside her. "How did it work?" she asked. "Did you summon the visions, like I had to?"

I shook my head. "They always came without any warning. I'd just sort of freeze in place for a minute or two, like I'd gone to sleep in the middle of the day," I said. "Your father put a tattoo of your familiar on my side. That was how he forged the connection."

Her eyes lit. "Of Cadno?" she asked. "Can I see it?"

I hesitated. But Ffion's curiosity was intoxicating.

I squeezed inside the tent and lifted the hem of my shirt.

"The day Osian gave me the tattoo was the day I had my first drink of bragawd," I said, feeling my blush deepen. "I was six—far too young for it. But the needle hurt worse than anything I'd ever felt."

I looked down at the red ink that spread from the top of my ribs to my hip bone, as clear and precise as Osian's own tattoos. Ffion just looked at me.

I was used to girls staring at me from the courtyard and giggling while I worked, though I'd never known what to do, or what to say to them. But I wasn't prepared for Ffion's eyes roving over my side—for her hands reaching for me without her even seeming to realize before she dragged them back to her lap. She cleared her throat. "It looks just like him."

"I know."

"Yes, I know you know." Ffion made a face, settling against Gruffudd. "Dafydd, you owe me a memory."

"What?" I frowned.

"A memory," she insisted. "You've seen me all my life. I only know what I've heard about you from Dad. So you owe me a story from when you were younger."

"What do you want to know?" I asked.

"Something that would have come to me in a vision, if the world were fair," she said.

For a moment, I considered.

I could've told her any number of lonely memories—life without my mother, life with my overbearing, disappointing father. I could've told a self-deprecating story, something that would make her laugh.

But as long as I was being selfish, I decided to tell her something flattering instead. "When I was a child, I used to let Tal win at everything."

Ffion's eyes widened. "What?"

"Training exercises. Knucklebones. Guessing games. Often enough he won on his own, but I never, ever let myself beat him." I paused. "I know that sounds like a fistful of sour grapes, but it's true."

"I know it's true. You're not vain enough to make it up. But why?" she asked.

"Because Dad ignored him." I stared at my hands, suddenly uncomfortable. *Wasn't* I being vain? "Tal didn't look like him. He was small, attached to his mother. I was also attached to his mother," I added. "I'd never known mine."

Ffion rolled onto her back. "I wish parents wouldn't have favorites. Arianrhod being Mam's favorite came between Arianrhod and me. Me being Dad's favorite came between Mam and me, *and* Arianrhod and me." She sighed. "Dad said once that Arianrhod didn't have the fire to be court magician. I agree she's too tolerant of Rhiannon's horrible behavior, but I wouldn't say not being able to hold your tongue is such a gift at court, either," she added with a significant lift of her brows.

"Not enough fire." I scoffed. "Osian's a blunt person who likes other blunt people; he's biased."

"We already knew that, though." Ffion cut her eyes at my side, where my tattoo lay hidden. The grimness of her smile made my chest ache.

Suddenly, though, I caught sight of—something. In the corner of my vision.

A little way north along the dyke, something was gleaming in the hedge. It was earthy, eerie, gentler and greener than forge light.

Was it magic?

My voice shook. "What is that?"

Ffion got to her feet, grinning. "Fox fire. Come here, I'll show you."

She took my wrist, not my hand. But my pulse raced at her touch as I followed her to a log grown over with mushrooms, glowing green in the night. "How?" I asked, wondering.

"Some people say it's fairies," she said. "But I think there's magic enough in the earth."

"Is there a difference?" I asked. Ffion smiled, but then the expression faded.

"Fox fire always makes me think of Cadno. He didn't like it," she said, laughing wanly, plucking a little for her cauldron.

"You'll see him soon," I said. And I knew she would.

"I've got five days," she said, looking up at the sky. In the uncanny glow of the fox fire and the thumbnail moon, she'd never looked more witchlike.

I wanted to kiss her. I wanted to keep her with me forever, to reinterpret all my doubts and make the world more bearable—simply by being who she was.

Like fox fire from the earth, it was just another expression of her magic.

43

FFION

I didn't know if it was the slow disintegration of my hold on magic, or the weeks of walking finally taking their toll, but my body felt like it was beginning to break. I felt every pebble beneath my feet, every thorn. My back hurt. My cold had come back in force. Most of all, my dreams were so vivid, I woke feeling like I was choking on dirt, like I'd hardly slept at all.

I wanted to give up. I wanted to be finished. I wanted everything to be over.

"You haven't sung all morning," Dafydd said kindly, coming alongside me.

"She's tired," Tal said flatly. "She doesn't sing when she's tired."

"I'm not tired," I retorted. "No more than everyone else is."

We couldn't slow down. Not with King Offa's Dyke beside me, pouring out power the way the sun above refused to pour out warmth.

Even with the blades, was I a match for the power in the dyke? Would it destroy me?

I climbed without stopping, imagining a water horse or a unicorn might appear and carry me away, imagining I was a raven or a dragon with the strength to leap into the air and fly instead of climb.

I imagined beating my wings, soaring on red or green scales or black feathers through the mist.

But as we crested the rise and looked down upon another viciously quarried hillside, I knew even the sight of Wales from the air wouldn't soothe me.

And as Tal snapped the reins and drove past Dafydd and me, I found myself wishing I were riding alongside him.

We made inquiries as we traveled, as many as we could without slowing ourselves down, always keeping quiet that we were from Powys. But we learned nothing until that afternoon, when we passed a village about a mile below the dyke and had to clamber down to meet it. I tried not to feel ignored as Tal walked past Dafydd and me into a mill and put our list of questions to a woman who looked to be the owner.

Is there a hedgewitch in town? Are there any close by? Have any hedgewitches left unexpectedly of late?

The woman, brown-skinned and in her late thirties with a kerchief tied neatly over her hair, eyed Tal dubiously as she said something Dafydd and I couldn't hear. But Tal's expression was euphoric as he walked out of the mill.

"You look like she told you the biggest piece of court gossip you've ever heard," I said.

"Better than that." Tal's eyes glittered. "She said there's a hedgewitch in town. And that they lost their last witch just a few weeks ago. Follow me."

We hurried after Tal along the river that ran through the village, past boats bobbing among the reeds clumped along its bank. That was where we found the witch—on the riverbank near the edge of town.

"Looks promising," said Tal as we drew near the hut. Dafydd pushed through the reeds clumped around the foundation, head bowed slightly as he tapped on the door.

"Come in," called a voice from inside.

The boy standing at the chopping block was about our age, with curly blond hair and a golden complexion. He gave us a quick smile over his shoulder when we came in. "With you in just a moment. Have a seat." While his back was turned, I made a hurried study of the cottage.

It was a one-room hut, round like Enid's, and it had probably once been a pleasant little place. The back window looked out on the river, and a hutch on the wall held a mortar and pestle and a collection of ordinary ingredients—sage and lavender, feverfew and stinging nettle, elder and spearmint. But the dirt floor was unswept, and the walls needed whitewashing, and the ingredient jars were dusty. Mam and Mam-gu both would've looked sideways at that layer of grime.

I frowned as the boy added a jar of chopped mushrooms and a jar of fresh rose petals to the collection on the hutch.

"How can I help you?" he asked, turning and giving another easy smile. I tried not to pity him when he turned it on me.

Tal spoke sharply. "How long have you been a hedgewitch here?"

The boy drew back, surprised. "A few months."

"And what happened to the witch who was here before you?" Tal asked. I elbowed him under the table.

"I've got a bit of a cold," I interrupted, grinning ruefully. "Can you mix me up a cure?"

The boy smiled again, looking relieved. "Of course."

But when his back was turned, my own smile dropped. "Something isn't right," I whispered to Tal, so close and low only he could hear me. He tensed at my hand on his arm, and I pulled away, refocusing.

I already knew this boy wasn't the witch we were looking for. But something else was going on.

I watched him like a hawk as he flipped aimlessly through a spellbook on the counter, then mingled a few ingredients with the mortar and pestle. "Take this, and you'll feel better," he said, handing me the whole undrinkable mess.

I made my eyes big. "How does it work?"

"That's my secret." He winked at me. Tal ground his teeth.

Enough. I crossed my arms, cocking my head. "Is it your particular trade secret that you used rose petals instead of willow bark?" I asked. "And I'd typically choose elder or feverfew, but the choice of poisonous mushrooms—that's interesting."

"Poison?" Tal shot to his feet, looking murderous.

"Sit down," I said, still watching the boy. "He didn't know what he was doing. Did you?" I asked him.

The boy looked like he might run, at first. But after sizing up Tal and Dafydd, he flopped back against the counter with a sigh. "No," he said. "I have no idea."

"Whose cottage was this?" I asked. "Some of those ingredients are good, but they haven't been touched in some time."

"My cousin was a witch here," he said. "She had an accident and died a few weeks ago."

"Did she teach you her craft?" Dafydd asked. He still didn't understand.

But Tal did. His mouth was a hard line. "No. He's a fraud. He's not a witch at all."

"Mam told me to get a job!" the boy protested. "And this cottage was empty, so—"

"So you decided to become a poisoner," I finished. "You could've killed someone."

"Sometimes they do get better," he said, sticking out his chin. "Am I really any worse than the likes of the Foxhall? They rode through a little west of here, wouldn't see anyone. I heard they charge you a penny just to stand at their door. Surely I'm no worse than them."

"'No worse than the Foxhall is a low bar," Tal said. "When did they ride through?"

The boy shrugged sulkily. "A few days ago. I don't remember."

"There are no real witches around?" Tal pressed. The boy shook his head.

Of course there weren't. The Foxhall was to blame for that, too. They were the reason this boy had been able to step into a role he wasn't qualified for.

Things had to change.

Dafydd had been the first to knock, and he was the first to get up to leave—but not before he approached the boy, looking serious. "Get some training," he said evenly, "or close your doors."

"Who are you to tell me what to do?" the boy snapped.

Dafydd's blond head almost brushed the slanting exposed beams of the little hut. In the whole, crooked cottage, he was the only thing standing up straight.

He bowed his head again slightly, and I thought he'd never looked more like a king.

"A blacksmith," said Dafydd. "I take my work seriously. You should, too, or give it up altogether."

For the rest of the day I gathered furiously, watching the sun rise and set as we walked.

I almost found it a pleasure now, to be so exhausted. My feet hurt too much for me to wonder if we'd ever learn who was Mercia's witch; my cold was almost too miserable for me to worry if I would succeed in raising Cadno.

The second night after we'd met the fraudulent witch, Dafydd and I deposited Tal and the wagon at a farmhouse a little downhill from the ruined hillfort at Pen-y-Cloddiau.

"Won't you come inside?" the round-cheeked farmer's wife asked me with a kind smile. Tal stood behind her, looking tired. Dafydd looked almost eager beside me.

"Ffion and I are all right," he said. "Aren't we?"

As the two brothers watched me, all I could think was: *Gwanwyn warned me about this.*

She'd softened a little, after she'd told me the Mari Lwyd story our last night in Mathrafal. "You're not a silly girl, Ffion. Don't pretend you don't see what's in front of you. Dafydd is softhearted. But Tal is vulnerable, too." Then her eyes had gone stern again. "Be careful with them."

And I'd promised I would be. Right before I had promised Dafydd a kiss and let Tal hold me in the dark.

Standing in front of the farmhouse, I imagined a night sheltering with Tal, warm and dry and quiet, and almost said yes.

"No, thank you," I said. "I have to attend to other business."

Besides, I told myself as we left, we were nearly to Prestatyn. And anyway, it was Dafydd I'd seen with me in the vision, not Tal.

I knew where I was meant to be.

As Dafydd and I set up a tent and a fire between the stones of the ancient hillfort, the rain bucketed down, and I let loose one magnificent sneeze after another. Gruffudd snuggled up beside me while I mixed myself an ordinary potion of honey and bragawd.

"How long have you had Gruffudd?" I asked.

"About four years," he said. "After I opened the forge, I kept finding him hanging around the fire. He was about three stone lighter than this, and if you think he's lazy now—well. I thought he was dead when I first found him." I frowned and cuddled Gruffudd closer, wrapping my arms around his shaggy neck.

"But I needed a friend," Dafydd said. "Just like you did when you summoned Cadno."

Instinctively, I searched the skies. But the moon was hidden for the moment, rain pelting the ground around our tent and dripping down its edge.

"You know," Dafydd said thoughtfully, "the weather's not even so terrible with both oilcloths. I think I could live happily in a hut, as long as I could find a dry patch to lie in."

"Dafydd. You live in a palace."

"But not by my own choice. When I have the opportunity to choose, I choose to work and live as normally as I can," he said. "You live on the edge of things. So do I. Neither of us quite belongs. That's why I think we understand one another so well."

"I don't sleep rough for fun," I said.

"Of course not. You do it because your morals require it."

"But I don't reject comfort because there's something evil about comfort," I said. "I left my mother's cottage because when I refused the Foxhall, she wouldn't leave me in peace. If I could go back, I'd do it in a heartbeat. And if you'd grown up like most people—" I broke off, shrugging as kindly as I could.

Dafydd flicked me lightly on the arm. "Even if I'd grown up that way, I'd still be myself, and no one could accuse me of loving comfort. Bite your tongue, Ffion vch Osian." He was teasing, but I could tell he felt stung.

"I'm sorry." I apologized as sweetly as I could. "Yes, Dafydd. You're very rugged. And that high man I goaded into telling the truth at the party did say you did well with your father's petitioners. What did you do?"

"Overthought everything. *Dithered,*" he said, eyeing me significantly.

"Maybe the people didn't see it that way," I said. "Maybe they found you discerning. Maybe they were just grateful to see someone was thinking about them at all."

I was only trying to smooth over the moment. But Dafydd's

posture eased just before his glance went to my lips. And as he shifted on his blanket, I remembered the way the tattoo had looked on his side. The way I'd almost touched him.

Well-built. Solid. That was Dafydd, and he was a comfort.

With the fire crackling and the rain outside, I thought I might kiss him right then.

"What would you do if I reached for your hand?" he asked quietly.

My breathing stuttered. "I don't know. It's a little terrifying, Dafydd, how fearless you are."

"I'm not fearless," he said. "But I want you, Ffion. I always have."

And as Dafydd leaned toward me, the look in his eyes was caught between want and fear—just as I'd seen in my vision.

Suddenly, I froze. He started to speak but I waved a hand frantically, my words barely a whisper. "Wait. Just wait."

For a moment, Dafydd looked hurt again. But then he heard it, too.

"Don't move," he said softly, and for once, I obeyed.

Dafydd peered out through a gap between the oilcloths, and cold ran through me as his face changed. "What is it?" I asked.

"Mercian soldiers." He crawled back to the fire, working rapidly, letting his fingers be burned as he smothered the flames. If we were lucky, the smoke wouldn't summon every Mercian in five miles.

"How many?" I asked.

"Too many. At least a hundred."

I peered out the gap and saw he was right. Leather armor and horn-scale armor and the flanks of horses gleamed in the sickle-sharp sliver of moonlight.

And they were coming nearer.

I was cold down to my bones.

I reached into my cauldron.

Bundling a dark stone and a fistful of damp grass into a pouch, I crawled in near silence from one corner of the tent to another. Near silence—but not complete.

Row on, my boys, row on
Row on, my boys, row on
The land behind, the sea beyond,
Row on, my boys, row on

And if we meet a blust'ring storm
Row on, my boys, row on
And if we meet a whirlwind tall
Row on, my boys, row on

And if we meet a pirate ship
Row on, my boys, row on
And if we've not got naught to eat
Row on, my boys, row on

With every word I sang below my breath, I willed the Mercians to keep walking. Then I clawed a hole in the dirt and buried the pouch inside. A stone the color of night and grass from the hilltop, in hopes we would be invisible to them as they passed.

"*Safe, safe, safe,*" I whispered, almost mouthing the words. "*Safe, safe, safe.*"

When I crawled back beside Dafydd, squeezing close to him and Gruffudd, his hands were red and blistered from raking through the fire. My own were caked with dirt.

Outside our tent, the soldiers' footfalls shook the earth.

I was so, so glad Tal was safe in the farmhouse.

Dafydd moved slowly as he wrapped his arms around me, tucking my head beneath his chin. I could've stopped him, if I wanted. But I didn't.

When I woke in the cold dawn, we were alone. The soldiers were gone. Dafydd had crawled away to sleep on the far side of the fire. I had dreamt again of being trapped.

Fear spiked through me at the memory. But as I lay there shaking, my head still unclear with sleep, I felt the earth beneath me draw a long, anxious breath.

Our journey was almost finished.

I dreaded to think what stood between us and the dyke's end.

44

TAL

On the Dyke, Gwynedd

I'd regretted leaving Ffion the moment I went inside the farmhouse, rain or no rain. And in the morning, as she told me about the Mercian soldiers who had passed their tent, I knew I'd been right.

It didn't account for why she and Dafydd could hardly look at each other, though. A hollow, pointless sort of anger built inside me as we traveled on.

"Anyway, they were moving east," Ffion said, panting as she climbed.

East, from deeper within Gwynedd. Whatever they'd been doing, it wasn't good news for us. "Do you think they were moving to join the camp Osian saw?"

"Hard to say." She grimaced. "Hopefully we aren't racing them north."

"How many days until the attack?" Dafydd asked.

"Two," Ffion and I said at the same time. He nodded, eyeing Ffion worriedly as her rattling cough slowed her climb.

I'd hoped my worry would drown out my jealousy. Unfortunately for me, it turned out that I could feel both very effectively at the same time.

The rain continued as we followed the dyke that day, closing the distance to Prestatyn, stopping in villages to ask after hedgewitches. Around midday, when Ffion's cough got worse, she sent Dafydd alone into a town to make inquiries. "They'll think I'm a plague victim and

I'll scare everyone off," she grumbled. "Besides, I can't bear to watch another fraud try to poison me back to health."

Dafydd gave Ffion's shoulder a quick squeeze and promised he would hurry back. From where she and I waited beneath the dripping trees, I could see a little row of half-timbered houses and another fouled lake, close enough to the dyke that I knew who was responsible.

It had been not quite two weeks since Ffion had purified Llyn Glas for Angws and the Mercians. I wondered if she would have the magic or even the physical strength for the same task now.

And yet magic buzzed around me. The smell of the rain and the earth, the phantom boil of a kettle; they were inescapable. Was it the magic of the dyke, or was there simply magic in the country, or was it both?

I didn't care. If this was magic drained from the land, I dreaded its return.

I thought again of the Foxhall, and how easy it would be to join Rhiannon. To have everything I wanted.

Everything but Ffion, of course.

A gust of wind sent water showering down over us, and Ffion yelped. "Come here," I said, beckoning her toward the wagon. She hesitated, but only a moment.

My palm sang with her touch as I pulled her up beside me. And when her knee bumped mine through her kirtle, as I adjusted the oilcloth over the two of us, I felt a jolt through my whole body.

Dafydd needed to hurry back.

"Were your mother and Rhiannon ever friends?" I asked Ffion.

"What made you think of that?" She sounded surprised.

"Nothing," I lied. "Just curious."

Just thinking about the Foxhall and the kind of pain they could save me. Just thinking about how friends lose each other.

Just curious.

"Well. Yes, they were." Ffion shifted. Beneath the hem of her skirt, I saw the soft, freckled skin of her ankles, the ivy she'd first wrapped around them at Merthyr-Tewdrig now little more than two bare vines. "They were close."

"What changed?" I asked.

"Well, obviously the separation changed things. A Foxhall witch being married to the court magician lent the coven legitimacy, which Rhiannon traded on as she built up her empire." Ffion paused. "But I always suspected Rhiannon felt competitive toward my mam, about how powerful she is."

I blinked. "Your mother?" I asked. *The woman too timid for sustained eye contact?*

"Wildly powerful." Ffion's voice was full of the satisfaction that only comes from delivering a good piece of gossip. "Just . . . incapable of standing up for herself."

This I acknowledged with a *look*. "I'm afraid Rhiannon is going to have to be dealt with someday."

"Probably," she agreed. "Do you think it'll be before or after my mother loses her mind and stages that coup you joked about?"

I laughed. "What's your mam's magic like? Is it like yours? Not her way of working," I added quickly. "I know she uses more material than you do. But does it . . . ?" I paused, not sure what I was asking.

"Sort of." Ffion sounded almost pleased. "I'm surprised you'd think of that. But yes, a little. Our work manifests slowly at first, and then it sort of appears."

"I've noticed that before," I said. "When you purified Llyn Glas. When you dug the well."

Ffion's gaze drifted through the dripping trees, finally lighting on my face.

Her throat moved delicately. When she shifted, her hip brushed mine. I swallowed hard.

"I forgot Mam and I had that in common," she finally said. "Thank you for reminding me."

I started to say something else. But then Dafydd came crashing through the trees.

"Didn't find anything," he called, sounding disappointed. Ffion jumped down from the wagon like she'd been stung.

I knew she and Dafydd would be suited, Osian had said. *In many ways.*

Not for you, he might as well have told me.

Ffion had chosen to stay with Dafydd again and again.

I wasn't my brother. I could take a hint. I knew when to have some dignity and give up.

"Time to move on, then," she sang out—too brightly—and I took up the reins, and we were off again.

From there, the day only got worse.

Ffion had done well enough moving downhill that morning. But she struggled up and down the next hill, and in a torrential rain on the climb above Pont-Goch that evening, she lost her footing and fell into the ditch.

"I'm fine," she panted as we raced over to help her out of the mud. "I'm fine. I was just looking at—look at this!"

A crack stretched along the dyke, about six feet long and a foot deep. Dafydd frowned. "What is it?"

"I think this means it's working." Ffion looked feverish, hair plastered to her cheeks. "The spell to break the dyke. It's working."

My stomach jerked unpleasantly. "It could be."

"It *is*," Ffion insisted.

She wanted it to be. I didn't. I wasn't sure either of us was being objective.

But at the moment, a crack in the ground that might be something or might be nothing wasn't what really mattered. Ffion picked up her cauldron again and started forward, wincing and trying to hide it.

"Ffion." I knew she could hear me, but she didn't answer. "*Ffion.*"

She hissed again, in obvious pain. Dafydd put a hand on her arm. And just as I'd known she would, she jerked away.

He looked surprised, and hurt. But I could've told him frustration made Ffion spiky. I already knew what was coming, what had to be done.

"I'm sorry," Ffion apologized to Dafydd. She stood grimacing beside the ditch, all her weight on one leg. "I didn't mean to do that. I need help."

"I'll help you," I said. "Into the wagon. We'll stop for the night."

Her face hardened. "No. Not this time, Tal."

"We have to."

"Tal, not again!" she said. "Twice now, we've been within five miles of our destination and you've forced us to stop. We're in spitting distance of Prestatyn. Not today. Not this time."

I held up a finger. "Our wheel got stuck on the way to Mathrafal. Not my fault." I held up a second finger. "And on the way to Black Darren, you were the one who suggested we stay with Enid."

"Tal, we are almost there." Ffion's expression was agonized. "We can get the blade and be done. Aren't you desperate to be done?"

I was. I was desperate to know if magic would be returning, and if my curse would hold. Desperate, I supposed, for Ffion to get on with picking Dafydd, so I could go back to protecting my mam and stop aching for something I couldn't have.

"Ffion." Dafydd's voice was gentle. "You can't walk another two hours. It's pouring rain. And we're in no state to be received at Prestatyn," he added, gesturing to himself.

"It doesn't matter, Dafydd," Ffion pleaded. "We have to."

I held up a hand. "I'll help you get to Prestatyn. I'll walk the whole way with you," I said. "If you can walk to that tree." I gestured to one about six feet away.

Lightning tore at the sky. Ffion clenched her jaw, but didn't move.

"You can't, can you?" I demanded. "Ffion, what have you done to yourself?"

"I'll make camp here, then," she said, angling away from me. "Dafydd, would you help me set up the oilcloths?"

"Will you stop?" I stared at her. "Ffion, you have to come inside. There's lightning, and you're sick, and you've done something to your ankle. This is ridiculous."

"No." Ffion shook her head, rain still pouring down her face and hair. "I need the dreams. I have to—"

"We have the blades!" I burst out. "You've walked the full length of the dyke! Why can't you rest? Why can't you just—"

"Because I have to!" Ffion hollered back. "Because I keep hoping the dreams will tell me if this will work, because if it doesn't, I will have nothing!"

"If you die out here, you will *also* have nothing!" I flung my arms wide.

"I don't care!" she shouted. "I have to do this my way."

"No." I shook my head, pushing my wet hair out of my eyes. "No. You do this my way, or you're free of our agreement."

"What?" Ffion drew back, startled. "You can't."

Dafydd stood silent, just watching.

"I can." I couldn't believe I hadn't thought of this already. "You come inside, and you care properly for your ankle. You sleep in a bed for the night. You eat hot food, not something half raw, half burned over a campfire. You continue our journey *in shoes*." I was breathing hard now, furious at her, furious at myself for letting her do this to herself. "You do this, or I am letting you go. I will pay you what you're owed. But you won't work for me anymore."

Ffion's thin chest rose and fell furiously. She was so near me I could have kissed her if I'd bent my head.

"Fine," she ground out. She was shaking with rage. But I scooped her up and carried her through the rain toward the lights of the pub in the distance.

I could smell her hair and her skin. I could feel her hip through her gown. Her mouth was only a breath from my neck.

I carried her up the Red Dragon's stairs, tossed her down on the room's single bed, and stomped away again before I could do something stupid.

Now's your chance, I thought at Dafydd as he hurried inside.

"I'm sorry, Ffion," I heard him say.

"I'm sorry, too," I said. "Sorry it took me so long to do this."

The door slammed shut behind me.

Blood boiling, I stomped down the stairs and slammed a fistful of silver on the bar. The innkeeper's eyes went wide.

"Evening," I said. "I need a healer."

45

DAFYDD

Ffion might have known if she was shaking more from anger or the cold, but I certainly couldn't have said.

"How dare he threaten to break our contract?" she asked, teeth chattering. Her hair and dress dripped onto the floorboards; rain pattered on the roof overhead. "How dare he, that snide, controlling, arrogant—"

I made a noncommittal sound, tossed her a dry kirtle, and turned away.

For all I'd been questioning Tal's judgment lately, he'd been unquestionably right to bring Ffion inside. I should've been the one to do it.

I wasn't quite ready to think about why I hadn't.

A knock came at the door. "Come in," Ffion snapped.

I expected to see Tal. But the latch clicked, and laughter and pipe music poured in from the pub downstairs as a woman ducked inside.

"Who are you?" Ffion asked, more or less politely. But I knew her face.

She was in her early thirties, with pale skin and plain brown hair. She'd asked a question that had troubled me when I'd met her on my first journey to Prestatyn.

If you and another adult and a child were starving and had no more hope of getting food, who would starve, and who would eat?

"You," I said. "I know you."

"From the Bwbach and Board. Dafydd," the woman said slowly, like she was recalling my face, too. She turned to Ffion. "I'm Canaid. Your friend sent me to you, to help with your ankle."

"My friend?"

"Tall, dark, irritable, handsome. Wears an expensive red coat."

Ffion scoffed. "I hate that coat."

"Tal agrees it's too much, but it's sentimental," I said, distracted. "Gwanwyn had it made for him right after they finally got rooms at Mathrafal." Ffion blinked at me, looking as surprised as I felt. I'd thought Tal was drowning his annoyance in the pub; apparently he'd been busy.

Canaid bent to examine Ffion's ankle. "It's a nasty sprain."

"I slipped," Ffion said.

"I see that." Canaid began salving Ffion's ankle, humming as she worked.

The last of the dragons have gone to sleep,
'Neath wings of scale and fledge,
The afancs and the gwiberod
Now lie beneath the hedge.

Ffion shot me a sharp glance I couldn't read.

"Do you always sing as you work?" she asked Canaid.

"Only sometimes." She cleared her throat. "It helps me gather myself."

"That's interesting. I always do," Ffion said. She paused. "And after all the looking we've done, it's interesting that Tal managed to stumble across the last real witch in Gwynedd."

Canaid stilled.

She didn't look like a witch, in her plain dress, with her hair braided. But the look she gave Ffion was confirmation enough.

"Quite a lot of us have gone south to join the Foxhall," she finally said. "I'm not the last of us, but only a few are left here in Gwynedd—me, my brother Iorweth, a few others. But we're here to help those who need it."

"Have you heard Mercia recruited a witch?" Ffion asked. "There's one traveling with their armies."

Canaid nodded. "I've seen magic at work east of here, beyond the dyke," she said. "But I don't know who could be responsible. There are so few of us left."

"Even for revenge against Powys?" I asked tentatively.

"Our relationship with Powys is strained. But even then—to betray our people to Mercia. I can't see it." She shook her head. "I'll keep an ear out. And you keep that elevated," she added, nodding at Ffion's ankle. "I'll be back in the morning."

Ffion nodded. I walked Canaid to our door, searching myself for money I knew I hadn't packed.

Canaid eyed me patting my pockets and frowned. "Your brother already paid me," she said severely. "I've warned you once about traveling without coin. Be shrewder, Dafydd. Time to grow up."

I nodded, flushing. Then I braced myself. "I've thought about the question you and Iorweth asked. And I have an answer." I took a long breath. "All remaining food belongs to the child. Every adult spends their last days teaching him what he needs to know to survive without them."

"Good," Canaid said. "A good answer."

The fiddle downstairs sang on as she left. I put out the candles on the table and the windowsill. There was only a bare sliver of moonlight filtering through the shutters.

Ffion lay on her stomach, eyes shut. "What does that mean?" she asked.

I didn't know how to explain, so I didn't. "It means we still don't know who's working for Mercia, and we have to think of a new plan tomorrow," I said. "You should rest."

"I'm not tired," Ffion said, sounding exhausted. "And here, I'm afraid I won't get the dreams, Dafydd. Everything hurts, but I could've done it. I could've stayed out by the dyke."

I steeled my nerves. Sitting beside her on the bed, I began to rub her back, feeling her muscles shift beneath her dress.

"You could've done it, but I think Tal was right," I said. "You have to take better care of yourself."

It irritated me to bring him up. But watching Ffion getting sicker, hurting herself—I knew I'd been romantic, before, about living rough.

I should've been the one to bring her inside, instead of worrying about not making her angry. Now I was just glad to have her dry, in front of a fire, with a properly tended injury.

"Traitor." Her voice was muffled by the pillow.

"I know. I'm sorry." I moved to her neck, trying to loosen all the tension she carried there. "I told you we're alike, Ffion. Your father had to make me see what my forge work was doing. And tonight—"

And tonight, Tal had had to make her see she had to stop. Because I hadn't been willing to tell her what she hadn't wanted to hear.

"What next?" I asked her. "What else hurts?"

Her hair was like liquid fire. The skin of her neck was soft.

I'd been this close to her the night before, on the hilltop. But fear had brought us together then. I hoped this was something else.

Gingerly, Ffion rolled over, and my heart began to thunder.

Her face was upturned to me now, cast in the faint moonlight, every freckle on her cheeks like the glitter of sparks in a fire.

"Kiss me, Dafydd," she said quietly. "No more talking. I want you to kiss me now."

I had always been good at waiting. At denying myself. But I was an utter failure at denying her.

And I had been dying to show her how it could be between us.

I had imagined a hundred first kisses with Ffion over the years since I'd learned who she was.

When I was fourteen, it had been at a dance in my father's great hall.

When I was sixteen, it had been in my forge, with her sitting on my workbench.

When I turned eighteen, I dreamt of finding her in Foxhall, of waking her beneath the hedge by kissing the dew from her lips and neck.

This kiss was all of those and more.

Ffion rose up onto her elbows, and I slid my arms beneath her. When I pressed my lips to hers, her mouth was warm and soft and searching beneath mine.

A kiss for the blade: that had been our agreement.

I desperately wanted to give her better than she'd bargained for.

My arms tightened around her, pulling her close enough that I could feel the rise and fall of her chest, and the kiss grew hungrier between us. Ffion gasped and slid a hand into my hair as my lips parted.

I had never kissed her before. But I let memory and the moment guide me, running my hand up her back, kissing her hair and her cheek and her throat.

"Fair trade?" I whispered in her ear when I couldn't breathe anymore. Ffion traced my cheek with her fingertips, looking dazed. She shook her head.

My heart was a riot in my chest. Her words came out a whisper.

"Nothing about this is fair," she said.

46

FFION

Long after Dafydd's breathing had evened, my heart beat a jagged tattoo in my chest.

The kiss had been part of our agreement, but fate had picked the time and place. I'd recognized the room from my vision the moment Tal had dumped me on the bed.

But even the fact of our bargain hadn't diminished what I felt when Dafydd touched me.

I want you, Ffion. I always have.

It was a heady thing, to feel his yearning. To be kissed like water drunk after an endless walk, like sleep after a long day.

Dafydd slept peacefully on the rug as I tossed and turned. Music played on downstairs. And still, Tal didn't come to bed.

The moon was dangerously thin beyond the window that separated me from the night outside. When it began its descent toward the horizon, I hitched myself off the mattress and made for the pub downstairs.

Y Ddraig Goch's public room wasn't as nice as the Dead Man's Bells, in my opinion, but it wasn't so different from any other pub. Warm light and a low-beamed ceiling, a crwth and pipes and old men playing knucklebones. Tal's glass of bragawd was more or less untouched when I sat down beside him.

"Why are you awake?" I asked.

"Because rural inns are their most fascinating when I can't hear myself think." Tal didn't look at me as he lifted something off the seat beside him and dropped it onto the tabletop with a *thunk*. "I got you shoes."

They were low boots, pretty and soft-looking. From the delicate tooling of the leather, they were obviously expensive.

"Thank you." My voice was subdued. "I just—I thought you'd be tired."

"Asking me why I'm not asleep is akin to asking you why you're not staying off your ankle like Canaid told you," he said, jaw working. "There's no answer that's going to satisfy both of us."

"Canaid. Hm." I stole his drink and took a sip. "And how did you find her?"

"Told the landlady I was looking for a healer."

"Hm." Another sip. "Healer, witch. Sometimes they're the same thing."

Tal nearly fell out of his chair turning to gape at me.

It was gratifying to shake him out of his sulk. Quickly, I related what she'd told us.

"So we're no further on that front," I finished. "Unless Canaid is wrong, or lying. Maybe she doesn't know every witch in Gwynedd. Maybe one of them would be willing to betray Gwynedd to punish Powys."

Tal looked defeated. "It would've helped to know who we were up against, but it doesn't matter, I guess," he said. "At least we've still got your original plan, to die a martyr's death on the road north."

I felt a flare of irritation. "I'm not—"

"Yes, you are," he cut me off. "First you say you have to walk the whole distance of the dyke. Then you add that you have to walk barefoot. That turns into an insistence on *sleeping* on the dyke, rain or shine. That's not method, Ffion. That's martyrdom. Why does your magic insist on you torturing yourself?" he asked. "Why isn't your work enough?"

"It doesn't," I said. "The magic doesn't care how I feel. It's just a cauldron that has to be filled—filled in less than two days, before Cadno and my magic are gone forever. And it doesn't care how I do it."

Tal turned, brown eyes entirely fixed on me. "That's where I think you're wrong, Ffion. I don't know much about magic. But I think it cares very, very much how you feel."

His shirt was unlaced at his throat, and the skin beneath was smooth and tanned. The embroidery on his red coat winked in the firelight.

"I told you before I've been having dreams, Tal," I said. "They're stronger when I sleep near the dyke." I ran a finger over the gold thread at his wrist, and he stilled.

"Dreams?"

"The first one was of a huge, cold sea. And in the second one, I'm underground. Everything's dark," I said. "I don't know what they mean. But they're connected to the magic in the dyke. And I just keep hoping they'll tell me what to do, what to hope for. But they're not clear enough. Or I don't understand—" I broke off. I was not going to cry in a pub after two sips of bragawd.

For a moment, he just sat, like he was lost in the wood grain of the table. Then he got up and made for the stairs.

"Wait. Tal, wait." I scrambled to my feet and trotted after him, struggling on my bad ankle. He must have remembered I was hurt at the same time I did, because he paused on the landing. "Why are you running off?"

"Nothing." Tal pressed his hands into his eyes. "I'm tired."

"You weren't tired a minute ago."

"Dreams, the dyke—for one hour, Ffion, I didn't want to talk about magic!" he burst out, voice still low. "We'll do our job. Try to get the blade, try to destroy the dyke. That's all you can ask of me."

"All I can ask of you?" I demanded. "What does that mean?"

Tal's laugh was hollow. He looked bitter and weary and breakable in the dark.

"Did you know that the plan the Foxhall proposed was the plan I set out with?" he asked, stepping closer to me. "I wanted to leave the dyke and magic alone, and focus on meeting Offa's attack. Then, when I told Rhiannon I had to destroy the dyke and restore magic, she suggested destroying it might not bring back magic at all. Maybe she was wrong. But that's what I've been hoping for."

I blinked at him. "You didn't want magic to come back?"

"No," he said. "No, I don't."

I'd lied to Tal, of course. But I'd lied to cover up my own shortcomings as we worked together. I'd been lying even as I was doing my best to help him win his father's favor.

Tal had been lying every time he said he was sorry I'd lost Cadno. Every time he encouraged or helped me. Because really, he'd been hoping all along that I'd lose everything.

It shouldn't have been a surprise. I knew how he felt about magic.

But after all our weeks together, hearing it cut me to the heart.

"Well, my magic's never been weaker," I said. "You might get your wish."

I threw the punch. Watched it land. It brought no satisfaction.

Tal bowed his head.

"Are you going to go find them?" I asked. "Are you going to join the Foxhall and your father?"

"I don't think so," he said. "I don't know."

I hadn't been able to stop thinking of Gwanwyn's story since I'd heard it. Fourteen-year-old Tal caring for his mother, facing malicious crowds, burdened with a curse.

"You don't have to carry that night forever, Tal," I said quietly. "Things can be different. The Mari Lwyd could be wrong."

"I do if magic comes back," he said. "If magic is restored, I will always doubt. Even if I become king, I'll doubt my ability to hold the throne. I will have no rest."

"You know, I'm not the only one martyring myself, Tal," I said after a moment. "Do you think your mother wants you to sacrifice everything to keep her safe?"

"You aren't safe," he challenged me, lifting his chin, and even with tears in my eyes I wanted to kiss his throat again. "You told me once you had magic that could stop my heart. Break my bones."

"Does my magic make you afraid?"

"Everything about you makes me a little afraid."

And when I stepped forward and put my hands on his chest, I could feel from his heartbeat that it was true.

"I don't mind," I said. "All those creatures you told me you were afraid of—I know you wonder at them a little, too." I swallowed. "Can't you trust that magic isn't either good or bad? That it's just a tool in the hand, like a hammer or a crown?"

Can't you trust my magic, weak as it is? Can't you trust me? I was really asking.

"Ffion," Tal said quietly. "I saw you kissing Dafydd."

I froze. "Tal—"

"No." He held up a hand. "It's the way it should be. The two of you suit."

He lifted my hands from his chest, brown eyes unhappy, and I thought again of the courting song I'd sung at the party.

I am for you, you are for me. I am for thou, we are for us.

It was a song about mismatched love. About knowing where you belonged, even if no one else did. But standing in the dark with Tal, I knew the words were just words.

Dafydd had always been intended for the throne. And I—I had always been intended for Dafydd.

"We should sleep," Tal finally said. "This will all be over soon."

47

TAL

The first time I woke up the next day, it was to Dafydd stumping around my mat on the floor. Gods' candles, he was loud.

I swatted his ankle and he jerked to a stop. *You'll wake her up,* I mouthed, gesticulating at Ffion on the mattress. She lay balled up beneath her blanket, only her hair visible.

Dafydd frowned. *What?* Finally, I staggered to my feet and dragged him out into the hall.

"You walk like you're fifteen people," I hissed, once we were outside. "You'll wake her up."

"Sorry." Dafydd winced. "Last night, where did you—?"

"I saw her kissing you." The words came out before I could stop them. "I came upstairs after I found Canaid, and you were sitting on the bed, kissing."

Dafydd looked away, blushing fiercely. "It was part of our bargain," he said. "When I agreed to give her the blade, she agreed to let me travel with you both, and to owe me a kiss."

I could still see Ffion, her hands in his hair, eyes shut. They hadn't even noticed me open the door and close it again. It hadn't looked particularly transactional to me.

"Some bargain," I said.

And then she'd come downstairs looking for me.

She'd cornered me just out here. She'd pressed me until I almost came apart, until I told her the truth.

The truth was, I'd wanted to hold still and let her break me to pieces.

"Do you love her, Tal?" Dafydd asked quietly.

I looked away. "She frustrates me. She doesn't tell me anything, until she tells me everything. She just . . ." I shook my head. "It doesn't matter."

"It matters more than anything," Dafydd said.

Infuriating as she was, Ffion was the truest friend I'd ever had. I didn't know if I loved her. I'd never have the chance to find out.

"She's meant for you," I said. "Osian told me that when we were children, he saw that you'd refuse the throne. Your connection to Ffion was supposed to keep that from happening."

He was supposed to see her as his witch. He was supposed to see her as more.

"I didn't understand any of that or what the connection was for until it was too late, and by then, I couldn't tell you," Dafydd said helplessly. "When he bound us, Osian only told me I was going to meet my best friend. At first, I actually told him no, because you were my best friend." He huffed a laugh, and suddenly, my throat was tight. "I only accepted because we had a fight a week later over whose pony could get to the city wall faster."

At that, I laughed, too, and found my eyes were suddenly damp. I swiped at them, blinking furiously.

I was so tired.

"I wish you'd told me," I said.

Dafydd nodded. "I wish I had, too."

I didn't know if it would have changed our circumstances. But it might have changed things between Dafydd and me.

"We should go back to sleep," I finally said. "Any minute now, she might pop up and start delivering marching orders."

"You go, brother," Dafydd said, clasping me on the shoulder before turning toward the stairs. "I couldn't rest right now."

I slept. In my dreams, I was back on the landing with Ffion, and I had another chance.

In my dreams, I told her yes.

The second time I woke, I knew something was wrong. The door to the pub slammed open and shut; footsteps ran up and down the stairs. Through the window came cries and wails.

My boots were on my feet and I was halfway downstairs before I knew what I was doing. "Tal!" Ffion's voice came from behind me. "Tal, what's going on?"

"Ffion, go back to the room." The pub was crowded with people—children wrapped in blankets, babies crying, men and women talking worriedly and clinging to their belongings.

"What happened?" Ffion limped to the bar behind me.

"You're not supposed to be on that ankle," I hissed, helping her into a chair.

"They've come from just north of Pen-y-Cloddiau," the landlady said, naming the town where we'd stopped the night before as she hurriedly sliced bread and served cawl. "Mercians set fire to their village. You can see the smoke in the sky outside."

Ffion's eyes widened in horror. "Then—the soldiers Dafydd and I saw at the hillfort—"

"They may have crossed the dyke into Mercia, but they didn't stay there," I said. "They *are* moving north."

"Did they have a witch with them?" Ffion asked.

"Not that I heard," said the landlady, grimacing. "But they did damage enough without one."

I glanced around the room again, frustrated. Ffion started toward a woman clutching a sprained wrist.

But I caught her by the arm. "I know you want to help them," I said. "I do, too. But the best way to do that is to get to Prestatyn and mount a plan to meet this attack. *Now.*"

"You're right. My magic—Tal, I might have enough left to finish this. But that's all." She grimaced. "Where's Dafydd?"

"He went to help the thatcher repair the columbarium," said the landlady.

"Can someone go find him?" I asked. The landlady called a boy over as I dumped another fistful of coins on the bar. "Restock your larder. Feed them in the meantime." I jerked my head at the crowds.

"You're a kind young man," said the landlady, giving a watery smile. "You and your brother. What a pair you make."

48

DAFYDD

The thatcher passed me beams up the ladder, and all I could think was that I couldn't have helped fix the columbarium if I'd been asked only a few days earlier.

After speaking with Tal that morning, I'd gone down to the pub and choked down the bowl of mush the landlady had offered me. I'd only been there a few minutes when a man came in.

"Branch smashed in the roof of the columbarium last night," he said. "Problem is, Bryn and his cousins and all their boys have answered Bleddyn's summons. And I still can't—" He made to lift his arm, but winced when his elbow got near shoulder height.

"Your columbarium?" I asked. "Have they—have the ravens—?"

"We live in hope," the landlady said, smiling resignedly. "When magic returns, we won't be caught napping. And anyway, think of all the rooks and unsighted ravens that make their home there now."

I cleared my throat, choosing my next words carefully. "I ask because I hear sighted ravens have returned to Mathrafal." Busy as I was pushing the mush around my bowl, I didn't miss the excited glance they exchanged.

Ffion and Tal were asleep in our room. I didn't want to wait downstairs until Ffion was ready to talk about the night before.

"I know blacksmithing, not building," I'd said, getting to my feet. "But I can help you, if you'll show me how."

So I spent the day with the thatcher, replacing the shattered beams and scattered thatch of the columbarium. The job had me at awkward angles fifteen feet off the ground, and it was no wonder that those left in Pont-Goch—those who hadn't been called up to serve King Bleddyn—weren't able to see to it. Curious children crowded inside the door as I climbed up and down the ladder inside the little circular building, replacing beams, securing straw bundles with hazel stick spars.

All around me were niches full of abandoned nests and gleaming black feathers.

"You ought to get someone to teach you how to thatch a roof properly," the thatcher said to me, not quite reproachful. "This won't be the last time you're called upon for it, to be sure."

I couldn't help it. I laughed.

The work was nearly done when the sound of hoofbeats and footfalls came thundering up the road. One or two wagons at first—but they were traveling too quickly, and then there were more of them. I gripped the ladder rungs and stared down the road.

Wagons. Riders. Runners with their arms full of belongings.

And far away, smoke rising.

They were coming from the south, most unshod or half-dressed despite the cold. Many of them were weeping.

I leapt to the ground, weaving through the gathered children toward the arriving number. "What's happened?" the thatcher shouted, and a woman in a torn cloak clambered down from her horse. I caught her as she fell out of her saddle, legs weak.

"Not me," she gasped. "My boy." The woman pointed shakily at the wagon behind her, where a girl of around twelve was silently sobbing.

I sprang into the wagon bed. "What's—"

But there was no need to ask. The girl was white-faced, almost as pale as the unconscious boy my age beside her. She had a ferocious grip on a wad of fabric, soaked with the blood pulsing from a wound on his leg.

I pointed to one of the boys hanging around the columbarium. "Canaid, the healer!" I called sharply. "Find her!" As he shot off, villagers began to emerge from their homes, expressions shifting from curiosity to horror as they took in the scene.

Canaid was at my side at once, and the mother explained that the boy had taken a bowshot to the leg when Mercians burned their village. We carried the boy inside a nearby home, and when Canaid had set to work, I went back to the girl still sitting in the wagon. "Come inside," I said. "It's cold."

"I didn't press hard enough," she said, staring at her bloodstained palms. "Someone else would have done better."

"You did your best," I said gently.

The girl shook her head. "Someone else should have done it," she said hoarsely.

I put myself on her level. My heart was beating hard. "Who else?" I asked, challenging. "Who else was there?"

"No one." Her words came out small.

"You could have cried the whole way here with your head in your hands, and he would have died on the road," I said, too fierce, but I couldn't help myself. "And no one would have blamed you. But you didn't. And why?"

She was pale and underfed, with two long childish braids and tear tracks on her face. But her voice was determined when she spoke. "Because it had to be done," she said. "And there was only me to do it."

I put a hand on her shoulder. "It had to be done," I said. "So it had to be you."

For a while, we could only try to manage the catastrophe. Children had to be consoled, babies fed, the elderly persuaded to rest. The old thatcher and I were the only men left in town who weren't too sick or frail to fight, and he was injured; it was up to me and a few others to move the wounded so Canaid could help them, to hold them down when she had to tend the worst injuries.

I didn't know how long had passed before a boy ran up to me. "Prince Dafydd! Are you Prince Dafydd?" he demanded, out of breath.

"Prince?" The thatcher goggled at me. "Dafydd ap Cadell?"

"Never mind. Yes, what is it?" I asked the boy. Canaid was salving the burns of a badly injured man, and he shrieked in pain.

"Prince Taliesin and the witch need you," he said.

I stiffened. "Is something wrong?"

"No, but they said to meet them at the stables."

"Tell them I'm coming," I said. In all the uproar, I'd forgotten we had another emergency.

The thatcher caught me by the wrist before releasing me, looking uncomfortable. "You said you were a blacksmith, boy. I'm—I'm sorry."

"I was a blacksmith," I said. "Sort of."

But he shook his head. "You're going to be king of Powys." He jutted a finger at me. "There's a war coming. Rise to the occasion. Keep us safe."

"I will," I promised, struggling to catch my breath. "I'll do better than my father. I'll be better." He nodded.

And I knew I could.

I tore back to the Red Dragon. "Ffion!" I shouted, my voice echoing off homes and rocks and trees. "Tal! Ffion!"

"Dafydd!" Tal reached down to me from the wagon seat as the horses came roaring out of the barn. Ffion sat in the wagon bed with Gruffudd.

I hauled myself up. "She's riding?"

"We have to get to Prestatyn," Tal said. "Before Offa moves again."

"If I can't destroy the last five miles of the dyke, so be it. We have to get the last blade from Bleddyn before we're out of time entirely." She turned to my brother. "Drive fast, Tal."

Ffion sang all the way to Prestatyn, about breadmaking and courting and highway robbery and faithless lovers.

The sky was clear, the sun blistering, the wheels rattling precariously over ruts and bumps. Ffion's hair blew behind her as she clutched Gruffudd and the wagon's side, as we raced past a dry riverbed beneath a Mercian dam and an abandoned encampment on a moor.

The ditch was always to our right.

Below the final hill of the dyke, Prestatyn Castle and the sea beyond rose to greet me for the second time. The sun shone off the waves and the gray standing stones, and King Bleddyn's afancs flew on their standards.

We rode through the gates, through the town, to the keep itself. At the stables, Tal helped Ffion down. The two of them were at the door before they realized I wasn't following.

"Dafydd." Ffion was breathless. "Come on."

But I couldn't move. "I should stay here. I should wait."

"No." Tal shook his head. "Dafydd, we do this together."

"I couldn't convince Bleddyn to form an alliance before." My voice grew desperate. "And I haven't told you why."

"That doesn't matter now. We don't need his armies. We just need his trust for a little while." Ffion squeezed my arm. "And who wouldn't trust you?"

I couldn't say no to her.

"Come on," Tal said. "We're out of time."

We ran. Or—we tried. When Ffion yelped and clutched her ankle, Tal and I each put an arm around her and helped her on.

I had always been good at waiting. But it was all too slow—the errand boy at the castle's front doors, the steward in the silver-painted entryway, the high man who met us outside the great hall and told us King Bleddyn was busy—and then recognized my face.

"You," he said, confused.

"I have a new proposal," I said quickly.

"You rejected ours." He shook his head. "And anyway, you're too late."

"What do you mean?" Tal asked. But the man didn't answer, and the doors burst open.

I had thought only Tal and Ffion would be surprised by what they learned at Prestatyn Castle, but I had been wrong.

My shock nearly knocked me over.

Because my father was waiting for us, and the Foxhall was with him.

He stood with Rhiannon and Arianrhod on the dais near King Bleddyn's throne, the sounds of the sea filtering through the grilles that covered the windows. "Dafydd?" He scowled. "Tal?"

"Father." I steadied myself against the wall. "I thought you'd gone to Ceredigion."

"I'm sure you wished as much." My father's voice was cold. "You told me Bleddyn denied your request for an alliance."

In a way, he did, I wanted to say. But there was no point trying to be clever. Not with Bleddyn standing right there on the dais, watching me with quiet curiosity.

"When I arrived, though, King Bleddyn offered me armies to confront Mercia straight away," my father said. "So long as we supported his campaign on their southwestern front."

"You mean his attempt to conquer Ceredigion," I said.

"I assumed you had carried this message back to your father," King Bleddyn said, speaking for the first time. "But when he arrived, I found him totally unaware of my offer."

Ffion and Tal studied Bleddyn, and I could see them taking him in as I had—thirty or so, slim and tidy, with an unassuming air and a reserved smile.

I had learned on my last visit not to trust it.

Gruffudd pressed against my side, sensing my anxiety. "You failed on purpose," Ffion said, quietly, wondering.

"I told you there would be consequences if you refused to try," Dad said. "Consequences Tal and his mother will meet when I return to Mathrafal."

Tal drew in a sharp breath. "Dafydd, what is he talking about?"

I ignored him. I could only handle one crisis at a time. "Bleddyn's condition for protecting us from our would-be conquerors was to help them conquer their own neighbors," I said to my father. "That's why I came home empty-handed two weeks ago. Conquest is an avenue I would never consider."

It had been true four years ago. It was true now.

"Weak," my father muttered, shaking his head. "Pure, and useless. Hardly even fit to be candler."

Unlike himself, he meant. My father would always choose the pragmatic way, and I would always choose my principles. And it infuriated him.

But my father was wrong about me.

I didn't understand how this would all play out. But I had spoken with the ravens.

I knew how it would end.

49

FFION

Prestatyn Castle, Gwynedd

I used to let Tal win at everything, Dafydd had said.

Apparently he'd never outgrown the habit.

I couldn't believe it. Dafydd had thrown away victory in his father's challenge with both hands. And he had been protecting Tal, somehow, all along.

King Cadell stood on the dais, six feet of muscles and braids and fury, just as my father had always described him. Behind him, Rhiannon, my sister, and a few other Foxhall witches waited, looking windblown and feral beside Gwynedd's tidy king, who had so tidily shocked us all.

I expected Tal to be humiliated by his father's words. But he stood straight-backed beside me, and spoke up unashamed.

"Father, please," Tal interrupted. "I have a boon to seek of King Bleddyn. I believe I can still complete the task you set Dafydd and me."

I would have told him not to speak. But without waiting for his father to respond, Tal turned to Gwynedd's king. "I am Prince Taliesin of Powys. This is my witch, Ffion vch Osian, the hedgewitch of Foxhall. We seek the blade belonging to Gwynedd so we can destroy King Offa's Dyke. We have already acquired Brycheiniog's blade and Powys's, toward this end."

Cadell blanched.

"To work her spell, over the last two and a half weeks, Ffion has walked the length of the dyke—apart from the five miles we drove from Pont-Goch," Tal said. "Because there, we met villagers from Pen-y-Cloddiau, which has been sacked and burned by the Mercians."

"Is that so?" King Bleddyn asked. He had beautiful hands, tucked lightly into his belt, and his hair curled neatly behind his ears.

"Yes," I said. "The Mercians are coming, Your Majesty. We beg your help protecting both your people and ours." If anything would convince Gwynedd's king, I hoped it would be the danger to his own people.

"My sons," Cadell sighed. Something knotted in my stomach at his expression, the smirk lingering around the edges of his mouth.

"First, we have Dafydd." He gestured at the son standing to my right, thatch in his hair, scrapes up to his elbows, and burns on his cheeks. "You're lucky I was able to secure the alliance you disdained, and that we haven't been forced to rely on the efforts of your brother—my second son, Taliesin," he added, dismissive. Tal stood on my left, sharp and beautiful, all flushed cheekbones and tanned skin and madder-red coat. "Tal, who has stooped unimaginably low, engaging the services of a hedgewitch who has more dirt than divination about her." Titters rose through the room.

I gritted my teeth. I couldn't care less what Cadell said about me. Tal was another matter entirely.

But apparently, my sister minded. "King Cadell." Arianrhod spoke sharply. "Ffion is my sister. Your forbearance, please." Rhiannon scoffed.

What are you all doing here? I wanted to ask her. *What is* happening?

"In any case," King Bleddyn said, "the alliance is struck. With their power and our armies, we will meet Offa's attack and crush his forces, and then I will take northern Ceredigion. And we will certainly not offer you the blade that has kept Prestatyn safe against previous assaults—interesting though it is to know you have taken possession of those belonging to Mathrafal and Black Darren," he added quietly, arching his brows at Tal. My stomach tightened.

I'd never given much thought to why Powys had never succeeded in cowing Gwynedd the way it had Brycheiniog. Was their blade the reason?

I stepped forward, trying not to limp, gripped with uncertain fear. "And what are your plans, Rhiannon?" I asked.

"We will stop their hearts as they descend upon us," Rhiannon said lightly. "A very effective spell."

"What did it cost?" I directed the question at Arianrhod. She only shook her head.

"A creature from the deep made a valiant sacrifice," said Rhiannon. "A great whale. One life, to save many. Though Bleddyn has kindly offered to lend us the dragon scale, if we have need of it," she added. She looked pointedly at a bracelet on Bleddyn's slim wrist, set with what I would've thought was red jasper.

Gwynedd's blade was a dragon scale. A relic from the protectors of Wales.

If the unicorn's horn was strength for the pure, and the raven's feather inspired truth, I could only guess the scale gave its bearer unimaginable power.

It would have made everything possible. It would have empowered my spell. It would have restored magic to Wales, and let me bring Cadno back.

And Rhiannon was dangling it over my head.

"Did you know Mercia has a witch?" I asked Bleddyn and Cadell, trying to keep the desperation out of my voice. "We've seen the evidence of magic in their camp. Are you prepared to meet this magician, whoever it is?"

"A single witch, against the coven under the hill?" Rhiannon raised her gray brows. "I think we'll survive."

I didn't look at her. I spoke to the kings, to Cadell pacing restlessly and Bleddyn with his hands still tucked neatly in his belt. "The

Foxhall's working will deplete what little magic Wales has left," I said. "And this is in line with their aims: to make magic impossible to work for those who reject them."

"You could have been one of us, Ffion vch Catrin," said Rhiannon. "But you were unwilling to make the necessary sacrifices." She turned to Cadell. "As I told you, unpredictable, undignified, and possessed of little magic. Motivated by a childish attachment to her familiar and a crush," she added, eyes wandering from Tal to Dafydd. I felt myself redden.

"I would see magic restored," Cadell said a little gruffly. "But my first end is driving Mercia out, however I must do so."

Cadell was speaking to his sons and to all of us; but Rhiannon spoke only to me. I locked eyes with her, standing a foot or so above me on the dais.

I was reminded of a song I'd heard my mam-gu sing once, and not one I liked. It was a song about two witches, one determined to possess the other, the other determined to be free.

The hedgewitch stands beneath the hedge,
Her feet upon the grass
The covenwitch beneath the hill
Holds riches in her grasp.

Well may you run, oh hedgewitch green,
Though to the wilds you go,
Before you've reached your fifteenth year,
You'll call the Foxhall home.

Away, away, cold covenwitch,
You're covetous and small,
You'd keep for coin my witching work,
You'd keep me in your thrall.

The hedgewitch held up dirty nails,
And swore she by the earth,
I would not be a Foxhall witch,
Not for our kingdom's worth.

The covenwitch, she raised her hand,
Her wand and spellbook fine,
You'll join us all beneath the hill,
Your witching work is mine.

The verses ran on and on. In some versions, the hedgewitch managed to flee. In others, she didn't.

I wasn't sure how the song would end today.

Rhiannon had failed to acquire me years ago; she had done her best to control my mother. Arianrhod was under her thumb. For now.

Nothing rattled Rhiannon. Nothing, it seemed, but the women in our family.

"It's a shame the hedgewitch has ensnared your sons," Rhiannon said to Cadell. "Prince Taliesin, at least, seems to possess the will to reign. He could join us, if he would accept your terms. You could offer him a second chance," she wheedled.

Beside me, Tal stiffened.

"We should dismiss them all," Bleddyn said, impatience beginning to creep into his voice. "Offa's representative will be arriving soon."

King Cadell ignored him, considering Tal. "You—you could come back, Tal," he said, almost a suggestion. "Your brother lacks the will, but you don't."

I didn't dare look at either brother. Their father's words were almost too much for *me* to bear.

Tal had admitted that he shared the Foxhall's goal. Would he leave me?

He hated magic. He didn't want it restored.

And above all, Tal wanted to be king.

I only just stopped myself from reaching for him.

The steward opened the throne room doors again. "Offa's representative, my king." He bowed, and King Bleddyn gestured, eyes inquisitive.

"Are they negotiating with Offa before the attack?" I asked Tal and Dafydd, confused.

"I don't know." Dafydd frowned. "We weren't meant to be given any warning."

Tal leaned close to us. "Then how—"

"Welcome, messenger of Offa of Mercia," said Bleddyn, as the envoy entered the room.

"Magician, in fact." The woman bowed before the throne, black kirtle and graying red hair swinging.

I gripped Tal's hand.

"Hello, Arianrhod," said the messenger to my sister. Then, to me, voice wavering, "Hello, Ffion."

It was my mother.

50

TAL

"Catrin?" Rhiannon's voice was almost comically shocked. "What are you doing here?"

"I should think my introduction made it clear enough," Ffion's mother said mildly, and I had to stifle a hysterical laugh.

King Offa's magician was Ffion's mother—Catrin the shy, Catrin the unexpectedly powerful. She hadn't taken over the Foxhall, but she'd done the next most startling thing. I couldn't believe it.

And my father wanted me to join him again.

"Do you know this person?" my father asked Rhiannon, now obviously irritated.

"She's our mother," Arianrhod said, nodding to Ffion. "And Osian's wife."

"Former wife," Ffion's mother corrected her.

"And a Foxhall witch," Rhiannon burst out. "A traitor to her coven and her kingdom!"

"Let the traitor wait, then," said my father, turning to me again, though for once, I didn't want his attention.

I didn't have the details, but I knew he had threatened my mother and me to light a fire under Dafydd. And now he was watching me almost warmly.

"I need an heir, Taliesin," he said. "Join the Foxhall and me. Put that keen mind of yours to our benefit. For now, magic can remain safely under control."

"Why now?" I asked. I hadn't meant to say anything. But the words slipped out.

Dad smiled. "Because you've proven yourself."

I watched him, studied him. Felt Ffion's hand grow more tentative in my grasp.

She was preparing herself for me to run.

"No," I said slowly. "I haven't proven myself. Rhiannon's simply decided the pragmatic son is likeliest to work with her, and she's doing all your thinking now."

I turned to my brother. For once, Dad wasn't looking at him.

For once, I wasn't going to let him pit us against one another.

It was two against one now.

"Actually, it's Dafydd who's proven himself," I said, watching my brother. "Proven he can't be controlled. He's proven his mettle, and you don't like what he's made of," I said. "You've defaulted to your spare, Dad. But not because you've suddenly decided you're pleased with me."

Dafydd met my eyes, surprised, and Dad's face hardened. "Can you blame me, Taliesin? To entrust this task to a hedgewitch? I've heard rumors," he added, surveying Ffion coldly. "I've heard more about her from Rhiannon than Osian let on."

Rhiannon spoke again, and her words were more of the same.

Unpredictable, undignified, possessed of little magic.

A childish attachment to her familiar and a crush.

Holding Ffion's hand, my palms began to sweat.

It was now, but I was there. I was in Prestatyn, but it was four years ago on Midwinter night.

Arianrhod gripped the handle of her cane. Catrin let out a hiss and moved to block Ffion from view of the dais.

"Liar," Dafydd burst out, stepping close to us. "Lies, all of it."

No one had helped me defend my mother. But suddenly, I wasn't defending Ffion alone.

And suddenly, I grasped what had escaped me for all these years.

I hadn't feared the magic of the Mari Lwyd that night. I had feared the mob that had followed her.

I had resented her curse, true. But it hadn't even been a curse; it had been a tynged, a destiny spoken over me. It had simply been the truth.

I would never be king. Because I would choose my walls every time.

I would choose my mam.

And I would choose Ffion.

"I won't join you," I said to my father. "My loyalty is to Ffion, and the future you and the Foxhall are building would break her heart."

The Foxhall couldn't offer me anything. Because the magic wasn't what I hated. Rhiannon was just the leader of another bullying mob.

"How do you feel about this, Dafydd?" Dad demanded. "She was intended to serve you, was she not?"

"I wouldn't force her hand," Dafydd said quietly. "It wouldn't serve either of us."

I knew the connection between my father and Osian. I knew what Dafydd meant.

Still. I jolted back when Dad swayed slightly on the dais, bracing himself on a chair.

When he lifted his head, one eye was rolled back so only the white was visible.

"My king." Osian's voice came out of his mouth. "I apologize for the intrusion. But I could not let you act without speaking."

"This is highly irregular, Osian," my father ground out.

"And so is aligning with the Foxhall," said Osian. "Their practices fall outside even what I can condone."

I stepped closer to Ffion, horrified and fascinated as my father spoke first with his own voice, and then his magician's, persuading and arguing with himself.

"Why so suddenly cautious, Osian?" Rhiannon asked with a sneer. "You've never been miserly in your working."

"Because of my daughter," Osian said, turning toward Ffion, and there was a bizarre kind of affection in my father's whited eye. "I do not deny that my methods throughout your reign have sometimes been excessive. But I could not have imagined how far Ffion would travel, or how much she would achieve through sheer mulish effort. My opinions have changed as I have watched her. And before the entire court," he said, glancing between Ffion, Dafydd, and me, "I was wrong to bind Ffion to Prince Dafydd without her consent."

We were in unfathomable danger. Offa was waiting to descend; we stood before at least three enemies in Prestatyn Castle's throne room.

But standing in front of a father who'd withheld attention and approval from me my entire life, I knew how much those words must mean.

"No magic need be spent at all," Ffion's mother said, speaking up again. "The petty kingdoms are tired of war. Our families are tired of rebuilding burned and ruined homes. Our women are tired of running with their children." Catrin's voice carried through the hall. She turned toward Ffion, her eyes shining. "Nothing is worth risking more death. King Offa is willing to move peacefully into the Marches."

"Why should I listen to a traitor?" my father demanded. One eye was still rolled back, but Osian was silent. "The guidance of anyone who can abandon king, coven, and family to serve another cannot be trusted."

"And yet you take counsel from the Foxhall," Catrin said evenly. "Or did you not know Rhiannon offered her services to King Offa first?"

Dafydd's jaw dropped. Ffion gasped. The three of us stared at one another, echoes of our shock moving through the crowd.

Dad turned to Rhiannon. "Is this true?" he demanded.

"It is." Catrin was smooth, controlled. I didn't even recognize the pale, shrinking woman I'd seen with Ffion at the Foxhall. "After Prince Taliesin's visit, Rhiannon saw which way the wind was blowing and approached King Offa. He offered her a price for her services, and she found it so low as to be insulting," she said. "And so the Foxhall went next to Mathrafal."

I couldn't believe I'd ever considered joining their side.

Maybe Ffion's mother was a traitor, but in her own misguided way, she was trying to avoid conflict and everything it cost. The Foxhall saw war as just another means to grow their power.

"I am trying to forestall this war," Catrin said, glancing again toward Ffion. "Offa will not be denied the Marches. But I want no more loss of life, from any quarter."

"She did this because of me," Ffion whispered. "She did this to keep me safe."

I exchanged a look with Dafydd. We both knew she was right. But there was something more than a mother's protectiveness at play. There was bitter pride in Catrin's face as well. And I couldn't say I blamed her.

On the dais, my father still hadn't spoken. I noticed then that he was murmuring to himself, first in Osian's voice, then his own. He swayed as he talked to himself, brows drawn low.

He glanced to one of his guards, and then another, summoning them with only the barest twitches of his fingers.

"I cannot say, Osian," my father said, so quietly I almost didn't hear. "Which do you believe?"

Dad straightened. But before he or Osian could speak, Rhiannon moved.

She ripped a lance from a guard on the dais and plunged it through my father's stomach.

51

DAFYDD

Was I screaming? Or was it Tal, or Ffion?

The throne room was chaos. Foxhall witches shrieked; Bleddyn bellowed orders; Prestatyn's court and Powysian guards jostled and shoved, all shouting accusations.

I wasn't sure who ran first. But the three of us tore through silver-painted corridors until we reached the beach. The sun was unforgiving, the sea pulling at the water around our ankles, the world seeming to sway.

I hit my knees, clinging to Gruffudd.

"He's dead," I whispered to Tal. "Dad is dead."

Tal fisted his hands in his hair, pacing. Then he jogged a few steps away and vomited.

"Rhiannon is a murderer." Ffion dropped into the sand beside her cauldron. "She killed your father in cold blood, because Mam told him the truth about what they'd done."

"I can't believe it. Osian said our father would die on an enemy spear," I said. "I just assumed it would be in open battle."

Tal wiped his mouth. "We all did."

Our father was dead.

"So who," asked a voice at our backs, "is king of Powys?" I jerked around.

Catrin was crossing the sand toward us, the brazen sun shining on her hair and throwing harsh shadows on her face.

"Mam." Ffion looked like she was struggling to breathe. "What—how could you? How could you go to work for Offa? How could you *do* this?"

"You couldn't be stopped," Catrin said simply. "So I had to stop the war."

"You finally stand up to Rhiannon, and *this* is how you go about it?" Ffion shook her head, disbelieving. She looked away from her mother, anguish in her face. "I was trying to restore magic so I could bring Cadno back. He was all I had. But I've failed. And now I'll lose everything, and we will lose Wales."

"We need a new plan," Tal muttered. "We just need to think."

"There's nothing to be done," Ffion spat. Tears filled her eyes. "We needed the feather, the unicorn's horn, and the dragon scale. Two out of three won't be enough." She glanced at her mother. "We shouldn't even be discussing this in front of you."

"Your secrets are safe with me, bach. But I have to go. King Offa will need to hear Cadell is dead." Catrin looked back at the dyke, squinting against the sun. When she reached for Ffion, Ffion didn't pull away. "Will you run?" she asked. "Now that this is finished, will you go somewhere safe from Mercia and Rhiannon both?"

Her voice was a mother's voice. But Ffion answered with a witch's words.

"It's not finished, Mam," she said. "I'm not done until Cadno's lost to Annwn."

Catrin sagged. "You've poured yourself out for this quest, Ffion. And you've come so far." She paused. "But it's time to let him go. It's time to let yourself rest."

"Never." Ffion's voice was low with desperation, or anger, or both. "Not while I have hair or nails or teeth or anything left in this world to sacrifice. Not while I still have a mouth to speak the spell. I will never leave my friend, Mam. And if you knew me at all, you'd know that giving up wouldn't bring me rest."

"I see." Her mother nodded, looking troubled. "I see."

With that, Catrin left. Tal, Ffion, Gruffudd, and I were alone on the beach.

When I'd heard the last of Wales's dragons was lost, I'd felt that a tynged had been pronounced over us—an omen, the doom of Powys. I felt the same way now, knowing my father was gone. That with the new moon tomorrow, he, too, would cross to Annwn, travel to the Otherworld, and that I would finish my life on this plane alone without him.

I had not wanted to become him. But I didn't know how to be without him in my life.

Who is king of Powys?

"I think your mother's right, Ffion," Tal said. "We run. We can go back to Mathrafal and collect my mother and take refuge in Northumbria. Or Wessex. Or Ynys Môn."

Ffion blinked at him. "But the kingdom—"

"I don't care." Tal's voice was gentle. "You have to be safe. I require that, and not much else."

Tal could only look at her. But I—

My head spun.

I got to my feet. Gruffudd rose, watching me, waiting to see what I would do.

"Powysian guards are waiting in that great hall," I said. "And Powysian soldiers are waiting outside it. They're waiting for orders from a king half of them don't even know is dead."

"Let's go," Tal said again, all urgency.

"I can't run," said Ffion. "For Cadno, for me, for Wales—"

"I have to go back," I interrupted.

Tal and Ffion froze. Turned to me.

"Are you out of your mind?" Tal asked.

"Offa's attack falls tomorrow night," I said. "We have to be sure the Welsh border is defended. Our father's death doesn't change that."

Tal gaped at me. "You refused to work with King Bleddyn two weeks ago—twenty *minutes* ago. What's changed?"

"I won't help with their campaign against Ceredigion," I said. "But I'll offer them something else."

"Dafydd, Rhiannon just murdered your father," Ffion said. "Bleddyn let it happen. Why would you go back to them?"

I had to go back because of what the ravens had told me. Because my father was dead, and because I loved Powys. Because the end had come.

I had to go, because I knew there was no one else to do what had to be done.

I thought of Osian, not afraid to change his mind when he saw what Ffion had accomplished. I thought of the girl in the wagon outside Pont-Goch, her hands shaking and covered with blood. She'd been terrified, but she'd saved her brother's life.

Because it had to be done. And there was only me to do it.

Maybe Gwynedd's demands and the Foxhall's schemes hadn't changed. But I had.

Tal would take care of Ffion. My responsibilities were different.

Ffion watched me, dread rising in her face. "Dafydd, they will kill you," she said harshly. "Just like they killed your father, just like they're going to kill so many other people. You are too kind and too soft, and Rhiannon and Bleddyn will use you up and throw you on the pyre when they are done."

"Dafydd." Tal put his face directly in front of mine. "I understand now why you set Prince Angws free. You were trying to protect me from a poor decision I was about to make. Please," he said. "Please let me do the same for you now."

"I've failed you and Gwanwyn more than I've protected you, Tal,"

I said helplessly. "It never occurred to me the Mari Lwyd might make trouble for you that Midwinter. But it should have. I should've been beside you, between you and that crowd. If not that night, then after. But I was so afraid to make a mistake, I failed to do the good that was in my power to do."

"You can't do this," Ffion said. Tears tracked down her face. "Dafydd, you can't be part of whatever they're about to do."

"What else is there to be done?" I asked. The wind picked up, tugging at Ffion's curls and Tal's coat. "Can I leave the Powysian army without a leader? Can I leave the defense of our border to Rhiannon?"

Neither of them answered.

"I know the Foxhall is capable of anything," I said, reaching to embrace each of them before I turned away, clicking to Gruffudd. "But so am I."

Five Days Ago

DAFYDD

I stepped inside the columbarium and immediately wished I'd come wearing my apron.

I knew my brother favored his embroidered coat when he set to work. It was Tal's particular kind of armor, a gift from his mother. I felt protected—purposeful—in the leather apron I wore for forge work.

And it was hotter than a forge inside Mathrafal's columbarium.

We are a forge, after a fashion, said the ravens.

Hail and well met, Dafydd ap Cadell.

My heart lurched at their voices in my thoughts.

I shut my eyes. This had been a mistake.

Do not hide from us, princeling. After all, you sought us out.

I nodded, eyes still shut tight.

Slowly, I opened them again. But I couldn't do more than glance up.

Sighted ravens were smaller than ordinary ravens. Their feathers were shot with emerald green, and their large ember-bright eyes were gold.

And inside the columbarium, they were everywhere.

Ravens filled the niches in the walls, perched on the beams below the domed ceiling. The sound of ruffling feathers sifted over me like snow.

My hands shook. But I got the sense they were waiting for me to speak.

"Will you tell me where to find Mathrafal's blade?" I asked.

I didn't know if they would. My motivations weren't pure. I had used the promise of the blade to bargain with Ffion for my own selfish purposes.

More sifting of wings. The ravens seemed to murmur among themselves. *The blade, the blade, the blade.*

You seek an icon of purity, Prince Dafydd. Your father lost it.

"I know he did."

Will you meet our gaze?

The moment I really looked at the ravens, I knew they would be able to really look at me. I didn't want to. But I had to.

I swallowed and looked higher, into those terrible ember-bright eyes.

It was a little like staring toward the sun. Difficult, and too bright to do for more than an instant. Afterimages seared the backs of my eyes.

Beneath their gaze, I felt trepidation, but no dread. It was terrible. But no more so than stepping out of a shadow.

The knots around my soul loosened.

You do not wish to be king. You wish to occupy a very small space in the world.

Why is that?

It wasn't a question. Not really. I resisted the urge to explain or justify. The ravens had seen all there was to see. They knew all there was to know.

You fear the dark, Prince Dafydd.

Not the dark that lives outside you, but the dark you know dwells within. And you are wise to respect its presence. To be cautious of it. To know its depth.

Because you are capable of anything.

My stomach twisted. I reached out a hand, clutched a niche in the wall.

The injured chieftain had described my father that way when he came back from war.

Devious. Grasping. Capable of anything.

I couldn't bear to be like my father.

My eyes stung. "Is that it?" I asked. "Darkness? That's what you see in me?"

We said there is *darkness within you, prince. Not that you* are *darkness.*

"Tell me what you mean," I begged.

Forget not that you possess darkness, Prince Dafydd. But forget not either that the light very nearly possesses you.

The ravens paused. I could hardly breathe.

You are pure of heart, princeling. You work hard, live humbly, and give with an open hand.

But you must be more than virtuous. You must also be brave.

"I can't," I pleaded. "I can't. Crown a raven. Crown a dragon. Crown a god. No human can bear up under this burden without failing."

We cannot wear your crown. But you can look to us for Sight.

Do not be afraid, Dafydd. You will fall short. And where you do, you must make amends, and master yourself, and begin again toward the light.

You will be king, but you need not become your father.

You are capable of anything.

With this, they fell silent, and so did my heart. For the first time in years, I felt something like peace.

Something like hope.

My hand brushed something cold and smooth inside the niche I'd grasped.

I took the unicorn's horn from its resting place and went back out to meet Ffion.

52

FFION

Welsh magic was lost. Cadno was lost. *My* magic was lost. And when the attack fell, we would have no way of facing it.

There was nothing left.

I sat on the beach, Tal at my side, and sang as the sun went down and the tide came in.

The last of the dragons have gone to sleep,
'Neath wings of scale and fledge,
The afancs and the gwiberod
Now lie beneath the hedge.

The dreigiau goch have breathed their last,
Their fires now all quenched,
The ceiliog neidr's eyes are closed;
He lies beneath the hedge.

Oh creatures wild, oh creatures fey,
We lift a drink in pledge,
We mourn you till we follow you
To lie beneath the hedge.

Tal took my hand when I was done.

"I can't raise Cadno," I said to him. "I can't destroy the dyke without the blades, so I can't bring the magic back to help me. And my magic is too weak to summon him without it. I don't even think I've gathered enough for the spell." Waves lapped at my feet. In the dying sun, the water and the sand and the stones were the silver of an afanc's scales.

"Are you still going to try to raise him?" Tal asked.

"Yes." I wiped my eyes. "I have to. I don't know who I am without him and my magic. But I'm—" I broke off, fighting back a sob. The tide rolled in farther and farther.

I wondered if the ache in my chest would ease if I let it catch me up and carry me away.

Tal reached into the cauldron and picked up the raven's feather, held it up. "You're afraid," he said. "I am, too. But neither of us is alone. I'm with you to the end, Ffion."

I dragged my hand across my wet cheeks. "The magic won't come back," I said again. I needed to see Tal react to my words. I needed the truth about what he felt.

Would he feel he'd finally been set free, with the magic doomed to fade? Would he see his path to the throne clear, with his curse no longer hanging over him?

I searched Tal's face for the relief I dreaded he'd feel.

I looked. But it wasn't there.

53

TAL

Ffion watched me with somber eyes the gray of the sea. Gulls cried overhead; the sun eased toward the horizon, as if it had finally given up on the day.

It was time to explain.

"For so many years," I said, "I've been afraid of magic, because of what happened with the Mari Lwyd. You heard the story from my mother." I swallowed. "I won't retell it."

"You don't have to," Ffion said. "I understand."

But I shook my head. "You don't," I said. "Because I didn't, either. Not until today.

"All these years, I've resented magic so I wouldn't resent the people I wanted to rule. I blamed the magic instead of the court that was cruel to my mother, and the town that shut us out. But today in Bleddyn's throne room, I finally understood. I'm not afraid of the magic anymore," I said. "And I'm not afraid of the mob, either, because I don't need them."

"No?" Ffion spoke softly. Her lashes were wet, and her eyes were red.

"No. Wales belongs to wild, fiery creatures," I said. "And so do I."

Softly, I kissed her hand, and then her cheek.

Salt on the air. Salt on her skin.

The taste of it was on her lips when she kissed me back.

For weeks, I had dreamt of Ffion's mouth on mine. I didn't resist as she pushed me back into the sand, hands cupping my shoulder and the nape of my neck. Water rolled up the beach, running up my back, catching the ends of her hair.

As her mouth moved over mine, I skimmed my hands up and down her arms, felt goose bumps rise on her skin and her fingers slide into my hair. I fisted my hands in her curls the way I'd wanted to so badly, red-gold running through my hands like water.

Her damp dress clung to her skin; my coat was soaked, but the cold couldn't touch me.

When Ffion kissed my collarbone, I gasped. "I have relived your mouth on my neck every hour since that night," I said jaggedly. "I thought I would die."

"And I have wanted to—" Ffion broke off, lips seeking out the mark at the corner of my mouth.

I grinned and gave a breathless laugh. "I've seen you looking at it."

"Haven't been able to stop. Stupid beauty mark." Ffion's voice cracked slightly as she brought shaking fingers to my cheek. "I can't stop with you, Tal. Ever since you walked into the Foxhall in that stupid red coat, you've lived in my every thought."

"It's the same for me." I gripped her waist, searching for words as my thoughts slid like waves down the beach. "I don't know what's coming, Fee. My father is gone, and I know you won't be kept. But I would keep you safe, if you would let me."

We breathed together, and I shut my eyes until I could bear the ache in my chest.

I had wanted her so badly. And here she was, in my arms.

"I never wanted to sleep rough forever, Tal," she finally said. She kissed my cheek, pearls of water sliding over her skin, and when she met my eyes, she smiled softly. "I was just waiting until it was safe to go home."

I kissed Ffion until the sun began to set. And then we set to work.

While the light lasted, we combed the beach and the ditch, filling her cauldron. We stopped when night fell, though, because although the sky was clear, the thread of moon left wasn't enough to search by.

We both knew what we found wouldn't be enough to raise Cadno. We both knew she'd still try before the attack fell tomorrow night.

We were together when we fell asleep beneath the hedge.

54

DAFYDD

The five of us sat in the throne room through the night and into the morning.

King Bleddyn of Gwynedd, who'd been surprised to see me return to take my father's place. Rhiannon, my father's murderer. Me and Gruffudd. And Arianrhod, Ffion's sister, whose argument in my favor had made my return possible.

"Without a leader from Powys, we cannot command Powysian armies," she'd said, round face serious. "If you require their forces, then you require Prince Dafydd."

It turned out King Bleddyn did need our help meeting Offa's attack—so much so that when I agreed to restore a Gwyneddian village we'd annexed, he agreed to the alliance against Mercia without our help conquering Ceredigion.

I suspected some of his generosity came from fear of Rhiannon. After all, she'd already put a spear through one king's stomach.

Bleddyn's men had carried my father's body into a spare chamber. I would have to bring it home when the battle was over, if I was alive to do so.

"The new moon is tomorrow night. We should fill the ditch tomorrow, so our vanguard will be able to meet Offa's armies," I said, gesturing to the model Bleddyn's advisors had produced.

Bleddyn rubbed his eyes, considering. "Will they come with siege engines? Do you think they will come prepared for battle in the open field, or an assault on Prestatyn?"

"I can't say," I admitted. "Unless—?" I glanced at Arianrhod and Rhiannon.

Arianrhod nodded. "Trebuchets. Breaching towers. We saw them when . . ." She trailed off.

When we went to meet with Offa, she didn't say.

"None of this matters," said Rhiannon. Her cool was restored now, though there was still blood in her hair. "I have the power to stop the heart of every soldier in Offa's ranks."

Arianrhod and I exchanged a glance. Her eyes were tired; her cheeks were flushed from arguing. And I didn't know how she managed to convey exasperation simply by how she handled her cane, but she did.

The others had begun to bicker again when it happened.

My body froze, as it always had during my visions of Ffion. I waited, wondering what I would see.

But the vision never came. I didn't see her.

I *felt* her, suddenly, as my eyes rolled back and my vision went dark and I heard Ffion's voice coming out of my mouth.

"Dafydd, they're coming," I cried—my lips, my tongue, *her* voice, *her* words. "Offa's armies—they're almost to Prestatyn."

They couldn't be. It wasn't time. My heart quailed.

But this was why I'd returned to the castle.

It was over in a moment. I coughed and choked as my sight returned. Gruffudd whimpered at my knee. Arianrhod, Rhiannon, and Bleddyn stared at me in horror as I planted my hands on the table.

"I am bound to my hedgewitch," I said to them, panting. "You heard what she saw."

"But it's too soon!" Rhiannon protested. "Osian said—"

I held up a hand to quiet her. "We have to move," I said. "We're out of time."

Interlude

Ffion dreamt of air.

She felt as if she were standing on a cliff, wind tearing at her skin, falling, flying. It was release. It was utter joy, cold and free.

And then came the fire.

It was vengeance.

It was justice.

It was glory.

Ffion woke beneath the hedge.

55

FFION

At first I couldn't distinguish the shaking inside me from the shaking outside. I woke to my heart racing—and the ground trembling.

"Tal!" I sat up, tugging on his arm. Could it have been only yesterday we'd woken like this, with the arrival of those who'd fled the raid?

But these weren't the cries of villagers. These were spears and shields clanking. These were pounding boots and hooves.

Tal sat up, wiping his eyes. "But it's too soon," he slurred. "The new moon's tomorrow. It—"

I searched the sky, choking as I tried to breathe. Smoke was everywhere, obscuring the stars and the shred of moon I'd seen in the sky the night before. "I know. I don't understand."

"Is it—" Tal coughed. "Is it because *tonight* is the new moon?"

I shook my head. "No. This moon still hasn't set. But I—"

I racked my brain, trying to remember. What had Dad said about the attack?

My sight was hazy, as if clouded by smoke.

I'd thought he'd meant his vision was fragmented, as mine had been; after all, he'd seen Cadell's death, but not where, or at whose hand.

But what if he'd been describing it literally?

I threw off my cloak and stumbled down into the ditch, my ankle throbbing.

Not once on our journey had I tried to climb King Offa's Dyke. But I threw myself against it now.

It was eight feet tall, covered in hedge and ivy and dew, and I was hungry and exhausted and clumsy with my sprain. I dug my nails into the dirt, crying out when my ankle rolled beneath me and the hedge tore at my skin. Muscles aching, I strained upward, Tal climbing beside me.

When we reached the top, we squinted into the sunrise, watching Offa's armies descend.

And behind them—fire. Miles away, a Mercian camp that had lain invisible by night was in flames, and the fire had caught and spread to a Mercian village nearby. Smoke choked the air, rising and blowing west on the wind, clouding the sky as it had confused my father's vision.

We were seeing what Dad had seen.

Even to the west where the sky lay dark, there was no moon. There were no stars. And there was no more time.

The attack had come.

"Tal, they're so close." I clutched at his shirtfront, panic gripping me. "What are we going to do?"

"Our armies aren't even assembled. Everyone in Prestatyn is in danger, the castle and the town." His chest rose and fell, and as we stared at one another, I knew we were both thinking of the people who'd fled to Pont-Goch the day before, whose own village had gone up in flames.

We'd had no power to stop the raid on their homes. We had to find a way to stop the attack today.

Then he froze. "Ffion. Your connection to Dafydd. We can use it."

"What do you mean?"

"If you warn Dafydd, he and Bleddyn can at least protect the town," Tal said. "Maybe even assemble their armies. Maybe they'll have a chance."

My heart was racing. I didn't know how to do what he was asking.

I had no offering. No spell to tell me what to do.

But I knew I had to try.

I stared into the billowing flames and reached for the bond between Dafydd and me, feeling my way toward our connection just as when I'd summoned my vision back at Mathrafal.

I stretched out toward my friend, toward the single stitch that bound us.

"Dafydd, they're coming." My voice was harsh and shaky. "Offa's armies—they're making for Prestatyn."

Please hear me, I begged the magic that bound us. *Please keep them all safe.*

Offa's armies were barely a mile off, thundering nearer and nearer. I limped down from the dyke, skidding in the dew and the mud until I landed in the ditch.

"Maybe he'll hear you," Tal said. His eyes were wild, terrified. "Maybe he'll hear you, and maybe now King Bleddyn will let us use the blade. Maybe—"

"There's no time!" I flung a hand at the approaching soldiers. "We'd never make it to Prestatyn."

I swallowed, scanning the landscape. A hill behind us, to the south, where we'd come from. The beach to the north. Thick woods away to the west.

But we stood alone on our side of the dyke.

No help was coming for us.

We could stay, or we could run. I saw Tal realize it the moment I did.

"We can't," I whispered. "We've come too far. Walked too many miles. Gathered too much magic—"

"Stop." Tal clenched his fists, thinking so hard it seemed to hurt him. "Ffion, remind me of the spell. Remind me of your mam-gu's breaking spell."

"A piece of what needs breaking, and fuel to do it. And contact."

Was that all there was? I thought hard, but the smoke fogged my brain, and there was no time to riffle through my cauldron for the spellbook. There was no time for anything.

"You've kept contact since Merthyr-Tewdrig, but for a few miles in the wagon." Tal counted off on his fingers. "You've worn the ivy around your ankles since we set out. And fuel—"

I shook my head. I could still feel the ground shaking beneath us, see the armies swelling as they drew nearer. I wanted to cry. "We only got two blades of three. We've only got—"

My cauldron.

My heart stopped beating in my chest.

Everything I'd collected to raise Cadno still sat in my cauldron—a little pile of roots and mushrooms, pebbles and petrified eggs, quartz and herbs and bones and shells. None of it intrinsically powerful, but potent by virtue of my efforts.

All that I'd stored up to resurrect my familiar. All my hopes gathered in one place, ready for me to try to bring him back.

Chest heaving in the smoke, I picked up the cauldron. I kissed Tal hard and staggered to my feet.

"I know what to do," I said.

I ran barefoot toward the beach, crying out as I limped on my sprained ankle. I ran through the haze, feeling every blade of grass, every thistle, every stone and flower beneath my feet, feeling the ivy that had traveled all the way from Merthyr-Tewdrig chafe around my ankles. I raced against my own heartbeat, full of fear and love for the land beneath me. Tears and smoke burned my eyes.

I knew I didn't have enough material or magic left in me to bring Cadno back as things stood now. He wouldn't return to me. But maybe magic could return to our home.

I didn't have the third blade. But I could offer up to Wales what I'd worked for alongside the raven's feather and the unicorn's horn, even if it meant letting go of Cadno forever.

I'd always been Foxhall's last chance.

This was mine.

Eyes streaming, lungs heaving, I sang.

The newborn sun is barely up
The mists have barely cleared
But baying hounds are on the run
And hunters are afield
Stay safe inside your cozy dens
Avoid the howling fray
Heed hunters' call, young foxes
"Tally ho! Hark away!"

Care not that you're mere kittens
Just weaned of mother's milk
With amber eyes just newly op'n
And fur like madder silk
They see not how a lambkin
And you are just the same
Stay home as hunters trumpet
"Tally ho! Hark away!"

O'er roots and under hedges go
'Cross brooks and grassy glades
Run fast as madder paws can fly
Keep not where hunters play
Run home where all is safe and warm
Where mother vixen waits
Your littermates are crying
"Run, Reynard! Run away!"

It was a song for a hunted fox. It was a song for a harassed people.

When I reached the beach, I staggered into the water, salt stinging the cuts on my feet and ankles. And suddenly, I was still, but I was reeling.

I saw the scene before me as I had in the dream. Gray-brown sand, blue-gray water, and sky and standing stones towering out of that water. Salt-heavy wind dashed itself against my face.

I *had* dreamt this. I had dreamt this place, had dreamt myself running here.

No time, no time, there was no time. I adjusted my grip on my cauldron and dug through what lay inside.

The sleek black raven's feather. The amber unicorn's horn. And all my small hopes gathered together.

I looked back over my right shoulder. King Offa's army was nearly at the dyke now. They seemed to fill the landscape, a meadow of men, a forest of men, a mountain of men.

"Stop!"

A loud voice. A kingly voice.

Dafydd was on horseback at the top of the dyke. Arianrhod and Rhiannon and Bleddyn and a small group of guards were gathered around him. Dafydd raised a spear in the direction of Offa's armies.

My heart stuttered in my chest. Hope rose in my throat.

They were an army of twelve or so, preparing to meet untold numbers. But my warning had reached him.

If I wanted to help them any further, it was now or never.

I lifted the cauldron high in the air. "Break, break, break!" I called, but I could hardly hear my own words over the din. I dashed away my tears, dragged in a breath. There was a hand on my elbow.

"Ffion!" my mother gasped. I whirled.

"Mam?" I demanded. Her clothes were wet from seawater; she was panting with the weight of the cauldron she rarely carried. "What are you doing here?"

"You were owed a blood debt, and you were owed more from me," she said resolutely, and dumped the contents of her cauldron into mine. "I'm doing what I should have done weeks ago."

It was everything I had seen in her chest back at the house. The untold riches of Rhiannon's coven. Grains of paradise, quartz, lumps of gold and silver. Turquoise feathers and ambergris and myrrh.

"You need your coven," Mam said, tears in her eyes to match mine. "And I'm here."

It was extravagant magic. It was now or never.

Together, we lifted my cauldron.

Together, we plunged it into the water up to our elbows, feeling the water bubble and churn around us.

Break

Break

Break

My words were a scream, a sob, a spell on the ocean air. I could hardly breathe for waiting to see what would happen.

But Mam was still at work.

She pulled a cedarwood poppet from a fold of her gown. A brilliant orange stone. And, as she began to sing—a fistful of foxgloves.

It was a song I knew. A song that wasn't my mam-gu's.

A song that was mine.

I am a witch of Foxhall
And I've come to beg a boon
My house it is quite lonely
Yet we're also out of room
I'm come to Foxhall Forest
And I hope not to offend

I offer you this poppet
And I ask of you a friend

Behind us, the shouts of Offa's army seemed to slow.

Confusion filled me. "Mam, how did you—?"

"Ffion. How many times do you think I heard you sing that song?" she whispered, running her hands over my face. "I'm your mother, bach."

"But the dyke," I said, frantic. "Two spells at once, how will it—"

My mother shook her head. "Stop. Trust me," she said. Then she smiled at something behind me. "Ffion, look."

I turned.

He appeared the way the sun does when it rises. The color first, and then the form. The sight, and then the substance.

Cadno came trotting down the beach, materializing slowly and then quickly as he came, red paws leaving prints in the wet sand when he was a little distance away.

Slowly, and then quickly. The way our magic had always worked.

"Cadno!" My voice broke as I dropped to my knees, throwing my arms around his neck.

Lost, and returned to me. Here, and whole.

Cadno licked my cheek, and I wept into his shoulder.

Mam crouched beside me, putting a hand under Cadno's chin. "Finish it, Cadno," she whispered. "Help Ffion."

Cadno drew back, considering my mam and me and my cauldron in the waves with those amber eyes I had missed so much.

When he pointed his nose to the sky, he gave a shriek that raised every hair on the back of my neck.

A strong western wind rose without warning, whipping my kirtle and my hair and pushing the smoke east across the dyke, leaving the sky and the air clear. I drew in a long, grateful breath.

The ground began to shake again.

On the far side of the dyke, King Offa's army was descending to meet Powys's and Gwynedd's forces.

And then Wales rose to defend itself.

It began with the earth. Molds spread, trapping the feet of the men who descended throwing axes and spears. Mushrooms sprouted, climbing over soldiers' legs and arms and weapons. Vines of ivy twined themselves around the limbs of men and horses alike, though more gently around the beasts' legs. The hedge on top of the dyke twisted and reshaped itself, pliable as resin as it herded men like sheep on a moor.

And then came the forest that had lain to the west. Willows and birches and spreading oaks and one ancient yew, old enough to have watched over kings and grandfathers of kings, surged through the army. The trees separated the soldiers, trapping them in their branches.

My hands shook. I gripped Cadno's fur, and he pressed himself against my shins.

Tal appeared at my side, clutching his ribs and panting. "What's happening?" he asked. I could only shake my head.

The ground suddenly began to churn again—but no, not the ground; it was overground, whatever was happening.

When I crouched lower to get a better look, a field mouse ran over my wrist, and I jumped back. Cadno wasn't surprised; he didn't even try to toy with it. Another mouse darted by, and another, and another.

Rabbits loped past. Badgers and moles popped their heads out of the ground, glancing around before darting up to bite the Mercian soldiers on the legs. Foxes streaked brilliant red over the churning green landscape.

Wolves. Stags. Bears. They began to race between the trees, coming from the south and the west, as if called from all corners of Wales by Cadno's cry.

And then—ravens, with bright gold eyes and emerald in their wings.

And then—unicorns. Horns and hooves gleaming like amber, their sides creeping with earthy life, they galloped through the moss and the mushrooms and the gorse and the trees, tossing Mercian soldiers with their horns, kicking out with their beautiful hooves.

More magical creatures came. Water leapers and water horses. Gwyllgwn bounding by and adar llwch gwin beating their huge hawk's wings. An enormous tusked boar and an even bigger cat, so large only a stable could hold him.

And then—the ground began to shake again.

"What more?" I gasped, turning to Tal. "What now?"

The dyke broke.

It began almost beneath my feet, a crack forming at the point where the earthwork met the sand. It raced south, spreading, spreading—all the way to Merthyr-Tewdrig, as far as I knew.

A claw poked out from the crack only a few feet away from where I knelt on the beach.

And then—wings.

And then fire.

"Ffion." Tal whispered my name, and I'd never heard him so afraid. He shouldn't have been.

"Dragons," I whispered.

I stifled a sob. Cadno nosed at my knee, and I wrapped my arms around him.

I saw them as I'd seen them as a child—as I'd seen them since in my memories, wrapped in yearning for what lay past.

I hadn't deceived myself. It had all been real.

They burst from the dyke, one after another. Dozens of them. Afancs, ceiliogau neidr, gwiberod, dreigiau goch. Scores of them. They were red, they were green, they were copper and obsidian and silver and gold, they were every color, as brilliant as the earth swarming around them. They climbed out, scaled legs followed by snouts and wings and flickering tongues. Shattered chains and frayed ropes hung from their necks and limbs.

Farther down the dyke, I could see more of them. One lifted its head with a scream, jaws bursting with flame, and my bones turned to water.

Tears poured from my eyes as the nearest dragon turned to face me. Its scales were a deep, deep red.

Arawn, came the thought, unbidden. Not mine.

My dreams raced through my mind as I met the dragon's deep gold gaze.

Water. Where I stood now.

Earth. Where they'd lain trapped, unbeknownst to all of Wales.

Air.

Fire.

My dreams had never just been dreams. The magic I had sensed in the dyke and feared for so many days had been the dragons, reaching for me, trying to guide me to where I was now.

The dragon—Arawn—crouched before springing into the air. He beat his wings joyfully, circling and swooping, tearing off his chains with gleaming rows of teeth.

Then he opened his jaws.

I wasn't the target of Arawn's wrath. But I felt the heat of his flame as he attacked the Mercian armies, targeting those who'd trapped him, carefully sparing the earth and animals who'd come to his aid.

It had been Welsh magic in the dyke. It had been Wales, drawing in a breath as I worked and walked. And it was Arawn, now, who blew that breath out, angry and full of fire, candling our land so that magic could return.

Staggering to my feet, I started out among the trees.

"Ffion?" Tal caught at my hand, wondering. "Are you sure you should?"

"It's safe," I reassured him, sounding dazed. "They've rescued us."

"You rescued us," Tal said, wondering.

"No. Tal, they came to our aid. We wouldn't have survived without them."

"No." Tal seized my shoulders, making me pause. "Ffion, you cast the spell. And they came—they came for you."

And as I looked around, at the plants and animals who had come to protect us and the fox who had summoned them all on my behalf, I knew it was true.

I loved the land. I loved its creatures and its magic.

And apparently, my magic was that it loved me, too.

56

TAL

Mathrafal Castle, Powys

If I'd had any doubts left, the battle would have silenced them.

As the creatures began to disappear from the battlefield—the dragons flying off to their homes in woods and caves and seaside cliffs, the unicorns trotting away to their meadows and forests, foxes and badgers disappearing into the brush—I found I wished they'd stay.

Later, a captured Mercian soldier would explain how they had imprisoned the dragons in secret—by night, just as they'd built the dyke. The sheer numbers of their armies had enabled them to trap the creatures in ropes and chains, even when they'd failed to take them by surprise. Many of their soldiers had died, but the loss of life was no object to Offa, intent as he was on containing Welsh magic.

King Offa himself was killed on the field, his armies crushed, his earthwork destroyed from end to end. Rhiannon didn't survive the fighting, either. Bleddyn did, but that was largely thanks to Dafydd and Arianrhod.

But the future of Powys's relationship with an unsettled and still conquering Gwynedd, a diminished Mercia, a hopeful Brycheiniog, and the rest of our neighbors was tied to a larger question: who would succeed my father as king.

Ffion, Dafydd, and I sat alone in the throne room a week after the battle to discuss precisely that question.

"I wonder what Dad would say if he were here," I said, leaning against the wall. Ffion lay on the flagstones beside me, Cadno curled up on her stomach, her hand in mine. Only Dafydd sat in a chair, Gruffudd lounging at his feet.

"He'd probably tell us he's disappointed in us again," Dafydd said, rolling his eyes. "For the way we approached his challenge. And for giving up that village to Gwynedd."

"Probably," I agreed.

"We did what he asked you to, though," Ffion said. "The dyke's broken. Magic is restored." Cadno licked her chin, and she laughed.

Ffion's magic had returned in full force the moment her familiar had, just as magic had returned to Wales when the dyke damming its power and trapping its dragons had been broken. A bitterness I hadn't realized she'd been wearing had fallen away, replaced by peace.

I was ready to know a Ffion at peace.

Dafydd shook his head. "You and Tal did what he asked. Technically speaking, you won." My brother wet his lips, bracing himself. "So what do you say?"

I knew my brother had tried selfishness on for size when he'd given Ffion the blade, and in the end he'd found it didn't fit. But my reasons for wanting to be king had always been selfish. Or personal, at least.

I still wanted to protect my mother and Ffion. But I wouldn't use the throne for that.

I'd do it with my own two hands. Just like Ffion had taught me.

"I say . . ." I sighed. "I say, no thank you. I say, I'll accept the lands I would have inherited, but not the kingdom." Ffion squeezed my hand.

"You know I don't want to be fair and just and impartial." I sat forward, meeting Dafydd's eyes. "I rejected the throne the day I refused to do what you did: walk back into Prestatyn Castle alone to lead our soldiers."

I had put Ffion first. As I always would.

Dafydd grimaced. "Tal, are you sure?"

"We won together, Dafydd." Ffion ran a hand down Cadno's back, looking thoughtful. "Whatever else my father got wrong, he was right about you. You're meant to be king."

Dafydd had told us what the ravens had said to him. But I knew what it must mean to have Ffion say it, too.

He'd also told me what Ffion had said when he approached her after the battle. That she cared for him, but not in the right way. That she was too prickly; that she would hurt him; that her heart belonged elsewhere.

I'd told him I was sorry. I wouldn't undo my own luck, but under other circumstances, I would have wished his were better.

It stings, he'd said. *But it won't always.*

"You're certain, then?" Dafydd asked.

"Will you protect my mother if you become king?" I asked. "Will you look after Mam and Ffion while I'm away candling the places that need to be restored?"

He nodded. "You know I will."

I did. He had already been protecting Mam and me by playing along with Dad in the first place, even when he and I were fighting.

He'd been trustworthy then. I could trust him now.

"Then—done." I shrugged. "The throne is yours, Dafydd. Take what you never wanted."

"Fine," he said, conceding with a wry grin. "You do the same."

Dafydd sat back then, obviously lost in thought. Cadno crept toward Gruffudd, still asleep. Ffion rested her chin on my shoulder.

"King's candler," she whispered. "We're going to have to get you some simpler clothes."

"I thought we agreed nudity was the most impactful uniform for me."

Ffion choked on a laugh, burying her face in my shoulder. "If you think nudity lends itself to working with fire, there's nothing I can do to help you." She sighed, smiling up at me. "Tal, why did you tell me you spent eighteen ceiniogau on that coat, when your mother gave it to you?"

"To annoy you," I said, and kissed her with a smile.

Candler and lord of some nowhere patch of ground, and Ffion there beside me. I couldn't wait.

Just then, the throne room doors burst open.

"Dad?" Ffion was on her feet. "Dad, is everything all right?"

Osian frowned. "Why wouldn't everything be all right?"

"Because you blew in like a—never mind. What is it?"

But Osian pushed past her to Dafydd. "Did it change?" he asked.

Dafydd frowned. "Did what change?"

"*It.*" Osian reached for Dafydd's tunic, impatient. When he yanked it up above my brother's ribs, all of us drew back with a gasp.

Dafydd's fox tattoo had changed. A tiny dragon soared beneath his heart now, beside a raven in a red coat. I rolled my eyes.

"And what's that?" I asked, gesturing at his side. Shades of pink and green stretched from the top of his ribs to his hip bones. "Is that—?"

"A foxglove," Ffion finished slowly, staring at her father. "Dad?"

But Osian had dashed back to the door.

"Arianrhod!" he called. "Come on. There's someone I'd like you to meet."

Epilogue

TAL

Mathrafal Village, Powys
Eight Months Later, Midwinter

Ffion bustled around the cottage, hanging rushlights and setting candles in the windows. Cawl was cooking over the fire in one cauldron, and something else—something I didn't care to ask about—bubbled in the other. Sausages were frying in a pan. A small keg of bragawd sat on the table beside a large bowl of wassail. Cakes and baked apples waited on the table, lamentably not out of Cadno's reach.

My mother's amber ring glinted on Ffion's left hand.

"Annwyl Ffion, are you hoping to light the cottage, or set it alight?" I asked, glancing out the front door.

"Annwyl Tal, either will do," she said idly, feeding Cadno a bite of sausage. "The bwbach will watch over the hearth."

"Is that his first or his second?" I nodded at the fox.

"Ask me no questions and I'll tell you no lies."

I rolled my eyes at her and was about to peer out the door again when a knock came. "Hello!" my mother sang out, bustling inside. Ffion abandoned both cauldrons to wrap her in a hug.

"Please, sit," she said to Mam, pulling her toward a chair, offering her a glass of bragawd.

It meant everything to have my mother safe inside tonight. It meant everything to see the way Ffion protected her. The way she protected me, this night and every other.

Another knock came. "Good Midwinter to you, Tal," said Dafydd, shaking snow out of his hair.

Gruffudd, Osian, and Arianrhod followed after him, and a chase between Gruffudd and Cadno and the bwbach began where it had left off on their last visit.

"Good Midwinter, Dafydd." I pressed a cup of bragawd into his hands. "Come get warm."

I was grateful he could be here with us this Midwinter, because Dafydd would have to roam far and wide for his throne. In the new year, he'd be visiting Prince Angws and King Meirion, bringing Enid back with him for a visit when he returned. As his new magician, Arianrhod would hold Mathrafal while he was gone.

Ffion was hesitant, still, of Arianrhod. I understood; I'd spent years struggling with Dafydd.

But Arianrhod had seen what Ffion's methods had done to the dyke, and she saw daily what it meant to have magic restored. What was more, Ffion had seen what it meant to have help that day at Prestatyn.

Above all, Arianrhod and Dafydd both knew where they would always be welcome.

More knocks came at the door, and Ffion answered this time. The twins tumbled in first.

"Tegan!" she cheered. "Taffy!" Ffion caught up both her littlest brother and sister at once, somehow managing to hold the pair of them on her slim hips. They kissed her cheeks and shrieked at her, clumsily demanding cakes and sausages and to pet Cadno, who backed slowly into the corner the little bwbach occupied. Hywel and Gareth followed after, Hywel looking shy and somber, Gareth cheerfully relieving her of Tegan's weight.

Catrin came in last. Osian hung back, but Ffion hugged her mother silently, tightly, and shut the door behind her.

Ffion's mother still sat beneath the hill, though the Foxhall had broken. The poison ivy that had been Ffion's curse on them had withered the day the magic came back to Wales, and their orange door stood open day and night now. And though they were only a small coven, with the combined resources of just five or six witches, they were known for offering help to anyone who asked. Ffion joined them sometimes.

Her home was with me. But Foxhall was her home, too.

Our dinner was not a courtly affair. We ate without any ceremony, lighting more and more candles against the longest night outside, talking over one another and telling stories.

We almost didn't hear the last knock at the door. But there was no mistaking the song.

Tonight, and oh, the longest night,
The longest night, the longest night,
Tonight, and oh, the longest night,
Come we now to your door.

Tonight, and oh, the coldest night,
The coldest night, the coldest night,
Tonight, and oh, the coldest night,
Come we now to your fire.

Tonight, and oh, the darkest night,
The darkest night, the darkest night,
Tonight, and oh, the darkest night,
Come we now to your lamps.

So open up your door tonight,
Make room beside your fire tonight,

Give houseroom at your lamps tonight,
No more than is your due.

But if you shut your door tonight,
Make no room by your fire tonight,
No houseroom at your lamps tonight,
The same, someday, to you.

Nobody moved. Not Ffion's family, not mine. Dafydd and my mother watched me, waiting to see what I would do.

On and on went the wassailers' singing, wavering up and down the scale. Bells jingled on the knees of dancers, and holly branches cut through the air.

I nodded at our friends, getting to my feet. "One moment." Then I ladled wassail into a cup and made for the door.

When I stepped outside, she was waiting in the snow—alone, though I'd heard other voices.

The Mari Lwyd.

She stood on her back legs, her spine hunched forward so she stood only a foot taller than me. Her eye sockets were hollow, and a wreath of greenery over a shawl on her head hid the place where her horn had once been. Green and violet and rose-colored ribbons hung about her.

I smelled earth and rain, heard the boil of a phantom kettle. All the scents and sounds and signs of magic I'd come to love.

The Mari Lwyd was stinking with life and magic. But it was nothing to the magic waiting at my back.

She cocked her head at me in curiosity, her sagging jaw hanging a little open.

Good Midwinter, Taliesin bach.

I hear Pendwmpian Forest has been brought back from the dead.

I hadn't told anyone that Osian, Ffion, and I had candled Pendwmpian Forest. That I'd sat in the middle of the logged wasteland for five hours, a stinking tallow candle melting in my hand, drawing and burning away things I could not see.

Osian, Ffion, and I had replanted acres of saplings there. And I had caught the smell of magic—so like the scent and sense of homely and earthly things, earth and rain and a kettle on the boil—before we left.

The morning after, Osian had woken up with a spark of magic lit inside him.

I see all from the place between, princeling, she added. And of course she did.

I poured the steaming cup into the wassail bowl she held between her front hooves.

"Your health, Mari Lwyd," I said.

Diolch. And yours.

"And mine," I agreed. "It's good to see you abroad again."

I reached for the latch and opened the door to the darkest night, welcoming it in beneath the rushlights and the candles. My family stared out at me, slack-jawed.

"My hearth is crowded tonight," I said. "But please, won't you come inside?"

Author's Note

A historical fantasy is a tricky beast to tame.

I have—as always—played a bit fast and loose with history in the construction of this story, in matters major and minor. For example, the Mari Lwyd—a real Welsh tradition carried out by community members and actors, and not a resurrected unicorn—goes walking on Twelfth Night, not the winter solstice; and Cadell ap Brochfael was a real king of Powys, to whom I've probably been wildly unfair. Wherever I've succeeded in representing Welsh lore, I'm indebted to Trefor M. Owen's *Welsh Folk Customs*, C. C. J. Ellis's *An Illustrated Guide to Welsh Monsters & Mythical Beasts*, and multiple articles on the beautiful Welsh concept of hiraeth. Paul B. Newman's *Daily Life in the Middle Ages* also proved an invaluable historical resource.

I'm further indebted to the rich supply of folk songs available on broadsides on Oxford's Bodleian Library website, which provided reference for many of the folk songs in this novel. For example, "The Workaday Song" was closely inspired in rhyme and content by a song called "All Jolly Fellows That Follow the Plough." "The Derby Ram," a song about a notoriously large sheep, became a song about a wonderfully fat, healthy baby for Ffion to sing to Deri; "The Fox Chase," a cheerful hunters' song, I inverted to represent the hunted foxes' perspective. Other songs provided inspiration and references in the form of subject matter, diction, and meter.

Finally, while many academics believe Offa's Dyke did not actually run the whole length of the Welsh border, it is a very real place, built by King Offa in the eighth century, and marked today by a very real and beautiful UK National Trail (much of which I have hiked). It is my sincere hope that this story will inspire readers to fall in love with Wales as I have: with their boots in its mud and their eyes on its hills.

Acknowledgments

So many wonderful people have contributed to telling this story—turning it from a pitch to an outline to a manuscript to a novel, and then to a book that can live on shelves. My thanks to:

Stephanie Stein: Thank you for somehow always seeing the vision I saw as I've designed and constructed these four stories, but especially this time, through a year when my brain sometimes felt like a strange and foreign place.

Elana Roth Parker: Thank you for your advocacy, perspective, and partnership, especially through these years of pandemic and new parenthood.

Elizabeth Agyemang and the rest of my Harper team—Meghan Pettit, Allison Brown, Audrey Diestelkamp, Jon Howard, Gweneth Morton, Lauren Levite, and Corina Lupp: I am so grateful for your support, your sharp editing eye, your design sense, your marketing and publicity work. Special thanks to Sophie Schmidt, for your tireless cheerleading of this story, and to cover artist Christin Engelberth. Your art is, truly, magic.

My One More Page friends—Eileen McGervey, Lelia Nebeker, Rebecca Speas, Rosie Dauval, Amanda Quain, Sam White, Eileen O'Connor, Neil O'Connor, Trish Brown, Lauren Wengrovitz, Sally McConnell, and everyone else: There's no place quite like our store. I love you all and so deeply appreciate your support and friendship.

The Pod—Laura Weymouth, Jen Fulmer, Joanna Ruth Meyer, Steph Messa, and Hannah Whitten: My friends, my dragons, I would be lost without you. You are a constant source of joy and comfort.

Sarah Batista-Perreira and Maggie Stiefvater: This story would not exist without the pair of you. Thank you for lending me your beautiful kaleidoscope brains throughout its development.

Sally Van Horn and Anna Sims: The seed that became *Hedgewitch* was a hike three girls of dubious skill and experience took down Offa's Dyke Path in 2018. I hold those memories of pubs and snow and tea very, very dear in my heart and my imagination. Thank you, my friends.

Wade: You are my home. Thank you for loving and looking after us every single day. You are the fun dad and best friend I always dreamed of marrying. I could never write a love story better than ours.

My parents and the rest of my family: Circumstances change, but you all don't. Thank you for constantly cheering me on. I love you all so very much.

Caroline and Anneliese: Oh, my sweet girls. You are the wildest adventure I've ever taken. Every moment with you is a joy, precious Caroline, and I am more excited to meet you every day, little Anneliese. Mama loves you both.

The One who keeps company with the lowly, the meek, the widow, the orphan, the sojourner, and the oppressed; Whose eye is on the sparrow; the God who came down: all glory to Your name. You are the Beginning and the End of every labor, every journey, every story.

And the sparrow who fell last year: Mama loves you, too. God keep you in His arms until we're together again someday.